What people are saying about *Without Wrath*:

After reading the first two books in the Harbinger of Change series, I could not wait until I got my hands on number three, *Without Wrath*. All three books are fast paced and take unexpected turns, like an olympic bobsled run. Great characters come and go and the story continues leaving you wanting more. Kudos to Timothy Jon Reynolds, a great new author has entered the ring.

—Rob Mckelvy

The third book, *Without Wrath* in Timothy Jon Reynolds series, the Harbinger of Change, has a vivid cast of characters and a story line with a lightning pace with numerous twist and turns from beginning to end. By the end of the book I was left wanting more and am definitely looking forward to Reynolds next read in this series, *Chesed*.

—M.R. Sandridge

Without Wrath was fascinating to read. Found myself hanging on every word. Tim Reynolds has an unique writing style that keeps you enthralled. Lots of storylines and characters to follow that comes to an impressive culmination. Can't wait to see what comes next.

—Rebecca Gumns

Other Novels from Timothy Jon Reynolds:

Harbinger of Change series

The Harbinger of Change
And the Meek Shall Inherit
Without Wrath
Chesed
And Thou Shalt Not

Others Novels

YOCTO

The Meth Chronicles

Rock

Without
Wrath

Timothy Jon Reynolds

AMERICAN PRIDE PRESS

Printed in the USA
ISBN: 978-0-9909779-7-1

Front cover art and design: Andrei Bat
Editor: Patti Whitman
Interior design and layout: Marian Hartsough
Research consultant: Adam Hochman

American Pride Press
1344 Disc Drive #372
Sparks, NV 89436

Visit us at www.timothyjonreynolds.com

CHAPTER ONE

Realizations

He could feel the hair stand up on the back of his neck. Matt Hurst was out of breath, hiding behind a large pine tree, close to panic. He'd never been spooked like this before, especially in the forest. Yeah, he knew it was unwise to hunt alone, but he'd always been at home in the forest and looked upon it as his friend. Not now. Now it seemed to have turned on him. Suddenly, he realized what it felt like to be the hunted, and he had to admit, he was afraid.

The morning had started rather uneventful. It wasn't until after he had descended to the bottom of a ravine that he caught a slight movement coming from near the top. He found shelter behind a boulder, and from there he sat and watched for a long while but saw no further movement. Just his imagination?

Moments later as he was traversing a small stream, hopping across rocks, he once again had the feeling he was being watched, that he wasn't alone. He had this unshakable feeling of being under the surveillance of a riflescope. He was still trying to pass it off as his imagination when a small glint off a rock sent his blood running cold. He quickly made his way to cover, sure the glint was not that of a bird watching enthusiast's binoculars. Someone was out here to kill him.

He sprinted a good stretch after coming around a bend in the creek bed he was following. He saw the glimmer of a lens reflected off a rock, sure it was not some miracle of nature. The sensing of this unknown presence was unleashing some very irrational fears in him. Really, it was surprising and almost irrational for a man of his experience, but still, he knew the forest offered unlimited places for a seasoned sniper to prey from—and who was to say there was only one? Just the thought had him ducking as he moved.

He tried to slow his breathing and listen, but his heart was still racing. In the back of his mind, he carried the hidden fear that one day one of his many enemies would follow him out here and finally rid the world of Mathew Hurst once and for all. He waited and listened for sounds coming from deep in the forest.

He had been receiving survival training these last few months, and some had taken place nearby in these woods. He had joined the President's little group and moved to Seattle where they were working with him, but he was far from graduated. He listened again . . . nothing.

There were always bears to worry about, of course. The experts often warned that hunting alone required a constant state of mental awareness and toughness, and hiking in or out in the dark was much scarier when you had no partner—no matter what anyone would admit to. It was a macho thing, he supposed.

Bears could be nasty on the charge, as they offered no place to get a kill shot with their head down running at their target at full speed. But Matt also knew that bears did not carry scopes. What if he were wrong; water had the ability to refract light and he was crossing a stream when it happened, after all.

He relaxed a bit as he could hear nothing, and was about to continue on when he heard a twig snap. Matt froze. Something was out there, for sure. He considered . . . if it were a bear or cougar, the best thing he could do would be to make noise and scare the animal off—unless it had him on the menu, there was always that. However, if it were an enemy combatant, then he would lose advantage by exclaiming, "Here I am!" But it was also possible it was a fellow hunter, in which case he'd want to be heard so he didn't get shot accidently. What a quagmire.

He considered his options as he shouldered his rifle over his left shoulder and reached his right hand under his left arm and drew out his Smith and Wesson 44 magnum from its shoulder holster. His normal sidearm choice was his Beretta 9mm, but not out here, not when he went hunting.

Of all the people in the world, it was his dentist, Dr. Vickerman, who had suggested the magnum and the logic behind it. It was Washington State after all, and a lot of people hunted, even one's dentist. Dr. Vickerman, who often went to Alaska to hunt, said he always asked himself what would be the worse case scenario out there in the wilderness, and in this case, it would be a grizzly bear standing over him, ready to kill. He asked Matt, "What gun could you guarantee would save your life?"

Matt had concurred at the time, as he did now, there would be only one: the 44-magnum revolver.

The trail veered to the right, so Matt faced the trail with his back to the creek bed. The tension was intense and the clock was once more ticking him toward some deadly encounter. Sensing the coming confrontation, he cocked the weapon, which had a hair trigger—less than a pound of pressure would set it off. Whatever beast or enemy lay on the other side of his gun was going to be annihilated in a loud and angry way. The discharge from the gun was violent; it literally hurt his hand to shoot, and even if it were a full-grown black bear or a man in full body armor, this pistol would kill its target on impact. It had taken Matt some practice to get proficient with it, but proficient he was.

The moment was upon him; his heart rate pulsing through his hand on the gun, waiting for the millisecond he needed to gain the deadly advantage. He assumed a semi-boxer shooter stance in anticipation. He was facing the game trail with the most intensity he could ever remember—when suddenly the barrel of what he could only assume was a gun came to rest on the back of his neck.

He froze. Then a very familiar voice instructed, "That was a good application of logic, Matt, but we really need work on the tracks you leave everywhere and how to watch your flank."

He lowered his weapon, easing off the hammer and replacing it in his holster, as he replied, "Yes, Jim." It was the only acceptable reply when his mentor had just taught him a lesson. Of course, it was an unscheduled lesson and now Matt realized he had to be "on" at all times, even out here.

He turned to talk to Jim, but he was gone. Matt sighed, and then continued on his way, a little more wise about hiding behind the tree his footprints led to, and watching his back.

* * *

João sat on the edge of his bed. Last night was a brain-cell killer… *so much rum*. He looked back onto the bed and spotted the girl he mated last night; she was maybe eighteen years old. She also had the perfect ass that was now slightly sticking out of the covers—and it stirred something in him even though his head was pounding.

He was going to replace the blinds today as some of the slats were bent and the sun's first rays always found his eyes, which was why he was up right now. He couldn't count how many times he'd planned to do this, but today was really the day he was going to fix the blinds.

He was pretty sure it had been over a year since he'd started trying to kill himself by partying too hard; over a year since he'd lost his best friend; and over a year since he'd returned to Rio de Janeiro and his Favela Nova Brasília.

He was currently the leader of "The Anthill Gang." Others had different names for them, but they were the "Anthill" as far as any of them were concerned, and that was all that mattered. Their Favela was part of the Complexo do Alemão, a place where there were many slums. João had no interest to know how many, all he cared about was their own, and those right next to them.

Abandoned on the streets at age nine, he had lived the life of a street child. He surely would have died had he not met Felipe soon after his parents had abandoned him. He remembered his early life with his parents always worrying about putting a roof over their heads. He remembered coming up Avenida Itaoca, the street that ran along the entrance to Nova Brasília where the businesses on both sides were abandoned, the buildings all stripped and broken, just like after a war. The drugs had not yet completely taken over things back then.

One of those buildings was the last residence João recalled having as a child with his parents. It had been a factory years before, but now even the roof was stripped. People had divided up the floor space and lived there, but rain was the enemy of that plan and it was short lived. He remembered the day he woke up and his family had moved. His mom had left him some bread and a blanket—and that was it. She couldn't write, so there was no note. She had never even told him his last name.

His best friend, Felipe, had suffered the same fate; only Felipe would still see members of his family. He was abandoned by his father, kicked out and told to go out and survive, while other siblings were permitted to stay. Felipe had to endure seeing his more favored siblings around from time to time. That was how he found out his papa was sick and he was able to let him know just how much he appreciated the abandonment—right before he killed him.

João had no such luck. He never saw his parents or any of his siblings ever again.

He walked over to the bathroom, relieved himself, and came back to the bed, positioning himself so to be out of the rays of the sun. He looked at his bed partner again. She was one of their whores. He had no idea how many they had at this point. Now that their rivals, the Reds, were gone, they were able to expand their place on the Hill and absorb all of the rival gang's assets.

It wasn't easy becoming *Premeiro Comando*. He and Felipe had grown up just floating around as kids with no place to be and no food to eat. They tried everywhere, but no place was for them. They were run off from any place where money could be found.

Then one day when they were fourteen they found themselves in a new kind of place in the flatlands—one the drug lords didn't control. They were both able to find vendors who gave them food for work. Life was good—for about a second. Hooked on getting high anyway they could, they sometimes found themselves sniffing glue, and although it made his head feel like it did now, a tube would last a long time and the world just disappeared when they did it.

The drug lords did not run this new town; it was the militia who did. The militia was a private group that extorted money from the locals for "protection." The protection part worked, but everything there was more expensive because of the "Militia tax." The main positive was the place was pretty safe for street kids—or so they thought—until one day they walked out from an alley where they had been sleeping. The militia had just caught an older boy of sixteen smoking pot. To their horror, the fucking *putos* took the kid out to the main square and shot him! That was it for them in the *Gardenia Azul*.

The next place they landed was Nova Brasília where the local gang, the Anthills, needed recruits, and they quickly rose up the ranks because they had learned a trick on the streets that the Ants hierarchy liked. After *Gardenia Azul* they met some Colombians who were smuggling cocaine and used them as mules. This was the best time of their lives to date because it was the only period when they ever had any money. Being old enough, then in their teens, they actually rented a room and had a place to stay. That was until the Colombians got busted, but not before teaching the two of them the trick.

The Colombians knew that most Brazilians could kind of understand Spanish when spoken, but what Felipe and João discovered was they couldn't understand provincial Spanish when spoken quickly. The Colombians used it as a way to communicate openly without someone deciphering what they said. Back then the leader of the Ants was Paulo, and he overheard them one day using it and liked the idea. Felipe and João quickly became intrinsic to the Ants ascension in the criminal world, and their impact never lessened until they ran the gang.

Other than the two years that he left Rio and had gone to Ecuador to attack the United States, João had never been outside of Brazil. Starting out as a foot soldier and ending as the co-leader, he didn't seek out to attack the U.S. He was brought into the attack as part of a team. His employer, a super-brain driven by God, recruited twelve of the Ants to carry out the attack; and João was the only one left to tell the tale. Everyone else was dead. After years of battling their rival gangs, the Reds and Ramos Naci-dos, the man/boy behind the brain changed their status overnight.

The man/boy was soft and looked so out of place, yet he spoke to Felipe like the most fearless warrior. He was after one of their whores. This was the part of the God thing that João just never quite understood. No one that knew them would have dared come in like that, but this man/boy, he later came to know as Pablo Manuel, just walked right in and bargained with Felipe for her. Such a deal would have been impossible for anyone else to pull off. Pablo said the rival Reds would all be dead by morning and the Ants could have their territory. Crazy talk as the Reds were connected to some serious prison gangs in São Paulo, the tendrils reaching all the way to their Favela.

It was unfathomable, yet it happened and it put them on a map of people never to fuck with. People spoke of their brutality now. When a gang perpetrated that kind of destruction, then they got notice and respect quickly. Suddenly, right after Pablo's people butchered all the Reds, the Ramos Nacido boys got real quiet and stayed off the Ants' turf. It had taken the Ramos boys this long to start their rivalry again. Apparently they were tired of hearing the rumors of how badass the Ants were now, and wanted some action for themselves.

Things were different now, though. As soon as they knew the Olympics were coming to Rio, the government started cracking down, especially on drugs and violence—the two things João stood for. He looked at his bedmate's ass again, still slightly sticking out of the covers, and added sex to that list of things that he stood for.

Nowadays, the UPP *(Polícia Pacificadoa)*, Brazil's peacekeeping police units, were everywhere, and that just would not do. So the Ants sent a message last week and shot one of their officers who was in the wrong place at the wrong time. Turned out it was a woman. Why the UPP would be sending a woman after someone like him he had no clue? But she was dead now and her upset brethren were buzzing like bees all around his Favela.

The Hill housed them and the Reds on the main facade, and above them the *Praca do Terco* (a flat terrace with no structures) prohibited the Ramos Nacido from coming straight down into their neighborhood on anything other than on foot. For the Ramos boys to get to them, they would have to use a car and come up the Avenida Itaoca, then turn up Rue Nova Brasília, and come right into the heart of the beast. So they had started the *galinha* (chicken) tactics.

Last week, some of the Ants were having a roof party when shots came from up the hill. No one was hit, but the party was over quickly. Spotters had been seeing the Ramos boys all over, driving by, and sitting up at the top of the hill staking things out. Once the Reds were dead, the Ants had taken over the territory, but that meant more territory to protect.

João rubbed the girl's foot as it popped out of the covers. She had short stubby feet, but they were cute. Not all whores were so cute. As a matter of fact, if it weren't for Pablo's "needed" whore, then none of this would have happened.

After Pablo had the Reds killed, the man/boy was back as promised for the whore, Vera. He took her and told Felipe to have fun for the next few months, but soon he would be back, and he would need twelve Ants for a mission.

At first they thought about refusing, but then they thought about the Reds and agreed, especially after seeing what Pablo had left to split amongst themselves—a duffle bag containing five million U.S.—and it put them on the map financially as a player.

Pablo's gift enabled them to finally buy *coca* from the Colombians who had that amount as their minimum buy. To this day, the day before the Colombians arrive for a delivery, the whole upper Favela empties except for the Ants. Initially, there had been some incidents that the Colombians had to deal with among the locals and the Ants stood back. But now the deal was in place and the shipments came every Friday.

João still marveled at Filipe. Filipe was a hard man, in fact, he was so hard that if one just looked at him, one knew his whole story, and that was why João was in place now. Like a prison gang, once their hierarchy was taken away to help this man/boy named Pablo Manuel attack the United States, Filipe just instinctively knew how to run things remotely: WITH AN IRON FIST.

He and Felipe had made the initial buys. Then they turned operations over to Carlos to handle while they were gone. To his credit, Felipe was amazing at controlling things from afar.

It turned out that the man/boy was a super genius. Pablo Manuel had come from Ecuador with a plan given to him by God, and somehow their whore was attached to the plan. Over a couple of years this genius had built a bunker inside a mountain attached to a rock quarry that he owned.

He also had built a drone army that ran on super batteries. They were silent, had stealth technology, and were internally cooled. And they were undetectable. He had two types—flyers and fish. The fish were of the five hundred pound Sea Bass variety and packed a wallop that could cripple any vessel. The flyers were of two different varieties: the boom and the electrical storm.

This genius then made it all into a video game to train the twelve Ants. They trained and trained and trained. Soon they were all really good at the video game, and they loved it. That was when it was revealed to them that it was not a game, but in fact they were actually guiding an automated army. Slowly the partying was tapered off and they got serious. They learned tactics, studying the attack tactics of both the United States and Ecuadorian militaries. Suddenly João was excited as it looked like the genius wanted to kill some people.

Then it happened, the first downside. Pablo separated the two of them—him and Felipe. He needed an Ant to be his right hand man, and he needed an Ant to be the lead to guide the other video warriors. João couldn't believe that Felipe accepted the right-hand man job without even trying to get him too, as co-right hand man. He just left him. They always did everything together. João was so hurt he turned down the lead video warrior offer.

This Pablo, super genius, had given them all their own rooms. They were four levels down in the mountain and João chose the room on the end of the long corridor, as far away from everyone else as possible. Felipe was out doing all sorts of things he wanted to do while he was stuck playing the stupid game, a game he used to love.

That wasn't what bothered him the most, though. What bothered him the most was Felipe's apparent belief that this Pablo had a relationship with God.

They had both seen and done enough to know that they didn't believe in God, and now this? He saw the adulation on his friend's face when he talked about Pablo, or saw Pablo. It was too much! And after that last visit with the *gringo* in tow, the two of them had needed to talk, especially after he gestured he was watching João after he asked him to stop getting high.

His head was pounding, and when he played it all out, it just got him angry and overloaded, which was why he was always getting high and drinking so much these days. He was self-medicating himself through the hardest thing he'd ever had to face, the loss of his friend.

João went over to the blinds, tried to adjust it, but ended up accidently letting in more sun than before, which caused his whore to stir and reveal a pair of tits that only youth could provide. His bedmate mumbled something and turned away to bury her head in the pillows.

The new light revealed a pair of eyes in the corner on the far side of the bed, eyes that were always watching him. As far as he was concerned, it was okay if they saw what happened in the bed last night. They could be witness to how heroic he was.

He drifted back again to his time away from the Favela.

Pablo had built special rooms that were rectangular in shape and about the size of a squash court. They had a console in the center that sat about two-thirds away from the far wall. The console was the game controller and the wall was the screen. The screen was dividable into four sections, all HD, and all very state of the art. After more than a year in the compound, however, João was going completely stir crazy—all he was doing was training, eating, fucking, and sleeping.

They each also had their own apartment and he kept one of the female Chinese workers they employed for his own. His girl resisted some at first, but he soon had her whipped into shape. Still, it was not enough. He'd realized that this was the longest he had ever gone without killing someone; ever since the day they stabbed that drunk in the alley more than ten years ago, they had not stopped.

That was when João went to Felipe and demanded he get him out of that room and let him have some freedom. Felipe's answer was to train João to be a helicopter pilot—not in the real world, but on a game that Pablo had created to get rid of his malaise. Pablo promised João that he'd made it just for him, and once he learned it, he could go anywhere he wanted.

It took weeks to learn to play the game right because one had to really fly the helicopter, but once he had learned and mastered all aspects of flying, the program let him go anywhere. It was a game like no other, but João had finally realized that those two had only tried to distract him. They figured because he got high all the time that he didn't know what was going on. But he did, he always did, and Felipe was just about to find that out when it all went down.

He got up and walked across the room to wash his face. He had a lot to do today, starting with fixing those fucking blinds. He looked in the mirror and realized how much he had aged in the past couple of years since it was over. He missed Felipe and had been trying to slowly kill himself ever since his friend's death.

No one had ever hit America like that before. It had turned the world upside down... and it all started with the Ants and the whore.

Pablo had needed to get vital information out of the United States and he used the whore to do it. Ostensibly, Pablo was operating off the belief the he was a messenger of God, and that's why he needed "our" whore. He was adamant that she was his destined partner.

Initially, they both found Pablo's story all a bunch of crap, and there was no way João was giving up his favorite whore. João fondly remembered breaking her in at a very early age when they found her on the streets, terrified. He loved it when they were terrified, like his former Chinese housemate was at first.

After Pablo took her away, he had trained her and sent her to the United States. She did come back with the stolen information, sure, but she also brought back that *gringo*; he turned out to be her lover. The *gringo* was then able to get himself appointed as Pablo's topside security man. It was all too weird. Felipe never trusted the *gringo* and told him so.

João had no idea who, but one of them betrayed the Ants and poisoned them. The only thing that saved him was that he was fortuitously locked in the stairwell getting high before the next round of warfare.

Luckily for him, he liked getting high before he played the game. In the few minutes he was absent, someone poisoned the Ant's rooms. Once he'd figured that out, he got away by riding an all-terrain vehicle, stopping only to get the *gringo*'s favorite guard dog on his way out of the compound.

Before that, they had finally had a chance to do some fighting. And once they started killing actual people, one couldn't have pried him out of his room with a crowbar. He was no longer jealous of his friend's freedom. He was a born killer and this was his chance to play the game of death. He just liked to be stoned when he did it—and now he was alive because of his love of being stoned.

He remembered the last time he saw Felipe. Felipe had been giving a pep talk after they'd destroyed an attack group of the Ecuadorian military and then crippled the U.S. Carrier Group the *USS George H. W. Bush*. João was so thankful that he took getting stoned so seriously. He knew that they were heading into some heavy action, and he knew he needed to be stoned to be at his fullest capabilities.

Felipe and the *gringo* made their rounds to each room for their little pep talk and then left. That was it—he never saw him again, alive or dead. Some asshole robbed him of the chance to set things right with his only friend.

He knew from the world news that after he'd fled, the United States seized the compound, but no mention of Pablo, Vera, or the *gringo*, Matt, ever surfaced. João saw one of the poisoned Ants die a horrific death right in front of his eyes, and he knew it wasn't the U.S. that did it because they hadn't gotten there yet.

At least one of those three betrayed the Ants, and probably lived to tell the tale. If João ever figured out which one was culpable, he now had enough money to do something about it when the time came. He also had enough money to leave here and never come back. But he knew he would never leave again.

He lit a joint and smoked it as he got the blinds right with some good old jerry-rigging. Guess he didn't have to go shopping after all. That was good because it was time to go back to sleep, but not before he investigated that ass sticking out of the covers one more time...

Carlos woke João up by entering his room; the alarm clock said it was three in the morning. Carlos was the only one allowed into his room or there would be trouble. And even then, he'd already learned not to move too quickly or try to touch him.

João uttered, "Shit, how the fuck did I sleep through the whole day and half the night, too?" *What the hell was in that joint*, he wondered? His whore was gone, he noticed. She'd escaped while he was in his coma, probably hungry. He looked at Carlos and tried to focus, "What's up?"

Carlos reported without emotion, "They're making their move, just like you said. They just parked two full-sized vans a hundred yards up the Rue Nova Brasília."

João jumped up and turned on his monitors. He'd been waiting for just this scenario. "Okay, go release my toys and take positions." Carlos left immediately.

He pulled up his super high-definition, night-enhanced, mini-rotating camera system. He had cameras secretly placed all over the entire Favela; after all, he'd learned more than a trick or two from his former co-conspirators. As he brought up the screen he observed the vans… and then he got *the rush*.

João was sitting on a big secret. In the history of the world, he was in the top percentage as far as people he had single-handedly killed in battle. It had to be in the hundreds, maybe even the thousands.

When they attacked the *Bush* Carrier Group, they were only supposed to aim for the propellers to disable them. But he purposely drove a five hundred pound bomb directly into the belly of the supply ship, knowing it would be loaded with easy kills.

He mused, imagine if the world knew he was alive and what he'd done. He would become the next Osama bin Laden. He might have been born poor and ignorant, but he was neither any longer.

The red light came on and his hand controller was ready. It got fun from here. He saw four men exit the vans, two from each. He could see they each had an AK-47 slung over their backs and a grenade in their right hand. So that was the plan, *they think they know where I'm staying and they want to blow me to pieces.*

João put false information out all the time as to where he was staying, so surely the grenadiers would have missed their mark tonight, regardless.

He saw them sneaking up the sidewalk, staying in the shadows. It was now time to have some fun. He launched the first RC car by them at forty-miles per hour. Slack-jawed, they watched it go by and zip right under the van holding six of the Ramos hombres. The van exploded with a thunder that shattered more than a few local windows.

All the occupants were dead before they knew there was danger. The street grenadiers were in no man's land now, not knowing if they should run for it through the inferno or continue the mission that was obviously blown? They didn't have long to decide before the second RC zipped by and headed for the other van, which was already on the go and was now turning around. The occupants in that van saw the black streak coming down the street and managed to get the side door open. Two of them actually made it part way out of the vehicle before the remote bomb blew them out, a good fifty feet away. The other four perished in the second massive explosion.

That was all the grenadiers needed to see; the battle was over before it had started and they ran as fast as they could back to the Avenida Itaoca, back to the their Favela Itarare. With the fire burning on the left and the middle, they had to go to the right. After they cleared the vehicles they stopped and gathered the two wrecked bodies that had blown out of the van, both tattered and bleeding out of their ears. They were carrying their brothers . . . really half dragging them, when they turned the corner right into the firing squad.

Before they could react, the Ants wiped them out, their unused grenades falling to the ground, as did their bodies and weapons. Without delay, Ants seemingly came out of nowhere, collecting all of the weapons from the dead Ramos soldiers.

Up the street, another group of Ants were collecting all of his wireless cameras that were mounted with magnets around the street. Just like that, it was over and they were gone, along with any traces of them. No one would dare speak against them in their Favela. The UPP could kiss his ass.

Even if they went door to door, all that they had used here were some strong plastics and some electronics, which the authorities would never find, as both had been incinerated.

João had five screens in all, and he was focused on the Ants' efficiency at removing the cameras in a timely fashion, which was up to his expectations. One by one they were taking down his cameras and he was losing views. He was still focused on his main zoom camera though, one that was well hidden and did not need to be removed.

He was so busy congratulating himself and lost in the rush that came from barbecuing those *putos* or he might have heard the small creak the door had made. Although he didn't hear the assassin, he felt his presence and by the time he turned around, the Ramos assassin's knife was a foot from him and coming down hard.

His reactions probably would have allowed him to get his arm up and take it from there, but he never got the chance. The black streak came out of nowhere, and his protector had his assailant by the wrist and was gnawing fiercely before the man knew what had happened.

As he was leaving the compound in Ecuador two years before, he had found one of the dogs the *gringo* had been training. The dog had been wearing a bulletproof vest and he looked so badass that João just had to have him. The dog came to him right away and accepted him as his new owner ever since that day, without question. João was a hundred and thirty pounds, and Gringo, his dog's name, was now a hundred and twenty. His assailant was his size and the fight was not going well.

Of course, by now he had his Beretta out and the fight was over no matter what, but this was a good time to give the dog a taste for blood and death. João gun butted the knife out of his assailant's hand and the Ramos assassin screamed in pain. He kept punching the dog in the face with his free left hand, but the dog would not let go of the right. He was screaming and then he tried to bite Gringo, but João gun butted him in the head and he fell back. That was it. He'd exposed his neck and the dog went for the kill.

To his credit the *gringo*, Matt, did not train these dogs to wound. The beast grabbed the assassin's throat and clamped down. His reaction was what João would have done—he reached for the dog's eyes. So João broke his fingers as Gringo crushed the gurgling man's throat with a syrupy kind of sound he would never forget. He called the dog off and sat him down. João noted that Gringo looked like a satiated lion after the kill.

João went out only to find his entire security detail dead—all of their shirts had a red dot where their hearts were located. He looked at his new best friend by his side and vowed to never again be anywhere without him. He went back to his monitors. There was one still lit up. He called a number, Carlos answered, and he asked if it was in position? The answer was affirmative.

Across the Hill, one of the Ramos runners arrived at their headquarters bearing a grave message for all, but he was so out of breath that he could barely deliver it. Finally he stammered out, *"Estão todos mortos."*

They were the last words spoken in the room full of Ramos leaders.

João's remote copter hit the window and its plastic explosive cargo took care of the Ramos boys and their entire headquarters. *That should slow down their growth,* João thought, and turned off his last monitor as the sounds of the madness he'd unleashed were unfolding throughout the city.

Ants came in and took away all evidence of the control station. They also had the ghastly job of removing and cleaning up his fallen security detail. Although João hated to admit it, he had learned a lot from Pablo as well. He opened his window and listened to the wonderful sounds of chaos. He heard a tortured scream come from far off and a large smile appeared across his face as he and his new friend lay back on the bed.

He lit up a joint and enjoyed the rest of the night, sounds of sirens and screaming and madness. Some people might like to hear pleasant words and sounds before they fell asleep to help them ease off into a peaceful night's rest. But João found the scene outside to be the most cathartic night he could ever remember, and for sure this was the most relaxing bedtime story he'd ever experienced. Actually, it was the only one he'd ever experienced.

An especially excruciating wail came from across the hill, yet it somehow made it through the cacophony of sound that was happening outside. João imagined it was the mother of one of the Ramos leaders. She must have just come upon the completely destroyed *casa* that João arranged and found her son dead.

He wanted this night to last forever, but unfortunately for him, he was back asleep some time in the middle of the helicopter search of his Favela.

* * *

Typical as of late, Matt went to bed around midnight, but here he was again up at five in the morning, *as usual.* His night terrors were too much for him and they inevitably woke him.

He looked beside him in bed where Jan was softly snoring, little Jon Jon on the guest foldout next to her. Jon had a cold and she never left him alone when he was sick.

Almost as soon as his eyes opened, his mind wandered to his past. For two years he had slept with Vera, ate with her, and loved her as deeply as he has ever loved anyone—until the day he killed her and their unborn child. Sure, the good ol' U.S. of A. had given him the best therapy money could buy, and Ray Callahan brought him back from the brink, no doubt about it. Ray was the best at getting into people's heads. Yet Matt had lied his way through the healing process and did what all Hurst men did since time immemorial, *they sucked it up and worked it out—alone.* Matt told them what they wanted to hear and what they wanted to hear was, "he was better, he was fine, that he'd found a way to cope with what he'd done." They got him to admit to the necessity of what he'd done.

It was then that the jig was up as he remembered the lessons of his past life, the ones where he was just a Loss Prevention Manager, catching people stealing and then being able to go home anonymous at the end of the day. Time after time he replayed the "if onlys" in his head. Especially the if only he had just finished that sandwich and let her go his life wouldn't be this clandestine mess it was now.

Once they started getting him to rationalize, he realized they were running a "by the numbers game" on him, just like the ones he ran on unfortunates that he had caught who refused to sign the confession. That's when the mind games would begin. Rationalizing is the number one way to break down emphatic denial. It's also the number one way to convince the population of a country to try to take over the world— just ask the Germans.

He knew Ray Callahan was sincere, but there were some things that just couldn't be fixed. So he became "the pretender." He played the game well; he always had.

Jan snored and rolled to the other side that Jon Jon was on. No matter their intensions, no one could make someone right who had done what he had done. He went from never having killed anyone to having killed over fifteen people in a little over two years. Ray might be the greatest mind Matt had ever known and for sure he was the reason Matt had come as far as he had today, but regardless, he couldn't fix this. This was one of those things that couldn't be fixed by words. This morning's awakening was right on schedule and he was beginning to think maybe even time would never fix this.

Matt couldn't stop the night terror wake ups. Every night his dreams put him in Vera's bed and every night she woke up terrified and brought him out of his dream sleep. He held her crying and sobbing and pleading *"não mais."* He couldn't even begin to think about the horrors she had endured—even in his dreams. Then, as it did every night, his mind went back to the control room. He was there with the gun and her angry and confused face filling his thoughts. She was defiant and crazed and he couldn't get through to her, even though he tried so hard.

He could usually get through to her, even when she was angry, but not every time. Once, when they were shopping in Quito some taxi driver bumped into their car. It was one of the few times they had ever gone out without a security detail. She wanted to go shopping for new clothes and talked Matt into the excursion. They had a wonderful day until the incident with the driver.

The taxi driver tapped their SUV and because he wouldn't make eye contact to apologize, Vera became incensed. Then the guy made the big mistake of dismissing her as a *puta*. He actually laughed at her, and the next thing Matt knew she was out of the vehicle.

The Taxi Driver was trapped in traffic as were they and couldn't pull out, so he tried to roll up his window. That cost him a punch in the face from a trained martial artist. Enraged he opened his car door and tried to get out, but no sooner had his foot hit the ground and his shoulder was breaching the upper frame than Vera kicked the door forcefully, breaking his leg for sure and probably causing some major damage to his shoulder. He was screaming in pain and she swung the door open on him.

The driver realized it wasn't over and went for his glove box, no doubt to retrieve his pistol. That move cost him a punch in the balls and when he sat up from that, a good face clawing. By the time Matt pulled her off him, he was a 911 call. But the most disturbing part was Vera's eyes, wild and crazed, he didn't know how to get through to her. She nearly attacked him too before she came out of it and they got the fuck out of there by employing the sidewalk as a means of escape.

That's what he was faced with in his dreams every night—that face, that crazed face. Matt could still feel the tension of that moment in the room, just as he had when he was there, just as when it was life or death. He continued to see it in slow motion, Pablo's hand reaching for the button. It is said that in the flash of life or death, one can relive an entire lifetime in that wink of an eye, and indeed, that's what happened to Matt that day.

As the shot he fired in the dream rung out he was ripped from his sleep every night. Often a new perspective came out of it, but it was the same hell every night. It might be just a new thought or word that was missed, nothing ever earth shattering. It was a never-ending cycle of sleep torture.

Vera had endured such a tragic life. Added to that, Pablo had enlisted her captors as his followers, so she had this constant reminder of that horrible chapter in her life.

He slipped out of bed and went to the living room computer, fired it up, and logged into his group, "Where's my America?"

His login was El Conejo and his avatar was a Rabbit. He was borrowing a little from his former captors, but also knew he was destined to have this moniker by a much higher authority. Today's topic was the former Occupy Protesters. The room was always diverse, there were people from all walks of life, but Matt knew the regulars, as they were his online friends.

Collectively they lived all over the United States. Phillybob74 was an obvious give-away as was BostonMike1. Matt learned that Picomann was from Los Angeles and TimberJustin12 was from his neck of the woods in Seattle.

His boss, Chase Viana, had moved him to Seattle at his request. Eric Barnett, Director of the CIA, was more than shocked when Matt turned down a job as an analyst, a job that would have fulfilled a lifelong sleuthing dream of his. But a visit from the President changed all that in a heartbeat.

Matt remembered he was asleep in the hospital, soon to be released, when he became aware of someone in his room. He accepted the fact that there were frequent intrusions in such an institution; it was a part of his life at the time; but usually not at that hour.

He turned and saw the newly elected second-term President. He was with a man that looked familiar, *was he an Actor?* "Hey Matt, how are you? This is Chase Viana, a friend of mine."

Chase leaned in and said, "It is my very special pleasure to meet you, Matt Hurst."

Caulfield spoke again, "Chase is one of the very few people who knows about you who's not in the Government."

"I see," was Matt's reply.

Caulfield pulled up a chair, as did Viana. In a more hushed tone, the President explained that Chase ran a clandestine organization, one that the President approved of, but not one on the books of the U.S. Government. Matt then became one of just a handful of people who even knew what TJAC meant. They were an Agency, but they were also a Paper Tiger. Sure they could hire outside resources to get certain jobs done, but that was a messy business rife with possible fallout. What they needed was an agent provocateur and seeing Matt had let Ray know he was choosing career and not the "lecture circuit," they thought they could offer him something a little better than an analyst job.

Matt pondered the moment. Back then, according to Chase, the President had been his biggest detractor but had subsequently become his biggest fan. They promised to wait and instructed him to turn down the Agency job. They handed him a packet that held his new identity. His new name was to be Thomas Mathew Holsinger; Jan and Jon would stay the same except for the surname.

The President put forth that the Federal Government would pay for some minor plastic surgery and put them into protection. The surgery would soften his features. His mother would recognize him, but probably not his third grade teacher. The offer was there and he took it, never hesitating for a moment.

Little did he know that his recovery would take this long. They seemed to know this ahead of time, but he was too stubborn to listen to anything he was being told. Chase figured it would be a year or more, while, of course, he expounded, "it would be more like a couple of months." Such hubris—that was a year and half ago.

Phillybob74 just hammered some newcomer for saying something he disagreed with. If one were outside his circle, Philly was an ass, his conversations were always aimed at all the conspiracy theory stuff.

Ecuador was returning back to the twenty-first century communications-wise, but there were still many questions to answer. The U.S. and Ecuadorian Governments were still dealing with all the ecological disasters caused by the sinking of the fleet and the resulting low-yield nuclear depth charge that had been fired in their coastal waters. Luckily the trade winds and currents spared the Galápagos Islands, but the coasts of Ecuador and Panama were not so fortunate.

Philly was having a very long field day with all the world madness, so the Occupy topic was not what he wanted to discuss. "They're no better than the zealot Sheep," he pontificated. Which, of course, sent the topic off in a million directions. Matt wanted to get it back towards the Occupy people, and fortunately, so did the rest of the room, so they ignored Philly's rants.

All agreed that the One Percenters were out of control, but no one could figure out a solution that they all could agree on. Pablo Manuel had taken the most extreme route—they all did agree on that—but what would have been the alternative?

Matt was creating these forums and think tanks trying to fulfill a destiny he didn't really believe in. Although this was no super educated bunch, they weren't stupid either. If you discounted Philly's incessant idiocy, the group was just a group of guys venting.

Picomann said that although he was Hispanic he thought there are too many illegals and that they were taxing the system to the breaking point.

TimberJustin12 thought we needed to legalize soft drugs and tax them, which Matt agreed with, but that idea was generally shut right down by the rest. Matt was talking about how he respected the Occupy people for at least having a cause, but they weren't in touch somehow.

And then it rolled out—Matt had been trying to connect the dots for a long time and then it just happened—he was able to articulate why they wouldn't succeed. He had the room as BostonMike1 egged him on to continue through Philly's rude comments on the Hispanic thing that was like ten minutes ago.

Matt commented, "When I worked in retail I observed a disturbing trend. The profit the store and company were expected to make was always more every year and it never seemed to have a ceiling. That's the problem," he furthered. "If you keep raising the ceiling, it's unrealistic. Everything has a ceiling. So the shareholders ask for more and some bean counters decide to trim some jobs, but the following year, there are no more jobs to trim here to reduce costs, so they move the factory abroad."

PhillyBob74 said, "How's that a solution, dipshit?"

Picomann then took a few minutes to tell Philly what a scumbag he was and how he was going to have Tom, who happened to be the site administrator, remove him. That finally got Philly to behave.

Matt, under the guise as Tom continued, "I understand it wasn't the answer Philly, but it is our doing that this all happened, we drank the Kool-Aid. That's why the Occupy people were sure to fail, because the One Percenters could care less if you're out there freezing your ass off for whatever cause it is you believe in, unless, of course, you are doing something to get their attention, something like, getting their quarter profit chart to drop."

BostonMike1 chimed in that, "We do this all the time. Talk, talk, talk, but we never do shit about it, we are dickless." He put an angry face on the screen. "Why don't we ever get out there with them and make it a really big movement, we just sit here and do nothing. Look at what Manuel did, he got moving and people who liked what he stood for followed. Really people, look at the millions of Sheep he was able to enlist."

"That's the reason they will fail," said Matt. "People aren't smart. America is dumbed down, and with two working people in every family, who has the time to protest? This isn't the Sixties where people had the job security or the wherewithal to protest. Pablo Manuel was successful because he was able to connect with a lot of people in a way no one has ever done before. Here's my theory, gentlemen, and it won't be popular, but I think seeing that we know that Special Interests are in the pocket of every politician and our immigration policies were made by these same politicians, it would not be a huge jump to say it was a planned policy to factionalize our country. Hell, who's to say that these Special Interest pukes representing a conglomerate are not foreign nationals! Who knows?

"The obvious plan is to divide us up and speak different languages to slow us down. Someone else has had this same failed plan and his name was God. He had this thought at the Tower of Babel and apparently our dear friends in the One Percenters agree with the strategy. Think about it? It makes it so much harder to rally the troops when we can't talk to one another. My thought is, the reason the Occupy protesters were sure to fail is that our country is so factionalized, polarized, and partisan minded, that nowadays it's impossible to rally the troops. I believe the 'powers that be' had a reason for this and I think you're seeing it unfold before your eyes."

"So we're fucked is what you're saying," said Picomann.

"Well, maybe not Pico, maybe we could find a way to get their attention. All we have to do is talk. There are people in society called 'connectors' and these connectors bring all sorts of people together from all walks of life. If we got a few of these people on board, real key ones, then it could start a groundswell. That's all any concept is really, just groundswell—enough people hitting 'like.'

"All we have to do is start a website dedicated to the concept of an organized boycott. We could call it "Boycott is Power." You can't tell me that if we got everyone to stop buying Nike for three months that the Nike executives wouldn't be more open to talking about bringing some jobs back. WE CREATED THESE BEASTS!"

SASPURSRULE29 came back with, "wouldn't that just run into the same problems? You still would have the 'whole factions' thing to deal with."

"Yes, Spurs, that's true, but we could get a select few minorities to join early on to help spread the word. All of us have minority friends, if we're not one, who we know and trust. It's just a matter of finding the right connectors to get past the tipping point. Once that happens, it will be like all other fads, it will catch fire. Don't forget, every empire that's ever fallen has done so because they failed to see the change at the bottom. Face it gentlemen, we're the bottom. Demographics is destiny and the former middle class has the numbers."

Matt took a break to crack his knuckles. "Here's the funny part and it's spelled out everywhere for us. I just watched the kid's movie, *A Bugs Life* with my son and I was stunned to see this same concept played out in a kid's movie! Spoken from the lead bad grasshopper in the movie, "If those Ants ever figure out they have us outnumbered a million to one, then our way of life is over." Matt typed one last thought, "It's there for us people. We just have to talk to make it happen."

TimberJustin12 broke in, "Deep, Tom." Matt always had a hard time remembering he was Tom now. Sometimes people would call him and he didn't respond, like the guy at the tire center who must have thought he was stoned.

He continued his thoughts online, "All we have to do is research a new target every three months and do it. At the end of the three months, they might want to come to the table, if not, another three. Corporate America is out of control, like a spoiled ten-year-old girl crying desperately for her parents to straighten her out.

"Don't forget guys, in the Fifties, if you would have tried this shit they're doing today, they would have been hung by the highest flagpole! What they're doing to us is the old boiling the frogs experiment. If you drop a frog in hot water his ass will jump out, but if you slowly increase the heat and boil him, he acclimates too easily and there is no more frog. Maybe quoting McCarthyism is a bit extreme, but not really, because the one thing that gets swept under the carpet in all this is the traitor aspect of this outsourcing."

For once, no one was bickering; they were listening, so he continued. "Since when is it okay to fuck over your country so you can make a buck? If you look up the definition of treason, it clearly states that anytime your actions help another foreign sovereignty prosper, especially to your own country's detriment, you are guilty of treason and that surely would have been true in any other era other than in this time of deregulated madness we are dealing with. We need to take back Washington and kick out the Special Interests, but that is going to be a near impossible challenge.

"So the one thing we can do now is target the corporations that think not having a ceiling is okay; that taking away our jobs, destroying our middle class, and having unrealistic margins is somehow okay because it's in the name of Capitalism. Maybe it is Capitalism, but it's Capitalism without conscience and the billionaires that make it run have now hedged the rules politically in their favor to allow for it to drain us like leeches. Irresponsible corporations have to be taught that they can't do anything they want without repercussions, that irresponsible Capitalism will be noticed and punished.

"We created it and we can stop it, all we have to do is start talking to each other and stop arguing. For me personally, the arguing is the worst part because it's what they want us to do. While we're all pointing fingers and standing our political ground, they are gaining ground.

"They have figured out that our parents had about thirty percent disposable income and they've targeted us to make sure we don't. We're under siege and too ignorant to see the elephant in the room. And gentleman, make no mistake about it, they are succeeding."

That set the room ablaze and the conversations went wild, but Matt noticed something, his core group was on board and did not enter the fray of thirty people going round and round.

Philly spoke next, "Tom Holsinger, I believe you are the true messiah, your words so inspire, how can I serve you?" It was PhillyBob74 being his usual flippant self, serving only him, "Seriously, Tom, how may I serve you?"

He wrote this about forty more times until Matt had enough and told him. "Okay, Philly, you want to help? Create the website of what we just discussed. Create a Mission Statement, make me the CEO, and make you and the boys the Board of Directors." He knew this would shut him up. "Just start caring about something other than yourself for a change."

TimberJustin12 slammed Philly with the old schoolyard, "Yeah bigmouth, do it, put your money where your big fucking mouth is."

"Yeah," Matt typed back, "Then we can start our quest for real and stop just jawing about it." Matt added one last bombshell for them. "Guys, you might talk about this stuff here because you're kind of concerned and then you move on to different stuff in your day. Not me. For me it's different and I can't really explain why. Trust me though. I do a lot of homework and this stuff is very close to my heart.

"If you want proof of my treason claims, Google up the 'hidden history of corporations.' It's a real eye opener. These guys are traitors of the highest order, but we're just too dumbed down and thinned out to fight back. Thomas Hobbes, the 17th Century Philosopher, wrote, 'Corporations are chips off the old block of the sovereignty.' It's insanity to argue it's not treason. It's like being covered in soot and trying to convince people you are not."

Matt left them with news about his big day coming today, "I have to go meet the new boss and find out my new work schedule."

Of course, everyone here knew him as Tom Holsinger, so everyone wished Tom good luck and before he logged off, Philly threw in a "Getting on it, Boss," out there. He was a card, but truthfully, he was right a lot of the crazy ass time.

Matt looked at the clock, it was nearly six o'clock and the ferry ran at 6:30 AM off his little island. Chase would be waiting for him at his safe house. He often thought about what had brought him here and he'd decided that it was fate, the way Matt believed all things worked for humans—through serendipity.

He had brought Jan up to the Seattle area to look around and see where they might like to live. They ate lunch in Mukilteo and took the ferry over to Whidbey Island. Matt was thinking island when they went over, which was translating to "small" in his head. But the drive across the island took almost an hour. It rained the whole way through thick evergreens on both sides. Every now and then a shotgun shack would pop out in a clearing, but that was about it. Then they came to one of the most beautiful places he'd ever seen in Deception Pass. They were lucky enough to get a break in the rain and were able to get out on the bridge of one of the most awesome views anywhere in the world. Matt remembered calling it the "Ninth Wonder."

They shot out to Anacortes and drove the quick trip back to I-5 and headed north towards Canada. They went through Bellingham and took a left at the sign that said Lummi Island. He discovered it was some miles out, but he just followed the signs.

Everyone has at least one inherent survival attribute and Matt's was sense of direction. He was never lost and once he'd found his way somewhere, he'd always remembered how to get back, even if the separation was years. He could see on the map that it was a short bridge from the mainland to the island and he liked the idea of living on an island somehow. He was an island in himself for over two years and somehow the thought of living on one just fit.

They made their way through an Indian reservation with the obligatory casino and fireworks stands. It was about twenty minutes since the last turn off when Matt spotted Tsunami Evacuation signs showing which way to drive to safely in case of emergency. That was something he'd forgotten about; they had earthquakes here, too. That was disappointing because he'd literally grown up his whole life living on the San Andreas Earthquake Fault and he felt it would have been nice to get out from that constant threat.

He pulled around a great sweeping curve thatched with evergreens on both sides until the populous and distant mountainous scenery returned to the horizon. He had been seeing only trees and the aforementioned signs for the last ten minutes or so. Soon he pulled up to a dock, but there was no bridge. It seems that they just dotted the ferry lines on the map; *lesson learned*. The ferry wasn't the large Washington State variety that carried hundreds of cars and people, like the one they had ridden earlier. This was a little ferry and he chuckled about the scene in the movie *Splash* when the guy went for the "little boat" and left Tom Hanks alone in a dingy.

Jan was just like him—they were forever quoting movies. It was one of their common bonds and she could totally keep up with him. So he said "I'm going for the little boat" and she said as a hyperbole, "the little boat!" Of course, it was delivered right on cue. This was surely the little ferry along those lines. The thing actually jostled when he drove onto it.

As it turned out, he was the front car. The operator kept telling him to move forward and he thought he was quite close enough. Jan was getting scared, he could tell by the nails biting into his hand, but the guy kept telling him to move forward and move forward until the bloody SUV was a foot from the edge of the boat. The stanchion for the chains looked like his hood ornament. The ride over was beautiful, though. As they headed to the island, the entire backdrop was an amazing view of the Cascade Mountain Range. The view was of the kind that always made him feel that only a very amazing God could have created such beauty.

The island was everything they had always wanted out of life. Quiet, quaint, and the houses that dotted the shoreline were breathtaking. He turned the car right and headed west off the ferry. They came across a charming restaurant and both being hungry they decided to check it out. The place was so homey, the centerpiece a wood fire oven that kept it toasty. The menu was pizza and burgers and Matt settled on the best-pulled chicken sandwich he'd ever eaten, the bun toasted to perfection.

They drove further up the island and found a charming school that they both fantasized Jon Jon going to. After a while they'd decided to go up another mile and turn around, they'd seen enough to know they loved it. It was time to find the real estate office and feel the pain. That's when they saw the "for sale" sign and pulled over in front of a house sitting high on the hill overlooking the Sound. It was a "for sale by owner" and the owner just happened to be walking out his front door, so they swung into the horseshoe driveway and pulled around to face him.

They'd learned his name was Chuck and he was a widower. He explained that it was formerly a bed and breakfast that he and his late wife had run. Chuck went on, "The lower apartment is nearly a thousand square feet and recently remodeled." Jan fell in love first, as it was the view from the Bay Windows that grabbed her. Also, the fireplace was set in a spot you could sit beside it and look out those same windows. The top house was a ranch style with three bedrooms and a very solid wood framing. Per the style of the area, the living room and master bedroom were elevated over the apartment below by stilts; sturdy looking, but stilts all the same. The bottom apartment was amazing though; it was done in a very modern style and two of those stilts were smartly placed to blend with the dark wood decor.

The apartment was heated by two hardwood floor heaters that did a nice job heating the place up when Chuck turned them on, but were cool to the touch. The bedroom had a wonderful elevated queen bed that looked out its own sliding glass window. Not quite the view as upstairs, but still an awesome view of the immediate lawn area that sloped toward the shore as well as the Sound.

The coup de grâce was the sauna room that was separate from the house. It had a wood burner and it looked like a cabin it was so big. The place was amazing, so they dared to ask.

Chuck could see they were in love with the place. They had already mentioned that Jon Jon was back in Seattle enjoying a visit to downtown with his Grandparents so he knew they were a family. But coming from the San Francisco Bay Area, Matt and Jan expected to just laugh after the next sentence and walk away, as surely this place was over a million. When Chuck told them five hundred and twenty thousand they both almost fell over. Matt looked at the little dock and pictured his future boat there.

Right now they had a little over seven hundred thousand in the bank and TJAC was paying him a salary he still couldn't wrap his mind around. He looked at Jan and didn't need to ask, "Chuck, we'll take it."

He noticed that Jan wasn't the only one wiping her eyes on the walk back up to the main house. Life sucked when he really thought about it. Someone usually died first, which left the other one alone like old Chuck, who was obviously selling this place because the daily memory was too much for him to take. Well, they'd try to fill it with as much love as they could and honor the obvious great memories Chuck had here.

After coming in and having some coffee and getting to know each other, a handshake deal was made and it was done. The wheels would turn and the people in the suits and ties would issue the checks. Matt sensed that in Chuck's perfect world this transaction culminated with a handshake from one family man to another.

They sat and talked with Chuck and discovered that he had three kids and he was needed in Southern California, specifically Orange County, for grandpa duty. As they were leaving, Jan hugged him and said goodbye a thousand times. She cried for a long time afterward and Matt knew why. Matt pulled out left onto the two-lane road in front and headed back to the ferry. He felt good, but would be lying if he said old Chuck didn't screw up his positive nature temporarily—the part that no man could shake was how long until that was Jan or him? He couldn't remember where he had read it, maybe Shakespeare in high school, but he remembered the words, "All great love ends in tragedy."

Why was he, such a young man, being so morose? Matt could only attribute it to all he'd been through, given all he'd seen, mortality was much higher on his list of thoughts than it should have been. He watched as Jan dabbed her eyes with a tissue and realized he was not the only one. He eased the vehicle onto the ferry deck, its nose coupled under the steel plate unsteadily.

He looked at Jan, and suddenly felt the need to have his hand in hers. At that moment he realized that if one concentrated on the end of everything, one would forget to live in the here and now, and it was in the here and now where all the great things happened.

Fortunately, on the trip back they were nestled in the middle of the ferry and had time to settle and enjoy the ride a little, although Matt longed to be in the front. They both loved this place. They decided to research the island to the max once they got back to the hotel in Seattle and if everything panned out with Chuck as planned, they'd just found their new home!

Shaking off the daydream of how he began his life on Lummi Island, the ferry pulled up on the mainland and Matt drove off, heading down his usual route through the Tsunami Sign Highway (his pet name). An earthquake was his only real fear, as he'd spent way too much time listening to informative TV this last year. He knew about the thrust fault that was out there and they'd practiced Lummi Island's own "run for the top" test numerous times. He shuddered to think.

Pretty soon he'd made it back to I-5 and headed for the safe house, although it wasn't so much a safe house as it was Matt's office. Tucked away in the woods, up near Whatcom Lake, it was a beautiful cabin style house that was to serve as Matt's headquarters until things changed in the future. It was nestled on a half-acre, not too ostentatious, but perfect for the privacy demanded in their work.

Relying on the old standby that good fences make good neighbors, he had a six-foot fence built around the place. It would keep out kids and if someone else wanted in they would find a way regardless. Among its amenities was a soundproof basement and science lab.

Matt had been absorbing a tremendous amount of knowledge from his multifaceted mentor. Every day of the week was a different lesson. Monday was computer training, Tuesday was global education and politics, Wednesday was self-defense/offense, Thursday was science lab, and Friday was a session with Frederick Tedesco, head-shrinker.

It was astounding the amount of patience and money TJAC (Thomas Jefferson Action Committee) was spending on him. As President Caulfield pointed out though, every single billionaire on the company's (non-existent) Board of Directors would have been decimated had it not been for him. Enough time had past, and bad sleep or not, his sense of fair play being what it was, he'd finally insisted Chase give him an assignment. Although his sleep had been shoddy, he had started to learn to just deal with living on only five hours.

Chase wouldn't allude to anything about the job on the phone, as was their protocol, but he was minutes from finding out as he merged for the turn off heading to the lake.

* * *

Lauren Betton was looking through her field glasses. It was another hot day in Ibarra, Ecuador and she was sitting about a quarter mile away from a store she'd discovered Matt Hurst used to frequent. It took heat, dirt, and showing his picture a million times, but she'd finally gotten a hit. Using all available assets, she found a man who could confirm that Hurst had been there. She didn't just bite on some stranger's information, however; she had to make sure it was credible. The source was a Veterinarian where Hurst had brought in a dog with a leg infection. She met the man by happenstance, as usually was what happened to a diligent reporter.

She was nearing the end of another seemingly pointless day looking for the man who had just disappeared. She corrected herself; she knew it had a point, many, as a matter of fact, as she had more than one horse in this race. She was showing Hurst's picture to a man on the street, asking, "Have you seen this man." It turned out the last guy she asked was an American who was visiting his aunt and uncle. He recognized Hurst.

"Why would you be looking for a dead man?"

She explained that she was one of the few people who didn't believe Matt Hurst was really dead. He gave her a sympathetic look and went on his way, shaking his head. She was resigned to going back to her hotel and having a cold shower when a man sitting at an outside restaurant asked why she wanted to know where Hurst was?

He was a very good-looking man, early forties, dressed nicely, but way too buttoned up for the weather; yet he wasn't sweating a bit. He was tanned, but not dark-complected, and he had soft features. He wasn't a laborer, Lauren could tell that right away. She loved his lips; he had the kind of lips people pay for. And he wore no facial hair; she liked that, too. She walked over to him. "Do you know him?"

"Well, my dear, by looking at you and listening to you, I know you're American. Why don't you sit down and tell me your story and then I will tell you what I know. I hate to eat alone and although you try to hide it, if you joined me, I would be dining with a very beautiful woman."

Lauren blushed slightly and agreed to join him. He introduced himself as Humberto Quezada. She introduced herself and sat down. He immediately ordered wine and they were off. She felt at ease with him, his nature was soft and she could tell he was no stranger to women. One could tell by his mannerisms and the ease with which he carried himself that he was a man of great self-confidence. She told her story . . . well, the part of it she wanted him to hear anyway.

She was born and raised in California and moved to New York when she was thirteen. She had always wanted to be a journalist and had been the editor for her college paper at Columbia. The summer she graduated was the summer that the story at Conceptual Labs broke. This is when her mission started. Her stepfather, Jerome Betton, was a man of means as he was a commodities broker, and they lived in upper Manhattan. She knew she could find a job and tow the company line, no problem, but she didn't want that. If she could talk Jerome into being the financier of the world's best investigative reporter, then she could be untethered to pursue her recently self-appointed goal.

She had taken his name even though she came into his life late. At first she hated Jerome because he broke up her mom and J.P., a music producer that her mom had met in LA.

Her mom had been in an abusive relationship with her real father, a struggling musician with a drinking problem. After another of many horrible incidents, she showed up at the studio looking for him—the man who didn't pay the rent and had left her to answer to the landlord. That's when she found J.P.

For J.P. it was love at first sight, a damsel in distress . . . no hell, two damsels in distress . . . and he swept them off their feet and showed them what normal felt like. Ironically, he had just shed himself of a similar relationship—the hard way. His wife overdosed and died in the bed right next to him. He had a son a few years older than her, she was 5 at the time, and they made a great family.

But it was never enough for Elizabeth Green. She could never be happy with a guy like J.P. because he was happy enough having what he had. Her mom's biggest fault was there was never enough when it came to money.

So when she met Jerome, that was that, and Lauren not only had to leave her stepdad and brother, but she had to go live in New York. At first she hated Jerome, he was staunch and really no fun at all. Then she noticed little things. Even though he had a very demanding job, he never forgot anything, especially sentimental things. J.P. had been in her life a long time and loved her, but he never did the little things with her that he did with his own son. She knew he loved her, but there was always this sliver of doubt that he never loved her unconditionally.

Not so with Jerome. Jerome lived by the motto that you loved what you spend time with and it didn't take long for her to figure out why her mom married him. He was much more than a full wallet.

He loved her mom and as a result of that, he loved her—unconditionally. She remembered how shocked she was seeing him in the audience of her school play during a weekday. He went to every showing of *Pride and Prejudice*, three of them to be exact, and it must have been rather painful for a man like him, but he never showed impatience. He even volunteered for chaperone duty at dances and all kinds of things men with jobs like his didn't do.

And the one endearing thing about him above all others was he loved to read as much as she did. He had books everywhere—one in the car, the bathroom, the office, and even the kitchen. That really bonded them. And he did the one thing she always wanted a dad to do above all else—he read her to sleep. He had the most wonderful voice and his narration put her to sleep in such a way that she never had nightmares again after meeting Jerome. He made her insecurities disappear with his absolute confidence.

Their first book was *Shogun* and to this day, it was still her favorite book. Within a year, she deeply loved her stepfather (she was not allowed to use that term) and asked him as shyly as possible if it would be okay to take his name like her mom had. She had never seen a man cry so hard as that day. He truly loved her and her words touched him and created a permanent bond, regardless of any future outcome of his currently wonderful marriage.

She could tell Humberto was gripped by her story, so she continued although his looks were distracting her.

She convinced Jerome to back her and she left for California right away. It was weird for her to be back in Northern California. She had lived in San Jose for eight years while growing up with J.P., but the circumstances had driven them apart and they didn't talk any longer. She'd tried, but he didn't return her calls. So she was alone, back in a place she had been just starting to get to know when she was young.

The first order of business was to investigate Conceptual Labs; of course, not from the inside, the place was like Fort Knox, but from the outside. Her first success came when she got a shot at Bill Westinghouse. Westinghouse was the CEO and owner of Conceptual Labs and had been shot during Chavez's escape. She knew that he would have a treasure trove of info, but she knew he wouldn't talk to a reporter. Fortunately, he didn't know her face, as she was new in town. It didn't take long scanning the faces of the drivers who came and went from the Lab to find Westinghouse. He was driving a new Dodge Charger with all the extras.

By the second week she noted that Westinghouse went out to lunch on Wednesdays and Fridays. Both Fridays he had gone up to a dive in the foothills above Menlo Park called Bucks. She had lunch at a booth on the other side of the restaurant and was partly shielded by a support beam, so Westinghouse was completely oblivious to her.

His waitress was blonde and in her twenties, very fit and tight, with straight blonde hair, and the right size boobs. One noticed she had them, but they weren't the main attraction. She had a very nice posterior and Lauren watched him track her with the most lust she'd ever seen.

She looked in the mirror and her green eyes stared back. She had straight hair too, but hers was red; not fire red, but this dull brick red that men loved. She had freckles, not massive freckles, but freckles nonetheless, and they ran into her cleavage. She had a little more than her competition there did, not too much more, and she always covered her looks at work. At five eight and a hundred and twenty pounds, she was fit, but had curves, too. She beat the competition by a hair in the boobs, but lost by a hair in the ass department. Both of their faces could be those of models.

So now she knew his weakness and she was going to have to step out of frumpy next Friday and see if she couldn't do the old "drop he hanky" bit on this obviously horny man.

Humberto was so into the story she was telling he jumped when the waiter arrived with dinner. She had chosen the *pescado* as Humberto had recommended it. Her story broke off for a minute for him to tell his. He was divorced. No big drama tale, no kids, marriage just wasn't for him. His ex was now a happily married woman with three kids at last count. He was a Veterinarian and had taken the practice over from his father.

Humberto insisted she continue her tale and she kept forgetting this was a lead she was following. It felt more like a date.

Acting on her "damsel in distress" plan she had come up with the week before, she waited for Westinghouse to arrive in the parking lot. She had a front spot and as he was approaching she got out of the car just in front of him, wearing a very flattering from behind pair of pants and a very cute and flattering top to show off the girls, just in case he like both floors, not just the basement. As she was about to enter, she wobbled her three-inch heels and went down.

She actually turned her ankle for real in the process and it really did turn out to be a rescue operation. He even carried her to the bench and set her down, but he limped and when he did, she could tell it hurt him even though he tried to hide it. She knew his right knee had had to be replaced as she saw him talk about it on *Meet the Press*.

She could tell he was smitten and when he insisted that she join him for lunch, she reluctantly agreed. She could see the confusion on her competition's face as she was taking their order. It looked like she hit the jackpot because it appeared he really liked freckles. He couldn't keep his eyes off of them.

Humberto gave a knowing smile at this that she didn't like. She looked at Humberto with non-approval and side barred. "Of course I knew he was married, I had his bio in my car. His wife's name is Candace, so he wasn't getting anything, but we hit it off and he wanted my number, you know, to join him the next week for lunch. I told him I don't give out my number, but lunch would be okay. I saw him for two months. In those two months, I softly got out of him all I could. The weekend before we had planned to sleep together on a getaway, I told him that I found out about his wife and dumped him."

Lauren took a bite off her plate, the fish was delicious, and she paused to ask Humberto some more questions about himself. She had already decided she was going to take him back to her room tonight. It had been a long time since a man made her feel this good on a date and technically this wasn't even a date! She was horny after her second glass of wine and could have finished now.

He wanted more, though; he wanted to know the reason she was here. Well, she decided a part truth was better than no truth. She continued, "After Westinghouse, I went on to the shopping center where the agents died and Hurst worked. It was at this point, Humberto, that this became more than a story; it became *the* story. This guy Hurst is the only one who really knows what happened, he's the only one that can say who was really involved.

"As I investigated those following weeks it became more clear to me that being as seasoned as Hurst was, he should have recognized it for an arrest. It got me to thinking. It would have been a great plan for them to be partners; and I wasn't the only one. Bill Westinghouse was still of the mindset that Hurst was a partner in this. So I became convinced that Hurst was the key to the whole thing and maybe not as small a player as everyone first thought.

"Then when it all unraveled and Pablo Manuel became the real villain, everyone forgot about Hurst or what role he played. Not me, though, because he is who I was following from the start and I like to finish what I start."

A couple of shots of tequila showed up and she wasn't shy about drinking one, making telling eye contact with this sexy man while she did it. He then gave her the lowdown on Hurst, how he brought in a dog with a bad leg infection from a fight. The dog stayed many days and Hurst was very concerned about him. Humberto also knew something else of huge value. Hurst had a friend.

Later, she laid back and looked at the ceiling fan spinning in her hotel room, exhausted from the kind of love making that Latin men were famous for. As she was going down that night she remembered how sometimes shit just falls right in your lap and how she felt now that she had finally taken a big step forward.

That was two weeks ago and now nothing; nothing but baking in her fucking van every day and peeing in a coffee can, which was okay the first couple of times, but the last one nearly made her lose it as it stunk so bad. It was time for a change of tactic; maybe she could reconnoiter a little.

* * *

He logged out of the chat site and looked around the remodeled library, so new and expansive. The old two-story building had literally been gutted to give the new library an open-floored design. It had crossbeam planters that ran across the ceiling of the second floor, the tendrils of the varied plants hanging down with beauty. The second floor had a railing that ran around the balcony and as you looked down to the first floor, you could see a statue of the Liberty bell with a wonderful ornate information plaque of gold lettering over the black marble.

The first floor had a cafe, a multimedia center for kids, and lots of books, both in print and audio. The second floor had private study rooms, but they were all glass and didn't appeal to him. Next to them were the public computers and periodical shelves. On the far side of the room there was a research and study area. He loved the modern library, but he missed the old one too—with its secluded nooks and long shelves that didn't quite go all the way to the end of the aisle to allow one to round the corner to the next aisle, and shelves that allowed one to hide there on the end cap. It was a quiet and calm place where he could hide from the outside world that came looking to bring its cruelty.

He would always hear them coming. They hadn't the ability to concentrate long enough to remember to be quiet. They knew he would be here because he wasn't out there. Then they would make too much noise and Mrs. Utley would chase them off. She was his biggest protector and the world's best librarian.

He went downstairs and bought a coke and thought about the stuff Tom Holsinger had been saying online as he opened his backpack and pulled out his brown paper bag and started to eat his peanut butter and jelly sandwich to which he had added a few chips. He had also added slices of banana today and it was a good move as the sandwich was awesome.

To do what Tom was suggesting would require a great cooperation from many people, but oh boy would that set things off. He imagined a movement like the one the Jesuit Sheep started. The Jesuit Sheep was his absolute favorite character in all of history and the fact that they named Pablo Manuel as the Avatar angered him greatly. By exposing him like that they removed the illusion that he could have been anybody. No one knew if he was a ten-foot giant or a five foot six, greasy-complected man with an inferiority complex.

Part of his problem growing up in a tough place like South Philadelphia was that he wasn't anything other than a nerd. He was German, Irish, Italian, and French, so he couldn't just blend into an ethnic group and be protected as, "their little friend." He was all alone and had always been all alone as both his parents were introverts and not very good parents at all. Once they came home from work, they would never leave the house. So he never had any kind of backup even from them.

He washed down the last bite of his sandwich with his coke and chucked the garbage into the trash. While he was thinking about trying Tom's idea, he realized that he would run into a lot of mean people who would disparage the idea until it seemed stupid. They would try to bully him right out of the picture—and he knew a thing or two about bullies.

His tormentors had come in every shape and color, for he was from one ethnic background that was bullied internationally—he was a nerd. He was only five-six and his skin had always had blemishes from the time he was twelve. His hair was oily by nature, so no matter how much shampoo or how many times he washed it, by that evening, it would be oily, and that was the best-case scenario. In the worst case, like in the summer time, just one hour after he showered he was a mess.

Robert had found out very quickly in high school that girls really don't like short greasy boys. Even the short greasy girls had standards. His face started at twelve, but his hair had always been the same.

He looked at his reflection in the cafeteria window; plain grey sweatshirt, grey sweats, and converse sneakers. No wedding ring. At thirty-nine he now added glasses to the greasy black hair and pimples that persisted to this day. He looked at his cap on the table. You couldn't wear a cap in school growing up, but he was an adult now and seeing as he didn't really have a job, the cap was a permanent fixture. He looked around again at his changed sanctuary. This place had been his only haven.

Although his parents never went out, they insisted he play outside. For a few years he'd hung with the neighborhood boys, enduring being different and always the butt of the joke. But then in the fifth grade Gerry Runnals moved in. Starting from that day, his life became a giant toilet bowl. First of all, Gerry was the biggest, meanest kid on the whole block and he gave the Irish kids someone to hide behind and find their own bravery, which was an irony since Gerry's brother was physically bigger than him. On Runnals' first day on the block, he'd beat up the biggest black kid there was in the whole neighborhood, a real bully himself, so Gerry's legend was built.

Robert remembered the first time he laid eyes on him. The gang was playing a spirited game of street "over the line" when he came out of the house into the baking summer sun. Well, he was pushed out actually, and as he came down the stairs in his thrice rolled-up jeans and white t-shirt, Gerry stopped the game to question loudly, "Who's this puke?"

His next-door neighbor, Andy Rusca said, "It's Robert Leme" and from that day on he was known as Robert Phlegmy. Runnals was merciless and mugged Robert whenever he'd come across him. There was no escape from this constant brutal nemesis who even seemed to have his school schedule down.

Robert grabbed a magazine and went to read it, but couldn't concentrate. He could never settle down when he thought about Gerry Runnals until he did it. He finally set the magazine down and brought out the folder from his backpack that he always carried.

He opened it and thumbed to the article. "Man killed in bar fight" was the headline. The story read that a man was shot and killed outside a South Philly Bar the night of August 6, 1999. Apparently there was a fight over a girl and the victim had punched a man in the face earlier in the night. Several hours later as he was leaving the bar an unknown assailant shot him several times before getting into a car and fleeing. The victim had been identified as Gerry Anthony Runnals of South Philadelphia. No arrests had been made.

Robert calmed down inside a little. Even after they turned eighteen the torture had continued as this guy never went off to any college and he'd certainly never kept a job. So every time Robert left his house, up until August 6, 1999, he'd heard the epithet "Hey Phlegmy" thrown his way.

He'd learned better than to disrespect him by ignoring him. If he did so, Gerry would burst off the stoop and start with the threats, "What, you think you're too good for me?" And the punching . . . there was always the punching.

Robert fantasized all the time about hiring a thug to beat him to death back then, and it had been such a comforting thought. In his daydreams he would watch from a safe distance and see Mr. Runnals teeth getting knocked from his mouth with brass knuckles.

Then came that wonderful day he opened the paper. He walked outside right away just to make sure. It was eleven thirty on a Saturday morning and Gerry would already have been out smoking, wearing his white wife-beater shirt and his Steelers cap. No Gerry. Wow, it must have been a wild night out in front, what with cops coming to notify and whatnot.

The way the neighborhood was built, everyone's bedrooms were in the back of the buildings so someone could get killed right in front and they wouldn't hear a thing, Robert could only imagine the horror felt by his mom and dad.

He looked at two kids playing in the library.

Maybe if someone would have reached out to him, maybe if he could have garnered even a single friend, then his life wouldn't be so unbalanced and lonely now. That's why he was so mean online, and he knew it. It was the only place where he could be the Alpha Male.

What confused him was the fact that it appeared that even though he was an asshole to his core group, that they still included him in talks. They still liked him in their own way. *Why would they bother to like me?* And Tom. Tom seemed so real. He even doubted that Tom would care about his greasy skin and hair. What kind of life was it when a man's only friends are people who think, "He's a bully?"

Robert looked around nervously because he was lost in thought. When he was younger, being lost in thought cost him a couple of times. His tormentors would sneak up on him, in school mostly, and that's why he hid here. Here it was they who stuck out, which is why he loved the place so much.

He was still safe in this library, but it wasn't the same. He could still hear the ghosts of Runnals and Rusca looking for him so they could continue the torture everywhere he went. But he also heard the voice of his savior in his thoughts.

She somehow sensed the trouble he was in, but never got the real story. Regardless, Mrs. Utley was his greatest childhood friend. He looked down at the refurbished front desk through the bars of the railing. It was there that he got the devastating news when he was twenty-three. Mrs. Utley had died in her sleep. He was so forlorn that literally a month later when the letter came he was not even excited at its prospects. She named him as her heir.

Apparently her husband was a man of means and left her no debt and with them having no children, he was the sole heir. After taxes, he received two hundred and eighteen thousand and a Victorian Home worth three hundred and fifty thousand. Having only been able to get small menial jobs, as no one ever seemed to like him for long, it was like God had shone a small ray of sunshine just for him, just to let him know he wasn't alone after all.

After all these years, he still came here every day he was able to. He came here every day so he could be where both of them were the happiest, and that was in the library. He thought about her at least once a day, as she'd saved him more times than he could count; and then she set him free, that sweet old woman. He grabbed his backpack and headed home.

As he exited the library he looked back, the remodel of the outside was done as an exoskeleton of steel framing. It was done by the remodel team as a means to leave the original building as intact as possible, giving it the look of having steel braces. Fitting for Pennsylvania, Robert thought. It looked a little awkward, but it did preserve the building just the way it was, as much as possible anyway.

He started down the street and there was a chauffeur standing at attention to the left. As Robert approached, the chauffeur swung the door of the limousine open and greeted him.

"Home, Sir?"

"No, Melvin, I need to stop by the office for something first."

"Very well, Sir, to the office it is." As the limo was pulling off he looked out and saw a plaque inscribed on the building. It read, "This building restoration was donated by Robert William Leme in memory of Librarian Eutice Utley." He sat back and put his mind to his new task, one that could bring sweeping change to an ailing nation.

* * *

The light was shining through the fucking slats again. He'd taped that motherfucker yesterday, yet somehow a sliver of sun was now shining directly on him. The hateful sun was waking his ass up too soon. João felt as if he had just hit the covers. He tried to hide behind his bedmate, but it was no use. The fucking tape must have fallen off. He tried to open his eyes but they were sealed shut with sleep crud. He wiped them and tried to find moisture in his mouth, but there was none. He'd partied hard last night. He turned away from the faulty blinds and saw only half a beer on the nightstand. Although he'd actually wanted water, there was none there and beer was better than nothing, so he gulped the remaining warm flat brew in a large swig.

When the voice said, "That's not good for you" he'd nearly jumped out of his skin. João turned to see who the dead man was and he could not have been more right. A corpse was sitting right in front of him, smiling that easy smile. He smiled too as he ripped the cover off Gringo, the one hundred and twenty pound Rottweiler who slept with him and yelled, "Help!" The dog was unresponsive. He yelled even louder, "Gringo, attack!" He kicked the dog, yet he remained unresponsive. His visitor held up a syringe and smiled. João's face fell as he observed the obvious chloroform towel near the dog's snout, "You killed my dog?"

"No, not killed, he's just sleeping for a while."

João observed that his uninvited guest was holding a pistol this time, showing him that his visitor was much less confident than the first time they'd met. The man pointed the pistol to the end of the bed and João saw a laptop sitting there.

"I brought you a movie to watch. Open the computer and it will start right away." His captor watched his face throughout the whole video and as suspected, it never changed expression, although inside, Pablo was sure João was freaking out. When the movie was over his attitude had altered toward the man holding the gun. His question was simple, "How are you still alive? I watched you die with the whore."

"Let's just say that I had a gut feeling so I hired a double for the last part. As it turns out, it was a good thing because I would have been captured. Of course, I never would have tried for the button as I knew the *gringo* would have shot me."

João looked at Pablo and the anger changed to something else, as they now had a common enemy. "He killed your Vera."

"He killed your Felipe," said Pablo.

Then he confirmed with him, "I just want to make sure that when I locate him I can count on you to fill Felipe's role, as he had intended all the time."

João said, "What do you mean?"

"He wanted you straight and focused because he wanted you to take his role with me as he was taking another."

João knew Felipe would not have forgotten about him, they'd just never had a chance to have that talk and now thanks to the *gringo*, they never would. He looked at the man who was no longer holding the gun and said, "Of course, you can count on me."

Pablo rose from his chair, "I'll send for you when it's time."

As Pablo went out the bedroom door, João had an angry thought. He got up and looked out into the living room. The last time someone had gotten into his room, his security staff was all dead, each with a silenced bullet to the heart. He looked out and found all three guards asleep and Pablo long gone. He was going to have to start locking his room, that's all there was to it.

* * *

The gravel crunched under his tires, making the sound that Matt had hated ever since he was eight. That was the day his tortoise got out of the yard and was in the driveway. He heard that sound then and ran out, only to see that his dad had crushed his pet under his two-ton work truck. It was more than his little mind could take so he ran and hid. To this day, though, that sound brought it all back; silly, but he hates gravel and always would.

He saw Chase's BMW and his stomach lurched a little. He'd asked for this assignment and now he was going to get it. He had to wonder what role he would play in all of this, and like most of his thoughts, he reverted to the movies. Remo Williams came to mind. It seemed more than probable that this was his path here. I mean, they weren't grooming him to play Bridge now, were they? There were only a finite number of things one could do with the skills he'd learned—and continued to learn.

He parked behind Chase's Beemer and went in. Damn his movie references, he always had to connect someone to an actor and Chase was a Robert Wagner doppelganger if ever there was one. He had the same prose, gait, and mannerisms of the actor to boot. He obviously stayed fit. At five eleven and no more than one hundred and sixty pounds, Chase Viana was a physically fit sixty-something male. Matt doubted he dyed his full head of hair, parted on the left.

He chided himself for his constant movie mind, finally concluding the same as his mother had, that it was all his dad's fault, as he had raised him on Westerns and movies of the Fifties, Sixties, and Seventies. Chase rose to greet him, and there it was. Matt had noticed that Chase, Ray, and even his mentor Jim Jensen, always had an air of pride when they met with him, like he would feel if he ever met Steve Young or Joe Montana. "Matt, how are you?"

"I'm fine, Sir, actually doing much better."

The conversation led all over the place, from family, to life on Lummi Island, to Jon Jon starting school soon. Of course, it steered to himself as well. After the small talk was out of the way, Chase started with, "Frederick says you're doing good, but still not sleeping well."

"I've learned to live on five hours a night, Sir, people adjust."

"I hear your studies are going well, especially in the computer lab."

Matt liked the computer lab, and the thought was, he was trainable as an IT person as he had the aptitude for it. "I particularly like that class, but this is all really too much, Chase. I feel so indebted in a way that I can never repay."

"Then you know exactly how we feel, Matt."

The next two hours were spent going over a file. There was an industrialist in Mexico who was not being a good person. He owned one of the largest bakeries in the world but he also was poisoning the U.S. by sending in drugs. "The DEA doesn't know about him, just us. He approached one of our board members, someone he thought he knew. The offer was a duel role and it was graciously declined, but not in a way as to cause suspicion. Our board member simply told him that she too had such a deal already, but they needed to talk again and hammer out some specifics of a future endeavor. They agreed to meet again in six months. This man is very well respected and no one has a clue about his double life."

Matt was a little confused and asked Chase, "So we're going after drug traffickers?"

"No, Matt, we're going after anyone polluting our country, and this guy is the worst of the worst, he must be removed with extreme prejudice." They went over it, settled on a game plan, and it was done. The troubling part to Matt was he knew he didn't have even half the ability of Jim Jensen, so why would they be using him for this?

After looking at the bad guy's file, though, Matt thought he would have little trouble shooting this fucker, and he certainly would not be losing any more sleep than he already was. But it just seemed odd. The one thing he liked about Chase Viana was he might have the chiseled good looks of any other pompous ass that seems to hold power and walk the halls of success, but once business was concluded one would never guess he was a billionaire. Chase Viana had the ability to talk to anyone on their level, whether it be a leader of a country or an over achieving ex-security guy who fell ass backwards into the world's most terrifying domination plot since the Third Reich.

He never just said, "Okay, Matt, I'll see you later." After hours they would always hang out and have a few beers while Chase schooled Matt in billiards and darts. The pool games were getting closer, but the darts were ridiculous. The guy must throw every day, Matt thought, as he lost another game of rotation.

Chase had real concern for Matt's father, Don Hurst. Matt had previously told Chase that Don had cancer but was now in remission. The local paper back home had him dying over a year ago, although he was fine and dandy, watching the Giants on cable and enjoying the last couple of years as a treasure of a lifetime, both as a grandpa and a baseball fan. His Giants finally had done it, and all it took was for him to move away, at least that's the barb Matt threw at him whenever he could, being an A's fan himself.

Don and Sherry Hurst were distant memories in America's past now that Matt was no longer the bad guy. The press gave up demonizing him when the President answered "the" question from a reporter during a press conference. The reporter worked for one of the TJAC board members, Jason Evans, whose communications group, Information Media Inc, had all the right connections—and all the right questions. That was why she was chosen and how the question was perfectly loaded.

The President spoke, pointing to Jason's employee, "Diane Hubbard, what have you got?"

Diane was ready and smoothed out, "Is there any evidence linking Hurst to any of this?"

President Caulfield's cooling reply was, "Well Diane, I'm glad you asked that. There has been no evidence in the investigation that shows Hurst was anything other than a victim throughout this situation. We've removed all warrants, both internationally and nationally, in hopes of bringing at least some peace to the Hurst family. Hopefully, for his family's sake, he's alive out there somewhere. Truthfully, his parents have always stood up to my administration and the press. They told us their son was a victim and not a traitor. Now this administration concurs.

"We reacted with prudence at the time and we apologize for the way the Hurst family and thousands of others were upended by this one group of people. I hate to use the term I'm about to use because it seems callous, and makes even a single life not worth saving, but in terms of protecting half a billion people, it's understandable that there would be 'collateral damage' in situations like this. Now think of how many others were collateral damage in this mess other than the Hurst's? Thousands, no doubt. Matt was just unlucky enough to be the highest profile. My heartfelt sympathies truly go out to everyone affected by this, even outside of our country.

"A lot of Ecuadorian soldiers died as well—let's not forget that. I'm afraid that history will have to sort out Matt's tale, but from our position, we reiterate our deepest sympathy to Don and Sherry Hurst and hopefully the press can find the decency to finally leave them alone."

That was it. The President had spoken, and Matt Hurst became a footnote, just another in the thousands that died or were destroyed one way or another by that horrible ordeal.

Chase had shown how much he cared about Matt in the coming months. Together, the TJAC Board members owned several media groups and Matt had received some positive press as of late, but only in small doses. If it became overkill, it would lead to scrutiny and that wouldn't do. Time passed and memories fade.

Several of the pieces were of the "What happened to Matt Hurst?" variety, one even mentioning the passing of his dad. Having never been found did give an air of "what if" to the whole thing, but it really looked like he was just a memory. America had a second Pearl Harbor to deal with now, and the man that was responsible for one of them was still alive, so it was easy to see how quickly the public had forgotten about Matt.

Pablo Manuel was alive and well as far as the American people were concerned and that gave them a new villain to hunt. But it was all smoke and mirrors. The U.S. Government did not want his followers to know they had killed him—they wanted no martyrs. So the search for Pablo had made the hunt for Osama bin Laden look miniscule. The U.S. had had to pretend to hunt for Manuel to make their ruse stick.

Unfortunately, that inadvertently led to the remaining Jesuit Sheep followers gaining a foothold of sorts, and it had to do with simple logic. Pablo still being hunted meant he was still alive, and if he was still alive, then there was hope. New websites, bumper stickers, and t-shirts seemed to spring up everywhere. There were even groups that had emerged in nearly every civilized country, groups that were waiting for their messiah's return.

Matt thought some of these peripheral groups might gain enough steam to make a difference, that they could persevere, but without leadership and more specifically, the charisma and cocksure of Pablo Manuel, the movement eventually stalled.

Coupled with that the fact that the U.S. Government was not finding the man they had already killed, people just went back to their normal lives and forgot about all of it. Which explained how the Hurst family was able to disappear in plain sight—that and a little help from the plastic surgeon.

Chase sank a three-rail bank shot to beat him for the third straight game of billiards, and that was it for playtime. The word "sank" jarred something deep inside of Matt, as he was constantly reminding himself of his reticence to act in the face of danger. As far as he was concerned, August 15, 2013 would be remembered as "a day of infamy"—a day that he was culpable for. He failed to act, plain and simple, cowardice under fire. He failed to push the button that would have stopped it all because he was afraid of death. Of course, "was" afraid was the operative word. Matt no longer feared his own death and it had more to do with faith than bravery.

The big difference between his mistake and Pearl Harbor had more to do with the now, as he'd created a situation where there was a mass underwater grave of American sailors that no one could visit, no place to see where loved ones perished. The depth of the water and the remoteness of the location made it near impossible to have any kind of permanent memorial. The entire *Bush* Carrier Group had been lost and with it over a thousand American lives.

Matt felt the weight of every family on his consciousness, and the one thing that weighed on him more than all others was inequity. People like Chase here had been telling him that it was not his weight to carry, but Matt knew things that no one else knew—things he'd believed the Lord personally communicated to him.

He could tell that Chase wanted to gauge his reaction to the news of his activation. He had that look like, "Now is the time to bail if you don't have the stones, Sonny." But truthfully it was a relief to Matt. He had been making a lot of money for doing something he loved and that was training to be TJAC's Agent Provocateur. He certainly wouldn't have made anywhere near this much as an analyst for the CIA. If this bad guy was really sticking it to the U.S., *then fuck him*. He looked through his packet—he was now going to be Norm Clausen from San Francisco, and Norman was headed to Mexico City.

* * *

Cecelia was stacking boxes of fans in the display window. They were the rotating kind and her father had gotten a good deal on them. Last time that happened she questioned why she even had to put them in the window at all, they had sold so fast. She was placing the last one into the display when she saw the *gringa* enter their small parking lot. She called her father, Mauricio, over and showed him. "Looks like Humberto's friend is here." She pointed at a woman who was talking to a man and showing him a picture. Cecelia gave her father that look of mischief that always got her into trouble, "Looks like she got sick of roasting in her van."

Mauricio looked out and furrowed his brow, "Why won't she give up?"

She looked at her father with that look again, "Maybe she needs a little encouragement."

He looked at her with great admiration. *With her incredible body and amazing looks she is the embodiment of her mother.* "Yes, maybe she does, my dear."

* * *

Lauren looked through her purse for all possible monies. She had thirty-eight dollars left on her person, with her bank account at a zero balance. She had checked out of her hotel two days before and her rental van was now overdue by three days. She'd changed her flight twice.

Although her mother was done with her endeavor and had dried up her financial well, her stepfather had been stellar, so she had tried working on his sympathy. She had begged for another month as this was a good lead, she was sure of it. The final answer was, "No more money." Of course, Humberto offered to let her to live with him temporarily and she almost took him up on it, but wisely chose not to. She knew what that would turn into and it wasn't necessarily a bad thing if you weren't chasing the story of a lifetime. She gracefully declined Humberto's offer.

She looked at her plane ticket morosely—her flight was in six hours. In six hours she would go home a failure with a giant hole in her résumé right out of the gate. She could just hear her internal narrative voice— which could be very negative at times—the minute she stepped home off the plane proclaiming, "And now ladies and gentlemen, if you focus your attention on the gangway, Lauren Betton will be coming home as the girl who gave up and failed." Yet it was also this critical internal voice that drove her.

She hated to lose and even worse, she hated giving up when she knew she was right. It was tough to continue to be upbeat and positive when the last nine months had yielded nothing other than a couple of worthy one night stands and more bouts of every type of stomach malady than one could name. That reminded her, as soon as she had money she was investing in whatever conglomerate that owned Pepto Bismol.

She started the van and pulled up outside the Mercado. She had thought about different tactics, but truthfully, she was out of time for anything other than an all-out blitz, one that she hoped would get some kind of reaction…anything that could extend her stay and keep her on the trail of the man she'd become obsessed with.

Although open for business now, the building looked like it could be converted into a fortress at a moment's notice, as the whole place was surrounded by a crazy amount of razor wire. The fence was solid wood and there was a big rolling gate that completed the fence once it was closed. She saw the parking lot was small and held only twenty spots, which was why she was always observing a double-parking madhouse outside most of the time. She waited until she felt the moment was right and made her move. As she walked into the parking lot she saw a man she'd seen several times a day talking with another. She recognized the two men as regulars.

Both men were middle-aged farmers and from what she could understand with her limited Spanish skills, they were talking about some kind of fruit trees. She waited until goodbyes were said and approached the man who remained, "*Hola*, do you speak English?" Unfortunately he did not, so she stumbled through with her barely passable Spanish as she heard her millionth denial. One of those doubts she had been suppressing was cracking though. She could feel its pickax just chipping away her confidence from the other side, just taunting her to get on that plane and accept what everybody else already knew. Matt Hurst was dead.

She slunk into the Mercado, her body language showing defeat yet trying her best to talk herself back into being positive. No story worth anything came easy—and she knew this—so why did she allow the doubts to sprout? She looked at her watch, five and a half hours until her flight.

The store was bigger inside than one would have anticipated from looking at the outside, a bit surprising actually. It was one of those "don't judge a book by its cover" type of places. It was kept neat and organized, which was also in contrast to not only the outside, but also the neighborhood as a whole. There were three rows off to the left that ran the length of the building and as she turned towards them a striking girl in the display window asked in English, "Can I help you?"

Lauren answered coyly, "Is it that obvious that I'm American."

The beautiful Ecuadorian girl answered, "I'm afraid so."

With a smile she introduced herself as Cecelia and her English was spoken very well. She explained that her aunt and uncle lived in Washington D.C. where she has gone to see them every year since she was ten. As she grabbed the last electric fan and put it in the window, Lauren saw what must drive men crazy. The girl had no body fat and a body like an hourglass. She was so fit and sexy that she was turning Lauren on and she had never been gay, not even experimentally in college.

Cecilia came back down out of the window and Lauren showed her a picture of Matt, "Have you ever seen this man before?" Cecelia looked at the picture and said, "Yeah, he used to shop here a lot."

Lauren was trying not to jump through her skin as she asked the next question. "How long since you've seen him last?"

The girl thought and said, "Well, let me see, maybe a couple of years."

Her heart sunk, but she tried not to show it in her expression, yet Cecelia picked up on it anyway.

"Why? Is he important to you?"

Lauren looked at her and thought *what the fuck do I have to lose?* "Yes, because I'm a reporter and he's the story of a lifetime."

Then the most incredible thing happened to her as she was going to thank Cecelia and leave for the airport. Cecelia said the most amazing words she'd heard in months when she uttered, "I know the girl he was sleeping with, we can go there now. It's not far away."

Cecelia had a Fiat sedan and she drove it like all the taxi drivers Lauren had encountered thus far. Lauren later learned that Cecelia's dad owned that Mercado, but at the time it appeared differently. When she told him that she was leaving, he'd protested, "There are still things to do."

When she responded, "Then fire me," and walked off, Lauren was speechless.

Lauren caught up with her and said, "I don't speak the best Spanish, but did you just quit your job?"

Cecelia giggled, "No silly, he's my father." She was quite the fireball as her driving was quickly showing Lauren, who'd been here in Ibarra for three months and had seen some crazy driving.

She knew Hurst had been in Ibarra because her old boyfriend told her so during one of their intimate talks. Lauren often fantasized about when her story finally broke and Bill Westinghouse came to realize that she was a reporter all along and that he had been had.

She winced as her new friend came way too close to a truck during an unanticipated stop. She had learned early on that there was a neighborhood in the eastern part of town that was to be avoided at all costs, and now it looked like they were headed straight for it. Lauren saw a few street signs, but damn if these chauvinistic bastards didn't name the whole town after men, and a lot of them started with Juan. They just passed Juan Jose Flores, and now she saw Juan de Salinas. As they turned right onto Eusebio Borrero, Cecelia noticed her concern.

"It's okay, I grew up here. The girl lives next door to my friends." That eased Lauren's mind a little, but she also knew the place. Three more right turns and a left and she was losing track of where she was.

In this part of town, the building structure was different as there were no more single story buildings. Here it was a four-square design like a mini-fortress. One giant rampart ran around the outer edge and was interspersed with periodic buildings and entrances. Most of them had courtyards inside which were all very different in design. Much like fingerprints, no two were the same.

A few had no courtyards, just had buildings throughout instead, but most went with an outdoor scene of one kind or another. Of the outdoor variety, Lauren had seen full-length basketball courts, soccer fields, and some even had mini-forests. Lauren knew this because she had canvassed here one day and stayed out too long, almost getting raped by two guys. The memory still haunted her and gave her nightmares to this day.

They said they had recognized Matt from the picture she showed them and they told her to follow them. She just knew something was wrong and started to back off, and that's when they got pushy. So she did the New York thing and "kicked balls and ran."

They were now in that same neighborhood and it gave her bad vibes. Cecelia pulled up at one of the complexes and parked. She looked at Lauren, "Don't be nervous, I grew up here." They got out and made their way into the complex through a gate that Cecelia had a key to. Once inside they were between two dark brown buildings heading up a shaded walkway. When they emerged, the sun was glaring in their eyes, so she shielded them and saw that this courtyard had a mini soccer field and no trees, but did have ten shaded park benches interspersed throughout.

They walked across the field and Lauren noticed the absence of any children playing? They headed toward a long building on the far side and then Cecilia lead her toward the right corner of the building that had an entryway leading inside. There were two benches near that corner of the field and Cecelia told her to have a seat and she would go get the girl and bring her out.

Lauren sat and looked at her phone; she now had four hours to get to the airport, but somehow she had a feeling that she wasn't going to be catching that flight after all. Her stomach rumbled and she realized that she hadn't eaten since she had some fruit that morning. She pulled her Ray-Bans out and placed them on as the sun was blaring, even in the shade of the bench awning.

On the distant corner of the field, five guys dressed for soccer were kicking a ball back and forth. They got out to mid-field and started playing a game of pass around. Lauren noticed that behind them were five girls of varying size. She looked away and checked the entrance into where Cecilia had gone, feeling a little uneasy. To lessen her unease, she decided to check her e-mails only to find her friend Scott Bailey had sent her one. Actually, it was a link to a story he had written, as he worked for the *Seattle Star* as the "Internet Watchdog."

Every time Scott wrote an article he automatically sent her a copy. They had gone to Columbia together and even tried dating for a spell. They were so good as friends that they decided they just had to try it as lovers. But that was where it all went wrong, as they ultimately wanted different things. She wanted to see what the world had to offer and do "serious" journalism, and he simply wanted to be what he became, and that was to snuggle in writing for a paper and become a "niche" guy that people would love and relate to.

It didn't take him long. Part of the original attraction was Scott's ability to bond with people and make friends instantly, but mostly he could make people laugh, usually by saying the stupidest things, especially when he drank. Each time she was tempted to write him off as an idiot, he'd say something profound and made her realize it was all an act. Actually he was a really smart, really funny guy, who sometimes even managed to be an "extremely romantic guy."

If she ever had the inclination to become a housewife some day in the future, she would run to him. At least she would never be bored.

Today's story was a diatribe on the video gaming industry. Apparently they had taken his sixty dollars to purchase the same game as last time, just slightly redone and now they would feel his wrath. His writing style was always so funny and she giggled to herself before she was brought back to reality.

She was expecting to see Cecelia connected to the voices she was hearing coming her way when she looked up. Instead it was the soccer girls who had come and sat down on the bench next to hers to watch their men play.

Lauren was troubled. She grew up in New York mostly and although she went to private school, she'd ridden the subway often. These five girls were all dressed the same. They had on jeans that were cuffed on the bottom, white t-shirts that exposed their stomachs and black and white converse shoes. All five had their hair the same as well—they wore it long, straight, and all had bangs. And they all had some kind of fusion of tattoos and piercings that made them look just like a gang. She tried to play off her discomfort by looking back at her phone and that got her a question from one of the girls, but seeing as she was looking down, she's not sure which one. *"¿Quién es usted?"*

Lauren looked up and answered, "I'm American; do you speak English?" That got a laugh from them and she saw the one speaking now, she was a little bigger than her other friends, and one could tell she was the first one to throw down. *"¿Acaso esto es los Estados Unidos?"* Lauren shook her head no and looked for Cecelia. She needed help. The girl got into striking range, her four minions closing in with her, *"¿Por qué estás aquí?"*

She fumbled in her purse and pulled out Matt's picture, her hand shaking badly. The girl snatched it and looked. She looked up at her, *"¿Cómo te atreves a venir aquí en busca de tu novio? ¿Sabes dónde estás?"* The tone of the girl was now crazy with indignant anger and Lauren quickly forgot all the training and role-playing she'd practiced on how to deal with these situations.

Now in the middle of it, she was reduced to a terrified child, crying, stuttering, and shaking, unable to remember how to reply in Spanish that she wasn't his jealous girlfriend. Worse for her, the one thing she did catch was the last sentence, and she did understand what the girl said, *and no she didn't know where she was . . .*

She muttered in English, "I don't know what you're saying." That was when the main girl called over to Gabriel. He ran over, dressed in shorts and a standard red soccer shirt, his white socks pulled up to his knees, and his soccer cleats new, white, and clean. The girl spoke angry questions to him in Spanish. He turned and in broken English said, "She want to know what you doing here. She says you looking for guy in picture, but how you get in here and why you look for him?"

Lauren said her friend Cecelia brought her here and she went to get the girl who was dating the man in the picture so they could talk. Gabriel translated and came back with two things. Why and Cecelia who?

Lauren answered Gabriel, "I'm a reporter and I don't know Cecelia's last name." Gabriel translated and she could tell the information was not received well by the girl as she was throwing a tantrum.

Gabriel relayed, "She wants to know what kind of friend don't know her supposed friend's last name? She thinks you lying and so do I, *puta.*" He said this as he was walking toward her, and without warning he two-handed threw the hard soccer ball right in her face, her glasses flying off but not before cutting open the bridge of her nose. She went down and when she did the pack was all over her. She was screaming, "Cecelia" throughout the beating until a vicious punch in the mouth broke one of her molars in half and that shut her up.

Then the kicking started. She felt ribs break and someone kicked her kidney so hard she almost blacked out. She was lying on her side, coughing out blood and teeth fragments when they started laughing and going through her purse. They found her airline tickets and she heard them laugh, saying that she was going to miss her flight.

She was in and out of consciousness when the leader came over and bent down in her face and grabbed her hair, pulling her face up by the ponytail. In the meanest cadence she spoke a diatribe in Spanish that was lost on Lauren. Gabriel came over and translated, "She says if she ever sees you again, you will die a painful death." She dropped Lauren's head back on the grass.

She was still on her side when she saw the player coming in dribbling the ball with his feet. The kick of the ball happened so quickly, even in perfect conditions, she wouldn't have been able to move or block it. It struck with the force of a large fist and her world went black.

She was in the deepest fog, but the fumes were too much for her to stay in the world of sleep. She started coughing and gagging as she heard the unmistakable sound of a bus pulling off and then the fumes got way worse. She opened her eyes to find she could barely see. As she tried to move she cried out in pain, something was wrong with her arm. She saw she was lying next to a tree on the street.

She sat up painfully and propped up against the tree. *Why couldn't she see very well?* She put her left hand up and felt her face. That's when she noticed she was only seeing out of one eye. She started to really panic. She was shaking so badly she could barely touch her damaged face and as she felt her eye socket she'd realized it was completely closed. It was weird to the touch and in the most painful thing she'd ever inflicted on herself she pulled her eyelids apart and was beyond relieved to be irritated by the sun. Her eyelids had been swollen shut like she'd seen in boxing movies like *Rocky*.

She could not believe that she was actually alive and she immediately thought about Cecelia. *What happened?* She then realized she was in her bra and panties. They had taken all her possessions. Something was scratching her stomach so she looked down and it was some papers tucked in the front of her underwear. She pulled them out as an *abuela* and her three *nietos* walked by looking at her like they just saw the devil. The woman shielded their eyes and ran off obviously disturbed at the sight of the devil woman whore that was ruining her grandchildren's innocence.

The papers were her airline tickets and passport and her thirty-eight dollars. She hadn't the wherewithal to process that before the headaches hit her. She put her left hand to her head, her right arm still didn't feel like moving, but she had no idea why. She resisted the feeling to take a little nap before she made her next move, but she didn't seem to be able to resist. Her eyes were closing when the taxi came skidding up. She heard, *"Señorita, ¿estás bien?"* and that was it, blackness hit and light wouldn't come again for some time.

* * *

The clouds looked so different here. They stacked in columns and when the plane hit them, it reverberated like it was gliding through an extra soft pillow. Matt looked down, the descent into Mexico City passed over a suburb. It seemed the standard of living in that part of town was good, the houses looked large and every home had a pool.

He'd done his homework before beginning the mission. His target had a file and like most people, his life had a pattern. One of his patterns was going to church. It was there that the hit would take place. This was the one opportunity to get him and if he missed and alerted him, they would never get another open shot again. He loathed and fought the idea of taking a shot in such a crowded place and worried about killing a bystander. He was going to attempt to do it with as little horror as possible. The plane landed and he lost the sun in some low-lying clouds.

Matt disembarked into the terminal and headed for the luggage claim. He found the carousal and waited and waited, but his suitcase never came out. So he went to baggage claim to file the report and find out what happened. He wasn't worried about any weapons he was bringing in being detected because everything he needed was already here.

This apparently was what they hired him for, to be a paid killer of the highest order, *the one who didn't miss.* Well old Jim Jensen sure took the place of Russell Peltz and then some. Peltz had been his first mentor, other than his dad, and he had high praise for Matt's skills with a gun. Jensen saw something else altogether, and it took him weeks to fix the hitch he had in his rifle shot. He had also picked up a bad habit of closing one eye and it took forever to get him to stop. Of course, now he could blow the balls off a squirrel at a hundred yards with no scope.

He used to laugh at the movies because the shots the guys were missing with rifles he could easily make with a pistol. What he could now do with a rifle was downright nasty and this target would be a comfortable two football fields out. At that distance, Matt was dead on. They chose that distance for just that reason. At four hundred yards or inside, if Matt had a rifle on someone, then that someone was a dead man on the first shot.

The dumb-ass airline clerk at the counter was telling him his bag was just behind on the next flight. He would have to wait an hour. He realized that this was an inauspicious start, but he shrugged it off and walked over to the luggage recovery area where he almost fell over a mountain of lost suitcases. It was a twenty-foot long, foot-high madhouse of bags of all sizes. It was the most backwards ass shit he'd ever seen and he was sure he would never see his bag again as he plopped down and waited on a bench.

He went to the pay phone and used his disposable calling card—the number memorized—to call Jan. She was not a happy camper and it almost reminded Matt of the old days when she would get so bitchy with him, but then she reigned it in. He tried to do the old reversal of roles thing, but it just didn't work as he had a calling that was only between himself and God.

Of course, before he embarked on his mission he took her out to their boat to explain why he had to make this trip. Matt had designed the perfect length rope to get them away from the dock and keep them out of harm's way on the Sound; this a result of Jon Jon getting out one night and heading to the dock when they were tied up to the dock making love.

Last night they'd zippered up the cabin to avoid the mosquitoes and made passionate love on the Sound. The moonlight was playing off the water and they could see the San Juan Islands in the West. The boat rocked with their rhythm and he reminded her again—in a non-verbal way—that he was different now, much more in control in every aspect. After lovemaking they unzipped the cabin and got out the sleeping bag. They both climbed in and just absorbed the universe as a whole. It was such a wonderful night, what with all the sounds of nature and God's breathtaking round night-light overseeing them, providing light where there should be darkness.

Matt never looked at a full moon the same since one of them saved his life. It was the night he and Vera fled the United States; they both surely would have perished if Doug Sharp had had to fly at treetop level in total darkness. Since that night, he never let a full moon pass without taking notice of its splendor.

They looked back at the house and it was all lit up, the bay windows in full glow with Jon Jon in the window closest to the fireplace, looking out with his grandparents behind. He understood why she didn't want him to go, but he wanted her to understand that he wanted to help make this world safe for their son. Matt Hurst was not going to just sit back and ponder the daily news until the day he died. At least this way he was attempting to make real change in the world that Jon Jon would grow up in.

Jan wanted to start in on him as he was leaving the next day, but she held her tongue and just let him go.

He was hanging up with her, hoping that she came to some sort of understanding of his obligation when he saw the handler wheel his bag up and prepare to throw it into the luggage abyss. He was up and running before it got added to the madness pile, as his bag had no tags left and was headed for purgatory when he caught up to it. After some heavy pleading and the use of his new language skills, he got his bag and headed out of the airport to get his car.

As he stepped out onto the sidewalk he was hit hard right in the face, his nose was on fire and he almost went down for the count. He steadied himself and exclaimed out loud, "Yuck, how can anyone breathe this air?" It was a combination of rotten egg and bus fumes and he would rather have ridden in a downtown cab in mid-summer rather than endure this horrid place one more second. It was quite literally incomprehensible for him to imagine living in this madness.

It set the tone for an almost unintelligible run to his hotel. With the rank odor, blaring noise, traffic and madness that is Mexico City driving, it took a few intersections just to get settled. After a few miles of GPS instruction he turned right on Calle Isabel la Católica. From his beloved *History Channel*, he knew that Mexico City was built to rival the great European cities. He saw French influence in the buildings architecture and remembered the style as Porfirian. He remembered them saying that Mexico City was known as the La Ciudad de los Palacios (City of Palaces), a nickname some 19th century guy gave it, but the man's name eluded him.

Great, now that was going to cloud his thoughts until he remembered or more likely, researched who had said that? The point, he argued with himself, was that the bloody place had lots of European influence. That was a time killer and before he knew it he was turning his rented Passat right on Avenida 5 de Mayo and a few blocks later, he was checking into his room at the Hotel Central on the Plaza de la Constitución.

Matt had been to Mexico before. His dad made a good living in construction and he had grown up not really ever understanding the true value of a dollar. His doting mom always was slipping him cash as he was leaving for any adventure. Whether it was a trip to the mall, a concert, or spring break in Cancún, he was always able to participate without feeling shy about not having money. They'd rented cars on their trips and ventured out into other cities and ruins.

Of course, it was nothing like this, but he didn't have the feeling he would have had if he'd just been set loose in Istanbul on a mission. Mexico could be a very strange and sometimes terrifying place, but he could think of a lot worse. Technically, he had been to Mexico City twice to change planes, which makes him almost a native. However, he had no clue about the three hundred pound gorilla that jumped you upon exiting to the street, otherwise he might have been more prepared for that. He wondered if other assassins took into consideration such things. *Other assassins?* He looked in the mirror of his room. He wasn't sure what looked back, but it surely wasn't an assassin. He did play the part though; he wore dark glasses and had a hat.

Over the last nine months he'd learned to speak provisional Spanish, but they also had fine-tuned certain conversations and taught him to use his body language to keep people from talking to him. Jim Jensen had a laundry list of things he'd taught Matt so far, and one of them was mimicry. He was so good and he could switch from Spanish to French, Italian, and finally Russian. He wasn't fluent in any of them, but he'd learned how to use bad temperament as a tool to get people to be wary and not want to engage him. Not anger, but a bad disposition and a bad aura in general. It could be done and it could be done effectively.

Jim Jensen stood only five foot seven—and had the tiniest feet Matt could remember on a man—so it was easier for him to blend without being remembered. Matt had no such luck, as he was a six-footer. Easy to remember is the big *gringo* standing tall, not so easy to remember is the same *gringo* when he's learned to hide his height by stooping and leaning on counters. He hid his European looks with hats and glasses and a beard. Although normally clean-shaven, he could grow a mean beard quickly. Matt learned to hide his warm inviting nature with a slight scowl and contemplative thousand-yard stare. Cell phones now provided excellent ways to be rude and not draw notice; just be another idiot in the masses, he was taught.

He doubted the desk clerk could accurately give a description of his physical appearance, nationality, or height. Matt knew something about that game from his former life as a Loss Prevention Manager. It was never easy to catch a crook when you look like a cop.

He pulled back the curtains and the Mexico City Metropolitan Cathedral was in his immediate view. His window was lined up with the street that separated the huge square that was to the right. It ran at least a couple city blocks long and one wide, like a mini-Vatican. The street that was in front was actually part of a one way that ran around the square, the top of which separated the square and the church. He looked from his current vantage point and sure enough, the church exited right onto the street in front of the square. At this distance his target would stand little chance.

He looked around the square, which was surrounded by buildings that were all obviously European influenced and all very high, and which afforded a lot of places from which to take a shot, that was for sure. He was watching people come and go and it wasn't hard to see why they had chosen this spot.

Matt heard a shuffling noise and looked to see an envelope slid under his door. He picked it up and found a key to a room one floor above. He picked up his bag and carefully headed to his destiny via the stairwell, making sure to keep his cap pulled down in case of some unknown camera.

The new room was a suite, whereas the last room had been a king bed single. This room had a living room and a bedroom, plus the vantage point a floor higher provided. Matt immediately noticed there was a case on the bed. He also noticed the French doors that led to a private balcony. He unsecured the bolt and latches on the door and went out onto the balcony before checking his suitcase, as he knew what it held. The view was impeccable and he certainly wouldn't miss from this distance. The car was parked half way up the block. After the shot he would use the staircase, walk to the car, and head out.

He'd brought enough food and water in his backpack that he would be fine until after he was done tomorrow—there would be no going out to enjoy the sights. TJAC's Intel had his target walking out the gate out in front of the church every Sunday morning at 11:20 AM. He would walk to the left once he was out of the church, away from where his assassin waited.

Matt walked over to the suitcase and opened it. His modified Ruger 10/22 stared back at him. After Jim had taught him to kill with the big fifty calibers, Matt thought, *that's how things went down, with a boom.* Maybe in a war. Jim taught him a lot of things go boom in a war, as there were plenty of reasons to make very long shots in a war. That was not the case here. Here he was going to make a shot in a crowded area and one wouldn't have the luxury and firepower of the boom. With his Barrett, even if a target hid behind a cinderblock wall, it would not matter.

This gun was different. Jim had made it from scratch so that Matt would be as "one with the gun" as possible. Actually, they had built two at once, the other one staying back in Seattle. They started with the stock. Jim had a friend who made every form of stocks: wood, plastic, metal, and graphite. Jim made Matt go through them one by one. He felt like Harry Potter picking a wand out before his trip to Hogwarts. Finally, he settled on a wood stock and then they went to see Jim's other friend, the machinist. What they walked away with was this amazing gun. Having a 29-inch barrel was the key here.

Once they got back and he attached the scope, they practiced using it on the range. Matt was stunned. Not only was this the most accurate gun he'd ever shot, it was also nearly silent, even with no enhancements. He estimated that the pellet rifle he'd used to use to keep the cats from killing birds at his mom's feeder was louder than this rifle.

Jim needed to sight it for distance, so they went into the backyard. The house was surround by the chain link fence, but the backyard had privacy slats put in so you couldn't see through. He told Matt he would have to take the gun to open ground to truly set it and test it, but he could come close here.

Their only neighbor was an old man a couple of parcels down and after that house, there was a deserted hill that was tall enough to catch the fallout of what they were about to do. Jim told Matt that the man had logged the hill to make money, but this was good for them, as there were no people hiding about. They had observed the old man previously—he was the type who was always trying to keep the local kids on bikes off his property.

At the end of his property he had a big apple tree that hung over the back of his house and patio. Spotting with field glasses, Matt was instructed to pick out certain apples. The gun and the man were amazing. Jim wasn't just dropping apples by shooting them through and through; he was dropping them off the stems. But the most incredible part was the sound. The spring sound was the most dominant, not the gun's report. This gun was a silent killer.

Then Jim blew Matt's mind. He pulled out sub-sonic 20-grain ammo and the impossible happened. The gun got quieter. They switched positions and to Matt's amazement, he dropped a few like that, too. This guy was like Russell Peltz in that regard, and he doubted he would ever be better, but soon he was going to give him a run for his money . . .

They shot a few more apples until one hit the old man's patio roof, then the old man came out on his porch and screamed out into the whole neighborhood, "You kids stop throwing rocks at my house!" That garnered a chuckle and they slunk back into the house to avoid possible detection. But the indelible mark had been imprinted. You don't need boom to be a killer. A 22-long rifle was a deadly and accurate gun in the hands of the right person. Then the right person assembled the gun and began the long process of the wait.

Matt double- and tripled-checked all aspects. The tripod was set, he turned out the lights, cracked the French doors and sat back deciding to "mock snipe" the passerbys out in the plaza, completely unaware of the scope they were under.

His beard itched. Jim taught him to grow a week's worth of beard beforehand and shave it after settling in. He also carried a small shampoo container with bleach in it for the cleanup. If someone did remember him, it was with a beard, not clean-shaven.

He lay in bed twisting and turning. The temperature wasn't right, the pillow wasn't right, the bed sucked. He finally fell asleep around two in the morning and there he was, right back in Vera's bed. Before the current madness had started, sometimes the dream allowed him to look at her sleeping. Even in his dream his heart fluttered when he saw her, she had such a spell on him. Then the madness started. Tonight's was especially bad and he awoke to the alarm clock at just past six in the morning. *I guess it's only four hours of sleep tonight.*

He had no computer or phone, so he didn't have even a game to take his mind off things. He sat and stared at the ceiling, reliving the last two years, as he often did. Sometimes life just did that to you, it dragged you out of your comfort zone and shoved you into a new zone. Growing up in California, and especially being there in '89 for the big quake, he knew what it was like to be fine one minute and fighting for your life the next.

The second he went out that door after her, there was no turning back. He had replayed that parking lot a thousand times and a thousand times he came back to the same conclusion. None of this would have happened if those two inexperienced agents had verbally identified themselves. The agent who was trying to kill him was under the presumption that Matt was her partner, and that he was attacking his partner. That was his deadly mistake.

The two must have had a hunch that she would try to get new clothes. How could it have not also occurred to them that a store detective might not let her do so. Most people never knew what it was like to actually die, but when the agent Matt was grappling with got free and spun around, he knew he was going to die and he still believed that just like in *Jacobs Ladder* he lived his whole existence in that moment. He broke out of his body, went to a parallel universe, lived a life there and came back before the agent could pull the trigger. She must have been very quick getting the gun from the man's partner, a partner that he had just killed who a second earlier had been containing her in a choke hold. If she hadn't, when he came back to this universe to face his fate, the bullet would have been flying for him. Instead, she changed his destiny as he had changed hers.

The elation was short lived, though, because then she trained the gun on him. He now knew that had he not gotten up right then and made it for his car, she would have killed him. She admitted as much while they were talking post coitus, and it was no bluff. That was at three in the afternoon. By nine they were making love in Tahoe. Somehow, what transpired in that parking lot fused them. He just didn't know how seriously at that moment.

At the time, he was just trying to stay alive and trick her as he could tell that something was going on in her head with regard to him. He never for a moment thought he would actually fall for her. When they were attacked in the airport hanger a short time later, he'd never thought he would have the kind of feelings for her that he had. Uncontrollable outrage was exploding in his head the moment before he pulled the trigger that ended her attacker's life. The man was on her, raping her, and its effect would have been the same as if it had been his wife of twenty years. From disgust to outrage to plain murder, he had always tried to reason out that it was all for God and Country, but the reality was, her outraged lover pulled that trigger every bit as much as the patriot Matt Hurst did.

It took months for Frederick Tedesco to drag that out of him, to admit that he viewed her as "his" even at that point. He still resisted the implication, but the fact remained, for the next two years he was with her and Matt could not deny her indelible influence on him. From her looks to her smell, his mind wandered into her arms whenever he daydreamed, for she was unique beyond description.

Although it was an amazing time, he also had become a household name, but not in a good way. For most of the last four years he was regarded as the worst traitor his country had ever had.

Once he returned home after stopping them, the God stuff started up with him. Subtle at first, then not so subtle, he was being told to be part of a higher calling. He was to do something different than those two, but still have the kind of impact they did. Matt had decided to just let God guide him through and take the paths as they opened up, not to try to microscope it too much. If it really were his destiny, it wouldn't matter what he did in the interim as long as he recognized the right path at the right time. Somehow it was that logic that had led him here today, to rid the world of another villain.

The clock now read half past the hour. He had burned thirty minutes on that trek down memory lane. He got up and looked out on the square. The sun was breaking over the tops of the buildings and life was beginning to waken out there. The square seemed to never sleep, but it was sparsely populated at night compared to the day. The weather was in the sixties, not a cloud in the sky, a perfect day for a kill. He had bided his time and now the hour was eleven.

He was in the final throes and it was twisting him, no matter how hard he tried to pretend it wasn't. Eleven fifteen. He was on the threshold and there was no turning back, a lot of people were counting on him to do the right thing. Then it happened, his target was in view. Fernando Vargas walked out with his entourage, but it wasn't the usual guards and such; instead it was the largest family he'd ever seen.

They broke off to the left and were inside the outer fence, closer to Matt's position. There were at least thirty of them, but he suspected it to be more. Vargas was a sitting duck. Soon the arranged distraction was to go off and that was Matt's cue. A blue van came around the turn that ran across the front of the church and Matt saw what looked like a red belt thrown out the window, only it was smoking. The next thing Matt knew, the firecrackers were going off at the edge of the Square.

At first it startled everyone, but then all the kids in Vargas's family ran to the fence to watch the excitement; all except one. Matt guessed that she was the man's granddaughter, as she was only about three and Vargas appeared to be nearing sixty. The girl was adorable in her yellow and white Sunday school dress with a yellow bow through her hair. Apparently she had an aversion to loud noises and ran to Grandpa when it started. He had a clean shot on his target . . . but the man was holding his granddaughter.

The firecrackers were still playing out while Matt had Vargas under scope, his finger starting to put pressure on the trigger. He was about to go a place he could never come back from and then it hit him. This was the same strategy of the two people he killed in Ecuador. Vera and Pablo thought they could change the world with such heavy-handed tactics and what did it bring them?

Vargas tried to console her and tried to move closer to the fence to show her there was nothing to fear, but she just buried her head deeper in his chest and started crying.

The time was now for the shot, but it was never going to happen. Matt just imagined the dime-sized hole in his head spurting brain and blood all over this little girl. If this is what Chase Viana wanted, then he'd picked the wrong man. He looked one last time at the villain who seemed to be a pretty good grandpa and shut it down. He only killed to imminently save lives and even then, his past hesitation in Ecuador cost a lot of people their lives when he failed to react in a timely fashion. He'd had to live with the guilt that his reticence cost many a life, and if he would have acted sooner back then, a carrier group would not be on the bottom of the Pacific Ocean.

TJAC didn't need to do this if they knew who Vargas was, there was a million ways to do it; they didn't have to destroy the lives of his family for his machinations. Plus, killing someone in front of a church? Well, this was the end of his career at TJAC, he was sure of it. He wondered if they would now try to kill him? Probably not, as he still had friends in high places now. If he disappeared, his new friends might do some investigating—he thought of Ray Callahan—but Chase wouldn't be happy nonetheless and Matt wondered what the true fall-out of this would be?

His movie mind went back to the scene in *Scarface* when the guy wanted Tony to blow up the car of the informant with his wife and kids in it. Tony wouldn't oblige and the Colombian Lord, Sousa, brought the whole drug army down on him. Matt was thinking of the actor's rage at Tony letting an opportunity get away, and he wondered if there was any Sousa in Chase?

For months Matt had been toiling inwardly over the concept of violence, and he was now sure that no matter what the Divine plan for him was, the path to answering God's Will would not have violence involved. If he'd taken that shot, he would forever be one of "them," a person who killed without provocation and without conscience. He was not that person.

He repacked and locked the suitcase. He went back to the window and watched the Vargas entourage walk down the block. If he was an evil shit, then Karma was going to catch up to him. Matt believed that to his bones. In a kind of stunned silence, he left the hotel and blankly walked back to the car, forgetting all the training he had on tails and how to move through crowded streets to ensure that he wasn't followed.

He popped open the trunk and threw the suitcases in and before he knew it, he was gone. He needed to dump the gun and he finally found a modern looking market that had dumpsters in the back. He took the ammo and threw it onto the building's roof, and then he placed the rifle under some rotted garbage, covering it with some boxes, hoping it made it to the landfill. Afterward he went around to the front to make a call to Jan from the payphone there.

She answered it on the second ring and she knew right away something was terribly wrong. He cut off her million questions and told her, "I promised I would never leave you in the dark again, so take the first flight you can to Cancún. Take a taxi to the Americana Fiesta. No questions, pack for a week, get cash, no cards, don't forget your passport, you need them for Mexico just like Vancouver. She said, "Okay" and hung up with no questions.

She was getting better at learning to trust him and not try to lead the dance all the time. He got in the car and headed for the airport. If they were going to kill him, he was at least going to get some snorkeling in beforehand. Jan hated when he became flippant in the face of calamity, but if she'd seen half of what he had in his life she then would have known that things would play themselves out.

If he were meant to die, then a second shooter would have done in Vargas, and his car would have went boom when he started it (he checked it anyway, not forgetting *all* of his training). He really needed to think and he wanted to see and feel the sun for a few days. No computers, no phones. Then he had another thought and reminded himself to look for the BofA logo—they couldn't track cash so easy. If they both went only cash for a while, it might give him time to think.

He pulled into the airport and as he got out of the car at the rental return building, the punch came out of nowhere. He stepped back in shock and reminded himself, if he ever came here again to bring a respirator. As his AeroMexico flight lifted off and pulled through what Matt knew now to be pollution, not haze, he was amazed once again to see the giant volcano jutting up like a hidden monolith, literally towering invisibly over the masses. *Adiós, Mexico City.*

CHAPTER TWO

Acceptance

L ocated in the heart of Los Angeles was the Garment District. It was just southeast of downtown and covered a good five square miles, the many businesses offering numerous types of wares. The alleyways and the streets were lined with vendors on both sides, some selling clothes they'd made, some fabrics so the masses could make their own clothes, others selling brand names for less, and then there were those who sold "knock offs" which the cops were always pointlessly trying to stop, as if . . .

John Fernandez worked as the Store Manager for the local supermarket, Alberto's. He grew up in L.A. in one of the roughest areas in the nation. His childhood was a mixture of joy and terror, but he had a great family. His father working at a local brickyard since the Sixties and when one worked in a brickyard, one tended to be strong. His father was John Senior and John Senior did not own one power tool. He bought the house in 1969 right after he'd returned from two tours in Vietnam.

He had been a combat soldier, but he didn't seem to have Post Traumatic Stress Disorder like many came home with. Anytime he had stress, he went to work on something. To this day, he also did not own one power garden tool either, so his house was his mind's retreat and it was the embodiment of his hard work. In the late Seventies the neighborhood changed and the gangs came in. That brought the terror.

John was just a kid in his teens, so he was an easy target walking home. He started hanging out with a kid whose older brother was in the Vagos street gang and before he knew it, they were planning to initiate him. That's when he ran to his dad. He was still not sure what exactly had gone on that day, but he'd once heard a spirited, rum-filled conversation with his dad's friends at a party. John swore he'd heard the word grenade involved.

Whatever his dad did, it gave him a pass that held up all these years. To this day, whenever he walked out and past the hangout near the corner, he was never bothered; he got a nod. In this neighborhood, that was bigger than one could imagine and he could only surmise that what his dad had done was of such bravado that he had became a kind of warrior legend and it just stuck.

As long as he was in "his" neighborhood, he was safe, which was why he bought the house right across from his parents. He walked to work every day. He did live in L.A. after all and it rarely rained here, plus his car was too nice to leave in the lot at work. His '69 Camaro was his dream car and it stayed in the garage unless they were driving out to Santa Monica Beach. He looked around at gridlock above at street level, *why drive in this madness when my store is just two miles away?*

He started working there when he was just sixteen and now at almost fifty he'd known nothing else. Being a Store Manager in such a unique area was interesting because the store served his neighborhood and was also the only grocery store near the Garment District itself. So he was able to make sure his corner guardians got the right kegs of beer on Friday night and that he found the right caviar for his Russian clients, clients who ran the fur warehouse and loved to give their friends discounts. As a result, his wife got a fur stole that she cried over. He secured the right beer and bratwurst for the German couple who ran the textiles warehouse where he bought his clothes and the right carne for the Mexican *taqueria* owner around the corner. Not to mention the Filipinos—oh man, some of the stuff those guys ate made *menudo* seem tame.

His own neighborhood was mostly Hispanic, but once you got into the actual Fashion District—as they liked to call it now—then it was all international, and he was the man that knew how to make them all happy.

He walked under the Harbor Freeway by the Convention Center, headed east up Pico toward his store. He began to think about the blog. He hadn't heard from El Conejo in about a week, ever since he went to meet his new boss. Same with Philly, and even though he was such an ass, things were not the same without either of them.

John hated that about the Internet, one could make real friends and then they'd be gone, and you'd have no clue what happened to them. He made a mental note to get some phone numbers tomorrow morning. His wife, Miranda, told him, "Who cares, you don't even know them." Then she would ask if he'd read to their daughter yet and any thought he had of time for himself was pushed in the waste basket, just like all married men the minute they had kids. He figured that women got away with this because no man wanted to leave his kids. And if one's wife was hot like his, then no guy wanted to leave that door open, either.

John liked Tom Holsinger. He could tell that he was a white boy, despite the Conejo moniker; but that didn't matter, his ideas were good. Tom had a way—even in writing—of carrying himself. He wondered if he was as enigmatic in person. He definitely was going to get phone numbers tomorrow. Miranda was wrong, he felt real concern and worry for his friends, cyber-world or not.

If someone could stop pundits from clouding the issues all the time, real stuff could get done in this country, but like Tom said, it's all being done on purpose. He walked across Broadway and into his store. He was expecting some special deliveries today for the German couple, and seeing today was Thursday, he needed to make sure his corner friends stayed happy for the weekend. He had the best home security there was—a gang that liked him. Such was life in L.A.

* * *

Lauren's eyes opened to another room. How many had she been in? This one was more like what one would think a hospital room would look like. She went to scratch but couldn't, her left arm was in a cast that ran from shoulder to wrist. She remembered somewhere from out of the fog that the doctors had said her arm was broken in three places. She'd been in and out of sustained consciousness for what must have been weeks. She had recollection of an emergency surgery and she remembered finding out from the doctor before they put her out that her spleen had been ruptured. They said they had to remove it right away. As she was going out, she literally thought she was never going to wake up again—but she did.

They had to keep her on morphine, as five of her ribs were broken, as well as her spine bruised. Every day she became a little stronger it seemed.

When they'd brought her in, she was near death as she was actually bleeding to death internally, yet some sharp doctor had saved her.

She became terrified as she recalled bits and pieces of what had happened to her. The more they cut back the medications, the more she remembered. Currently she remembered enough to know that when she got better, there was one place she was going to pay a visit—the local Mercado where there currently worked a snake in women's clothing.

She wanted to adjust herself so badly, but her left arm was in traction and the right one had an IV line in it that ran from a bag on a pole next to the bed. Of all the things she loathed, being stuck in this entrapment was number one, as the need to scratch an itch was maddening.

What I wouldn't give for one of those telescoping back scratchers and the right man to do my bidding. Hell, even a woman. She'd gladly switch teams for a good scratch. She was about to try to wiggle her butt over a little bit, which of course meant she had to suffer the rib pain for her trouble, but at this point, satiating the itch in her ass crack was going to be an equitable trade off.

Then she smelled it. And it was unmistakable. It was a slight drift of many light scents, but the one that stuck out was the sandalwood. She knew someone that used to use a very expensive and rare sandalwood perfume once upon a time. Although she hadn't been talking much, she mustered a pain-free throat clearing and managed to get out, "Hello, Mother."

The reply came from behind the bed, so she didn't see the respondent, "Hello, Dear," was all that was said.

"Did you come alone?"

With an expulsion of air to signify the insanity of the question, Elizabeth answered, "Of course not, Dear, do you think I would come to this ghastly place on my own? I would be terrified beyond my wits. No, of course not, Dear, your father brought me."

Lauren thought about her next words carefully, "Why are you here?"

Her mother came into view as Lauren spoke, "I just meant that if you're here to take me home, then save yourself the speech and effort. Please go now because it will not be happening."

Her mother looked at her in anguish. She was seeing what a mirror revealed to Lauren the day before when the nurse held it up for her. Her beautiful face was broken. Aside from two broken teeth, she had a fractured eye socket and it looked horrible.

The doctors confirmed that she would get her vision back, but it would be a long road to recovery, as would her spine injury. Tears started rolling down her mom's face. Elizabeth was a strong woman and sometimes a very cold woman who was capable of writing people off that she truly loved in order to grab a better position in life. She finally spoke in a calm but convicted voice, "You can't keep this up, Lauren. You were nearly killed; this is no longer healthy."

"I understand your concern, Mother, I do, but do you realize that the people who did this to me were stopping me from looking for him? I was close, Mom, and I won't stop until I find him."

"And then what?!" Her mother suddenly snapped, her voice way too loud for the setting. In more of a hushed tone now she reiterated, "And then what, Lauren? He's no longer a fugitive. President Caulfield exonerated him, and the world is focused on what happened to that madman/sheep leader who attacked us. Meanwhile you're focused on a ghost."

"That's not fair and you know it, Mother! You know why I can't stop."

"Lauren, he's dead, you need to let it go."

Lauren could only hope the feelings that she had raging inside of herself right now were being conveyed through her facial expressions, as well as her words, but her face was so lumpy that she could only hope for the best, "You know never to say that to me, Mom. You left them, but I never did, I never turned my heart off and left them. So when Matt Hurst killed Joe, he only killed half of the team, the other half has a score to settle."

"Lauren, listen, you don't get this now because your young, but J.P. doesn't want this. He doesn't want more blood to flow. He would never forgive himself if something happened to you."

Her eyes were tearing up; she was unable to think about her half brother without welling up. Matt Hurst had put a bullet though Joe with his own partner's gun. He was cut down in the Stanford Shopping Center in front of a women's clothing store called Stor. They shot him and he died right in the parking lot.

Stor was where Hurst worked and where her investigative reporting led her to believe he was guilty. Her time spent with Bill Westinghouse confirmed that even a man with his connections and insight didn't believe Hurst just fell into this. She was going to pay back the man who killed her brother and there was nothing anyone could do to stop her. "Mother, I think it's time for you to go."

"Well now, is that any way to talk to your own mother?" J.P. walked in holding two coffees and handed one to his ex-wife. "Your mom tells me you fell down. Looks like you scraped more than your knee."

Lauren could see J.P. hadn't changed a bit. He still had straight long blonde hair, less illustrious than his youthful days though, she noted. She wiggled a little bit and the pain shot through her like a bolt. Her face told the tale and J.P. ran over quickly to help her out adjusting herself. He shifted her ever so gently and asked if that was okay?

She smiled and said, "Yes, that's fine, but one more thing, can you scratch my ass for me?"

The next few minutes were not so intense and they caught up a little. J.P. admitted that he climbed in a bottle until Elizabeth had recently dragged him out of it. The death of Joe was too much to handle and he just didn't care anymore. She was crying while she listened, as she knew what was coming next.

"We came here to take you home, Lauren, this is over. You don't need to do this."

She sobbed and looked into his broken soul and said, "No, J.P. We all have something we need to do in this life that defines us, molds us into what we are to become." Her mom moved in and grabbed her right hand, "Mom, listen to me, those people would have never bothered to scare me off if they weren't hiding something. This is actually a break."

Elizabeth looked at her battered daughter and said, "You call this a break? You call this scaring someone, Lauren? What will happen when they're done scaring you?"

The room focused on a man with a familiar voice when he appeared from her blind side. He was tall, dark haired and was dressed in slacks, a button up short sleeve shirt with smart leather loafers. He was fit, with no stomach bulging out like many of his contemporaries, and had the air of a man used to success. He wore only a watch and a wedding band as jewelry and J.P. noticed the band with a bolt of pain.

Two hours prior J.P. had finally met the man who'd broken his family apart and stolen the only women he'd ever truly loved. The man signaled with a nod that he wanted to spend some time with his daughter alone. J.P. noticed that the man had no compunction as he had called Lauren *his* daughter earlier. It was painful to swallow for any man, but a man so freshly out of the bottle was already one leg back in it at the sight of this obviously prosperous man.

Elizabeth and J.P. left the room to go sit in the lobby and let the two of them talk. J.P. felt just about as insignificant as he felt when Elizabeth left him for this same man. Now he was being excused from conversations with someone he called *his* daughter as well, but now things seemed to have changed and he was treated more like uncle or something.

After they were gone, Jerome pulled up a chair and looked at his daughter and said, "Okay, what have you gotten yourself into now?"

Jerome listened to an amazing tale, one that shocked and scared him as the story unfolded. She was truly lucky to be alive. He also saw that one level of naiveté had been removed, as his darling little star had become jaded just a little more than she had been, but wiser too. She wanted more money and time, but his fear was that Elizabeth might have a breakdown worrying that something like this or worse would happen to her again. Lauren was convincing and compelling, and in the end, he was convinced she was unstoppable. So he had the choice to either get on board to help her or he was going to have to get out of her way. She may not have been born to his blood, but she was surely his daughter in traits.

Today he had to admit that J.P. had left his mark on the girl, too, giving her a sensitivity that was unique to her personality. He would have to remind the man of that. She would heal and she would find her bank account full again when she got out.

Jerome already had her transferred here to this private hospital; she just didn't know it yet. His only problem was going to be the two in the hall, although the calm truth was usually the best way to handle things. They would have to adjust to the fact that Lauren was a warrior and she would fight to survive. And he was confident that she would survive. Jerome contemplated his daughter and realized that revenge was the fuel that had kept her fire lit, but it was the type of tenacity it took to sustain such a fire that was more interesting to him. Put to other uses, it could become quite a force in his world.

He had many, many millions, and he would be damned if he saw this precious gift in his life killed here in this third world abomination. That was why he went to a CEO friend of his who had needed some elite protection after 2008. His firm had been targeted as a possible source of management misuse of retirement funds. Ever since, he'd had to have some tight security as he had a big target on his back, albeit truly not earned, as he was an honest man.

Jerome was referred to Depee Protection Services, and a referral was the only way one could get an appointment. Once referred, one had to be vetted, as things got ugly in their world very quickly. The word *discreet* was priority here, as they were often covertly found on foreign soil and needed to remain anonymous to the world. Depee Protection didn't cover Rock Stars or deal with the paparazzi; they specialized in protecting rich people's family interests. Oftentimes children of the rich did foolish things and needed a guardian angel. So Jerome thought, *yes, she was free to carry on her business, but she'll do it with a shadow.*

Jerome listened to her finish, kissed her on the head, and assured her that he would support her and would do as she requested. He left to go get Elizabeth and J.P. so they could all talk together, but he would have a small private talk first, intent on setting their minds a little more at ease.

* * *

Robert Leme walked into the meeting and all the chattering voices quieted. It was just about one year ago that he had walked into a similar meeting, but that time the voices didn't stop.

His team of ten was working on the follow-up game to his Internet sensation, *Top of the Heap.* The follow-up game was also a Sim game, but with a unique concept. Like most Sim games, a virtual city was built, down to the last detail.

On opening day, the city would open up and it would be a "free for all" thing. Players would need to keep their characters health up, as well as all other aspects of living. The key here was balance. Once you had secured the job you wanted (you had to click it and apply for it), your job responsibilities would immediately pop up. Then you'd have to do the same for living quarters because if you didn't rest correctly, then drones in the game would randomly meet you on the street and ask, "Are you're okay?" If you continued to get that message when you met certain drones, usually street vendors, it was a sign that your character was not balanced in some way. You needed to eat and rest, and if you continued to neglect yourself, then your game character would collapse and need to be hospitalized.

The city and game were designed for a cap of half a million people, but that would also include an eight percent unemployment rate. Once the jobs and housing were filled, you could turn to the game's Social Services to help out. But if you had any chance of winning, you had to stay balanced so drones would give you information instead of asking if you were okay.

Hidden inside the new game would be ten thousand drones, each placed in a different capacity around the city. Of the ten thousand, only eight of them would have a code. There was a code building downtown, next to City Hall, and all one needed was any five of the eight drone codes. The only problem was you had to truly be resourceful as the codes were very difficult to obtain—one drone might be a traffic cop, or a waitress, or even a killer in prison looking for pen pals.

The code building was out of place in downtown, as it was ornate in the way of a golden palace. The walkway to the entrance was paved in gold and led to a front door that didn't exist. All that stood was a sealed entryway with a single screen and keypad. Each player was limited to twenty tries per a player's life, and no more.

The first two people to gain entrance to the building were going to be awarded a seat on the, "Counsel of Power." Those two would also win a very grand prize in the real world: $100,000.

There were eight chairs at the table for the Counsel of Power, but there were only two openings as part of game, as the rest of the counsel chairs were already filled. Once the two seats were filled, the community they rose from would hold an election to decide which one got the grand prize of one million dollars. With one week allowed for campaigning, the two prospects had to go out and get other gamers to vote.

People who stayed in the game and interacted in the election process would randomly be awarded thousand dollar prizes, so it paid to stick around even if you didn't win one of the chairs. They were handing out over two hundred thousand dollars. And whoever got the most votes would win the million.

The video drones would only give you the information if you did something to impress them, or forced them, as they were designed to crack under duress. Duress was the key word, as rough prodding would yield you nothing, and some drones were designed to fight back. If that happened, you'd need to go to the hospital and get re-balanced.

As in the real world, there were good sides and bad sides to the video town with drones placed throughout. One could choose any path one wanted, as all the jobs were open within the city. Once the game started, it was a free for all, yet within the game, the current laws of the U.S regulated life.

A person could be killed. If that happened, then the person who did the killing would either get away with it or get caught, as in the real world. There was a prison in the game, staffed by jailers and wardens, etcetera. Justice would be meted only if a witness testified, and it took multiple witnesses to convict for a prison term. The victim would have the ability to resurrect himself as anyone they chose, complete with all previously saved data.

The only stipulation was you couldn't bear witness against your attacker if you died. If you did not die, then of course, you could claim the attack. Murdering others will not likely win you the game, unless maybe you became a prison gang leader and used your tendrils to do your game work. But even then, you would be sharing info with other players.

Consequently, it was also possible that the code you needed was being held by a criminal and you chose to take the honest route and become a cop. Then your street smarts might earn you the respect you need to get the code... or just the opposite, you might alienate yourself and never get it. It was advisable to not make enemies, for cooperation was the key to winning the game. But one could try any route, it was a free-will game after all.

However, if one went the bad route, there was a perk. Any drone that was imprisoned for more than one minute would reveal its code to get away, as drones could not be kept prisoner for more than a minute in order to keep the game fluid. Of course, that path could just as easily get you hospitalized for messing with the wrong drone. If one chose this route, you could also build street cred and gain fighting ability to take less damage from an attack drone.

Naturally, the news of this follow-up game had built momentum, as it was similar to *Top of the Heap*, but different in the biggest way possible. This game was going to offer two executive jobs as a perk of winning.

Robert Leme had started with four programmers, then he expanded to eight, and now it was nine, down from ten because of a bad egg.

The day he walked into the meeting and the buzzing didn't stop was because an associate he'd hired had figured out his neurosis and had begun to manipulate it in little ways. Like all bullies, he tested his waters and when he perceived he could get away with anything he wanted, he took it as a sign of weakness of Robert's and he decided to try to take over as the boss.

Robert was already sick of Craig Mathews' mouth, as he could hear his too loud voice from everywhere in the building and it annoyed him to no end. Of course, Craig didn't realize that Robert had an ace in the hole as of late, one that gave him some much needed real world strength now, strength that he's never possessed before he'd met Melvin.

That day he sat down, fully expecting the meeting to come to a reasonable quiet; but it didn't. Craig kept telling a story about himself in some bar arguing with a drunken patron, even when Robert cleared his throat. Craig actually raised one hand and proceeded to finish the story to the discomfort of the associate seated next to him. Robert had had enough. He had a new sense of power since he hired Melvin.

Their encounter was chance, but Robert likened it to serendipity. It was months before, and he was driving through his old neighborhood for some morbid reason. As he was sitting in front of his old house letting the memories flood back, he suddenly saw something across the street. He saw Melvin come out of the Runnels residence. He then realized after watching this huge, sad man that Gerry Runnels had at least one more victim he had permanently damaged—and that was his little brother, Melvin.

Little brother was an oxymoron as he was just slightly smaller than a tractor-trailer. He stood probably close to six foot seven and had to weigh three hundred plus pounds, yet he was not fat per se. He was country boy large and by the looks of it, forlorn. This neighborhood had a way of doing that if one stayed in it too long. He remembered Melvin from his 4th grade class, a simple child who was not the smartest but not the dumbest kid in the class either. Robert remembered that Melvin never picked on him directly, although he was present while it was going on, and laughed when it was time to laugh, yet somehow Robert always felt Melvin had been just going along.

In the boldest move he could remember ever making, Robert got out of his car and walked over to talk to Melvin. At first Melvin was stunned to see Robert because he said if he were Robert he "never would have come back to this place again."

They got to know each other that day, and Robert found out why he was forlorn. He had lost both his parents in the course of the previous two months. Without warning, he was left all alone in the world to try to fend for himself, yet he had never even learned to cook. He was eating out of cans.

Melvin went from having a family of four to just himself in just a few short years—he was now alone. Before the day was over, Melvin was alone no more, as he was now working for Robert as his new limo driver. Well at first he was, but then it became more. Now he was also an important member of the office staff and a self-appointed bodyguard.

Their business was in a very closed environment; even the mailman used the slots on the office door. Their office was entered "by appointment only." Melvin became Robert's ability to deal with the outside world and became the fixer of all Robert's direct people interaction problems. As a result, Robert was no longer invisible and no longer afraid to go out.

Of all the things that bonded them that day, nothing was more binding than the fact they were both the perpetual victims of the same bully; Gerry literally dominated their lives, and poor Melvin had to live with him.

Fortunately, Robert hadn't come out of the ordeal with any lasting mental damage. His complex was mostly of the physical variety, not that they didn't torture him emotionally, but he hated the pain of being hit. Not so for Melvin. Apparently, Gerry had learned his cruelty from their dad, and from the time he could remember, Melvin was called stupid, beaten, and basically ridiculed on a consistent basis. Melvin got beat plenty of times, but he could take that. It was the degrading message of his stupidity that was what damaged him the most.

Truthfully, Robert found him to be just like he was in school, not the smartest, but not the dumbest by far. After a very short time in Robert's constant company, his intelligence level went up as much as Robert's confidence in the real world had, and that was a whole lot. They had a truly symbiotic relationship.

Although he still felt stupid inside, Melvin had figured out that his physical presence was enough in most circumstances to deter any words from outsiders hurting him. And he had no problem punching someone's lights out. Robert thought how lucky that must be as his own stature was such that a mouse could provide shade for him.

That fateful day, Robert was finally convinced that Craig was a bully of the highest order, and that was when his hand hit the buzzer. Robert called for Melvin to please come in and escort Mr. Mathews out of the building, as he was no longer employed there. That stopped the meeting right away, and Craig said in a condescending voice, "You've got to be kidding me, Robert, you're not firing me for finishing a story, are you?"

Robert's voice did not crack as he replied, "No, Craig, I'm firing you for being a bully and worse, for being disrespectful to me, the man who writes your check." Melvin walked in and stood by Craig.

Robert had never seen Craig lose his cool in such a way, but he was definitely a scared little boy in the shadow of the giant Melvin. "Oh, I get it, you can't do things yourself so you have your goon here do it for you."

"No Craig, that is wrong, I'm doing it right here, right to your face and if you refer to Melvin as a goon again, I'm afraid you will regret that, as he might make that accusation a reality for you." Robert gave a knowing smirk. "Melvin has told me several times that he doesn't like you, Craig, as you are nothing but a condescending turd to him. Now you will please give him your keys, ID, and company credit card so we can move on with our meeting." Robert finally added, "Your last check will be sent to your house tomorrow."

Craig tried to think of a way out of the situation he'd just created with his arrogance, but there was none, so he did what all bullies do when they're out of options, he made a threat. The threat was one of getting a lawyer to file suit and that was all Robert needed to hear. On his order, Melvin then unceremoniously bounced Craig onto the street like a good doorman would do to a bum. One minute he was a programmer on the hottest game cart going, the next he was on the street, literally. The effect was stunning on the other nine, and now when he walked into a meeting, it got very quiet very fast.

He looked at his group and asked the question, "How long before we can get this up with my new modifications?" The group had apparently chosen Cole Wyman as their spokesperson and it wasn't a bad idea as Cole was one of his original four and Robert liked him.

Cole cleared his throat, "We think that your request of thirty days will push everyone to the very limits, maybe mistakes will get made."

Robert looked around the room of uncertain faces. It sucked to be in their shoes. One minute they were riding a cruise ship called the Robert Leme Gravy Train Ocean Liner and the next Captain Quig was weighing the strawberries. Each and everyone one of them at the table thought he was going Howard Hughes on them and they were terrified to hear what was next.

Robert answered, "Your point is well taken Cole, but in the time you've all worked here you have never been taken to task. Sure, we've worked hard and accomplished much, but we've never really had a serious deadline. Those days are over, as this company is my dream, my vision, and you are all simply helping me accomplish my goal." His voice was cracking with emotion.

Melvin sat his tea down next to him; then retreated into the corner where he sat back and watched. It was his way of reminding his friend that he was there to support him and he could do this. He could make them follow his dream or get out of the way.

Cole spoke the question that had to be asked, "Why do this, Robert? We're days from releasing our hugely anticipated second game and you throw this curveball? Why Robert? What's really going on?"

Robert stared hard at Cole, "I'm only going to say this once more, so you better all be listening. This is not a democracy. You are here because of me, and you have jobs because I started this company." He rose from his chair and placed his fists on the table. "When it is said and done, this will eclipse our wildest dreams. But I will not have a naysayer in my midst." He pointed to Craig's empty chair which he had never refilled and said, "He's gone because he didn't believe in me, and anyone else who doesn't believe in me can get one year's salary as a payout right now, no questions asked, and then they are out forever. Now is your time, who wants it, tax free even, I will pay Uncle Sam for you?"

When no one raised a hand he then let them all know that anyone staying would be getting a 10% raise, and he further let them know that only real loyalty would be rewarded in this house.

Melvin held the door as he made his way out of the boardroom and through the work cubicles. Soon they were outside, and as soon as Melvin let him into the limo and they drove off, Robert had a mini-nervous breakdown. He was gently talked back in off the ledge by this supposedly average man he was quickly finding out was anything but.

* * *

Jan was yelling at him to stop, but of course he wouldn't, he just kept right on climbing up and saying, "It's okay, don't worry." According to Jan, Matt always had to go find some form of danger to get into. She had to pretend she was not stressing as that would freak out their four-year-old son, but she was still stressing nonetheless.

Matt found a man who dealt in cash as he had taken a sizable amount out in Mexico City. Then after just one day, they rented a car and left Cancún, Matt finding a new place to stay about a hundred kilometers up the peninsula. The further they got away from Cancún, the more sparsely populated it had become and when he turned down a deserted dirt path, Jan was sure they were never going to come out alive. They went a mile or so until they cleared the jungle and the road opened up onto this amazing white sand beach, the shoreline of which was littered with small cottages, most of which had docks.

Matt had rented one with a dock, but as they had no boat, they spent the last couple of days on the beach, sitting on the dock, and staring at the soft white puffs the waves made as they hit the reef. Jan was still learning about her man. Yes, she knew him, but when you do new things together for the first time, it always opens doors of enlightenment of one another. Sometimes it was no more than cracks a hairs width wide, but it was in that place that one saw into the true soul of one's soul mate. What kind of parent were they, how thoughtful of a person were they, and what kind of lover.

The last thought brought her a blush because Matt was really on his game the night before. If one spent enough time with another, there was no hiding who they really were, and she was sure that this Vera, the woman who had her spell on his mind, never got to see this side of her man because she believed with total conviction that Matt would have never shown it to her.

The days were too wonderful to be true, except for when her son and her were intermittently struck with horror and pride as daddy climbed the cliff or snorkeled all the way out to the reef, which looked to be a quarter of a mile or so. That day they sat and worried for an hour, and when he got back they both told him not to do that again. Jon Jon was still a little touchy about daddy going away, even though he wasn't making permanent memories when Matt was gone, he still had separation anxiety as a result.

So after that Matt stayed closer and spent time introducing his son to swimming lessons off the dock. That was their routine until today. Today they traveled to the ancient ruin of Tulum, a Pre-Columbian Mayan walled city that had been a major port, sitting on the edge of a cliff. It was very close to where they were staying. They took the tour, but they didn't pay; instead they just waited for a bus and blended in.

Matt loathed tour buses more than anything and several days earlier he'd used one as an example to his family on how thinking like a sheep could lead one to missing so much or worse, as the world almost found out by following a madman—a madman who would have brought more destruction than any person in the history of the world.

The day of the lesson they went to Xel Ha Park and for the first time Jan was in awe of what he'd taught her. Sure, he'd taught her things in the past, but she saw for the first time that he'd past her up, that she needed to tap into the experiences of a man who had a great book to write one day.

Ever since she'd known Matt, all he did was talk about snorkeling in Cancún any time a discussion about the ocean came up. He'd wanted her to see it so bad for so long. He would fill her head with stories and one of them took place in Xel Ha. Xel Ha was the world's largest natural aquarium, a natural harbor that hosted more fish than one could imagine. One could see them right away by just standing on the edge of the water.

He had been diving there years before and found this mushroom shaped rock out in the middle of the harbor. When he'd held his breath and went down he found this whole species of bright green fish that were backed up against the rock, hundreds of them. It was just such a spectacle of nature that he had retold the story a few times over the years they were together. Now was his chance to show her, along with their four-year-old in tow.

Of course, once Matt got an idea or wanted something, it was going to happen or there would be no rest. His answer was to take off for an hour while his wife and son ate lunch and looked at iguanas and simply buy a life vest and a small inflatable raft/boat for his son. When he returned, he taught Jan how to snorkel in the shallow water nearest the first cove. There were so many fish right there, it was breathtaking and Jan was hooked. Snorkeling was a quick learn for her as she was a very strong swimmer having played water polo in high school. Once she had it down, they practiced close to shore with Jon Jon in the boat.

He stayed put as instructed, plus one of them was up top with him at all times, they weren't stupid. Once it was a go they slowly just swam out and started looking for his story. The one thing about her husband that always blew her away was his memory and sense of direction, he was rarely lost and once he had been somewhere even one time, he was going to be able to find his way back, even if years stood between the experience. In less time than she could believe he found the rock and dove down only to come up thirty seconds later like a kid in a candy store announcing "they're still here!"

She got her turn as he stayed with the excited boy and sure enough, according to Jan, it sure was a spectacle of nature. "So beautiful" she announced. They each went down a few more times.

Even though they were explaining it to Jon, he was feeling left out so Matt had an idea. They went back to shore and he left them and went to a tourist shop. A few minutes later he returned with a disposable underwater camera. Swimming back out alone, he dove down and took pictures for his son.

Soon they were tired, it had been a long day. They all lay on the shore soaking in one of the most amazing days they'd ever had. Then the day's lesson rolled up to a halt and gave a big hiss. The door flew open and it gave way to the "Tour Group." These people were not equipped to go into the water, so Matt surmised that this was just a pit stop for them. There were pathways that led up to the mouth of the harbor. The path itself was a tropical bouquet of indigenous life and flora that was by itself worthy of admiration, a place that deserved a nod just for its natural beauty and aesthetics.

Instead, the group that got out dispersed in different directions with a grumble. Then, this sixty-something couple from Oklahoma, Matt was pretty sure, wandered up, looked out over Xel Ha and exclaimed in their signature twang, "Why in the heck did we stop here for? There's nothing here to look at."

Matt and his family politely waited until they'd left and then they made sure they dissected this proclamation made in front of them because it meant so much. In the second it took them to make that statement, one of the small fissures into their souls revealed man's biggest threat to his continued existence. Himself. It also revealed and personified the fact that life was about perspectives and the perspectives of the ignorant were terrifying in ways that would continue to reveal themselves and destroy humanity for future kind. They vowed then and there to never be, "Those People."

Now that she had thought about it, Jan hated tour buses just as much as Matt, but the bus tour guy at Tulum had information about the place that they wanted to hear. When they had heard enough about the temple, they broke off from the group.

Before his cliff climbing adventure, they'd decided to stay and check out the beach below the ruin. As they were walking down to the beach they saw one group of sheep coming and one loading onto their respective buses. Matt observed that it was good times in the sheep hauling business.

As it turned out, there was a popular European beach below and Jan was able to go topless and that made her happy. That was until the incredible blondes giggled when Matt walked by them on the way to water, their twenty-year old breasts acting like they had helium in them.

That put a damper on her spirits a little until he played it off that he hadn't even noticed them. Of course, he caved while under interrogation later, but it was sweet of him to pretend.

Of course, interrogating him was really pointless if he wanted to lie; yet maybe something in his psyche made him unable to lie to her. She was going to have to get used to that, as he really had changed everything about himself in order to survive, even his body, so now she would never really be able to tell when he was lying—or at least not one hundred percent.

Of course, with Matt, everything had to be an adventure, which was why she was worried about him right now, as one minute he was splashing with Jon Jon and the next she was pleading with him to come back down as he saw a cave half way up the ruin cliff and just "had" to go there. Was he addicted to this type of behavior? Men like that rarely lived or stayed faithful, and it worried her. It didn't take long to get a list of the recent men who had died going through her head. *Great. Something new to worry about.*

The water was actually pounding the bottom of the cliff, so Matt had to climb up at the sand and shimmy over to get a straight climb to where he was, but once he got going it was an easy climb to the cave. He was on the beach looking up when he'd noticed a single palm tree had grown on the cliff face. He almost missed that it was covering up a secret, but once he saw it had a secret to reveal, he wouldn't stop until he unraveled it. She loved and hated that about him; and felt that their future was super-uncertain right now because of his impulsive nature.

But in reality, only the future of his employment was in peril, their love was as solid as could be. The last few days had sprouted several bouts of intense lovemaking.

When they got to the beach house, Jan was amazed that it was so beautifully decorated inside. The whole house was done in Spanish tile with very modern furnishings. Jan truly loved the sunken living room, as it received the setting sun through a stained glass western facing window and it cast the most cathartic glow on the room, especially when enjoyed with sangria.

One of the things that excited her—and angered her at the same time—was that her man had been gone for two years with another woman. And when he came back, he was minus all his baby fat and was experienced in things he was not before. He had a six-pack now, and she felt like she was cheating with another man sometimes. It didn't help that he had new moves as well, things that he did now that he had not done before.

Like the first day she got Jon down for his nap and she tried to make her way into the sunken living room. He blocked her path and the match up of his face and her pelvis were met with a vigor she had never encountered with him before. Her toes literally grabbed the tile step so hard she thought she was going to crack it. So it both excited and angered her as she tried not to think of the things this Vera had brought out in him that she had failed to.

Then she reasoned that if she would have had the time she would have brought all this out too, but she was robbed of the opportunity. She tried to not let the past eat away at her because he was hers now and no one was ever going to get between them again. He made his way down the cliff from the cave and smiled that stupid smile of the idiot who can't help himself. That garnered him a solid punch in the arm, she was never going to stop being "that Jan" when he needed it.

Jon Jon was super excited, however, at how cool his dad was. But then he proceeded to lie to the poor kid and tell him that he used to be "Spiderman," but had retired when he became a dad. His kid was so thrilled at that he almost split open; and then he made his own path to healing, and it was amazing. Even though he didn't actually remember Matt's absence, he must have remembered the sadness it brought Jan, which then caused some sort of an instinctual animosity for his dad. So it was with cathartic relief that he asked, "Is that why you were gone from us, because you were being Spiderman?"

Matt wasn't as up on children's psychology as he should have been, but he knew the right answer for his son at that moment, "Yes, son, that's exactly what I was doing. I was Spiderman, fighting the bad guys." That somehow meant so much to the boy that the lie had to be told and Jan looked at her man with new eyes. This time she saw through another crack in his facade, but this one was not a hairs width, this one she could stick her head through.

They went back to the house and fell asleep, just like the day they went to Xel Ha, except that day when they woke up from their nap, she was alone with Jon Jon. Not five minutes later, she was sure that she had the best man there could be. He had not napped, but instead traveled an hour to find a place where he could get some one-hour photos done, and then make it back just as they were waking up. Jon Jon was so happy to see the photos of what he had missed. What a magical day both were, but her favorite was today because Matt was able to give his son an explanation of his absence in a way that worked for his developing mind.

The night before Matt had told Jan that sadly they would have to go back sometime.

Two weeks later, they forced themselves back on a plane and returned to Seattle, although for the life of them, they could not figure out why? Matt had decided to leave TJAC and take the CIA analyst job that was and always would be open for him.

Of course, they could have just stayed. They had plenty of money so she was sure that wasn't going to be a stumbling block. Hell, Matt could write a memoir and they would never have to work again. She wondered if they had stayed if she would have ever become sick of the perfect life.

Time flew by so quickly that it wouldn't have mattered if they were there for a day or weeks, it all felt like a day in the end. Her long sought out life in paradise ending far too quickly. She was happy about the CIA job—at least she knew whom he'd be working for—and that they for sure were working for the good old US of A.

They would have to move to the East Coast now, of course, but according to Matt, they had a power-couple friend right off the bat in Ray Callahan and his wife, Kim, the President's Chief of Staff. Looks like they were going from snorkeling in the ocean to snorkeling in a shark tank.

They had talked about so much over this last month and she knew Matt was everything she could have ever wanted in a man. Her life had been a rollercoaster for long enough and she was glad he was doing the sensible thing. As the plane pulled up and they were about to leave behind a piece of time she never wanted to end, she turned her head as she was starting to cry.

When life got this good, one just wanted to freeze the moment and keep it forever, for one knew that soon it would just be a memory and memories slipped way with time. Plus, it was the law of all things—there was no continued joy in the universe. Jan pondered that maybe that was what heaven was, you were allowed to pick the happiest moment of your life and go back and stay there. She would pick this moment, for the last few weeks were as good as her life had ever been. She wiped her tears and turned to see Matt's misty eyes glued to her, as he knew her all too well. They locked hands and said goodbye to some place very special.

Matt had traveled under his alias, but Jan hadn't, she traveled under Jan Holsinger, which was the surname the Government assigned them when they disappeared, which, of course, he realized was also was an alias.

When they got off the plane at Sea/Tac they were gathering all their carry-on things together when a man they never saw took their picture. It would be a picture that would change the course of their lives in the same sudden fashion as the day he was plunged into infamy in the parking lot of the Stanford Shopping Center a little over three years before. But the Hurst's were too immersed in joy and elation to have even noticed him, even though he was wearing socks with sandals, khaki shorts, and a Free Tibet t-shirt.

* * *

As soon as he walked in he could smell breakfast and knew he was going to be forced to eat. He used to exercise for the fun of it, now he was running for his life. When he chose a provincial Swiss country girl to be with he hadn't thought out that part all the way through. They lived in a former Bed and Breakfast that her parents used to run and one had to expect some pretty heavy foods, but Pablo would never have thought he would see what he saw when he got on the scale. He had gained ten pounds!

After that it was smaller portions and more running. He quickly showered and got to the table as his food was hitting. His Eva believed in timing and food was best-served and eaten with steam coming off of it. He pulled up his computer and was reading a tech blog by a writer he liked in Seattle. It was an interesting article about a group of Americans led by an investor from Philadelphia who designed the Internet game *Top of the Heap*.

The investor was going to release his second game as a new concept platform whose underlying premise was a grass roots movement for national economic sustainability. He was about half way through the article when he noticed the profile photos that the writer had taken. Apparently, it was a local Seattle man who had created the premise, a man by the name of Tom Holsinger. Another local Seattle man who was listed on the Board of Directors was Justin Parker, a retired police captain. But Pablo's interest zeroed in on Tom Holsinger. He swallowed his food hard as he realized just who he was looking at. It was *El Diablo* himself!

He took a drink of coffee, realizing he was going to have to leave his Eva home alone once again, but this shouldn't take too long, especially with his little friend to help. Time to send a message and a helicopter to his little friend. He didn't know it, but he was a top-notch helicopter pilot, one that Pablo would trust with his life; he just needed some real world practice. He took a hearty bite of eggs, sausage, and toast whilst laughing a maniacally inward laugh, for he wouldn't have to worry about God's guidance on this one, the bible was pretty clear on that one. *An eye for an eye.* It was time to make some travel plans to see an old friend...

* * *

Lauren was happy she was getting her arm cast off today. Rehab had been slow until this last week when her appetite returned with vigor. Since then her physical therapy had been working wonders. Actually, much to her surprise, her libido had returned as well.

Her therapist was Rodrigo, and he was a hundred and seventy-five pounds of solid muscle. Rodrigo was able to pick her up and move her with the ease of a paperweight, and it turned her on to no end. His hands were as soft as they were strong, and his accent had her melting on most days before they even started.

She loved his smell and his touch, and it had really helped her along, she believed, because as soon as she was able to she was going to jump his bones. She had spent the last few days actually chronicling all the events that had led to up to where she was now. One of the things she had decided on was that maybe her last hook up wasn't as innocent as she had thought.

Maybe Humberto tipped off Cecelia and that was how it all came apart. Either that or Cecelia was really close to Hurst and she figured this tactic would work on any sane person; *they just didn't know I'm not sane.*

It had been nearly impossible to get her mom to leave. Of all her flaws, Elizabeth did have very protective instincts once the chips were down. That was a good thing to know, she supposed. Jerome and J.P. were wonderful and although she could see they were scared for her, they were stoic around Elizabeth and that helped. Not much, but it helped.

She was formulating a plan. She was even thinking of kidnapping Cecelia and extracting some information out of her. The reality was, however, she had no idea how to put that together and it would also make her a criminal. But at this juncture, even irrational thoughts got a place in line.

J.P. gave her some heartfelt advice—and that was "to be a reporter and to be professional." Jerome told her more directly that, "Revenge is the strongest path to blind stupidity and mistakes. You've already had a couple of tastes of how revenge clouded your judgment and now you need to start working smarter."

Well, she certainly would start working smarter, so kidnapping that bitch and beating the truth out of her was out, but that didn't mean she couldn't be tricked into thinking she fucked with the wrong person.

When the cast came off her arm, it felt like it was floating to the ceiling. She now had a scar on her left forearm as the ulna had a compound fracture and they had put a plate and a pin in. She discovered that Jerome had been handling things and taking care of her medical bills almost from the start, so she had received excellent care. Her fingers moved well—which made her happy because she wrote the old fashioned way, she typed it all out. No word encryption software for her.

Rodrigo came in and gently washed the sticky stuff off with soap and warm water. She was still unable to do it herself, as her spine still wanted nothing to do with twisting. Everything still had to be straight forward for her, so Rodrigo had to maneuver around her to do his job.

This Rodrigo was one cool character. He never acted attracted to her at all, except the one time she'd caught him looking lustfully at her in a mirror. That had thrilled her to no end, as it meant he wasn't gay. He must have had so many women, Lauren thought, a real Casanova for sure. He was always talking about something pleasant, too, never about anything negative.

After the adhesive removal, he talked her into a body sponge bath. As she was living temporarily in heaven, she decided to look at her phone. It was amazing how one could think they could not live without something, but when one got things put into perspective, that thing seemed so inconsequential. There were no Twitter cravings when one was fighting for one's life.

That is . . . until Jerome went and bought her a new phone and then added all her multimedia information into it. Now she had some curiosity. She recalled a certain freak out she'd had not long ago when she thought she'd lost her phone while eating. She ran back to the restaurant but couldn't find it and was just about to have a meltdown when the waiter walked back out with it. Her relief was equivalent to getting a lost dog back. So transforming from that to not even being too excited to be able read her emails was a big jump. It was nice to read her emails though, she would admit.

The swelling had gone down in her left eye so she could now see almost normal again—she'd had an eye test that morning.

Rodrigo found the spot on her spine while gently massaging. Oh man did it hurt—and feel good at the same time. Unfortunately for her, one of her deep erogenous zones lay just off her hip centerline. Every time he hit it, her back gave a suggestive twitch, which hurt as the spasm slightly tweaked her spine. But there was no way she was going to tell him that it hurt. When Rodrigo reached over to get the towel he had placed there earlier, she felt just how much that back twitch turned him on.

Her phone made a familiar sound, it was programmed to make the Austin Powers voice, "Oh yeah, baby," whenever Scott posted a new article. It was her one super joy since getting her phone back. She did not notify him of her situation, as she knew he would be the one person who would not have taken no for an answer, he would have come and taken her home. And quite frankly, she believed she would have let him.

Rodrigo hit the spot once more and it was more than she could take. She turned around slowly, not covering up. His eyes became sparkled like he was getting to have his wildest fantasy come true. She asked if they sell condoms downstairs and he only smiled as he pulled out a condom. Of course.

He looked like the cat that ate the canary as he closed her door and pulled the protective curtain around. He was definitely a Casanova of the highest order, as she soon found out. Scott's article could wait.

The week went well as she was making an amazing recovery and soon she would be released. Rodrigo was giving her another back massage—actually it was his last as today they would be moving her to a rehabilitation center for her final institutionalized stint. This pleased and saddened Rodrigo because it meant his over-sexed American friend was leaving his care, but it also meant she was getting better.

And it was too bad she thought, because she'd finally found a man who had not only found her G-spot, but had become close and personal friends with it. He'd made love to her the last four days in a row, and she had to admit that he had set a new standard that might be hard to achieve for the next man she was intimate with.

Rodrigo could have ruined her for all she knew, she couldn't remember ever meeting anyone beforehand who had had this kind of impact on her. But alas, what the hell would they really talk about at the end of the day. She knew that Scott would be the only man who could keep her mind happy as well as her body.

Then she had a start. She'd forgotten to read his last article. Fortunately, this massage was Rodrigo doing his job, as they'd already had sex earlier. She was very relaxed already when this massage started. She was now reading a very interesting Scott Bailey article.

Robert Leme, the creator of the Internet sensation *Top of the Heap*, was set to release his much anticipated second edition of the franchise when he'd suddenly decided to collaborate with some new people and came up with a fusion of his game based upon a vision of a man named Tom Holsinger.

Holsinger's idea was to challenge true American patriotism, which he claimed was not dead. His mission would be to not only award the winning prize of a million dollars, but to also add two people to the board of directors for his new game franchise, *American Pride*.

The idea was to grow this into a new type of political party. They wouldn't be entering politics per se; they just wanted to have a voice. Leme was crediting the inspirational idea of this to Tom Holsinger from Seattle, as well as listing four others of the creative team who fine-tuned it.

Scott concluded that such a game, one woven from such a loved franchise as *Heap*, could have a real chance of doing just that, creating a voice rising from the Comicon sect. Scott ended the article with, "it appears that Leme is trying to make a virtual Occupy Movement with some cash incentives for joining—never a bad idea and a lot better than freezing your ass off in the street. This writer gives a 'thumbs up' for ingenuity and a patriotic heart."

There were two file pictures at the end of the article, one of a mousy looking Robert William Leme and one of Tom Holsinger. She'd almost glossed over them as Rodrigo had hit "the spot" on her back again (the little rabbit), but alas, he had already conquered her today, so the answer was no.

Then she really focused on Holsinger and she just about had a heart attack! It couldn't be?! But it was . . .

She used to go to sleep every night looking at his picture, dreaming of the day she would kill his fucking ass for the heartbreak he'd caused so many people. She looked again, and yes, it was he for sure. Apparently no one else could see it as they didn't have this guy on their every thought like she did. Rodrigo moved to the side and his bulge gave an indication that he was up for round two before they moved her off.

Tempting as it was, the vacation was over. She *had* to get out of here soon, and although she thought the sex had helped rather than hindered her recovery, she now needed her mind focused. She was heading back to the U.S. with a purpose.

She gently let him down and told him she was sore. He was a sensitive lover and although she accused him of being a Casanova, he declared he wasn't, and that he only loved one woman at a time. He used the word loved, and she was pretty shocked by that. She'd found men to be the much weaker of the two species. Sex didn't always have to lead to love, and if the rest of the world would get that, maybe the divorce rate would come down.

They moved her to the rehab wing and a forlorn Rodrigo left her to the care of a new set of people that were going to accelerate her recovery. She told them she wanted to be on a plane to Seattle as soon as she could and her new doctor said it might be possible within a week.

She'd settled in her new bed and tried to control her rage to a point where the coming week wouldn't feel like a couple of years, but the reality was, she knew it would now that she knew the truth. When one wanted to stop the clock, no chance, and when one want to speed it up, no chance there, either. Clocks only worked at one speed, the speed of reality.

* * *

Chase greeted his visitor with enthusiasm, as it wasn't everyday one got a visit from the President's Chief of Staff. Of course, Kim Callahan was anything but a visitor to Chase, she was his protégé. Chase had her marked since her sophomore year in college. She was amazing and his agency wanted her loyalty so they set out to prove themselves to her. For fifteen years she had the luxury of getting any job she wanted. If she applied, it was hers. It led to a great many discoveries for her, and ultimately landed her in the position of a lifetime at the age of thirty-five. Of course, it wasn't the CEO's chair he had groomed her for, as his life took a more political turn.

She might have been the youngest to take the seat, but she was hardly the luckiest. Almost as soon as her name was on the door the trouble started. Kim was as good as there was, and she helped lead the U.S. through arguably one of its roughest patches. The U.S. and all militaries lost a certain amount of swagger that year—a single man had brought them down. Not any man, Chase reminded himself, but a renaissance man, the kind that happened every century or so. But unlike most of his predecessors, he got away from the war to tell the story.

Pablo Manuel was a very special man, and actually Matt had given him the moniker of man/boy, as had many others due to his angelical features. His brain was anything but adolescent though, and his automated military had not only caused massive loss of life, it also tried to sink a nuclear-powered aircraft carrier.

Because of the acts of savagery and death cast upon his family by a drug cartel, Pablo's head had became filled to the brim with hate and revenge, and then by fate he was given access to the information that enabled him to change the world.

Chase was so proud of Kim for getting his other protégé through the crisis. TJAC (Thomas Jefferson Action Committee) was founded to defend their country when no one else would or could. It lived because the few that sat at the table truly believed that the world needed ultimate right to battle ultimate evil, and evil was casting its shadow over every land.

Privileged all, contrite none, they had been trying to do what they could as a collective of good, even if at times in underhanded ways. They talked Lawrence Caulfield into running for President and helped him win, but pitting those two against a whole playing field of Special Interest was turning out to be a losing battle.

The problem wasn't with Lawrence's Administration, or Kim's ability to handle the next crisis. *No*, Chase chided himself, *we can put a person in the office, but we can't make the most powerful office in the world effective anymore*. The American political system had clogged arteries, and Chase was bothered because the answers were not going to be easy. It was going to take a major bypass surgery to get Special Interests out of Washington.

Kim approached wearing a smart brown skirt, tailored perfectly for her body and a beige top. Her hair was in a bun as usual, but this meeting she was sporting two new things. He held out his hand, "Hello, Kim."

She gently replied, "Chase," and retrieved her hand, not missing his gaze upon the ring. He looked smarmy, and Kim hated smarmy, especially when she knew its root was based in her flowerbed.

Chase almost sniggered, "So how's married life treating you."

It was no secret that she was a staunch supporter of "the single life." She had seen too many Washington careers clash with romance and wanted no part of it. As a matter of fact, she'd apparently said it enough times that friends starting doing impressions at her wedding. Even retired CIA Director Bob Thompson got in on the act, and it was a real knee slapper she was told.

"It's been wonderful, Chase, and thank you for asking."

He was bursting with the laughter from a secret inside joke and then he asked, "Are those prescription glasses?"

She was trying to find a good story, but Chase was like a father to her, so lying was pointless, "Ray suggested I get them."

He looked puzzled, and asked again with too much smarm, "Ray suggested?"

Kim exhaled a patient trying breath for her mentor, "Yes, we were driving and I missed an exit sign, so he thought I didn't see it. So we argued and he made me agree to see an Optometrist."

"Don't tell me, he was right"?

"Yes, Chase, he was right, and now I need glasses to drive."

Chased smiled, "Well, it's your fault for marrying a spook anyway, you'll never get away with anything again."

"He's not a spook and you know it, he's 'the spook.'"

Chase had to agree with that, her husband was a legend. He was the last line of defense to ensure that the wrong person didn't end up in America's most secretive agency. He was also the one who'd figured out that the American citizen, Matt Hurst, was kidnapped by the man/boy and that he was not duplicitous in the crimes committed on our soil.

In fact, it was Ray Callahan who figured out that said citizen Hurst then enlisted himself into the CIA and drove a stake right through the heart of the man/boy's plan to destroy the records of all the money in the world. Stock markets, banks, militaries—all were plotted to go down, except their own captive stopped them cold in their tracks.

This was also the reason for their meeting, as currently Hurst was missing. Kim opened a folder and looked at the note, "He came back in through Sea/Tac three days ago."

Chase thought about that, "Three days, huh?"

"Yeah, and he had his wife and kid with him, but he traveled under the alias. What do you make of that, Chase?"

Chase had to think long and hard about what he thought about it, as he was the one who had sent Matt to Mexico. The job was simple, go in and extract a Drug Lord that was polluting the U.S. with his toxic waste. The only thing was, that Drug Lord was an actor, as were all the people there in his entourage. It was a family all right, but they were hired to play a part.

Matt Hurst was supposed to pull the trigger and end a life, even if there were small children around, yet the gun would not have fired, as the bullets had no primer. The gun they'd left him did not have a firing pin, but instead had a sensor in it, and every time the trigger was pulled, it would register it.

Chase knew that he had been testing the gun the night before as the sensor went off more than twenty times while Matt was practice shooting people in the Square. The reason he had to put Matt through this ordeal was because the other members of the TJAC board had a rare disagreement with Chase. Their contention was that he had gone too far around the bend, and once one did that, it tended to change a man in a bad way. He either became shell-shocked and withdrawn or he became a hardened killer.

Matt had to go deep undercover to bring down Pablo Manuel, and in the process fell in love with one of his sycophants—he had even impregnated her. It had taken under twenty people to operate an automated army that took out a carrier group, yet Matt Hurst killed them all single handedly—well, almost.

Chase wanted to show his loyalty to this great American; to be able to give him something that could never be acknowledged in the history books, yet would be a salve for his future.

Unfortunately, the other board members thought him too damaged to be their agent provocateur, too prone to senseless violence. Even after he went through training with a retired West Point instructor, getting his stamp of approval in all areas, they still were not convinced.

Of course, now every one of them had a guilty conscience because they were culpable for pushing Hurst too far and he snapped. Chase knew that he would not take that shot, but he was the only one who had that conviction. No one on the counsel wanted to face the fact that they were wrong, and worse, that Hurst suddenly did not like whom he was working for and was going to leave, something that had yet to happen in their organization.

Chase knew where Matt was located the whole time, as Matt had kept the gift Chase had given him the last time they were together. Chase had given him a key chain with a small but powerful, hardened steel, impact resistant laser pointer. Matt commented that it looked like a mini-mag light.

When Chase gave it to him, he showed him how to activate it, and impressed upon him the gravity of the action. It was only to be used if his life was in mortal danger. Chase didn't fully allude to what kind of help was going to come, but he showed Matt how to make it come. He told Matt that he wouldn't have believed him if he told him anyway.

Then again, Chase considered, thinking of where Matt had just come from, that was a silly thought; but the information was to remain classified anyway. So they left it at that. Matt assumed that Chase was a man of his word and apparently he hadn't given up on him enough to throw the pointer out.

Of course, he didn't let Matt know they could ping it at any time, but he should have assumed it given all he had been taught already. Matt had been in Cancún, which was confusing at first, but once Jan and the boy joined him, Chase got what it was about. The one thing his people somehow didn't see in this man was his heart.

Chase had been at the funeral of Vera Maldonado, Matt's lover he killed because she stood in the way of a madman about to bring on the big hurt to the world. He saw the man's anguish, and he heard the man's words at the eulogy. He knew the man, and normally that would have been enough, but with so much on the line and his role to be played out throughout their ranks periodically with different board members, they had to know without a doubt that he possessed the judgment and temperament to do the job they needed him to do.

If he had pulled the trigger, then he would have been retired at an early age by the Board. But he didn't pull the trigger. Yet instead of being handed over his new title as planned, he took umbrage and unexpectedly decided to disappear.

Well, at least it seemed that Matt had decided he was done with clandestine agencies and associations for a while. Now he was back and Kim came to tell Chase her thoughts. Her husband, Ray Callahan, had a huge personal interest in the whole thing, as he was about the only one who believed in and stood up for Matt when literally a whole country was against him.

Ray would be very disappointed by this turn of events, as her husband was a psychologist and Matt had been under his care until he had transferred him to his mentor in the civilian world. No, Ray certainly didn't know about this. He thought Matt was done with this life and had taken his family and just checked out. In reality he was lying to Ray when he turned down the CIA analyst job and joined TJAC, and so was Ray's wife lying.

That was the real reason she was here, Chase wanted to ask her point blank what she intended to tell her husband if the subject of TJAC ever came up? It was another point that had become a source of dissention in their usually placid organization. TJAC had carefully chosen Kim Sullivan because it looked like they were never going to have to deal with her having a spouse. Now they were facing a new name of Callahan, the surname of one of the CIA's greatest minds.

TJAC was a closed society of billionaire philanthropist who had his or her own view on how philanthropy should be meted out. The organization itself was only known to its board members and four outsiders: one was a West Point legend, one was sitting in front of him, one was Matt Hurst, and the other ran the free world.

He broached the question and became more concerned with the answer. She simply stated she wouldn't lie to her husband, and since he was a clever guy, he'd probably figure it all out at some point anyway.

Chase almost recoiled at the revelation, as it was so troubling on many fronts, but the main one was that they were doing things that the CIA might take umbrage to; after all, it was "their" job to be defending the sovereignty of the United States, not the Thomas Jefferson Action Committee. Or at least that was how they would see it.

Chase brought her up to speed, as all she knew was that Chase wanted to know when Tom Holsinger re-entered the country, and have a picture of that re-entry. The thought occurred to Chase that maybe Matt did give away his laser pointer, and they were looking at some donkey walking around with it in its saddlebag.

Then when it got on a plane, Chase thought that maybe it was in some tourists backpack that Hurst had slipped the pointer into. But sure enough, it was he in the photo at Sea/Tac, plus they pinged him again and it showed Seattle as the pointer's location. So he was back. But still no word.

Chase finished his meeting with Kim, but he was so distracted with his thoughts about Matt that he was barely listening. His true reason to have her here was really just to gauge her reaction when asked the magic question, and now he knew. It was now dinner for two apparently. Unfortunately for Chase, Kim was brought into them as dinner for one, and now he was tap dancing.

Chase had to face the fact that his fellow board members were right about this, and now they were a breath away from being known by five people instead of four. The unnerving part was the fifth was a wild card, and that let into play something no one at the table would tolerate— being exposed.

Every one of those people would disappear from that table and their aid, which was desperately needed to the world, would be pulled. It would be a serious tragedy that sadly no one would ever know about, as no one knew they existed.

Kim left Chase to his thoughts, and his thoughts were that he hoped Matt came to his senses and came back in from the cold. If he just came back in and talked to him, then he would become a very powerful and trusted man. They were not vetting Matt for a job; they were vetting Matt to take control of all of TJAC's operations. They were going to use him as an agent, but only of the intimidation kind, they didn't want to rub people out. If they ever really had information on a drug cartel, then the right people would get that information. On the other hand, if they got information that an American industrialist was doing things to undermine the interests of the United States, then they would decide if that person was going to get a visit or receive other means of retaliation.

Matt was going to have the keys to the operation handed to him, but the keepers pushed too far. Now he looked unstable in their eyes and his window of opportunity was shrinking by the minute. If he'd just come in and explain that he was not some arbitrary killer, he would not believe the doors that it would open.

It was always planned for him to join them, but he had no idea in what capacity for which they wanted him, and he certainly would not have guessed that another chair was being made at their table for him.

It was unfortunate that Matt's only way out of the situation in Ecuador was to eliminate everyone involved, because now he had the daunting task of removing the stigma he'd placed over his head. He needed to change the perception they had of him and that was not looking good at the moment. It looked like he just plain snapped.

CHAPTER THREE

Revelation

There it was again, his wake up call. Vera was screaming at him, and those eyes, those crazy, glassed over eyes, just like every night. No matter the pleasantries initially, the dreams always ended the same, with her accusing eyes judging him, so betrayed and furious. As always, the shot rang out that ended her life and he awoke. The clock read five fifteen. He pulled himself up, no need to just lie there and try to get back to sleep; sleep time was over.

He looked over to see son sleeping soundly. Jon Jon was sick again. Sooner or later they were going to acclimate to this region, but for now at least one of them seemed to be sick at all times. He was getting to be such a big boy and was beginning to protest Jan's methods, but he was not winning that battle, as Matt had found out the hard way. This was probably his last night in their room.

Matt sat at the computer and turned it on. It had taken a month to get back into any kind of normal routine, and he was sure his old discussion group had moved on, seeing he had, but he sure did miss them and hoped to at least find one.

He logged onto the group he had created, "Where's my America?" The topic was the economy today as the group had taken on a life of its own long ago, but before he had a chance to get into any kind of discussion, he had given a "thumbs up" on a comment and was immediately mobbed by all of his old guys.

Picomann was the first to say, "HEY CONEJO, WELCOME BACK, WHERE HAVE YOU BEEN?"

The rest all did similar greetings and he had to explain that his job took him away for a while; he even traveled out of the country. He apologized and gave Picomann his phone number. Apparently his absence had a more profound impact than he would have thought and he realized he should have checked in.

Sometimes life did that though, it took one in directions that one never saw coming and then one quickly forgot all non-essential things. They were all having a great time until PhillyBob74 showed up. Matt wasn't sure he really missed *him* too much, as he had never really like bullies. Philly asked him how he'd been, and actually said he had been worried about him and almost sent out a search party.

El Conejo said thanks and meant it, it was a rare day to get sincerity out of Philly. Matt started to get into a good mood and decided to have a little fun with Philly seeing he was in such a good mood himself. He wrote, "Hey Philly, as I recall, you had a mission to accomplish and then I never heard from you, either. Where's my organization to run?"

Philly then broke off into a private chat with just El Conejo, PhillyBob74, BostonMike1, Picomann, TimberJustin12 and SASPURSRULE29.

Philly led with, "Hi guys, I just wanted to say that you need to keep an open mind here, as you're about to step through the looking glass." Next appeared a link, and he asked that they all count to three right now and click on the link. He implored, "Please, this is no joke."

The next thing Matt knew, he was in a virtual world. His screen lit up with full animation and he found himself in a boardroom where at the head of the long conference table was a portrait of this virtual company's CEO—and the picture was of him.

His character looked around by using his mouse, he was walking with the arrow keys. There were five other characters in the room as well: two were Caucasian, one was Hispanic, one was African American, and last was an Asian American. The graphics were so unbelievably lifelike. A short nerdy white guy walked up and said, "Hi, Tom, I guess I have some explaining to do."

The words appeared in a bubble above him and Matt responded with "Yeah, you do." They were all asked to take a seat. There were eight seats, four on each side and one at the head of the table. Their moderator was PhillyBob, it appeared, and he told him to approach the chair and hit F4. As Matt's avatar approached the table, his name lit up at the head, but as Tom Holsinger, of course.

They all sat at their respective places, the only problem was, it was their real names that lit up and not their usernames that everyone used in the chat room.

SASPURSRULE29 was the first to speak up, "How did you get my name Philly? I never mentioned my name—on purpose."

Robert's avatar was the only one not sitting. He responded to SASPURSRULE29 with a request for patience. He claimed that although he had been a jerk in the chat room quite often, it was mostly an act, a way to vent his anger at the world.

Robert let them know that everyone in the room was scaled to their physical self. Matt remembered looking down on him when they met a few minutes ago in this virtual boardroom.

Robert began with his life story, describing his early childhood. Everyone at the table winced at the real world torture he had endured. Picomann finally interrupted with, "Okay, Philly, but what has this place got to do with it? How do you know what I look like, this thing looks like me?" With that everyone erupted into havoc and Philly had to rein them in.

He raised his hands and implored, "Please just listen to what I have to say, then after, if you want to leave, you can go. I will erase your avatar from existence, I promise. That quieted everyone, mostly because everyone's curiosity was so high. Philly continued, "Forget PhillyBob74 people, and just listen. My story didn't end with being tortured, it began there." For the next thirty minutes—two had to call in late for work—Robert filled their heads with an unbelievable tale, right up to the point where Tom empowered him to create this.

Matt was blown away, "Robert, I don't really know what to say. But at the very least, I need to tell you that there is a lot about me that you don't know, and if that is true about me, then it is probably true about everyone here." Matt continued, "I'm not saying I'm a bad guy, but I'm not saying I wanted to be this guy, either."

Robert spoke back, "Tom, this is all your doing. You're the one who so passionately pointed out what must be done. Well, here's your chance." Robert then addressed them all, "I'm a millionaire many times over. I don't have to do this, I already got my break. But Tom was right last month, it can be done."

He turned his avatar to Picomann, "John, your family has lived in Los Angeles their whole lives. You work in a store on the edge of the neighborhood you grew up in, which also serves an international community where you are quite popular. You know so many people and you don't even realize how many you could touch if you wanted to.

"All of you, you're all capable of the same things, I checked you all out. I know why you don't want your name out Griffin, it's because you're the Head Physical Education Trainer for the San Antonio Spurs." He had their attention now, Matt noticed, and Robert continued, "I know you all have a lot to lose, but from the retired Fire Captain in Seattle to the Pharmaceutical Rep in Boston, all of you have more connections than you can ever imagine." He asked them to rise and they followed to the stairs where they all climbed to the top, several floors up.

The mapping of the game was amazing and the stairwell looked very real, like nothing any of them had ever seen before. They came to a window where they could look out over the empty city.

He said to the group, "Once the game starts, people will flood this place and they will all be trying for those two empty seats, and while they are doing it, we can prime our agenda."

Matt could see that Robert had it all worked out, but the one thing he hadn't figure into the equation was that Matt could not afford Tom Holsinger to become a household name. Once his likeness hit mainstream, someone would put it together. He could change his hair, unsoften his features, but he was still Matt Hurst.

Many a time in public he caught people giving him a double take, and then he would always get the comment, "You remind me of someone?" Only no one had yet put two and two together.

He turned and told Philly the words that he didn't want to hear, "I'm sorry, Robert, I guess I'm just full of shit, but I can't do this. I'm just not as brave as you are in real life. Please do as you promised and remove my likeness and avatar from here. I believe in you guys and I wish I could tell you why I can't do this, but that is not possible either, but trust me, I can't."

While Robert was trying to pitch his case, Matt's avatar disappeared and Robert and the group were left standing with one burning question. Why?

Matt turned his computer off, stunned. How the hell did that just happen? The shit just kept piling up and now he was starting to feel that old pressure again—the pressure he'd felt before he enacted his plan two years ago when he thought he would be discovered and killed by his captors as a saboteur. It was a feeling of foreboding, as the clock just kept moving forward until it ran out of time.

Eventually time is the foil in every situation where one wants to stall the clock or to simply stay where they were in time. He went back to his room and spied on Jan. As usual, she was sleeping peacefully while right in front of her things were reverberating in another realm that could upend the apple cart one more time. How many more apple carts topples would this girl endure before she got wise he wondered?

He knew he needed to get out and be alone with nature, so he scribbled her a note, packed the hunting gear, and left. Today was the last day for Mule Deer. The drive out was quiet.

He took his boat over to the mainland so he had to wait for no one today. They kept a slip on the other side along with a car, which enabled them to get off the island when the ferry wasn't running. It was at Jan's insistence when they moved that they had these two back ups. Of course, the boat had provided a floating hotel when they wanted privacy, too. Those were some good times he mused.

He had gone out the first day of deer season and almost got an eight-point buck. He had been hunting his whole life, but had never gotten a trophy buck. He had also never been the shot he was now—but the buck smelled him that day and got spooked.

Matt was hunting out near Baker Mountain. It was a large swath of forest he would hunt occasionally when he did not want to travel up near the Canadian border. Just the word border made him always think of that night many years ago—a night when he made a mad small plane dash across the Mexican border with the U.S. Military hot on his trail. He couldn't help but think that the wiser path would have been to have headed up through Canada, it was so sparse.

He passed the heavily wooded area where TJAC's training safe house was and proceeded around the lake. Of course his thoughts immediately drifted off to Chase, and the confrontation he was avoiding.

Jan was going to be up soon. Jon Jon had an early doctor appointment and then they were going to go play at his favorite children's park near downtown Seattle. His cold had waned and he was feeling better, but she just wanted them to listen to his chest to be safe. She thought that if he felt up to it, she would take him to the park to play afterward.

He dialed home. She answered on the second ring, sounding a little put out. Apparently she was already up. "Why are you going to go kill Bambi when we need you to go with us?" He chuckled at the joke, and said, "I'm not going to kill Bambi, just his dad. Today is the last day of hunting season and you know I've always wanted Bambi's dad's head on my wall."

Jan burst out, "Not in our house it won't!"

Matt chortled, "Well, we always have the guest house."

In her most condescending and irritated tone, Jan imparted, "Right, Matt, that is going to fly with Sherry, to have some dead fucking animal in her living room."

She had used the F bomb, and right then and there, he knew when he wasn't going to win, "Look, Babe, I got some things on my mind, okay? I'm sorry, and I promise to be back by three or so."

Couples knew, friends knew, and especially family knew how to swing low and connect on something painful. Jan knew the things he hated more than anything, so she just had to say, "Whatever," and then hung up on him, which was the other thing he absolutely hated.

As far as Matt was concerned, the word "whatever" should be banned as a word for all time, he fumed, but he knew better than to call back. Every now and then, old Jan came around and it was best just to stay clear. He still had ten minutes more to drive, so he hit play on his iPod. Cage the Elephant tried to rock his irritation away while he tried to absorb the gravity of Robert's actions. He broke away to think, but not as a childish response to some crisis he was running away from.

What he did in Mexico was what Jim had taught him: never make a life changing crucial decision on the spot if you don't have to. And if you don't have to, break away, clear your head, and really think things out. He had a whole other set of procedures to follow if time was not allowed, but for now, he would stick with the regiment that Jim ingrained into his head.

He was really starting to soften toward TJAC, hell, he could turn around and be there in fifteen minutes. But he still felt the need to stay away, to make Chase understand just how much he disliked the disrespect of his nature and abuse of his patriotism. He had already played the patsy once, and was lucky as hell to have survived.

* * *

She waited below the main platform and it was killing her. She had wanted to scream, "be careful," but she knew that was breaking their pact and would elicit a harsh rebuttal, so she resisted. No matter how many times they did this, the torture never stopped for her. She would always irrationally imagine him plummeting to a painful death after losing his footing on a ledge that was only inches wide.

Next he expertly shimmied up a pole and made it onto the platform. From there he gave the thumbs up sign and disappeared back out of view on the platform, her anxiety heightened.

After a few moments he showed up in a hurry and launched himself into the escape tube and down to the extraction point. She was waiting for him at the bottom as he slid right into her arms, "I love you, Mommy."

"I love you, too, Jon Jon."

He looked at her rather antsy and said, "I have to go pee-pee real bad."

Jon was not old enough to go to the restroom on his own yet, so they went to the Women's side. She carried a backpack instead of a purse and coupling that with their jackets, and the fact someone went out of their way to make the stall as small as possible, it was a rather a tight fit. She realized in the middle of her grousing that he'd soon be making this trip on his own and she got sad at the notion that she wouldn't have to do this hassle much longer. She supposed she was just crazy, but then realized that she was crazy like every other mom in the world.

Thank God little boys didn't have to sit on anything. She didn't think having a girl would be too much fun, at least at this age, she would be hunched over.

After he was done she had to step out backwards as there was no turning room in the stall. She took her backpack off and placed it on the sink and had the boy stand right outside the stall while she went number two. Even though he came out of her, she still couldn't poop in front of him. They were having a nice conversation through the door about his favorite toy store. They were heading there next, and somewhere between wiping and flushing, she didn't hear his voice any longer.

She said, "Jon," but there was no answer, so her anxiety heightened quickly. She burst out of the stall and ran out, leaving the backpack on the sink. She turned the corner, scanning, and immediately saw her son, as he was only twenty feet away, looking at a butterfly hop around in a flowerbed.

"Jon," she admonished, "Why did you do that? You scared mommy very badly, you know to never, ever, leave me. She reached down and picked the boy up and as she was turning to go back for her backpack she abruptly bumped into a short man wearing a fedora and dark glasses. He bumped her so hard that she almost dropped the boy. She automatically protested, "Hey, watch it," when she smelled something almost sweet. The man said, "Sorry" in heavily accented Spanish and was gone, but suddenly, she was feeling very light headed.

Jon complained, "Mommy, I don't feel so good," and it was all she could do to set him down before she face planted unconscious on the sidewalk, the boy on her side, both unresponsive.

* * *

Doug cleared his throat before he addressed the cabin. "Um, this is your captain speaking. This is flight 1812 to Oakland. It will be a one hour and forty minute flight gate to gate. We expect to have clear skies and a pleasant flight, so just sit back and let us get you there in Southwest style."

It used to be that he only flew as a means to meet women. He never really loved the craft and he feared that it was only going to get worse after he started flying for the big boys. He had read that many pilots equated themselves to underpaid bus drivers and he was sure that would be him, too.

Previously, flying was definitely only a means of getting laid, but now he actually enjoyed the flying. He loved the initial inertia that one felt upon lift off, for it made one feel that one was doing something to defy the limitations that the earth tried to place on all animals except birds. From flying squirrels to flying fish, every animal wanted to fly and the reality was mankind was different enough to make it happen. We were placed here to break all those barriers.

That was the only sappy part though; the other was the great responsibility and he supposed he loved that as well. It was his validation of being part of society, and not just a flying sex machine.

They were third in line to take off, so he had a moment to daydream, as things were moving a little slow at Sea/Tac today. Prior to that night, he had only flown cargo planes. Of course, the night he was abducted, everything in his life changed. The minute those two kidnapped him and made him fly them at treetop out of the country, he became a footnote in American history.

At first, the traitor threats started along with all the other anti-American shit for not letting them kill him before he flew that plane. Then he went on *Nightline* and William Kerr thought he would press him hard on the fact that he flew that plane out.

Doug began carefully with Kerr, but the fact he wasn't afraid was evident. When men went to war, they didn't come back with less confidence, unless the horrors were too much for the mind to bear. Mostly, they came back with a bit of swagger. Doug had been to war.

He had decided to carefully turn the tables on Mr. Kerr. "Okay, William, I'm going to do a little roll-play with you, if I may." Kerr hesitated to answer, but Doug went on anyway, "Let's pretend that you are me, and you just met a beautiful woman who takes you to see her new plane."

Kerr, still hesitating, but answered an unsteady, "Okay."

Doug continued, "It is going way better than you could have hoped for and you start making out with her because wow, who wouldn't, and all of a sudden a guy shows up and knocks you out with a series of martial art moves you are defenseless to stop."

Kerr immediately started another line of questioning, and Doug willfully snapped back control, "You wake up to the sound of a cork being popped on some fine champagne, only it wasn't, it was the sound of a silencer. The guy who knocked you out is now dead and only has part of his head left to show for it."

This was where Kerr decided he was going to draw the line, yet it still didn't work as Doug out willed him and forced him to face facts instead of wild speculation. "The man that just ended the other man now walks over to you and says that you are flying him and the female out of the country at tree top level via Southern California to Mexico."

Before Kerr could rebut a word Doug continued, "You say 'No,' and the man shoots the ground inches from your hand, the cement burned into your hand and arm and the acrid smell of cordite fills your nose as he tells to you, 'That the next shot is through your head.'

"Okay, William, go. Now take in mind that it was an unfolding story that no one had the whole picture of, and these two looked different than the two that the public was looking for. Not to mention, you have a concussion. Now let's hear your hero move. Unlike you, William, I'm going to give you all the time you need to answer."

That was it, Doug sat silent as Kerr tried to regain momentum, but he had no snappy comeback. And after that show, it all changed for

Doug, as he went from traitor to accepted victim. Now it was regarded that he was a lucky ass guy to be alive. After all, two people who were regarded as putting very little value on a human life abducted him. Not to mention the U.S. tried to shoot them down and failed. That was all before the U.S. military found out that they were up against a new kind of enemy, a shrewd and calculated one built on stolen technology.

His flight crew was finalizing all their checklists and instructions with the passengers, and his was the next plane to go. Doug thought back to when he saw his dad for the first time after the *Nightline* taping. His dad knew his motives in life were of the selfish variety and he detested the way his son flaunted convention and opportunities and was never the guy to be exceptional. He finally got to see pride when his father saw him reach his potential.

When he applied to the airlines, he figured he would be treated like some kind of plague, but no way, he got offers right away. He chose Southwest as it seemed appropriate somehow, after all, he had lived in the region his whole life.

He sped down the runway and there it was, the second they went from people held to the earth by gravity to people that literally had the sky as their limit. He felt it, that unmistakable feeling that one was part of something bigger than themselves, yet somehow one that was helping to make mankind's progress happen.

How lucky we are, he thought, *to be part of something that was obviously the beginnings of man reaching farther than this planet.* As Doug had learned earlier in life, asking rhetorical questions was not something he should ever do.

As they were gaining altitude, something oddly familiar shot past on the port side and a microsecond later, the engine light was on following a rumble that reverberated through the plane. He stabilized the plane, but before Doug could look for a visual on the port engine, another object flew by and the starboard engine light came on also.

Doug was now floating a sixty-ton boat anchor and he was about to learn firsthand what the other Captain had to do to survive in New York. The plane hadn't risen high enough to get out to open sea, so he was going to have to put it down in Puget Sound. Kingston was on the port and Seattle was on the starboard. He made the commitment and steered the barely responsive dead weight toward the Sound. That was when he saw the ferry . . . yet there was no turning back. It was going to be close.

* * *

Tim Smith and his wife, Julie, were standing on the observation platform of the Kingston Ferry. They were going to go have lunch and spend the day hanging out in Kingston; they'd brought their bikes and were excited to have a whole day to hang out. Tim hated bringing his car over as so many times he'd had to wait for a second ferry for the return trip. There were just too many people; there were just too many cars in this world.

On their last visit, he finally figured out that if they had parked on the mainland and took bikes, none of the waiting would be necessary.

They were standing on an outcrop made for photo opportunities, an extension of the observation deck that resembled a gunwale on a whaling boat, only this one had high rails. The observation deck itself held about thirty outdoor seats on each side, but was recessed in shade whereas the narrow platform was in the sun on the side of the boat. It wasn't more than ten feet wide yet it allowed enough room so their ten-year-old twin daughters were able to play with some miniaturized toys at their feet.

Tim saw it first; it was off to the left. A plane had made an unusual noise, a grinding sound, and then a puff of black smoke started billowing. Then he heard and saw it again, something had flown into the other engine and now the plane was powerless. He could see two trails of smoke that looked like black jet trails—they were coming out of the engines.

The plane banked left towards them, and then was coming down fast. Julie looked up and joined him. To Tim's amazement, she was quick on her feet and immediately went to the lockers under the benches on the deck, retrieving three life vests. She called the girls, who had still not caught on that something was amiss. The second she yelled with sternness, they both caught on and came right over. She quickly put the vests on and returned to Tim, as white as a ghost.

She instinctively said, "We have to warn people!" As she was turning, her husband's arm shot out and grabbed her. Tim Smith was a Seattle Fireman, and he knew it would do no good to warn people, it would just cause wide spread panic in the last seconds of their life, and Julie needed to be here.

"How far down do you think it is?" she asked her husband.

"I don't know, maybe fifty feet."

His worried wife asked, "Can we survive that?"

"Yes, no problem." He looked back up to survey the situation and heard a scream come from up where the cars were on the top deck. It started—widespread pandemonium unfolding, but before anyone who wasn't already in place could do anything about it, the moment was on him or her, and just like Tim had said, there was no time.

The plane came in howling, an angry ghost town in a windstorm howl. The maw of both engines looked like a mouth that had all its teeth knocked out, and the air passing through was making a sound effect that Tim would never forget. He had both girls and Julie on the rail, legs over and he was ready to push them, but it looked like it was going to barely miss the ferry. Right before he pushed them over, he had hesitated as the angry jet howled overhead in a terrifying moment that anyone who had witnessed it would never forget.

It was so close that it scraped off the communications antennas and masts, the debris raining down on the cars and spectators. In a moment of indecision, Tim did not push them over and the plane missed the ferry and slammed into the water with the force of a thousand killer whales. After the huge splash of water and mist cleared, they could see the plane was intact. It was a miracle.

* * *

Just as Doug had committed to the channel, he saw the ferry right in the middle. His options were limited as time was no friend. In his quick assessment, he determined he would clear the ferry as it was moving west at a good clip. He could hear his howling engines, sounding like some fucked up haunted house. The stick was dead, but at least he had it lined up. Then the moment was on them, the plane was coming in. He had already warned the passengers about a water landing and the crew was bracing for the impact.

In his best initial estimation, he figured they would miss the ferry. But as they approached, he had serious doubt and pulled the stick back with all his might. The plane cleared the top of the ferry by feet as he could feel the collision with the mast as it vibrated the through the dead stick.

The jet hit the water with a tremendous jolt and roar, the ocean vehemently resisting with all it had. Once Doug realized they were alive and intact he immediately went into action, leaving the cockpit to get to the starboard door and stop anyone from opening the middle doors.

When he exited the cabin, he heard a small applause, but he quickly extinguished it as he opened the port door and the slide came out. He could see the ferry and the commotion that was transpiring and was glad to see that they had sustained no major damage.

Then without any warning the explosion knocked him right off his feet and he waited for the quick death he knew was coming.

Only that nanosecond did not yield his untimely death by explosive fireball. Even though he could feel the heat and hear the screams, they weren't coming from his plane, initially anyway. And then they started from his plane as well. He stood up and was looking at a scene unfolding, never in a million years thinking he would ever see such a sight. The ferry had literally split in half.

There was a mass of people, fire, and hysteria that would only be analogous to a water-borne 9/11, a scene from Hell. Doug's mind could not begin to wrap around it. What could have done that? Then he had a chilling thought—maybe a different plane hit it?

Then he reasoned that a plane would have had to have been right on his tail, but his proximity radar had not gone off nor had the tower interjected. So if it wasn't a plane, what could have done that to the ferry? It was sinking fast in two pieces. He would have loved to be able to throw all their floating devices out there to help people, but his plane was full and they might need them. Doug knew this was an area with a lot rescue personnel stationed nearby, and thankfully he could already hear them coming.

He was initially thinking that a bird strike did this, but after he got the plane lined up he was able to sneak a peek at the port engine and saw that it was blown out. Something hit the engine, and it was explosive enough to blow the engine out, but not sheer off the wing? When the projectiles zipped by, they had an air of eerie familiarity. Once upon a time the U.S. Military had tried to kill him while he flew a Cesena. He remembered two of those things zipping by, and then two more. The next thing he knew, the U.S. was out two jet fighters and he was in Mexico.

Those were the first sightings of Pablo Manuel's drone army. If these were the same things, then why him again, and why not just use big ones and wipe him out of the sky? What a fucked up thing, to be so elated at their survival and then immediately horrified at the death and destruction two football fields away. He now knew what it was like to be on the ground for something like the Hindenburg tragedy or 9/11.

* * *

Matt parked out on the edge of Reese Hill Road and started hiking up the public access trail. He was still fuming about Jan hanging up on him and it brought back another thought. The last time he was here he had lost his buck because of Jan. He had bought all the gear for hunting including deer urine. For some reason, the deer urine triggered some irrational thought in her and she forbade him from wearing it. She swore that if he wore it, she would not touch him for a month. So he abided by her wishes and sure enough, just as he was lining up the shot of a lifetime, the wind shifted, the buck caught a whiff of something it didn't like—most likely him—and bam, it was gone.

He surely could have shot it on the move, but the shot would not have been humane, and if he missed the deer, it would never come back to that clearing again. All he could hope for was another day. Of course, he didn't talk to Jan for a full day when he got back. That was when they had The Great Urine Talk.

He had fought his case valiantly and in the end it was agreed upon that he could use it as long as it nor any of the clothing it ever touched came into the house or garage. The next day he bought a three thousand dollar shed and it was over. That was surely a victory—he had convinced himself.

Some avid hunters had placed a blind up here and he'd found it where the guy in the sporting goods store said it would be, and it was now his favorite spot. Of course, this late in the season, he doubted his eight-point buck was still around, but he had to try. It was a short hike in, and although late by hunting standards, Matt had a feeling. At just after ten in the morning, lo and behold, his buck came back home.

Matt was going to bag him, dress him, and hike him back to the car the old fashioned way. Then he would have a great hunting tale and trophy to show his old man, who himself owned such a trophy. Venison was not a flavor he could endure, its gaminess too much for him, Jan wouldn't even try it, but he had an Indian friend who ran the fireworks stand who was going to be very happy tonight.

His friend Big Mike was on disability and was just getting by. Matt had to drive by his place to get home and of course Mike had the stuff of boy's dreams, so the two of them were destined to meet.

That first day they met was Jon Jon's birthday and he had stopped in for some birthday fireworks. Of course, Mike and Matt got to talking. Matt just carried that air of openness about him, because it seemed everyone always wanted to talk to him, at least that was what Jan said, only she didn't say it as a compliment.

He lined up his shot. He could see the neck perfectly as he controlled his breathing. As he was gently squeezing the trigger, his phone started to vibrate inside his breast pocket. He hesitated, lost focus, but got it right back when the very unexpected happened.

He had inadvertently placed it on ring/vibrate and now that the vibrate portion was done, his ringtone of "American Woman" burst out across the glen. The buck shot straight up in the air. When it came down its legs were moving like a cartoon, and much like a cartoon, it wound up running smack into a tree.

It got up stunned, but still panicked as Matt stopped the phone, which read "Jan."

As before, its legs were moving faster than its mind could control and it ran right back into the same tree, this time though with a cracking sound. It righted itself again, seriously wobbled, and with an unbalanced gait it made its way back into the forest like Dean Martin's reincarnation.

He could see as it staggered its way up the knoll, that it was no longer an eight-point buck. In its last tree encounter, it broke the left rack. More than irritated he answered the still ringing phone with, "I hope you realize I won't be talking to you tonight unless something is really wrong."

He listened and turned white.

The woman on his phone was saying his wife and child had fallen unconscious and were being loaded into an ambulance right then. She said she was at the Woodland Park Playground. Matt replied with total shock in his voice, "Okay, please give her backpack and phone to the authorities and thank you." He ended the call and was already out of the blind and running before his phone was fully put away.

* * *

Tim Smith came to with a jolt. He was in the water—and it was cold and hot. What happened? He saw the jet was still intact and that confused him even more? He had felt intense heat on the top, and it contrasted to the intense cold of Puget Sound on the lower part of his body. Then the mind fog cleared a little and he became super panicked.

He was searching his mind; the last thing he remembered he was hanging onto the donut shaped buoy, but Julie and the girls had put on life jackets, right? He couldn't remember Julie putting one on, but she must have, they were on the outer railing.

Rescue boats were everywhere, and they already had a spot where they were ferrying people to on the shore, then coming back for more. Tim realized those were not official rescue boats but local people coming to the rescue. Then he looked left and almost fainted. The entire ferry had cracked in half and was sinking fast. He did a quick assessment of his body and found all his parts intact and working. He had either been blown or drifted about fifty yards from the wreckage, and he still saw people coming to the maw of the sinking ship halves and jumping for it.

He saw a guy jump badly, hit the jagged bottom of the boat, and then began a horrific screaming that Tim would never forget. Realizing his positioning saved him from serious injury, he went into action, looking and calling the girls names out as he swam toward the carnage. The closer he got, the more bodies he found strewn about intermittently, some blown apart, yet he still had to check them for life.

Thus far, none were alive, but none were his wife or daughters either, so he kept it together, he kept looking. The water was starting to get to him and he wondered how long he had been in the water before he had burst awake? He had this feeling that he been treading water in a semi-conscious state for five minutes or so, and it would explain how civilians rescuers were already on the scene.

He came in as close as he dared to the ferry and found a woman who needed assistance. She had clung to a buoy in the Sound, and Tim came from beside her and hugged her into the buoy as she was very weak.

By this time the official rescue units outnumbered the civilians, and a Seattle Fire team arrived to help them. Tim identified himself as he clung to the buoy, hugging the woman against it. Soon, the two of them were on board a boat and heading over to the dock where he had seen people being shuttled. There were ambulances on the Kingston side, and triage had already started.

That was when he saw them in a small crowd on the dock. The fact that they had their legs hanging over the rail probably played a big part in him ever seeing them alive again. He ordered the boat's driver to go over toward their dock and he jumped out before the vessel could come to a complete stop. Tina and Tammy grabbed him first around the waist, then his wife next as she pulled back and chided, "Show off."

They turned and saw that the two halves were nearly sunk all the way now. Tim did not know the answer to his wife's question of how deep the Sound was. His was thinking about how a lot of people saw the ferry as a city bus and never even bothered to get out of their cars. The divers were going to find a lot of entombed people, he feared. And then his mind raced to figure out the cause of all this destruction.

The civilian rescuers were still needed as the plane was being disembarked now with their help. But that still left out the cause of this? Tim had seen with his own eyes that something had hit the remaining plane engine. Plus he had heard the first one.

His head was bursting from the noise of the explosion, as were Julie's and the kids'. When it was their turn to be given blankets and be checked out by the medics, they were told that the kids needed to be seen by a pediatrician to have a hearing-loss assessment done.

His head was also screaming for answers. He couldn't take his eyes off the carnage. It was the main reason he had become a firefighter, as he loved to help people. So to make him watch this and not be able to help was a special kind of torture. Soon the Coast Guard, Navy, Fire, and Civilian crews were able to get all survivors out of the water and headed to hospitals. Tina had suffered mild hypothermia and had a slight concussion, but Tim made the call to not have her go to the hospital as it was going to be a nightmare there, and one he didn't think they needed to deal with. He was a trained professional, after all.

Too soon they were ferried over to the mainland and were in their car headed home, the luckiest family in America. Every one of them was in some form of shock, but none more than he, for he had the greater scope of all things worldly.

When the world had gone crazy two years ago, he had dealt with some real frightening things. First of all, Julie and he had always been city people—not suburb people, but downtown city people. Julie was a real estate broker who specialized in corporate moves when a company had outgrown their britches. Tim worked at Station 12, which was near the Space Needle. They worked and lived downtown.

The building they had lived in was all glass and exposed to the world. He had always felt a bit uncomfortable, but Julie loved their apartment somehow, even though a person with binoculars could actually see right into their house with little difficulty.

However, after the madness of two years ago, they began to reassess what was important. One of the support rallies for the Jesuit Sheep leader, Pablo Manuel, was held right across the street from their building and it terrified the girls and Julie to the point that they no longer wanted to live in the building.

From their vantage point, they saw and heard many varying viewpoints, some of which were revolution, and Julie figured correctly that if it turned into an angry mob, the big glass building right in front of them was going to be toast. That was when they made the call to move just outside of Everett. It gave them both a commute they'd never had before, but they were able to buy a private property with a fence and a gate and even Julie had to admit, the safety factor was huge for a good night's sleep. The girls had a yard to play in when it wasn't raining and they got a dog to boot.

Their life had been going very good, but now that had all changed. Tim was sure he was going to have to set up some family counseling. He looked at his wife and she knew that as soon as they got home safe, he was gone, back to where he was needed. Julie Smith knew the life of a fireman's wife and it hurt her just a little that everyone else always counted more than they did, even when *they* needed him, too.

Normally his predictable actions would lead to them arguing, but after what she had just seen, she understood it was selfish of her to withhold her man from doing what he was meant to do. Watching her husband suffer in a situation where help was needed and he sat powerless to provide any was a look she hoped never to see again in her lifetime.

* * *

Robert's head was racked. In the computer and math world everything made sense. Nothing was ever a surprise and nothing ever fell out of the predictable; but not people. People threw you curve balls. People did the unpredictable. They pissed away chances of a lifetime, for what? Was Tom a criminal? Why would he run? He was the loudest and strongest voice they had. After he left, you could feel the air sucked out of the cyber room.

It was a serious letdown and Robert went into a little funk. They'd decided to meet back in his cyber boardroom at 11:00 AM East Coast time today. It was 10:30 and he was not feeling so good. First of all, he had done some pretty heavy research on Tom Holsinger and found nothing. He was no stranger to finding people and keeping tabs on them.

In his backpack was a binder with the profiles of every bully who had ever lived on his block, any person who had run with Runnels and had been part of chasing him down and hunting him like an animal even in his sanctuary. He started off with fourteen live bad guys to keep track of and now he was now down to eight in just a few short years. There had been a car accident, then a construction accident, and a shooting. This was South Philly after all, and his backpack held the proof of what it can be like for a young man bent on destruction. It also held the proof that he was good at finding people and that he had many resources, yet it was like Tom Holsinger just popped up out of nowhere.

It was very troubling, as he had invested so much in the word of a man who was probably a criminal. Hell, he might even be in jail right now and that call was from prison. They get computer time there. The worry on his face was so obvious that Melvin could not be at ease. Normally he left Robert in the library alone, as he was still ashamed of the times he hunted Robert in here like a scared little animal. Not today though, he knew that this meant a lot to him, and hopefully the others would find their own voice and resolve.

They had twenty minutes to go, Melvin was reading *Newsweekly*, and Robert was tooling around the Internet when came across an article that was written about his new game. It was an article written by Scott Bailey from Seattle whom he liked and had corresponded with by email the month before.

The article was flattering, and as he neared the end of it he observed something that he hadn't expected. There was a file photo of him, and one of Tom Holsinger. He had told Bailey that Tom was from the Seattle area and *Bailey had been able to get the picture no problem*, thought Robert. *So why the mystery then?* If this reporter had caught a photo of him, then he must not have been a criminal, at least not behind bars?

Robert now had an amused smile instead of forlorn, and Melvin asked what the change in attitude was about?

Robert said, "It's nothing, just that the reporter in Seattle snapped a picture of Tom Holsinger."

Melvin was up quickly and came over to see. He looked for a long second at the photo and then his face turned into a smile as well as he started smacking the rolled up the newspaper in his hand.

Robert noticed immediately that his friend had something. He was holding out. Melvin did not let him off the hook as he returned to his seat humming and maintained a look like he had the world's biggest secret, but he wasn't telling.

Robert played along and said, "Okay, let me guess, you know him?" Melvin grinned and said, "Oh yeah. We all know him."

Melvin turned the page of the article he was reading around so Robert could see it and Robert almost fell out of his chair exclaiming, "It can't be!"

Melvin smiled a rarely used smile, showing an awesome set of teeth and said, "Oh, but it can, and it is."

Robert had to sit and compute. Melvin knew the look of genius working and stood by silently. After a few moments he came out of it and said, "We need to go to Seattle and talk to him. If we can get him to come out and do this, it will be the tipping point, don't you see it, Melvin?"

He realized that although Melvin had come a long way, he still was not quite an erudite scholar either, so Robert explained as a mentor. Robert chose his words carefully so his friend could understand the true gravity of this revelation.

"Melvin, Matt Hurst was a national scorn, but ever since President Caulfield exonerated him, he has become a national curiosity. Not only that, Melvin, he is also someone who had been up close and personal with Pablo Manuel and his sycophants. We are talking super-immersion.

"One could spin it that the sheep did it the wrong way, but Matt figured out a way to make sweeping change without all the warfare. We could parlay that into being the catalyst of a great movement, maybe picking up sheep followers looking for direction. We'd have a movement with real power, one without wrath. No rioting, no name calling, just good old calculated decision-making that is for the good of country. Pack your bags, my friend, we're going to set out on a journey, and the end result could be the biggest thing to ever hit this country—a new kind of power that is apolitical."

They both saw it was time to join the others in the cyber world that Robert had created. Melvin inquired, "What will you tell them?"

Robert answered matter-of-factly, "The truth, of course, and like the Man said before they killed him, "And the truth will set you free."

Melvin asked, "What man was that?"

Robert said sincerely, without the slightest hint of a patronizing tone, "Dr. Martin Luther King, Melvin, and one day you and I are going to sit in this very place and discover together why he was much more than a Monday off of school and work.

* * *

Madness was not the word for what Matt was feeling. It was more like crazed insanity. His Explorer could go way faster than the eighty-five he was doing, but not safely now that he was on I-5 and headed the ninety miles to Seattle.

He was trying to remember exactly what the lady had said on the phone, something like, "The lady whose phone this is and the small boy with her both passed out and the ambulance is finally here. It took a long time but when one showed up there were no paramedics or police."

Confused, Matt asked the person he was speaking with to give the cell phone to the authorities, thinking that they were going to show. But now he was concerned that it didn't happen as no one was answering the phone. He had tried three times now and he foolishly had not gotten the good Samaritan's name or number.

He decided it was time for some deductive reasoning. First, he would call his parents at the house, just in case someone had tried there. He would ask his dad to walk upstairs and check his machine. His parent's house was under theirs. They were living in what used to be the guest quarters when the house was a Bed and Breakfast.

No luck. He tried the cell he'd bought for his parents, and of course it went to voice mail. Finally he tried the house and got his answering machine. He wished he would have set the auto-retrieval code, but he had decided he would never use it. He wondered how many times doing things the lazy way had cost in him in his life? His mind started reasoning. Why would they both have passed out? Jesus, he thought, TJAC wouldn't have gone after his family, would they? He needed answers.

He knew they went to their favorite park after Jon's pediatric appointment and that was right near Northwestern Medical Center. Children's Hospital was also nearby. He started with Northwestern. After the preliminary computerized options were forced upon him, he pushed zero and the operator answered. He explained his dilemma succinctly and the operator said words he didn't comprehend. She said that unless his wife and child were in imminent danger of dying, they would have been referred away; they were only handling life-threatening issues at the moment. Matt asked, "Why?"

The operator said, "Because the ferry blew up today, where have you been?"

White as a ghost, he turned on radio and didn't have to search for the story as it was on every channel. The news was unbelievable, it left him dumbfounded and grasping for comprehension. How could this be? What horrible timing for his wife and son, and now he had no idea where they were or who had even taken them?

Now it made sense why no emergency personnel had arrived, they were all at the ferry. Out of options, he dialed 911. He got put on hold. After five minutes on hold, he got an operator who gave him the name of the ambulance company they had been forced to use. It was another five minutes on hold until they finally answered. They didn't have her. He hung up and screamed in the car at the top of his lungs. He slammed the dash and tried to rip the steering wheel out while he was driving, swerving into the other lane as he did so.

He was the only person in the world who could go out for a cathartic moment in nature and get pulled out of it by something so horrific as this. Why didn't he get more information from the stranger? His stress level was at the point where he'd better not have any faulty vessels in his head or he would stroke out. He was going over ninety now weaving through traffic when his phone rang. The caller ID said "Jan."

He answered with a frantic, "Yes."

It was the ambulance attendant. He had Jan and Jon, they were still unconscious but stable. They were being rerouted all the way to Anacortes as the hospitals in Seattle, Tacoma, and Everett were all inundated with casualties from the ferry explosion. Some were going as far as Portland. The attendant's name was Jerry and he worked for Tier Ambulance.

He said they were mostly involved in Medical Transportation for non-emergencies, but a few of their personnel, including him, were EMTs. Jerry explained that when they were pulling away from the park a woman flagged them down and said the backpack was Jan's. She also said there was a phone inside and she had called the husband and informed him.

According to Jerry, the severely injured were counting in the hundreds, so there was no hospital to take them to except for Anacortes. That was the call their boss made. A call was placed to Anacortes and they were waiting for them now. All vitals had been sent ahead.

Jerry further explained that the witnesses who had stepped forward said they both just fell. No one was around them or could have assaulted them. They had no external injuries except abrasions to Jan's face that occurred when she fell. Matt took it all in, thanked Jerry, and told him to please keep him apprised if anything changed on the way to the hospital.

According to Jerry, they were coming up to Everett, so Matt whipped off on the next exit. Although he had passed the Anacortes exit ten minutes back, he knew another way through the town of Skagit. According to Jerry, their vitals were good and he had no idea of why they lost consciousness or why they wouldn't wake up now. He had never seen anything like it.

It was a fifteen-minute drive out to Anacortes, but, of course, there was some backed up traffic in town, too many people driving on a sixty-year old system. He had the news on low volume, but he had been listening and was shocked to find out that the ferry was only half the story.

Apparently, a Southwest flight had gotten into trouble and lost both engines. The pilot landed the plane in the Sound, barely missing the ferry. It was after the plane water landed safely that the ferry blew up, literally splitting in half.

There had been some physical contact between the plane and the ferry, but the initial reports were that the plane sheered off the communications tower and mast of the ship, causing nothing more than superficial damage. Matt's head was spinning. Why was this happening? Was it coincidence?

And there it was. When he was an investigator, he learned something very valuable—through trial and error—and that was that he didn't believe in coincidences anymore.

Suddenly he got a very bad feeling in the pit of his stomach. If TJAC did this and made him out to be a homegrown terrorist, it would start all over again for him. Maybe their payback was going to be to set him up and pin this on him—Jan and Jon's situation, too.

His similarities to Oswald were mounting again. He even left the country there for a while. Expat with a grudge, Hell, even the President himself was tight with Chase and had recommended this path for him over the CIA.

He was very confused as he thought about all those close conversations with Chase and Jim. He really couldn't believe that they were doing this to him. They were supposed to be representing the side of good here, the side of social justice and the better of the community.

He made his mind up right then and there. If he saw this thing spinning that way or anything that would lead him to believe that he was to be made into some sort of patsy, he would disappear, and when he reappeared, he would live up to their wildest media spin of Matt Hurst; especially if anything happened to Jan or Jon.

It occurred to him that maybe he had been part of a long-term con, a grift to build him up and then turn him into a killer—either set him up, or set him off.

Damn this world was full of fucking evil people.

He was now merging with the road coming from the north heading to Anacortes. But his mind was in that place where one just didn't know what the hell was going on, or what was going to happen. Matt's imagination was running wild, and then he thought of his parents. *What the heck is going on there?*

He left messages on every machine the Hurst clan owned. He called their apartment again. No answer. He called their cell phone. No answer. And finally he called his house. No answer. With each and every no answer his blood pressure increased until it was now boiling over, his apprehension of the unknown was mounting. He was so frustrated. Why did everything have to be like this in his life?! He was sure others had uncomplicated lives. He saw them everyday, going about their business with not a care in the world. No one was seeking them, and no one was trying to make them a killer of men.

Not him, though. He just had to be the guy a whole nation wanted to talk to—while they were able to go home to their families and live their lives.

The news was softly reporting in the background that the ferry scene was one of total devastation and surely hundreds of lives were potentially lost. The ferry was particularly full as a lot of people were attending a concert in Kingston.

As fate would have it, Matt turned off the increasingly redundant news radio just as the reporter was talking with Southwest pilot, Douglas Sharp, who said he observed two objects buzz by and then his engines were gone.

When pressed about what he thought those objects were, Sharp reported, "I couldn't exactly say, but it was probably a flock of birds. I guess the investigators will know soon enough."

* * *

Ray Callahan looked across the CIA compound, his office overlooking the old headquarters building. So far his day was going well. He had gotten up at five thirty to run and his wife, Kim, actually joined him, which thrilled him to no end as they had such little time together. They lived in a gated and guarded community near Georgetown, and although Hillandale was exclusive and patrolled, they had another patrol in tow as well, albeit one they rarely saw when jogging. Having two high-ranking government officials living together did pose a possible National Security Risk, so they had to live with the shadows. Ray hated the reality, but understood the necessity, especially since he'd finally become the director of something.

The CIA was a very structured organization. There was no room for someone outside the four established divisions (Intelligence, National Clandestine Service, Science and Technology, and Support) to exist. That was until Bob Thompson took over.

He'd needed two people under him who created a balance for abilities he personally lacked. But it was more than that. He also needed two people outside the box to be able to spot things others in the agency didn't think of or were too close to see. One of those two had to be a wizard in the quick-analysis department. Bob was an individual who liked to think things out and Ray was the best at instant assessments.

Bob also lacked one other thing—and that was ruthlessness. To fill that void he chose Ken Beck, eventually deciding it was he who should get the Deputy Directors seat. Only Beck wasn't designed to be a bureaucrat, he was a field agent who liked to be out among the people. He was Thompson's heavy, the one he sent in to bully teams not performing. But it all backfired on him when Beck went Norman Bates.

When Bob was later pushed into retirement, Ray was suddenly the odd man out. He was technically in the support division, but he had his hands everywhere, especially the Farm. Ray had a way of sniffing out a person's weaknesses and he would expose those weaknesses that could be exploited until the person broke.

With Eric in charge, there were no more inter-departmental jobs. In fact, Eric thought it to be utter insanity and Ray could sense a demotion coming, even though he had saved everyone's butt more times than he could count.

That was when Eric surprised him and did the right thing, promoting him to Deputy Director NCS (National Clandestine Service). It was a job tailor made for Ray and actually gave him the ability to traverse to other realms inside CIA just as he had before; only he could do it in the right way.

Of course, all this and the fact his wife was the President's Chief of Staff, made getting time together very difficult. They had good pacing with each other, so it made running with her easy; just like being married to her, he just found it very natural.

Ray was brought out of his daydream by the fax machine going off and shooting a paper into the tray. He came back to his desk from the window by rolling his chair across the low carpet, then spun around and brought his computer out of its sleep mode. It was just after lunch and his computer was still on the last Internet page he was on before lunch. He had been shopping for new running shoes.

In this day and age, there were times that the news media got to a breaking story first. Apparently at 10:03 AM PDT a plane went down out of Seattle and an adjacent ferry exploded. He looked at his watch; it was 1:19 PM EDT, sixteen minutes later.

Ray's personnel were already in scramble mode, and assessments were coming in quickly, but before he got lost in the beehive that was their main control room, he needed to have a serious one-on-one discussion with Director Barnett. He had his own instant assessment the Director needed to hear.

He hit Eric's direct number, the Director answering right away. Ray asked, "Got a quick second?"

The Director replied with some incredulity, "Right now, Ray, we're both needed for assessments."

Ray did not back down, "Eric, we need to talk."

One minute later he was in the Directors office. Eric Barnett was a man of medium height, carrying a few extra pounds that showed in his face. Not overtly, but his face seemed to have a furrow to it that Ray was not sure would be there without the extra thirty pounds he carried, especially in the eyes area where it gave him a hangdog look. His baldhead was shining in all its glory like he'd just stuck it in a bowling ball washer.

His looks belied the fact he was a great white shark, not a blue or a leopard. He was strong, fair, opinionated, and in charge at all times. Unlike his predecessor, he did not need people under him to create balance. He was the balance and everyone else fed off of him.

Ray was instructed to take a chair after he closed the door. Eric spoke first, "Ray, there is a situation that you need to be brought up to speed on. It was a need to know basis, so please don't get indignant at the news."

Ray raised his eyebrows as Eric uttered the next words, "It has been discovered that Pablo Manuel did not die that day when Matt shot him. A hair brush left at his school in France confirmed that the person Matt killed was a double."

Sometimes a sentence had so much impact that even a great mind like Ray Callahan's could not comprehend all its meaning until it was put under the microscope. This sentence had the effect of throwing a brick in the middle of a lake. Ray was not of the ilk to respond to even the most outlandish news with expletives, it was one of the things that made him a legend around here, that and his ability to multitask. His first response was one Eric expected, "This would have been nice for the Director of NCS to have known."

"Ray, I agree, but other than the technicians who did the work, the circle of people who knew this had to be very controlled. From my ears to the President, it was his call that no one else was in. President Caulfield figured that the world already thought Manuel was still alive so all the preparation they'd done for this was going to happen anyway. His thinking was to hide Hurst and make pretend that they thought he was dead, from every level of Government."

Ray had seen a lot of horrible shit in the last few years, but what was unraveling here was too much, "Are you telling me you staked Hurst out as the sacrificial lamb knowing that a killer was going to go after him and his family? You took our single greatest hero since Audie Murphy and put him out there to be killed?"

Eric looked hurt at the accusation, "First of all, Ray, it wasn't my call. I have a boss and he has a mind, you of all people should know that. The President had reason to be scared. With Manuel alive, he feared his ability to cyber strike us was still in play, not to mention the possibility of something like the shit that happened today. His thinking was sound. If the new attack didn't come right away, then Manuel knew that Hurst betrayed him and would want revenge.

"So they decided to play it by the numbers and act as if he were really dead. That meant hiding Hurst. Of course, we couldn't put a permanent detail on him, but we are loosely following him, mostly through cyber space, although we did GPS his car and boat.

"We also figured out how he was made by Manuel. Your boy likes to blog and you're right, he is a Patriot for sure, Ray. Some buddies and him got an idea together for a website and he accidently got his picture taken and put on a web article."

Ray was still miffed, "Eric, all you're doing is convincing me that I'm right, you hung him out to dry and didn't even tell him that a person who wants him and his family dead was alive and kicking. All the while, Matt thought he had killed him."

Eric reassured, "We have a detail on him right now. They're staying way back and will know when to make their move. Least I remind you that the man we seek did this today. Ray, use your power of analyzing and be objective. If Manuel was not dead, then we knew this was not done. Can you imagine an American public that knew what this guy really intended? The depths he was able to penetrate our Government have never been seen and the President made the right call Ray, even if we sacrifice Hurst and his family. Our goal is to protect our Sovereignty. So we wait until Manuel comes after our boy, then we kill him."

Ray's expression was beyond apprehension. It was a fusion of absolute rage and total fear, but, of course, he had to temper it when he addressed Eric, "Aside from the fact you are running covert operations out of my department without my knowledge, Eric, all I'm going to say is I hope you sleep good. If we knew this, we should have informed Hurst and moved him under deeper cover. Yes, I see the national implications, but that still doesn't make it right, and all I can think about is it sure doesn't pay to be a hero around here, the way we treat them it's a wonder anyone ever steps up."

Eric's line buzzed, a meeting of the Joint Chiefs of Staff was being called and he had to attend. He addressed Ray in a more relaxed manner, "I'm sorry Ray, but you know how this stuff works. Some of it is pretty dicey and we blur the lines of right and wrong in the pursuit of national interest. That's our mandate and you know this. You've gotten too close to this and that's another reason why you were left out. It's not that we didn't trust you to do your job; it just creates a conflict of interest because you have too much personal time invested in Hurst. Now that you're in, I need your help, so I will talk to you as soon as I get back."

Ray choked back what he really wanted to say and replied in the politically correct way, "Okay Eric, I'll be here." He got up and left.

* * *

Nudging into the seat was uncomfortable. Just carrying one very light travel bag had been a burden. Her back was on fire and, of course, she had had no choice but to take a middle seat for the flight to Houston. There, she was to switch planes and she would be in Seattle a mere six hours later. Dr. Gonzalez pleaded with her not to leave so soon, her back was just getting better and he warned her that if she did anything to aggravate it, she would have a much longer recovery.

She wore some loose pants that resembled pajamas and a simple tee-top. Her hair was short now for the first time since she was a kid. One of her attackers had mutilated her hair with a switchblade. Lauren remembered her attacker touching the blade to her face and then was complaining that she got blood on it. She then cleaned her blade on her hair, which of course turned out to be a backstreet haircut. She tried to lose the thought and the guy next to her fixed her problem by opening a deli sub and start noshing on it before they were even in the air. She was very glad she had taken two muscle relaxers. *Stinky sandwich guy will be a distant memory soon.*

She had called Scott and told him she was coming to Seattle to rehab, that she wanted to be near a familiar face. He was more than receptive, but slightly confused by the news, as he knew that she was obsessed with her story.

She told him she "needed a break."

Of course, he was elated after that, and he was counting the minutes until they saw each other again. She sure hoped he was still talking to her when he figured it all out; not that she didn't want to see him as well, but this was about her revelation.

Her pills were kicking in and the disgusting man with the even more disgusting sandwich were becoming less offensive by the second, which meant she was minutes from sleep. Her mind was drifting off in that way a good buzz would help you to sometimes, where you are relaxed enough to step outside yourself.

She thought about lying in that hospital for two more weeks like they wanted? But there was no way she could wait two weeks to get on this. She was able to get through the first week after her discovery and she tried to listen to the doctors, but by the second week, it was too much to take. She'd decided to stop acting like a girl, so she womaned up and took the pain, leaving the hospital early, much to the dismay of the staff. In an adoring move, Rodrigo had heard she was leaving her new facility early and traded his day off so he could take her to the airport.

He really was so sweet. He got her to the security checkpoint without any drama. She swore he had a small tear when she left? She was so wrong about his nature and felt a twang of guilt for not allowing him to be anything more than a great coital experience. Her last thought before she dozed off was, *it's funny how that works sometimes, people are not always who they seem and sometimes their true nature gets discovered.*

When she awoke later, she had forgotten this sentiment, but had she not, it would have soon become the biggest coincidental thought of her life.

* * *

Scott finished his blog and then he spell checked it, afterward sending it to his editor Tina Polaski. Scott loved Tina because she was easy going and had a sense of humor. She was in her sixties, but still had that hippy girl earthy charm that some were able to pull off to a very late age. He'd seen pictures of her in the Sixties and she had been a major babe. She probably liked him because he came to meetings in shorts and hiking sandals, or one time even wooden clogs.

He wore a goatee too long, and whatever shirt he could find, usually wrinkled. He fondly remembered the kid he cut off accidently on his bike the other day referring to him as a "hipster douche." So being a hipster douche had also endeared him to a lady who could be nasty if you were on her bad side, but career advancing if she liked you. And she happened to like Scott.

Contrarily, one would just have to ask Dale Couler of the *Financial Report* for his opinion on how life was on the other side of the fence. Dale was an acquaintance of Scott's from NYU and his "know it all" personality had a completely different view of Tina's ability and scent of her vaginal area than Scott had.

He looked around his apartment and shame befell him. It was bad enough that he hadn't done anything more that go to IKEA and put together some prefab arrangement of furniture, but he'd also put on ten pounds of ice cream and chocolate weight since the last time they had seen each other. He used to be eclectic, picking up pieces with a story. Now, most of those things were still in his moving boxes from two years ago.

He'd actually given up on women for the time being—and along with that mindset was it was okay for him to let it all go. He figured that if one didn't stand a chance at five foot nine, sporting his particular brand of cool, then one might as well go out in a blaze of glory.

Actually, by using this technique he'd inadvertently learned a new way to talk to girls, as it seemed some liked a man looking like the cat just dragged him in. But he just wasn't into it, and he secretly knew why.

Who could ever match up to her? *No one that I had met so far, and Seattle is a pretty big city to find women.*

Scott shut his computer off. His palms were sweating, and his heart was racing out of control. Lauren was the only girl who could make him feel that way, and he would swear off ice cream forever to just spend one more night with her. Somehow in college, he was under the delusion that another woman of her caliber would come along. After all, he got her.

What he found out was he got her by *not* trying. She was out of his league and he knew it, so he never tried to hit on her. He'd learned to get to know her for who she was—and fall in love with her from a distance for the person she really was.

Of course, there was the other stuff too—the playboy looks, and the most amazing freckles that mankind had ever laid eyes on. *Oh man, the freckles.*

She was a perfect ten, and he was a possible five; right now he was ranking more in the three-range. He called the maid service he used and put in an emergency request and got lucky—they would be out today for an extra $25.00. He headed out the door to get his hair done and his disgusting car washed and cleaned. Among his other bad habits as of late, he'd been eating fast food and leaving the containers in his car.

He was headed to his barbershop when he stopped at a red light and had a second to think. He thought that it was still odd that she was coming and he hoped that this "visit" had nothing to do with any kind of angle for a story. He could take betrayal from anyone else but her.

His apartment was on N. 59th and Linden N. and he needed to go up N. 59th and turn right on Aurora Ave N. to get to Downtown. The first intersection was Phinney Ave N. It was the corner of the Children's Zoo and Playground and he could see a scene happening in the area where the jungle gym equipment was.

Some kid probably fell off or something, he assumed. He could see a crowd and he normally would have let his curiosity get the better of him and gone in for the answer, or story—he was a reporter after all. It looked serious, and based on the crowd that had gathered, something awful must had happened. He pressed on. He needed to get things done today, so the story in the park would have to be for someone else.

He turned right onto Aurora Ave N. (U.S. Highway 99), and as he was heading over the Aurora Street Bridge he nearly crashed into the middle stanchion, as off to his right he could see an Airliner smoking from both engines and heading for the Sound. He crossed over the bridge stunned and turned right on Queen Anne Dr., went back under the freeway and started heading north again on Aurora. He zipped up Aurora and cut over toward the Sound to about where he estimated the plane would have gone down.

The problem with Aurora was there were no exits or ways to make a left turn for quite a distance. So he was quite sure that he had gone past the actual crash site when he finally found a left turn.

It looked like he was going to miss all his manicuring appointments today. *What the hell,* he thought, if she ever loved him at all, it certainly wasn't because of his appearance, of that he was sure. He weeded his way up toward the crash via side streets, his mind was spinning, of course, because what he thought he saw was hard to fathom.

The reporter that had been alive in him before he'd lost his passion for adventure was stirring. He hadn't been close to any real action since college—and it had been Lauren who had dragged him into all of that. He lived vicariously through her after college, for sure, and now he was getting ready to host Ms. Indiana Jones. He turned right onto Richmond Beach Drive, and found a left-turn onto what looked like a levy road with the refinery on one side and a construction site on the other.

Unbelievably there was no fence or gate preventing him from going through, just a warning sign. Ignoring that, he drove right up the elevated road through the middle and out to a long dock that also was unbelievably accessible. Once he got out and made it to the front side of the dock, he could see the horror up close and personal using his equipment. One thing he never shed was the need to have his photography gear with him at all times.

Scott Bailey, Reporter, had a unique photographic vantage point during the last ten minutes of the real life and death struggle going on. He caught all the drama as the two halves of the ferry slipped under, and the last people pulled out alive were saved. Scott mulled, *did the plane do that to the ferry? How did the plane manage to land after causing that?*

* * *

Matt pulled into the hospital and found several cars blocking the parking for Emergency. He looked to his right and found a spot in the one-hour parking. He jammed the car into reverse and deftly backed in. He was out and running, but before he got out, he put his pistol in the center console of the car and made sure it was loaded. He would have taken it with him, but he wasn't sure if they had metal detectors here or not.

Inside was a little more crowded than one would have expected for a mid-sized community hospital. Matt was attributing this to the patients coming from the disaster zone. Inside the E.R. was a TV, and that's when he caught his first glimpse of the horror.

He stepped back outside to wait until he saw their ambulance arrive. As they were being unloaded he identified himself and went in with them. They brought them in together, mother and son, unconscious.

The doctor who was looking them over was of Indian decent, about five eight, short dark wavy hair, and no facial hair. He had the soft features of a man in this early thirties, he also had very little accent.

He began examining Jan and looked up when Matt entered after washing outside. He stopped his examination and asked if he were her husband?

Matt answered, "Yes. What happened to them?"

The man, whose nametag said Dr. Arshad Singh, approached Matt with an inquiring mind. He was looking deeply into Matt's eyes and he asked, "What do you do for a living, Mr. Holsinger?"

Matt stumbled for a second, as he always wanted to answer to his real name and profession. He replied, "I'm in sales."

Still not satisfied, he asked, "What do you sell?"

Matt did not like these inquiries at all; it was just the thing he was on high alert for. "I sell electronics, why?"

"Because I believe that they have been exposed to a chemical agent or some other neurotoxin. I'm not the E.R. doctor, Matt. They called us off our rounds in the hospital. I'm a resident, but in my country, I was a neurosurgeon."

Matt didn't just come off the farm, and it was no hidden secret that even if you were a neurosurgeon in India, it translated to nothing in America without the credentials, but that didn't mean the man was not a neurosurgeon. "You're saying they were poisoned at the park?"

The doctor responded, "I have no idea where they were poisoned, if that's what this is."

Matt realized that he had just made himself a suspect and he needed to get this doctor to realize that he was not a suspect, he had no time for police interactions.

He made serious eye contact, "Please listen, Dr. Singh, I implore you, I know what the implications of what you just said mean, and you and I know that the cops will do their investigation into this." He reaffirmed his eye contact and said, "From man to man, please don't believe for a second that I had anything to do with this. It's not like there is anywhere I can hide in the modern world. This is my family, we have no issues and I am not in any way culpable." He looked at Jan and the boy—he'd been avoiding doing that—and started to cry.

Dr. Arshad Singh could read people like a book. He used everything from their breath to the eye contact they made in order to ferret out untruths. He knew that was easier if the person was under duress as people could not help but expose their true nature under duress without realizing they had a tell, just like in poker, his favorite game. He could see this man was not lying. "Okay, Mr. Holsinger, ignoring all the protocols and police procedures that will happen regardless around us, I believe you, and I am sorry this happened. I will make some calls and see how long it will be before we can get them back to Seattle. Once there, we can get them into a neurology department, as our community hospital does not have one."

Matt thought about that and the atmosphere of Seattle hospitals right now and said, "No, you said you were a neurosurgeon and you're a resident here. If what we're dealing with is a neurotoxin, won't most of your work be lab work anyway? I want them admitted under your care. With the madness going on in Seattle and most of the State, I want them with you until we can figure this out."

"That's a flattering suggestion, Mr. Holsinger, but we are not equipped to handle such cases and we would have to defer them to Northwest in the best of circumstances. It is hospital policy," he explained to Matt, as he could see for himself, their vitals were very strong, so transferring them would be no issue. Dr. Singh continued, "I have to make some calls and then we will have a plan. Please be patient as nothing is going to happen fast today."

Matt was left alone with his thoughts, his paralyzed family lying comatose next to him and his parents missing. His head was swirling. *Who did this? Why did they do this? Why not just kill me?*

He thought back to Mexico and his target. If he could have just ended the man, then none of this would have happened to his family. If only he could have just become someone he was not, for the people who were using him. Then he would have been free.

What kind of skewed thinking was that anyway? He knew better. Once he pulled that trigger, then he no longer would have ever been free again. He buried his face in his hands for a while, then slid his chair between the two exam tables and stretched out to touch them both at the same time.

After almost an hour Dr. Singh came back in. "Tom, I'm sorry to tell you that the situation in Seattle is much worse than even the news has said. There is no way we will be transferring Jan and Jon there in the foreseeable future. I'm trying to arrange a medical-flight to San Francisco for them as we have the injured from the Southwest flight coming here. For now, we can go and have them admitted into a room, as you had wanted, but it will be a temporary situation. How far do you live from here?"

Matt answered, "Lummi Island, it's about 45 minutes home," less he thought as he had taken his boat over in the morning."

"Then you should go home, pack, and be prepared to be gone for a while. Let's get them moved into a room so you will know they're safe until you get back."

Matt thought about that. His mom and dad had not called him back yet and it had been another source of anxiety all day. He needed to pack a few things, but mostly he needed to find out what the heck was going on with them now as well. He replied, "Okay, I'll go and be back in two hours. I need to get a hold of my parents anyway. Let's hurry up and have them moved, please."

Dr. Singh left, and Matt got up and caught the mirror. Since he was a teenager he had worn a stainless chain with a cross on it. Mostly it stayed inside his shirt, but in the tussle of the day it had come out and he saw it, and the elephant in the room bellowed a thunderous chord as there was a real possibility that God was smiting him.

He could have chosen to break off right now and write a book, hell, he could have written several: one on deep cover and long-term espionage tactics; one on how to survive combat and overcome fear; and one on God and how he communicates to us.

He had spent two years in the presence of a man who maintained he had been instructed by God to bring change to the world. He'd not only had the instruction but the means to carry it out. Of course, Matt stopped him and ever since then, all the signs appeared that he was supposed to take Pablo's place as the Harbinger of Change.

For well over a year now he had been waiting to see what new sign was going to appear to get him to jumpstart this change, but there had been no directional signs on the road.

Then it actually happened. Robert turned out to be an agent of God, able to bring that kind of power. Yet he ran away. He was always running away these days. Did he have a more serious case of Post Traumatic Stress Disorder than he thought? He sure was afraid to face Chase and more afraid of where Robert wanted to go.

All of a sudden he couldn't face his problems anymore. He pondered that. Some super spy he would have made, the pressure of this situation was enough to make him fold right now.

He had two people to call in this situation, and one of them was his dad—who wasn't answering his phone. He pulled out his phone and dialed Ray Callahan. Ray had believed in him from the start and had put him back together after it was over. Well, as much as could be done with him. The phone rang and like everybody else this day, Ray's phone went to voice mail. *Just great.*

He was about to nervously dial his dad again when Dr. Singh came back in with a team of orderlies and two rolling beds. The move took twenty minutes and Matt signed all the paperwork. His insurance was being paid for by the CIA for life, which, of course, was a Godsend right now.

Dr. Singh did not attend the move, but a nurse practitioner oversaw the whole thing with a watchful eye. Matt kissed and blessed Jan and Jon, and then left the building on a near run.

He exited the main entrance but as he was heading to his car adjacent to the E.R., he saw personnel helping people off a charter bus coming from the flight. Dr. Singh had said they were on the way. Then Matt saw something that made his blood go cold. He could swear that he just saw a familiar face in the crowd.

He saw a man pushing an older woman in a wheelchair and they had just entered the Emergency door. The compulsion was too much and he broke for the E.R. at a full run. When he got there and went in, the woman in the chair was there but not the man who had been pushing her. He looked around and sure enough, it was Doug talking to the admitting nurse. *It can't be.* His knees went weak and he almost fell over. *This was all too much! What could this mean?*

More people were being brought in, most in stable condition, some complaining of severe back pain. Doug left the attendant and came over and talked to the woman. Matt saw a door that led to the main hospital and went over to Doug and asked if he could talk to him out there for a second. Doug looked startled and asked, "What's this about?"

Matt just placed his arm on Doug's and said, "Please."

He said, "Okay," but with a look like he was about ready to call for security. By the time they got into the lobby of the hospital Doug was asking, "Do I know you?"

Matt didn't have time for games, so he pulled his hunting cap off and said, "Doug, it's me. Matt."

His eyes got as big as quarters, and he quietly exclaimed, "No fucking way."

"Way, Doug, and seeing you here creates a big problem, one I hadn't thought of before and should have." Matt quickly tried to catch his friend up.

Doug sat with a look less stunned than he should have had, "I knew you were alive, I just wondered when you were going to pop back in my life."

Matt asked, "Doug, what really brought your plane down? Was it the same things we saw before?"

Doug's answer was a grim, "Yes, and worse. They're keeping it under wraps right now, but soon the mainstream media will have it. Matt, do you really think Pablo would attack innocent people like that?"

"Truthfully, I just don't know. If I tell you what I'm about to tell you, it will put you in peril."

"You don't think I have the right to know, Matt?"

"Okay, Doug, but I wouldn't plan on ever telling anyone what I'm going to say." He looked at Doug with sincerity, "I killed Pablo, Doug, two years ago in Ecuador, so this can't be him."

Doug thought before he spoke again, "Do you remember what you said to me when our faces were in the dirt and crazy assholes were holding machine guns to our heads in Mexico?"

"I do, Doug, why?"

"Because the way you said your turn was next, I believed you, even though you were about to be killed, so I'm not going to act too surprised by that revelation. But the question still remains, who is doing this? Have you made any new enemies or done something to someone that would give them a reason to do this to get to you?"

Matt wasn't about to get into his situation with TJAC, he needed to get going now, but one day Doug would hear the whole story. "No, Doug, I have no idea who would want to do this to me or my family;

maybe Pablo's followers. My wife and son are upstairs right now and it seems they have been poisoned and are fighting for their lives. I have to go to my house now and get some things as they are going to transfer us to a hospital in California ASAP."

He let Doug know where Jon and Jan were and asked him to please look out for them until he got back. Doug said, "Okay," but then asked if he didn't want some company for this quick trip to Lummi Island to get his stuff.

That's when Matt snapped at him, "Doug, listen to me and listen good. Everyone who comes into contact with me ends up dead. Whoever this was tried to kill you today, you weren't supposed to live through that, my friend.

"Then I was supposed to see it in the news. You need to listen to me my brother. If you want to live to an old age, then you need to forget you know me. Someone has chosen me to be the world's biggest patsy and just the fact we're talking right now might have already done you in, let alone watching my family. Which in retrospect doesn't sound like such a good idea for you. I can't keep from cursing the people who are close to me."

He got up to leave and Doug wanted to say something, but there was really nothing to say. Matt leaned in and told him that, "Maybe one day I can write the truth because as it looks like now, they are going to take away everything I have that would stand in the way."

Doug retorted, "I've heard you out, now you hear me out. I'm in your corner and it's obvious by my jet being brought down that they already know we are close. So you won't be scaring me off, Matt, I'm in this 'till the end."

"Thanks, but you know that I can't ask that of you, it's not in me."

"I know, and that's why I'm telling you!"

"You know, Doug, when a man has nothing to lose, he can be dangerous. Of course, the minute I open my mouth, I'm a marked man for life, but if something happens to those two, then I'm going to sing like a canary."

They exchanged cell phone numbers just in case something happened after he left. He felt beyond anxious to find out what the heck happened to his parents.

Doug watched him hurry off and sat there trying to process all that the last ten minutes had disclosed. Sometimes whole worlds changed in the course of a few minutes and he felt that his world had just experienced such a transformation. He was elated to hear that Matt was alive, but the current circumstances and the fact that someone must know that the two of them were close and then had tried to get to Matt through him, was proof enough that he was already in this way over any point of backing out. Matt was just too stressed to see that now, but it would come to him. This was war.

Matt's mind had never spun so hard. If he were Pablo, he would have sorted all this out and had a plan for each contingency as they popped up, but he was not Pablo. Yes, he had survived that horrible ordeal and in the end outsmarted the smartest man the world had ever known, but it could not be that man.

He'd had a nice, simple one-dimensional plan four years ago: infiltrate their group, garner confidence and trust, and then bring them down. He had never had to deal with so many variables in his first life or death struggle, and as he reached for the door of his car, his fear for what he was going to find out about his parents was nearly too much for any one human being to handle.

He got into his Explorer, and put on his sunglasses with his left hand as he was using his right hand to turn the key, no motion or millisecond wasted. Just as he put his hand on the shifter, a shot came through the window.

Matt found out first hand what happened to a person who was nearly hit by a supersonic round. The glasses saved his vision, as the impact of the flying safety glass off his face was enough to crack the lens on his wraparound glasses. He had also learned something from what Peltz taught him. Bullets shot at you at that velocity make little super sonic shock waves as they fly by and even though Matt was four inches from the shot, it felt like a punch in the face. He immediately (and a lot quicker than he thought possible) crouched into the driver's well; the second shot would have been a kill as it burst the front and back window right over his head.

Glass was raining on top of his head. He was too crouched to put the car in gear so he did the only thing he possibly could, he opened the door to create a diversion. His thinking was the next shot was going to be through the engine block and into the well, so he was banking that the shooter would instead redirect and hit the door. And that's when he would slide up and try to pull out before he could re-sight. Basically he was hoping the shooter was less skilled than he was, or this was it for him.

Just as predicted, the shooter took the bait and hit the door. So Matt pulled himself up with all his might and jammed it into gear as he was punching it. The next shot came right through the metal of the window frame and exited in the passenger window behind him. He peeled out of there expecting one more through his side of the car, getting him in the back, but the shot never came. Maybe his movement changed the shooter's perspective?

He checked the rearview mirror, no one was coming, but his face and head were bleeding as his hat fell off when he ducked. His hands were shaking so badly he could barely hold the steering wheel. He made his way out to Highway 20, heading to the terrifying prospect of what he was going to find on Lummi Island. Then he had a thought.

He dialed 911, and when the operator answered, he reported the gunfire and lone sniper on the grounds of the hospital. That would send in the troops to occupy the place. He also placed a call to Doug. He wanted to ask him, even if he had no right to do so, if he would go to Jan and Jon now and look out for them. No answer on Doug's phone. *What is up with that today?*

Doug watched him leave and his heart twanged. That poor guy was destined to be road kill. Most people would have never have believed that story, yet he knew it was true as he drifted toward the door to watch his friend run for his car across the parking lot.

The glass in the hospital was smoked so anyone on the outside wouldn't know he was on the inside and that was a good thing. As soon as Matt made it to his car, he witnessed someone shooting it up. The next few seconds were hard for Doug to comprehend as the boldness of such an action in broad daylight stunned him. He watched as Matt got away again, seemingly unscathed, although this time he could hardly believe it.

Doug searched for the shooter but couldn't see anything. People were coming out and there were other witnesses who saw what had happened, pulling out their own cell phones. Doug turned and immediately headed to the front desk to find out what room Matt's family was in. He had no weapon, so he didn't know what he could do if someone showed up who did have one, but he'd be damned if he just stood by and watched Matt's family be killed.

Matt told him that he figured they were just using his family to get leverage on him, because if they wanted them dead, they would be. Doug concurred, but that didn't mean that they wouldn't change their minds once they missed their target. He knew the cops would be showing up soon, so if they were going to do something, it would probably be now.

Doug got to the room and the boy and his mom lay still in separate beds. He closed the door and moved the heavy chair in front of it and sat down. After a tense fifteen-minutes he got up and checked the window. Hordes of cop cars were everywhere and soon thereafter came a knock on the door.

He moved the chair out of the way and let the two cops come in. They let him know they were conducting a room-by-room safety check as someone had discharged a gun in the parking lot. Doug let them in and they searched the room and left. Doug left the chair where it started.

He walked over to the window again, which just happen to look right down on the crime scene. When asked, he told the two cops he had seen nothing. The CSI people showed up and he could see they were digging slugs out of the wall of the rehab building.

Then something off in his horizon caught his eye. It was a seaplane that landed in the harbor just a few short blocks away. He had never flown one, but he assumed its takeoff would be like one of his old cargo planes when it was laden—sluggish and heavy. He turned and looked at Matt's wife and child, so helpless. Matt wasn't much better off. Who knew what the guy was walking into all alone? He had a feeling starting to build, and a voice in his head that needed to be addressed.

He also felt that there was little he could do here that mattered. It would be a very high profile kill if it were done anytime soon and Doug seriously doubted that the bad guys were within miles of here now. The more he considered it, the more his impulse to help his friend was growing out of control. He felt for sure that was where the danger was now. It looked like it was time to shit or get off the pot. He reluctantly left Matt's family's side to go and do what Matt had warned him against; Doug was going to get involved

* * *

Matt was over the edge and driving over ninety now. He was beyond rational thought and would stop for nothing, so he hoped he encountered no cops. The wind was howling through the glass and his cracked wraparound sunglasses were causing all kinds of visual problems. Also, flecks of glass were randomly breaking off and flying in, and he was pretty sure one just cut his earlobe. It was not safe or sane to be driving so fast with a shattered car, but he was beyond caring.

Matt considered that it was a good thing that the fucker who shot at him was not as good as Jim Jensen or he would be dead. Then the epiphany came. If TJAC had been behind this, then he would be dead, because they would have sent Jim to do it, and Jim did not miss.

So if it wasn't Chase who wanted him dead, then who? He looked at his keychain and he'd remembered. When it was handed to him, Chase had told him that if he were ever in imminent danger, he should activate the locator. And when the danger was life threatening, use the laser pointer, and keep it on the target for ten seconds.

He promised when and if Matt did that, help would be on the way. Matt had to trust. Throughout his recovery, trust was the one component that was nearly impossible to get back. After all the things he had seen and had been party to, a part of him became a hard-core cynic.

He exited Slater Road just outside Bellingham and started to make his way home.

Matt was now running on raw emotion and adrenaline. He also realized that he'd been setting his training aside and doing the thing whoever was herding him wanted him to do. Then he thought about what Jim would do right now and he'd decided he needed to start being smart and bury his emotions for the time being.

First, he would activate his locator and let TJAC know he was back and where he was. Second, he would not run straight to his boat as he had intended. As one approached the edge of the woods before the harbor came into view opposite Lummi Island, there were a few houses that faced his property. He knew from previous observations that one of them never seemed to be occupied.

He noticed this house during Jan's and his excursions into the sound to have loud sex (something they could not do with mom and dad living below). This particular house never had lights on, and Matt had never seen anyone there during the day, either.

He still had his hunting rifle, so he decided he'd get a peek at the house before committing to breaking and entering. Then he had another thought and pulled over. He got out and searched the undercarriage of the Explorer and found it on the back left bumper. It was a GPS tracker. He did not smash it though, instead, he brought it into the car. He came across a produce stand, stopped and bought an apple, leaving the tracker on a couple's car he had seen coming in from the west. It had Canadian plates.

He saw it now. Someone was playing a game with him. Someone wanted to toy with him before they ended him. He made the turn for Lummi and made note of the Tsunami Escape Path signs. That was exactly how he felt, like he was running from a tsunami.

Whoever was doing this to him wanted him running in a blind panic, and so far he was obliging them. But now his organization would be in on it, and if he wasn't reading the situation wrong, then he still worked for a group of people who would like to see him stick around. As he was nearing Fisherman's Cove, he saw the house and pulled in. He was able to pull all the way back and over as the driveway had a small dogleg down near the end that allowed him to get out of sight.

He parked and gathered his thoughts. Someone was trying to make him think that Pablo Manuel was alive. No one else would carry that kind of a grudge, unless it was a sycophant who still lived. Matt had poisoned his people, *so maybe now the payback was they poisoned my family? I killed our woman and him, but somehow not all of them, and now what?*

He looked across the Sound but could see no sign of life. Matt got out and went to the back of the SUV, retrieving his rifle case. He had just purchased a Bar ShorTrac Hog Stalker Realtree Max-1. He almost refused to buy it because of that ridiculous name, but Jim told him to just ask for the Browning tree-camo 308, the one with the pistol grip.

Sure enough the guy at the counter brought him his favorite gun to date, without the tongue-twisting name. From the second it hit his hands it was a part of him. With a pistol grip and 10X fixed scope, it was a dream come true in his hands. The scope wasn't as sophisticated as the scope that Jim had him use for sniping, but that scope had mil and other advancements that he didn't need for deer hunting.

He brought his rifle out of the case and went over and sat on the ground right in front of the truck and brought the rifle up. His house was deserted yet still in one piece. There were no signs of broken windows or mayhem. His head pounded with the thought of *what the fuck is going on?*

He wouldn't have been able to see his parent's car, as they usually parked in the horseshoe at the front of the house. The clock was ticking on him, though, and he figured whoever had put that tracker was going to be frantically looking for him now. Anyone he saw on his property was going to die quickly. He kept his ears peeled for the sound of revved up engines speeding around. Nothing. No movement of any kind on the opposite shore. He'd had enough. He needed to get home and get answers.

He went back to the car, placed his shoulder holster on, and put his Beretta snug in its home. He put on his windbreaker and headed to the shore, rifle slung over his shoulder. It took ten minutes to traverse the shore and get to the boat.

Then he'd realized that he still had to go home by his boat, but if they were looking for his car and it was headed to Canada, as long as the one he thought they'd have planted on the boat didn't move, then they wouldn't come here. It took him five minutes to find the GPS locator they'd hidden under the ledge on the port bow. He placed it on the adjacent boat, "Mother Theresa," which was berthed right next to him.

The trip over to the house was quick and he leapt up the grass to his parent's apartment in desperate bounds. Their door was locked so he used his key. The house looked untouched and he quickly looked around. They weren't there. He ran out around the side past the sauna and up to the horseshoe driveway. No cars were there.

He went back to their house and looked around. On the table was the news that he dreaded he was going to find—well not this exact news, but some lead as to where they might have gone. There was an open letter on the table and it said that his parents had won a raffle they had submitted who knows when. They were invited to lunch in Kingston and the two tickets enclosed were not there. Matt thought, *it's impossible for one man to be this unlucky all in one day.* He dialed his dad's number again and it went straight to voice mail like before, but now the mailbox was full.

Then he heard a buzzing coming from the coat rack and Matt walked over there and found his dads light jacket. In it was his cell phone with all Matt's missed calls on the screen.

He looked at the call log and there had been a call to the main house just after ten. Jan would have been long gone by then. He re-ran back up to the house, entered, and got to the answering machine. It was his mom who had called, and her message was a joyful. "Hi, Dear, your father and I won a raffle contest for something or other, and the prize was a first class lunch at Prizzis over in Kingston. You know how your father loves good Italian, so we're going to travel over there for lunch as I finally got your father to agree to ride the ferry."

The call ended after that and Matt found the nearest chair to collapse in. He'd finally been beaten. Someone had finally made him give up. If they burst through the door right now, he'd have let them shoot him without a fight. Thunderstruck, he wondered if his parents were really dead?

He was falling down a well of despair when he remembered Jan and Jon. There were times in life when life handed one too much for one to handle. Matt never remembered saying he was cut out to handle any of this? True, he had considered himself smarter than the average individual, but he was never equipped to handle such abstruse matters as these.

The situation was mind-boggling. And if his unseen opponent was trying to cause the utmost in confusion and terror in him, then that person had succeeded. Matt moved to the bathroom to treat his wounds. He cleaned them and then used liquid bandage on the multiple places from which he was bleeding. He was looking in the mirror when he had another epiphany.

He'd been so caught up in his own misery that he'd forgotten his literary lessons. In *The Count of Monte Cristo*, which in his eyes was the ultimate book of revenge, Edmund Dantes goes about executing a plan of retaliation that was unrivaled in length and details. He systematically broke Mansour Villefort down to a nub. By the time he'd revealed himself, Villefort was so badly broken that he literally went mad at the discovery that there had been an unseen vandal who had been secretly behind every horrible thing that had been happening to him. And as it turned out, it was a person with a legitimate grudge.

Matt now knew that whoever was doing this to him was trying to have that moment. They were trying to make him go mad. How foolish was he to just blindly plod around. He fell right into whatever they had going. Being that child of the movies, he also had another thought—a James Bond thought.

What was the name of the bad guy who had the white blue-eyed cat? Blofeld? Matt remembered that in the movie, *Diamonds Are Forever*, he died at James Bond's hands. But as it turned out, Bond killed his double. At that very moment, as he realized that Pablo did not die that day, a helicopter thundered over his house and a very powerful machine gun roared to life, essentially cutting his house in two.

* * *

President Lawrence Caulfield watched his meeting prep tape that his Chief of Staff, Kim Callahan, had just streamed it to him. He was no stranger to planes being brought down, or boats burning and bombed until they sank. America had suffered a great deal of loss while he sat at the helm.

Despite his shortcomings, the country rallied behind the man they observed was strong enough to return for more of that punishment. In what had to be the cleanest campaign in U.S. history—no one wanted to mud sling in the country when it was so fragile—he won by a good margin and reclaimed the acid pit that was his office. Well, the office wasn't an acid pit, but his stomach had been most of the time that he had worked there. He just connected the two.

The current intelligence information was that the downing of the Southwest plane and the attack on the ferry were not related to each other as far as the explosion was concerned. Whatever happened to them had happened independently, as two different projectiles damaged the planes engines and they had missed the ferry almost completely.

Initially, it was the pilot who was the one who reported that two objects had zipped past before his engines went out. And now they had received a report from a Seattle fire fighter who was on the ferry. He heard the first strike, and then he saw the second. Whatever it was blew the engine out as the plane passed overhead, the maw of the turbines were in tatters.

That information was disturbing enough. But it had now been discovered that this particular Southwest pilot was the same pilot who had flown Matt Hurst to Mexico four years before. *A weird coincidence?*

Soon the news would break that the plane had been both piloted by him and shot down by some sort of drone. Of course, the public as well as numerous government agencies would all jump to the conclusion that Pablo Manuel was culpable.

Little did anyone know that it was the CIA that had created the fake video of Pablo Manuel threatening to come back and exact revenge if the world did not fall into line and act accordingly. Of course, when they'd shot that video, they also thought this "new Messiah" was dead. Only afterward was it discovered that the body they had in their hands was not that of Pablo Manuel.

The world thought he was still alive because their video made it appear so, and as it turned out now, they were not lying—according to the DNA that they had obtained. In the fabricated video, the CIA audio teams pretended to be Manuel and stated that he would come back if he didn't like what the world was doing.

It was now dawning on Lawrence that Pablo might have taken that as a challenge. Divers said the hull of the ferry was ripped apart like a torpedo had hit it. President Caulfield was aware that Matt Hurst thought he'd killed Pablo that day in Ecuador, but DNA showed later on that he did not.

Only a handful of people kept the erroneous secret that Manuel was really dead, including Matt's handler Chase Viana, and an even smaller circle knew he was really still alive. That circle was government only, and even then, it was the smallest circle Lawrence ever had. TJAC was the catalyst behind his presidency, but anything about Manuel was highly classified information.

Lawrence just figured that if Matt went to work for TJAC, then Jim Jensen would train him and he would be as prepared as anyone could be to face whatever the future would hold. It now appeared their enemy found Hurst and it looked as though he needed to get a hold of Chase and let him know that he needed to bring Matt in.

Eric Barnett had warned him about this, as he was one of the few in the know about what had really happened, and Eric thought Hurst had the right to know he killed a body double, that his bad guy was still out there.

Lawrence begged to differ, and was just doing what he thought best, as Pablo Manuel had been able to hack into all their government sites without a problem. Lawrence wanted to make Matt a ghost, out of the reach of the ever bumbling bureaucracy of the U.S. government. Although he could have been in witness protection, he would have been in a system somewhere and Manuel would have found him. Not that his plan had turned out any better.

He opened his locked drawer and retrieved the Blackberry that Chase had given him. It was no average Blackberry though, as it had special encrypted software that could not be traced. It only worked between the two of them and only after he punched in the nine-digit access code. *Even Presidents can have secrets.* He texted Chase, "We need to bring Hurst in, he's in real danger, we believe Manuel is alive and caused the Seattle situation."

The text back was not pleasing, "We concur something is wrong.

Hurst activated his GPS locator thirty-two minutes ago. As you know, he has been AWOL for weeks. Jim is checking it out as we speak, the signal is local."

Lawrence knew that if Jim Jensen was going in on this, then he could count on it being taken care of and reported back promptly. He texted, "I have the Joint Chiefs gathering. This has the signature of Manuel and I know Matt is living up there under an alias. Kim believes his alias was compromised three weeks ago. We have a picture of him linked to a story of a new type of video game that is supposed to inspire people's patriotism. He was listed as the CEO of this game company and we believe that photo sparked this attack."

Chase texted, "He activated the locator. If he activates the pointer, we need to be on the same page."

The President stoically responded, "You prepared him for that even-tuality, correct?"

Chase responded with a cold, "Yes, he knows how serious it is, the question is are *you* prepared to handle the fallout?"

President Caulfield answered his mentor; "I won't have much choice so you guys had better make it count."

The next sentence was a difficult question that could have been answered with unending ambiguity, but he saw no point in lying to the man who got him elected. Chase asked his friend and the leader of the free world if he knew Pablo was alive all along.

Lawrence typed one word back that said it all, "Classified."

* * *

Doug didn't have a car as he'd come with the airline transport vehi-cle to the hospital. His intention was to stay with his passengers, which, of course, he had now abandoned with only a meager explanation. There was a Southwest Regional Manager running the show, and Doug knew all along he was just a figurehead, so that was justification enough as he was definitely heading off.

He could see from the Hurst's hospital room that the harbor was only blocks away and he began a light jog there. By the time he arrived he was in more of a run. The Harbor was big and he needed a break in finding what he needed. Right then he found that break, a maintenance guy who looked of retirement age. He had grey hair, wore thick glasses and a smile on his face as Doug approached him in his cart, which was laden with the obligatory tools of the trade and a grey trashcan in the back bed. He asked the guy if knew where the seaplanes docked?

The man's response was, "There's only one, hop in and I'll take you there." His name was Ed Trinidad, and he was a retired Navy guy from Bellingham. He, of course, noticed that Doug was still in uniform and it wasn't long before he put two and two together as the word Southwest could be heard just about every other second on the news.

It turned out to be Ed's pleasure and point of curiosity when he dropped him at Luke Slate's place. According to Ed, "Luke runs a private sight seeing and charter company and is as ornery as they come—to anyone not looking to go sightseeing that is."

Ed wished him good luck and Doug could see was still wondering why a pilot that just barely survived one crash would be in a hurry to go back up? Before he pulled off, Doug stopped him and asked that he please not reveal his whereabouts. Ed looked Doug sternly in the eye and apparently liking what he saw said, "Okay by me, son, looks like you've earned a break."

He drove off looking for answers and Doug thought, yeah, *good luck.*

Slate's Sightseeing was an office not attached to the land. It had a small bridge that went over to it, as it stood on stilts. The building was good sized and as Doug entered he saw the plane hitched to their dock. It was red with their logos all around. The door chimed when he entered and a few seconds later a man who introduced himself as Richard Luke Slate came in. He preferred to be called Luke, Doug later learned.

He was a six-footer with brown fading hair and wore only a mustache on his face. He was wearing a hat that Doug thought looked like a safari hat, but he took it off at the introduction, and off it stayed. He wore hiking boots, khaki shorts, and a khaki short sleeve button up shirt. He certainly looked the part of an adventurer.

Doug pumped his hand as he was introducing himself, but Slate immediately retorted, "Everyone knows who you are, Son."

Doug replied, "Those with a good memory."

Slate responded with a heartfelt laugh, "Memory? In case you didn't know, they just broke the story of what happened to your plane today, not five minutes ago. Couple that with the information that you escorted a group of passengers to the hospital here and memories don't have to be long.

"On top of all that, the connection has been made that you were the pilot who was forced to fly Matt Hurst out of the country four years ago and everybody's memory just got refreshed in a big hurry. Believe me, they're looking for you, Son, the paparazzi have questions for you. Last I heard, they were converging on the hospital up the street."

Knowing that the information would be coming out at any minute, Doug had been preparing for the discovery of his past, but Luke's words were still like heavy blows. It had taken forever for people to stop talking about him before. He lived in the shadows of life now. He had never desired a spotlight even before this, but less now.

Apparently he was broadcasting his emotions and Luke said, "Sorry, I guess you didn't know about it. I thought you were running here from them or some darned thing."

Doug had really good eyesight and Luke had left the door to his office open. Doug's uncle was a war hero in Vietnam, so he'd seen a Silver Star before—plenty of times at his Uncle's—and now again, in a frame on Luke's wall.

Doug didn't know where to begin, but the truth was a good start. It was a long story but he broke it down to fifteen minutes. Luke had his listening hat on, so things were not repeated a whole lot. After Doug was through he thought he would have seen more amazement in the man's eyes, but it wasn't there. What was there was belief, much to Doug's disbelief. Luke's only interruption was when he stated rhetorically, "Matt's wife and kid lay up the street right now, as we speak, huh?"

Luke was a, "get to the point" kind of guy, so he asked, "What do you need from me, Doug?"

The answer was the plane, of course, but he wasn't expecting Luke to hand over the keys to his livelihood, so he asked, "Do you want to take an adventure?"

Much to Doug's disappointment the answer was, "No."

Luke explained that he wasn't the pilot any longer, but his son was and he was gone for the day. "The Doc grounded me, Doug. I developed fainting spells and bouts of loss of equilibrium. Fortunately no one was ever hurt," he added.

Doug didn't know what to say, as he wasn't going to ask the man to lend him his plane. "Do you know anyone else who can fly me, Luke, anyone at all? I need to help him, even if I have to drive over there, but it has to be now. I won't ask and wouldn't accept your rig right there, so don't even suggest it."

Luke chuckled, "I wasn't going to, sorry, as it's not mine to lend. He walked out onto the dock and headed left to a slip with a thirty-foot covered yacht. On the other side of that yacht was a floating piece of canvass. They stopped and he told Doug, "This I can lend you."

* * *

Scott had stayed with the ferry until after the fantail sank, and fifteen seconds later came the video that would win him a Pulitzer Prize, he had no doubt. A man had gotten free of the vessel and managed to swim through the undertow of the sinking ship. He'd burst up out of the sudden calm like a banshee, startling everyone around before he was pulled to safety.

Because of the configuration of the rescue boats on the other side, the area was basically obscured by rescue craft, and Scott was the only one with an unobstructed view. With his zoom lens, he shot a very important video for the authorities as well. It was gripping.

He set his camera on record so he had a video, but throughout the video he had also used the photo button at several opportune times to snap stills.

He stayed and photographed the disembarkment of the plane and after three hours his stomach started to rumble. He remembered he had a multitude of things to do to prepare for her arrival, and then he'd noticed it. There were no planes in the air.

He needed to get home to at least freshen up and change. He tapped his pocket to check her flight status on his phone. Oh great, my cell phone is in the car, *what an idiot!* Scott ran back to his car and, of course, there were seven missed calls: four from newspaper colleagues, one from his mom, and two from Lauren.

He listened to hers first. She was in Houston and her flight to Seattle had been delayed indefinitely due to what was going on. He noted a sound of desperation in her voice. The second message was that she had secured a flight to Portland and would drive to Seattle, rather than sit around like an idiot.

She'd given him the flight information, so he started his car and hurried back to his house as fast as safety would allow. Once there he could see that the cleaning people had come—that was one off the list. He turned on the news to get the story. He had thought about turning on the car radio and blasting it on the dock, but he never would have heard it, and he would have had to leave his keys in the car, so no. Consequently, this whole time he'd been in the dark as to what had happened? He checked the time and saw that he had no reason to be antsy; it was still early in the afternoon. Then he'd realized just what a pussy he'd become. No wonder he'd lost her the first time he had her, he was a hopeless pussy. After everything he'd witnessed today, he was still feeling the Lauren butterflies. Why did this girl have such a hold on him?

Apparently he must have the same affect on her, as she needed to recoup her relationship with him. He was her safe haven and her safety net when the world fell apart. He was the backup plan also—not that he was unhappy to be her backup plan. He would have basically worn women's clothes and talked in a bad Welsh accent for the rest of his days just to spend his nights with her.

The station showed up to retrieve a copy of his video, as he had called Tina right away. He gave them the video and the still photos that he wanted to share, making sure to keep some doozies for himself—especially, the man breaching the water, just like a Pulitzer Whale.

He headed back out around two, and Seattle was obviously still shell shocked. Traffic was very light. When one lived where he lived, everything one did was predicated on traffic. You hear about the traffic of Los Angeles, San Francisco, and New York, but the greater Seattle area had to be right behind them. Not today though, the streets were nearly empty.

Word was spreading that this was an act of terrorism, and the President was going on at five to address the speculation.

He still needed to get his hair cut at the very least. Hopefully he would hear from Lauren soon. He got right in at the shop, oddly named Ralphz Hare. It was a large place with no rooms, just a wide open shop with ten chairs. This place had only male stylists and was set up to be a "No Woman Zone."

His man was Axel, and Axel "got him" hair wise. His name was probably Bruce or something in reality, but regardless, he looked like a modern James Dean, and Scott felt a little cooler just being around him, let alone getting his hair cut by him.

He requested the usual and Axel was on it. Obviously, the only thing on Axel's mind was the crash and he was waiting to get off work and get home to see the President. Wanting to try out his new elite status as "News Reporter," Scott let Axel in on the fact that he was at the right place at the right time and got it all. When Axel got home, he would be watching Scott's video on the news.

He elaborated that he was there, but not happily. It was kind of hard to call it the right place when a bunch of people died and the Sound became a massive graveyard of innocent people. Scott mused sarcastically to himself that Axel wasn't exactly the intellectual type, what with all the exclamations at the right juncture in the story. He had "Whoa," then there was the timeless, "Gnarly," and finally a, "Dude!" It was like telling the story to Bart Simpson.

If he would have come up with a "Rad," then a puppet would have dropped out of the ceiling and presented today's prize. Scott wasn't so jealous of Axel anymore, and he let the haircut continue while he went into his mail. He was reading a comment on his article about that concept Sim Game out of Philly. The Blogger wrote, "Why don't they just hire Ted Kaczynski to be in charge of shipping, too."

Scott was annoyed. He knew this troll, some diehard Mariners fan whose screen name was Grif4ever24. He was sure the douche just spotted some simple error he'd made, and then made it out to be the biggest deal ever. In one rant, he called for Scott's removal from the newspapers staff.

So he meticulously went over the article while Axel was shaving his neck and evening him out. The article was clean—and then he saw what this man was talking it about. It appeared that Tom was a near doppelganger for another famous man. Scott had attached file photos of Robert Leme and Tom Holsinger, the latter of which he took himself when he and his wife re-entered the country from Mexico.

The one real reporter-like contact he had was his Uncle Tim. Uncle Tim worked for the Department of Homeland Security's TSA division. It started innocent enough. He tried to contact Holsinger, and his mom said he was out of the country indefinitely. He thought it odd because Leme assured him the guy would talk after he got him warmed up. Now he was out of the country indefinitely? At the time, it added enough intrigue to get him to call Uncle Tim.

Tim couldn't find out anything about Tom himself, but his wife and kid were due to come back in three days on United Flight 1147 from Mexico.

Scott sat and waited for a good half an hour for the Hursts, who he had thought were the Holsingers. He had to buy a refundable ticket and check in before he could enter past the security area. While he hung around, he ate fish and chips and drank a pitcher of beer in the process. He allowed the beer while working because this wasn't a high intrigue, life or death case, he just had a need to do better than anyone and the guy was right here in his back yard.

The plane disembarked and there he was with his wife, or she was a cheating whore, one of the two. He knew it was the Holsingers as he checked her seat location, and she would be the fifth person off the plane. After he took the picture, he had followed them back to an address on Lummi Island. Once he had the address, then the property records were easy enough to check, and the property had been sold to a Tom Holsinger. At the time, Scott figured the omission on the flight was a simple clerical, but now that he was looking again, he wondered if he should stop drinking while he worked, maybe he would have thought to make sure.

He paid for his haircut and headed to his car when the full weight of this revelation rung his bell.

She knew.

He had sent her all of his blogs and she read them, he knew that for sure. So she caught onto this, and instead of trusting him with the story of a lifetime, she lied to him and made it seem like a personal need. *What a fucking bitch.*

So she was really rushing here to get her scoop and leave him again, just like before. Not this time, he thought, this time would be different. He looked at his freshly shaved baby face in the car mirror and came up with an idea. He really had believed a few short minutes ago that the story and pictures of the ferry tragedy were going to be the highest rung he was ever going reach, but he was wrong. This was now his story, as long as he had the balls to stand up and take it.

Lauren was using him when she should have trusted him. He would have done anything for her, but he refused to be used like this by anyone. He was going to fight back. He dialed his editor and Tina answered on the second ring. He didn't introduce himself, he just spoke, "Do you want to get nationally famous?"

CHAPTER FOUR

Hellfire

K im's cell phone vibrated right in the middle of her meeting; not her work phone, which was on the desk in front of her, but her private phone. Only a select few had the number and even a more select few would dare to call it mid-day. It was a text, not a call and it simply said, "lunch." The sender was her husband, Ray, and the only other time she had seen him so curt was with someone else, never her.

The situation in Seattle was getting a lot of attention as they now knew it was an electronic device that felled the airliner. Lawrence was going to have to go on national television in a little while, and they needed a cohesive story to throw out there until someone could figure out what the hell was going on.

By the initial looks of it, Pablo Manuel was back. She looked at the phone again and grew more concerned, as Ray of all people knew this was not a take lunch kind of day. His office had to be busier than hers because the President was waiting—in other words, she expected a report very soon from the Foreign Threat Assessment Head.

She picked up her iPad next to her phone and sent her aide, Charlie Mayfield, a message to cover for her, as she had something urgent that she had to follow up on. He agreed without question because that was what he was paid to do. Kim then got up and exited without explanation.

They usually ate at a Greek Deli on 19th Street, so without actual lunch instructions, she drove the block while her detail waited outside. She walked in and was very surprised to see the look on her husband's face. She sat down. It appeared that he had already ordered, although she doubted they would be doing much eating. Before he could get it out, she cut him off in a very hushed tone, "It wasn't my call."

Ray never took his eyes off her, as she him. The two of them in a stare-down situation like this was Ali versus Frasier, and seeing this was their first real fight, make that an Ali/Frasier one. "I knew you were going to say that, Kim, and my reply is, some boys back in Germany had a similar thought back in '39."

He super-lowered his tone and played off his body language. He quipped, "You know I consider Matt my family and I cannot believe you sanctioned this sacrificial lamb behavior. You should have told me, Kim. We've always respected each other's jobs and have done a very honest job of keeping up moral obligations, but this was different and you know it!"

She knew he was right. She knew she should not have let them make Matt a decoy to draw Manuel out, but what could she do? President Caulfield assured her that precautions were being taken to ensure Matt would be okay. "Look, Hon, you know how things are. I was not at liberty to discuss it with you or anybody other than your boss and my boss. That was it. Now, the information I was given was that he was going to be just fine and he didn't need your overseeing. Lawrence figured you had enough to worry about with your new job and all."

Ray admonished, "If you're trying to tell me that what's going on right now isn't wrapped around that decision, I'll eat my hat."

"You can't know that for sure, Ray."

Ray replied condescendingly, "Sure, Kim, I'm known for misreading situations, built my name on it."

Kim tried to control her emotions. Ray was the only person who knew she had them. "You realize this is not the place to do this and we'll both answer for it."

"I don't care, Kim, this is bigger than that. We have this life where we're supposed to be married. But then you can carry such a devastating secret like it was no big deal? You and I know, as far as I'm concerned, our friend was more than a big deal to me. He was the most broken person I've ever met. The fact he was able to pick himself up after the trauma of that ordeal is a miracle, and he needed to be left alone. Not only did you guys not do that, but then you decided to use one of the greatest American heroes in all of our history."

She looked at him with deep concern, "You think I'm capable of doing that? I did nothing. If anything happened like that, it came out of your neck of the woods, not mine. Maybe you should be having this conversation with Eric and not me."

The food showed up and Jenny, the owner, asked, "What's wrong?" They ate there every week and she had a private table set aside for when they came in. Kim was a good tipper and Jenny knew who they were.

Ray answered, "Nothing, just work."

She looked at him and said, "You of all people should know that you need to leave work behind when you leave the building." Then she looked at Kim and said, "Both of you. If you're going to make working together work, you have to have a set of rules," affectionately looking at her husband and partner of thirty years, "even if you run a Greek Deli and not the Free World."

Ray knew her story. She and her husband, Tom, immigrated here and worked hard doing many jobs and living sparsely to get enough money to open this place. They'd run it successfully for twenty-five years together, and Ray knew that she was right. Jenny had such pretty blue eyes and even though she was approaching sixty, she still looked great.

Jenny left them and Ray looked at his concerned wife, "I guess we knew this day would come; it had to happen when we had a conflict of interest. It's why our bosses cringed at the notion of us together. That doesn't mean I have to like it, though."

She nodded her agreement and took a bite of her Gyro. After they ate in silence, only checking their phones, she said, "What are you going to do?"

As they rose, he pecked his wife on the lips and said, "I'm going to help him. I have that power now. Looks like you have to keep more than their secrets now."

She gave him the look that she reserved for only one man other than her Father. He could be infuriating at times, but ethics were so important to Ray, and it always made her feel that if he used that much effort to stay honest and true in the world, then he would surely do it within their marriage.

"I can live with that. Be careful, we still have bills you know."

They went their separate ways, but would soon see each other in a threat assessment meeting where only a few people knew what the real threat was. Ray was sure his wife was truthful, but this part of government was such a waste. All their resources should be focused on Matt, but a ghost is hard to explain. Ray got in his town-car and asked to head back to Langley. He had something he could put into play there, something he'd recently learned about and the timing and placement couldn't be better.

Ray was walking back to his desk. He had one hour until his meeting at the White House, and his staff meeting was starting now. He told his assistant, Wanda, to start without him as he was running late. He knew his excursion would put an extra burden on both their days, but he had needed to hear it from his wife, that she was not duplicitous in setting Matt up like this.

He was hurrying down the hall when he almost trucked his boss over. Eric was carrying a coffee and deftly maneuvered his wrist to avoid spillage. Ray said, "Sorry, I'm late for my staff meeting. I take it you just came from the White House?"

Eric always had a hangdog face, but it hung a little lower right then. "Ray, we need to speak in your office. Susan Mason from the NSA is waiting for me in mine, and the minute I show up, there will be no peace as the list of things I have to accomplish today is a mile long."

Ray agreed, and they headed back to his office. Once past his Secretary, Mitch, they settled in to talk. Ray's office was littered with tidbits of the world's greatest minds, including a framed doodle from Einstein of the equation PI that Ray treasured dearly. Eric avoided getting sucked into a conversation about some of Ray's conversation pieces, as he needed this meeting to be succinct and get out of there quickly.

Eric looked at his Director, "Was it necessary to go and do that, Ray? Was it necessary to go and pull Kim out like that? You two are already walking a fine line, and even something this innocuous can have one of you sidelined. And I don't need to tell you who it will be."

Ray looked at Eric with that look that he was known for. Not snarky, but so assuredly right it was impossible to not look smug, "I've figured this all out, as you must have known I would. I'm just wondering what the plan is now?" Ray straightened his posture as he continued, "You guys underestimated who Pablo would go after. You thought he would have been happy just going after Matt, but now we know that Doug Sharp was the pilot of the Airliner. That pretty much seals it; he wants to destroy everyone Matt knows. You guys are in over your head. You have an inside secret that the threat assessment teams don't know about and it will skew what they advise, wasting time and resources. Eric, if you don't know it yet, now is the time to let me take over; it's not too late."

"Just what did your wife tell you, Ray?"

"She didn't say anything, just like you, this is a listening conversation. I know what went on here and I'm telling you that it's time to pull the plug on it and let's bring him and Jan in right now. We know they're not safe."

Eric responded with passion, "Do you think I like this shit? Only a select few know just how powerful Manuel probably still is. One sniff of this and all those followers are going to start up again everywhere. This is bigger than you or me or your buddy, Hurst. No one wants to be the first guy on the suicide mission, but that doesn't mean if you survive that it will be your one and only. Hurst was hidden well, it was happenstance that exposed him."

"Well Eric, we see what Pablo really wants and we either literally dangle them out there or we pull them in. What's it going to be? One other point I'd like to make. Those soldiers you speak of went knowingly on those suicide missions. They may have been drafted, but free will drove them up that hill, that and fighting for the man beside them. Not that Matt wouldn't have volunteered, but you guys never even had the decency to ask him."

"Your naiveté is surprising, Ray. I assumed you had this figured all along, what with that great analytical mind of yours. But I suppose you are right at this point, it probably would be prudent to bring him in."

Relieved, Ray asked, "Do we know where he is?"

Eric pulled his phone out and requested someone's presence. A few moments later, after getting sucked into a discussion about Ray's autographed copy of *Will: The Autobiography of G. Gordon Liddy*, Jeff Walton came in carrying a laptop.

They set it up so they could all see the screen and it showed a GPS blip of Matt's marker on a map grid. His dot was heading toward the Canadian border. Agent Walton commented that Matt went up that way all the time, and in fact he had been there this morning.

Ray asked, "How big is the team covering him?"

Eric answered in a less than steady voice, "We keep two Agents at the five mile marker."

Ray looked at Eric and Jeff and asked, "How's that coverage?"

Jeff answered, "Hurst goes up there all the time and as it's sparsely populated, we have to lay back."

Ray had that look again, "How often does he go into Canada?"

Jeff answered, "He doesn't, why?"

"Because unless I'm mistaken, that dot just crossed the border."

Agent Walton became very interested and picked up his phone. He instructed the five-mile team to make a visual. Being this close to the border, Walton's team had passports, as he was no rookie. It was a tense thirty minutes that passed by them running their offices off their mobile devices. Finally his phone buzzed and he was patched into a live video feed of an old couple driving a large sedan. The beacon was right on, so Hurst or someone else switched his tracking device to another car.

The agents were being rerouted back to the U.S., but it would take longer to get back heading south.

Agent Walton turned to Ray and said, "This shouldn't have happened, we've had this tail for months."

Ray impatiently explained, "Exactly, Jeff, agents become complacent and they forget about the little things, and the next thing you know, the cat's out of the bag, your cover is blown, and you're chasing down old people in Canada.

"How one's cover gets blown on such a loose cover job as this I have no idea, but it happened. Maybe there was shoddy placement of the tracking devices themselves. Either way Jeff, it's done. Now please reroute the agents to the Hurst property ASAP. They are to retrieve the Hurst family on the highest alert level."

Agent Walton looked at Director Barnett who barked, "You heard, Ray, Jeff, get a move on and see who Seattle can spare, get a chopper up there for Christ's sake." Without hesitation, Agent Walton did just that. Eric looked at the smartest man he had ever personally known and said, "Think you can really get us out of this, Ray?"

Ray quipped, still slightly wounded, "I'm the best hope you've got. I also happen to have an ace in the hole."

"Oh really, do tell. What is that?"

"Now, Eric, if I told you that, then I might as well let you know what your 'tell' is when you lie, and where's the fun in that? Do I have control or not?"

"Yes you do, Ray, and if you succeed, the President will owe you once again."

"I'm doing this for Matt Hurst, Eric, and the American public."

They parted to head to their respective meetings, but Ray had ten minutes to make a call and he did just that. The call was to Frederick Tedesco, Matt's current therapist and a specialist in Post Traumatic Stress Disorder. They had been friends for many years and Frederick worked with the Agency a lot.

They were more than contemporaries, they went to College together and Frederick had beaten Ray at everything since the first day. He was his literal nemesis at every competition. He was also very rich, as he chose a private practice and his fees were exorbitant. But as in the case with Hurst, he had to fly across the country to see him twice a month.

Because of their friendship, and the fact Matt was a transferred patient, they compared notes and future treatment schedules. They had built a working relationship and Ray often wondered where its boundaries lay. Well he was about to find out.

They had been talking last week and before they discussed Matt, Frederick had brought up Malcolm Ward, a patient who was done with acute care and was now being sent back to Seattle where he lived. He was assigned to Frederick and now he could see him in Seattle at the same time he visited Matt. Malcolm Ward was an Agency assassin who had just come back from Afghanistan and his legend was not a thing unknown to Ray. According to Frederick, he had no PTSD symptoms that were preventing him from a return to active duty.

They were sending him home for a while, though, to get some R and R. It was a privilege of their office, every now and then they got to bend the rules and do a good turn for someone like Malcolm Ward. His kills weren't what earned him legend status. What got him legend status were the three Marines he pulled out of a nasty firefight. First, he dispatched their most immediate threat, as his Barrett fifty-caliber sniper rifle blew an orange sized hole through a brick wall to get the ambusher. Once that was done, he was able to make well-placed shots inside the enemy position to back them off, then in between, ran and drug a single Marine over to safety.

He did this successfully two times, and on the way back from the third attempt, his enemy got wise to the ploy and he caught a round in the calf. Emboldened, a move was made on his position. He dispatched the four combatants advancing and it was back to a stalemate, but not before he ran out and got the third Marine back to safety. He held down the position and triaged the four of them, saving lives in that process as well. He'd actually gotten one more combatant through a second story wall as the man was peppering their location with sniper shot. Ray noted, *and that was how legends were born.*

Frederick answered his private cell on the second ring, "I thought you'd be too busy today to be talking to the likes of me, what gives?"

Frederick found it important to be intuitive. Ray was almost tempted to say "Nothing, just wanted to say hi," but of course Frederick was right again.

"I need your help, Frederick, it's a matter of life and death. This is not inside the lines, though, and it will be breaching some normal protocol. I have a feeling after you hear the story, you'll understand the need."

* * *

The sun shone where it shouldn't be shining. Not only was that a pun for the area, it was a serious fact about his roof. In the most terrifying moment of his life, Matt now knew what it was like to be under fire from a heavy caliber machine gun.

The chopper was now off to the left adjusting, which meant he had to make a move. But what move? If he went out the door, he would run right into it and although he had his Beretta out, it would do little against an air assault. He was oddly frozen. If he went out the newly destroyed bay window, he would fall twenty feet to a rolling slope, and there was no chance of escape that way without injury.

He wanted to get to his boat, as he had the firepower to deal with them there. His indecision was handled for him as the machine gun now cut the house in half from the west, the answering machine and phone table now obliterated. He'd had enough and dashed out the front door, and around to the west side of the house. He sprinted down the hill to the dock, careful not to over run and stumble.

He could hear the chopper coming around again loudly just as he got to the boat. Matt grabbed his rifle and turned, but of course, the damn thing was in the sun; still he put five rapid shots right in the shadow he could see in the sun, and sure enough, it seemed to retreat.

He started up the boat and headed back across the Sound to where his vehicle was. He made it half way when the sound of the chopper was heard coming across the water. The next thing he knew, heavy machine gun fire was cutting in front of his boat and forcing him out toward the San Juan Islands, and away from his car.

The chopper was getting very low and aggressive, and Matt knew that he was being herded. Those shots could have killed him. He powered off the engines to full stop and grabbed his rifle. He still had two shots left. He brought it up and as the chopper turned Matt saw a ghost in his scope.

Pablo was alive. That was the only thing that made sense. Finally. Unfortunately, he was so distracted at the revelation that he failed to take his best shot. Plus, he'd realized that his enemy wanted a showdown of some sort.

Well, for poisoning his family, it was the least Matt could do. He was being herded out to the Salish Sea, but that would not do, nothing but open water. If they were going to get him to play, it was going to be on his terms and it wouldn't be at open sea.

He fired up the boat and made a hard port turn once they cleared Lummi Island. His chosen destination was a mile away at Matia State Park. Truly, it was a rock with trees and a dock, but Matt knew it like the back of his hand and it had cover. He also had ammo in his vest. He had put it on when he left the car at the house near the docks. He just needed to live long enough to make it there.

Pablo slapped his soldier on the shoulder, "You see, just like I told you, he knows the island offers hope. I'm never wrong."

"I just don't understand why we don't end him now?"

"Because in two minutes he will be close enough to taste freedom. He thinks he's going to get away and then at the last second, he'll learn that he's not. He'll know how it feels to be so close to something and have it taken away."

João shouted, "I just want the fucker dead now!"

Matt was approaching the island, no doubt counting on the benefit of fighting on his home turf. He came around the point and had the dock in sight. At this point, Pablo had had enough with the life of Matt Hurst, the betrayer. He lowered the sixteen-inch barrel of his Adcor Bear defender automatic rifle out of the choppers open window. Its 7.62mm rounds brought a big reality to those on the wrong end.

Pablo detested guns and killing Hurst this way would have been unheard of until they found out he liked to hunt. That opened up this little scenario in Pablo's mind, and then he made it happen, just like anything he desired. The hunter would now become the hunted. *How classic.*

Pablo spoke, "First we'll make him dead in the water. Pablo suppressed the trigger and the amazing gun destroyed the boats engine in a flash. Matt's boat now laid dead in the water. João had pulled the chopper back as he saw Hurst going for his gun. Pablo had already reloaded and was squeezing to put an end to this once and for all.

Matt saw the dock and had a hope that thirty seconds from now he was going to be on that dock, well at least next to it. Then he heard the roar of the gun over the crafts engines and his motor was blown to pieces until it functioned no more, sputtering to its quick end.

It looked like this was where the final battle was going to happen. He reached back for his gun, ready for whatever happened, determined to make his shots count. He had loaded five shots while steering and heading for the island. He got the weapon in his hand and turned.

* * *

Doug was impressed. Luke kept his old plane in an amazing state of readiness. Luke was a mechanic and although he was retired, he loved her and said, "If you don't keep up with what you love, then you are a fool with lousy stuff." Luke kept her there at a ready state to back up David, just in case he had mechanical problems on his flagship plane. In this line of work, one gets the double whammy, not only a loss of a day's revenue but the repair costs as well.

Of course, the real reason he kept her so ready was in case he ever needed to get out to his son on a rescue. He paid a lot of money for David to become an architect at Cornell, not to fly tourists around Puget Sound. Like most kids, they had their own idea of what they should do to fill their days.

As Doug was ready to go, Luke disappeared back into his office. When he reappeared he asked Doug, "Ever take off in water before?"

Doug found it to be a reasonable question, as indeed he had never taken off in water before, "No, I was hoping to get some pointers right now."

Luke replied matter-of-factly as he handed Doug what could have only been a service issued Colt .45 in a leather holster, the straps looped around it, "I was hoping to give some 'in-flight' lessons."

Doug thought about that, "It could get dangerous."

"Thank God. If I have to live one more day without some kind of danger, I'm going to implode. My life was nothing but excitement for forty years, you get addicted to it."

Doug fired her up and she felt strong. He had a pit in his stomach like he was heading out to quarterback the team in the big game. It was almost nausea, but nerve related. Luke's instructions were clear. Take off into the wind. Verify there is no other cross traffic—that was a new concept to Doug—and go. He told him to hold the elevator control all the way back and apply power smoothly, while maintaining directional control with the rudder, of course. When the nose reached its highest point, ease back the pressure to allow the seaplane to come up on the step.

Luke elaborated on how to establish the optimum planning attitude and allow the seaplane to accelerate to lift off speed. Luke furthered that in most cases the plane lifts off as it reaches flying speed. Occasionally it may be necessary to gently help the floats unstick by adding a small amount of backpressure to the elevator controls or by using aileron to lift one float out of the water, but that rarely happened he told him. The pit in his stomach subsided as the plane rose on its own and they were soaring into the western sky.

His copilot had a pair of binoculars around his neck; he was a man who came prepared. They had banked from southwest to a true west heading and were currently passing over Guemes Island when Luke queried, "So Matt Hurst really is a war hero of the highest order, you say, huh?"

"Luke, trust me, he got kidnapped on purpose and he did it to become a poison pill to whatever those guys were up to. I knew he lived because he sent me a message not to fly on the day the *Bush* fleet was sunk. Things aren't always what they seem, Luke."

"Son, I served three tours in Vietnam. I've seen shit happen the worst of the movies don't cover. I've also seen what happens when the black bag guys show up. Those sons of bitches operated with impunity and if any of us ever got caught up with them, we always got the worst of it. It's a lot to take in because all these years I've refused to believe Hurst wasn't duplicitous in this crime."

They had already passed Guemes Island and were heading to the eastern tip of Lummi Island. As they flew over the eastern top of the island they could see the small Lummi Island ferry halfway across the Sound holding several emergency vehicles, all with their emergency lights flashing. It made the ferry look like a fourth of July float in some water parade. The string of emergency vehicles already on the island was focused on a house to their left. The place was swarming with personnel.

Doug went past them and was making a sweeping view of the area west of the island when his copilot exclaimed, "There!"

Doug looked off to the southwest and saw a helicopter at low altitude chasing a small boat. He immediately banked left and headed for the action, which was heading for a small island.

* * *

Pablo had him in his sights. Matt was able to get to his gun up, but this was it, Pablo fired the roaring weapon and it struck the water right outside Matt's boat. The line was dead on and all Pablo had to do was bring it up steady and he would cut both Hurst and the boat in half. As the first bullets struck the water, a seaplane came out of nowhere and narrowly avoided contact between the two flying crafts.

João jerked the yoke in response and Pablo's shots were all wide left, albeit he had blown the bow into splinters and the small boat was now taking on water. By the time he righted and tried to locate his target, Hurst was in the water and was halfway to the dock, swimming on his back holding his rifle out of the water.

João righted their position and Pablo brought the reloaded weapon around on Hurst just as the plane was back. This time, now understanding the near collision was no accident, Pablo emptied a clip on the plane; hitting it mid-section and making it retreat.

Pablo reloaded and they refocused on Hurst, who had now made it to the dock and was climbing up. João brought the chopper in a herky-jerky dive that concerned Pablo for a second until he gained better control. Matt was running on the dock at full speed as Pablo brought the final blow to him. He fired and the dock started exploding. Just like before, his line was right and all he had to do was raise the gun slowly.

This time though, the distance between the bottom of the planes floats and the choppers blades were inches, not feet. It actually created a small wash that João overreacted to, and while he was trying to get control back, he stalled the craft.

They were thirty feet off the ground when the stall occurred and the Chopper hit the water hard, but because of the floats, it wasn't life threatening. The dog in the back seat got the worst of it as he had no seat belt and ended up on the floor, but you can bet he didn't cry from the pain. Pablo was most impressed with João's dog.

Of course, Pablo had not come all this way to fail. He actually had what he desired most, a game of chess on a playing field that was only so big. Not many places to hide. He followed suit and went into the icy water and swam with his weapon and ammo over his head to the dock. He instructed João to get the chopper started again as they would need it. Matt's boat had half sunk by the time he headed out into the islands interior.

Already Pablo could tell his adversary was not worthy, as he'd made it to the tree line without incident. It was the perfect place to make a stand and Matt had failed to utilize the advantage. João had a similar gun and he was instructed to cover him on the advance, but still, to make no attempt to shoot him at his most vulnerable place, which was at the dock and beach, was a huge tactical error.

On his trip up to coverage he saw something that energized him, and might answer the lack of assault when the time was right. There were copious amounts of blood, both on the dock and in the sand.

So angry at the interference, Pablo wanted to blast that insipid plane, but it disappeared. Pablo could only guess that it was Matt's pilot friend, but how he ended up in his game he could not compute right now.

He realized Hurst probably thought he had an advantage here, but he did not. Pablo had also been trained in combat now. He figured it was worth learning, for one day he might have to fight outside of a chair and controller. Plus, he had the machine gun. Knowing that Hurst had a high power weapon with a scope added to the drama, for sure, but his had steel jackets and he could shoot a lot more of them.

As he was making his way stealthily across the thickly wooded forest, Pablo heard quite a ruckus, the kind one wouldn't make unless one was in real trouble. It was too overt for a decoy and seemed spontaneous. Pablo scanned the terrain ahead and found the path that would provide cover as well as gain him ground. He thought he knew what the sound was, and it was his chance to gain the upper hand.

As he was making his way quickly toward the sound, he almost made the same mistake as his adversary. There was a sudden ledge and the forest floor gave way suddenly to a steep embankment. One had to adjust quickly to the downward slope or one would be in trouble. He looked to his left and there was Hurst, trying to get to his feet. Apparently he was walking backwards trying to use his scope and fell down into the leaf-covered ravine.

Pablo walked around the tree to the left and came into his view, "Next time you're fighting for your life, you shouldn't scream out your location and that you're in peril. Oh wait. There won't be a next time for you, Matt. This is one of those lessons that cost you your life."

Matt lunged for his fallen rifle, but his right ankle was damaged and he fell to the ground at least six feet short of his gun. He rolled over just as Pablo was bragging about a fact that he had been unsure of until now. "Your wife and child will die. The neurotoxin is slow working and gradually shuts off all their vitals. I just wanted you to know that. Oh, I almost forgot, your parents were on the ferry also, in case you didn't already figure that one out. Looks like your lucky friend lived though, but rest assured, after what he did here, I will hunt him down and kill him, too."

Matt reached into his pocket during Pablo's diatribe and retrieved his keys. He pointed the laser pointer at Pablo and turned it on. Chase always told him that once he activated it, they would know he was in mortal trouble. "Only use the pointer to bring the troops in," he had said.

Matt aimed the pointer at Pablo, its beam finding his chest. His hunter laughed a mighty laugh at this move. "Scrappy Matt Hurst, fighting any way he can until the bitter end," Pablo shielded his eyes partially, "only this time there is no one to save you, Matt. You killed her remember? And now you must pay."

Pablo looked at his chest and realized the beam was focused there and no attempt was being made at blinding him, which would have been the only point of such a move.

Matt, being a child of the movies, was watching the end of a good one here. Only this movie had not been titled yet, and Matt was apparently going to miss the end.

Pablo raised the gun and fired. The light was much brighter than Matt thought it would be. He was told when you die there was a bright light, but he was never told it would be so hot. Then it was done pulsing. The light was still bright through his closed eyelids, but the heat was gone. It was still there, even though he couldn't feel it anymore. His eyes were blinded, the light was so bright that he feared Heaven was experienced as a blind person.

He kept them closed, trying to let the brightness stop. It wouldn't. It took two full minutes to get even splotchy vision back; and he then realized he was still in the forest, not dead and in Heaven. He was nearly blind, but he could move so he checked his body. He was not injured. This time he took Pablo's advice and did not scream out. In two more minutes his vision returned to shades. In two more, he could focus enough to try to move out of the ravine.

He carefully nudged his way along to his rifle and picked it up, his vision really only semi-clear for about five feet. Using this tunnel vision, he made his way up the embankment. It took a good ten minutes, what with the hobbled ankle and the impaired vision.

In that time his vision came back a little more, and he could see what his nostrils had been telling him. There was a fire of some sort. He looked at the hill where Pablo had been and the ground was smoldering. He walked over and the smell was disgusting. It smelled like burnt hair. There was a charred area about six feet in diameter and on the outer ring of that was a rifle, melted in half. The stock, up to the bolt, was gone.

Matt was still in a form of shock when he'd realized that this was the troops Chase was talking about sending in? Matt remembered his words, "Be prepared and be away from the target."

Now he got it, he just wished Chase had mentioned he should look away, too. When he was given the pointer, he remembered the gravity to which Chase said the conditions of its use were. "If you use it, we're going to be peeing in some pools and make no mistake, it will cost a lot of money."

Matt turned to go back to the harbor, forgetting another lesson, and that was, always watch your flank. This was not his tactical day, and Jim would be shaking his head right now. He looked up to find one of the tattooed maniacs from Ecuador holding a rifle on him and he had a very familiar looking dog with him.

Matt jumped back as the tattooed killer spoke in accented English, "Drop that gun, Motherfucker! Damn *gringo*, you brought that shit from sky? I thought that was his thing." He looked over the melted earth and said, "I guess he really dead this time, huh? That too bad 'cause I wanted to be the one to kill him. You both caused Felipe to die—and for that you both were going to pay."

Matt's mind flashed to him grabbing Felipe and plunging a knife into the base of his skull, scrambling his brain and discarding his lifeless body to the ground.

"Well, here's the difference between me and him, asshole," he said as he pointed the gun at the melted Pablo, "I don't fuck around." He started to bring the gun up and Matt saw his life flash before his eyes yet again. This time he threw himself to the ground, his face away from his attacker, forcing him to shoot him in the back.

The killer from Ecuador ordered him to turn around and take it like a man. Unfortunately for him he never saw Matt blowing the whistle around his neck, otherwise he might have taken the right action, but he didn't. Instead he reached in with the barrel and jabbed Matt's back, ordering him to face his death, actually poking Matt in the butt as well.

Matt heard the action start a second later. He had kept Storm's protect whistle around his neck since his dog disappeared two years before. He had almost lost hope of ever seeing him again—until now. He turned quickly to see Storm had locked onto the forearm of his attackers trigger hand and was shaking profusely. As a result, no rounds were discharged.

Using his good foot, Matt deftly swept kicked the short man right off his feet where he hit hard, dropping the gun, which went down the very slope Matt had tumbled down earlier. His left hand was free though, and his attacker reached for his knife, which was on the belt of his wet Chinos. Matt gun butted his hand and threw the knife far away after pulling it from its sheath. Storm had now severely wounded the right forearm and the attacker made a move for the eyes.

Matt saw the side arm on his right side and knew what that move was about, the weird part was the whole time, the guy was yelling for Gringo to *alto*. Apparently he had named Storm, Gringo. And when the initial attack happened he had that look of betrayal on his face reserved for people like Pablo and him.

It was almost comical that this overconfident psycho was going to his grave more upset about the dog than anything else. Matt's gun butt cracked João square in the face. This was not the time for anything other than lethal actions and the result was the dog gained a deadly advantage and took it, going for the neck.

It was not lost on João in the waning seconds of his life that he had previously killed someone with the dog in the same manner. As he was fading out he saw Matt smiling and holding the dog whistle, "Adios, Motherfucker," was the last thing João ever heard as the dog crushed his windpipe. Matt noticed he ended up sprawled on the exact spot Pablo was incinerated and it felt fitting somehow.

He called off the dog with, "*Niza.*"

Matt looked at his savior and with heartfelt pride said, "*Aquí.*" Storm obeyed both commands and come proudly to his side with a look on his face that indicated he'd just finished a long-range mission and he knew it would end up like this. No questions asked.

Matt's ankle still hurt badly, so it took a long time to get back to the dock, hobbling along, nearly falling twice and having to use his rifle as a crutch, an action which made his stomach ache.

On his painful journey he had time to think. He now knew for sure that Jan and Jon were going to die. Maybe the certainty of knowing Pablo used a neurotoxin could help Dr. Singh, although Matt remembered he was already leaning that direction.

* * *

Jim Jensen had the auto-track locator on. It not only showed where Matt was, but a digital trail-line to where he had been in various colors so it did not all become one blur. It was very advanced software. He saw Matt's signal was stationary right now, on an island not far from there. He pulled into the driveway that showed as a previous Matt location and went to the end. There was a big green and red trimmed house on the right with lots of big trees around the house and property. Shade abounded everywhere. At the end of the driveway was a dock and a fairly nice sized boat tied up to the dock. Jim saw Matt's car and his first piece of the puzzle came into play.

He pulled out his digital field glasses and hit record as he watched the excitement across the Sound. It was furious over there and he could see Matt's house was tore up. There obviously was a gun battle, but the way the roof was hammered, the fight was from above, too. The tracker showed from here he went across the sound, presumably in his own boat to his own house. Then back out and south into the Sound just minutes ago. He eyed the house, it had Hurst's car off to the right and no other vehicles or activity. Jim walked up to the back door of the house and tried the door, it was locked and alarmed he noted by the sign indicating so.

The cops were too close for the alarm to go off and him to get away or worse, they'd think he was part of the action across the way. He looked up to the second floor, there was a bathroom window slightly ajar, and it would appear that the homeowners must have overridden it to set the alarm. He climbed one of the many helpful trees and was inside in no time. The boat keys were on a hook in the kitchen and something else of interest hit him as he passed through the upstairs bedroom to exit.

This was an operative house of some kind. There was surveillance equipment aimed at Matt's property. He could see it was recording, and that wouldn't do. He stopped the recording, took the memory chip out and pocketed it on his way back out the window. He was on the small roof ledge going back to the tree when he saw the laser strike. It pulsed blue for five seconds, *just like the operating manual said,* and then the Krypton laser stopped, impressing him with its immense power and spectacle. *That's going to get some attention for sure.*

His time was now limited, but it had Jim wondering what transpired that would make Matt use it? That satellite was TJAC's biggest secret by far, so Jim could only imagine. He noticed that the shot didn't go unnoticed across the Sound either, with several people in uniforms on Matt's dock trying to see over the hill south.

* * *

Matt hoped that someone from TJAC was heading here to extract him. Just when he had this thought he stepped on an odd shaped rock and almost went down again. He was wondering who that crazy-ass pilot was when his question was answered. Sitting in the cove was the plane. Doug and a tall man in his sixties who looked like a jungle tour guide were on the beach, Doug still in his Southwest uniform.

He spoke to the elder man, "You see, I told you we didn't need to look for him, he's a survivor." Doug saw Matt limp and started to run for him when a very large Rottweiler ran between them and got in a defensive posture. Matt told it, *"Niza,"* and the dog stood down with a whole different demeanor.

Doug and Luke hurried to him and as they started heading back for the plane, Matt said, "I was reacquainted with a few old pals. Fortunately, my dog was one of them." They got in and Matt pleaded with Doug to make post haste in getting back to Anacortes.

Doug saw he was ashen. He also knew he was no friend to flying. He brought the plane around into the wind and started the takeoff procedures. The downed helicopter and sunken boat were soon left behind in the natural harbor.

He didn't need to look to know that Matt was scared. He forgot to tell Luke that bringing the plane out of the water felt very similar to bringing a loaded cargo plane up; maybe he would later over coffee. He looked at the magic man. The last time they were together in a prop plane, a whole nation was looking for them. He never saw him scared during the combat parts of their journey, but a couple of times during turbulent flight situations, he saw fear. The plane lifted off and Luke introduced himself and asked before Doug could, "Was that a laser that shot out of Space?"

Matt looked at Doug and hesitated in answering Luke.

"Matt, providence brought me to the only man with a Silver Star on his wall, adventure in his heart, and a seaplane; I believe we can trust Luke."

That was good enough logic for Matt, "Yes Luke, it was a laser guided by a smaller laser on the ground. You know, a pointer. And thank you for saving my life, both of you."

"I used to do a lot of black ops, Matt, and pointing a laser designator at a target is no new invention, but pointing one at a target inside the United States that is then connected to a megawatt laser in Space, now that's a different story all together. I take it you work for the CIA?"

Matt looked at Luke and he was sure sick of the lies and subterfuge, this man just risked his life for him for God's sake. "I work for a secret group of patriots, backed by money you can only imagine. I was given a keychain and told if I'm ever in mortal danger in the northwest, then activate it and point the laser pointer at my target, and then be somewhere else, but keep it on the target for as long as possible. Only thing was, no one told me not to look."

Doug asked, "How close were you? That thing was bright from the cove?"

"I was twenty feet away down an embankment. No elaboration here, it struck right as Pablo was pulling the trigger to end me. He had me compromised. So I actually thought I'd died and the laser shot was the white tunnel of lights I've always heard about. I thought I was dead. I heard a sound best described as a bug hitting a zapper, and then a hum for a few seconds, and then just white. I could smell that smell one gets at the dentist when he uses the drill for a cavity. When I came to, it took a good ten minutes to make it up the embankment, as my sight was slow to return. Once I saw Pablo's gun melted into the earth, I figured out what weapon this little designator unleashed. Matt held out his pointer.

Luke chuckled, "Yeah, it brought the whole can of whoop ass son. That is for sure."

Matt laughed an odd laugh, "First I was obsessed in getting my vision back, and then I wanted to see the body or remains. I forgot to watch my flank and his henchman was able to get the drop on me. Only he had my lost dog at his side. He apparently stole it when he escaped in Ecuador."

Matt pulled the whistle out and showed it to them, "I always carried it, I really love this dog, and I never believed he was dead. This whistle got me through some tough times."

Luke liked this boy, but he had a lot to take in. So much history involved Matt Hurst, and it was like being in a plane with a warrior king of legend.

"So then what happened?" Luke inquired.

Matt stared off out the window while he answered, "He was about to blow me away, saying he wasn't the type for long goodbyes. I recognized my dog; Storm was the strongest and smartest of my kennel. During training missions, he was always the dog that was in the attack lead. He was also a bad boy and bullied the other dogs.

"He has two light brown patches on his head right where the devils horns would be. The joke was that's where we cut them off. So once I saw him, I remembered the whistle. Hoping the killer was the type to want to see who he shot I feigned cowardice and flung myself to the ground. He didn't realize I was blowing Storm's protect whistle. Before he knew it, the tables were turned and I helped Stormy here end his lowlife, flesh-peddling ass."

Matt continued looking out the window, emotion welling in his eyes, "They killed my parents. Pablo informed me before he died that he gave Jan and Jon a neurotoxin that will kill them slowly, no hope of a cure."

He tried to kill you, too, Doug, you were never meant to survive that attack. Pablo's plan was to make me realize he killed everyone I loved and then kill me."

The plane's cabin was silent. Luke knew Matt didn't want to hear about what a hero he was, just like he didn't want to hear those words on missions when he'd lost good friends. So he came up with something Matt did want to hear, "I'll watch your dog while you go to the hospital and deal with things. You can be sure he'll be safe with me."

"Thank you, Luke, this whole thing was unbelievable of you to do. This block of time you are gaining for me might be the difference in me seeing my wife and son alive again or not."

Those were the last words spoken on the flight.

* * *

Jim Jensen started the Edgewater Console powerboat with the acquired keys, she was a two-engine rig and he was soon powering toward the San Juan Islands, her gas tank full. The tracker said Matt was moving from the center of the island heading toward the islands harbor.

From what Jim could ascertain, some kind of battle happened at Hurst's house and bled over to this island. He could only assume that Matt led the attackers away from his home to a place that he knew had cover he could use. He wondered where his family was? Jim rounded the Point of Lummi Island and pulled out his field glasses from his pack. He could see a chopper lying in the water at the mouth of the harbor, his field glasses always recording for review later. He knew the bird wasn't the target as it was still of this earth. Had it been the target, it would have been incinerated.

He opened up the throttles yet didn't go as fast as he'd wanted. Out in the more open water, the Sound was offering up some choppy conditions. The outrigger came out and slapped down, came out and slapped down, for what felt like an eternity. Finally he covered the few miles and as he was pulling up on the chopper, a seaplane took off and headed southeast. He went past the downed bird and found Matt's boat half sunk and destroyed by heavy gunfire. A quick tour yielded no bodies.

He looked at the tracker and it was showing Matt was now on the path of the departed plane. He thought about finding the laser strike site, but chose against it. The troops would be coming to check that out soon enough. He pulled out of the harbor and headed southwest, following the tracker. He was going on the presupposition that a plane with floats had to land in water. As a graduate of West Point, he was trained to observe things calmly in battle, things that others might miss. He headed southwest at full throttle hoping that Matt's family was okay.

Jim Jensen pulled out his phone. It was time to make a call to Chase.

* * *

Lauren's plane had landed a little too rough. This was going to be a day she would never forget. Everyone was jumpy as hell with the speculation that Seattle was a terror attack.

Of course, everyone immediately focused on Pablo Manuel and his zealot followers. He had ended his last communication to the world with, "If the world doesn't straighten out, I will be back, and like Jesus, I will come back with wrath."

Was that what this was? The flight attendants were instructing people to wait until the plane came to a complete stop before undoing their seat belts. She reached in her purse and turned on her phone. She was in no mood to jostle with people. Although she was in a hurry, she was in no physical shape to join the fray getting out, so she took the easy route. The attendant showed up and helped her to her waiting wheelchair. She got in and they were off. The wheelchair attendant dropped her at the car rental shuttle bench after retrieving her bag.

She had gotten one of the last rental cars available for the day, and it turned out to be a monster GMC SUV, way bigger than anything she'd ever driven and nearly impossible for her to get into. If not for the small ladies step, it would have been undoable. As she headed north up I-5 toward Seattle, she wondered if the plane and ferry had anything to do with Matt Hurst? Otherwise, it sure was a giant coincidence.

The car was fully loaded and she synced her iPhone to it before she left the airport. She had three messages. The first was from her mom, the second and third were from Scott. In the first message he mentioned the genius of going to Portland now that they knew it was a terror attack. The third was right before she landed and it was just Scott checking in on her.

She cut the phone off. *Good old Scott, always looking out for me.* She wondered how he was going to take it when he figured out that in a small way she was using him. She hoped he understood that a secret this big could have no leaks, not even him. If he really loved her then he would understand.

Her stomach rumbled and she felt queasy from the meds and lack of food. Up near Castle Rock, Washington, she saw a taco place and that was the tipping point. She'd been eating corn tortillas, rice, and beans for so long now, it had become a staple for her.

She was now an official *carnitas* connoisseur, so they'd better bring it. The place was called Los Perrico's, but it obviously was a true American cafe once upon a time. It still had the obligatory counter and rotating dessert case, which was now filled with Mexican pastries instead of pies.

Lauren ambled to the end counter seat, as they sat higher and she could get up without exertion. There was a TV on, and she was trying to pick up the news while she ordered her chicken tacos with rice and beans, which of course made her stumble through her order. She'd realized that she had to get to know a place before she trusted them with her *carnitas*. It was hard to fuck up grilled chicken.

She was munching on some chips when a breaking story came out of Seattle. She was now glued to the small TV on the shelf behind the counter. The story was actually out of Bellingham. Apparently a house on Lummi Island was the scene of a massive police presence. Cops and news crews of every kind were there. Before news crews had arrived there was a blue flash in the southern sky that witnesses said looked like a laser.

It appeared that the flash was either shot at—or from—Matia Island State Park. Lauren's tacos showed up and she ate quickly. She was going to have to get a news station on in the truck right away. She had left a message for Scott and he still hadn't called her back, which was kind of unusual. Her pills were wearing off and her neck was stiffening up.

The TV news was of course repeating itself over and over. The speculation was that the police action on Lummi Island was tied to today's terror bombings. She scooped some rice and beans on a chip and put some salsa on board. She was in food heaven, as this place was really good, and as it was in her life, every time she allowed herself a moment of joy, for whatever reason, it was always followed by something bad to counter it.

Before she could get away from a really good lunch at a reasonable price, Los Perrico's became the place that she would always remember in infamy. She would always know where she was when she heard the

news, like people did with the Kennedy assassination or the Moon landing. Seattle's NBC affiliate broke into the news with a live broadcast
from within their NBC studio in Seattle.

Stuart Blackburn was Seattle's top news anchor, and they gave him
the lead in for this breaking story. Stuart was announcing that he was
going to be interviewing the *Seattle Star'*s tech reporter, Scott Bailey, and
his editor, Tina Polanski.

Blackburn settled in on one side of the studios coffee table, with Tina
and Scott sitting across from him on a small couch. "Scott, we understand you and your editor, Tina Polanski, have some breaking news you
would like to share with our viewers."

Scott spoke very unevenly, obviously not used to the camera, "Yes,
Stu, I'm the Internet Watchdog for the *Star* and I run a daily section on
"All Things Tech." Two weeks ago I ran an article about a new game
startup by Robert Leme, creator of the SIM game sensation, *Top of the
Heap*. In my article, Leme named his new CEO as a local Seattle resident.
I was able to get a photo and place it in the article."

Blackburn further led the interview, "So is that particular article
intrinsic to this story, Scott?"

"Yes, Stu, it is. There is something very interesting about Mr. Thomas
Holsinger, game creator and CEO of Mr. Leme's new offshoot brand."

"And what's that Scott?"

"We believe, that is, I believe, and my editor stands beside me, that
Tom Holsinger is really none other than Matt Hurst."

Blackburn looked stunned, "That's a wild accusation. Do you have
anything to back that up?"

Stuart had a look like he'd just fucked up by taking this "Exclusive
Story." He could just see John Stewart having a field day with this mate-
rial on the "Daily Show." It was live TV, he was trapped, good thing for
him they were on the level, but that would come out later, for now it
was anxiety time for Stuart Blackburn.

"Stu, the police action happening right now on Lummi Island is at
the home of Tom Holsinger, we just confirmed. We've brought file photos of Hurst from the past and now Holsinger from the present. The
changes in him are small. They are effective unless you are thinking Matt
Hurst, then it becomes quite easy to spot.

"The day I took his photo, Hurst had traveled back into this country,
not as Matt Hurst, but as a Norm Clausen, whom later research revealed

does not exist. If this is not Matt Hurst, then Mr. Holsinger wouldn't mind coming out and explaining that I am wrong. But I have confidence that this is our man."

As Scott said that, he looked into the camera with an extra smugness that was reserved for her. Scott could be acid if crossed. Lauren often saw him getting Machiavellian revenge on hapless waiting staff that crossed him, especially while shopping. He was so good at it that she thought he was gay at first, he could bring a person to near tears with words. Afterward, when it was just the two of them, he would have this special satiated look on his face. That was the face he was showing right now.

If it were possible, she would have split open and exploded chicken tacos all over the place. The level of deception, the depth of dream destroying bad ethics was unfathomable! Tears were welling up as she headed out to her beast of a vehicle and she vowed that Scott Bailey would not get away with this outrage! *How could he do this to me?!*

* * *

Ray's phone went off and he picked it up on the second ring. It was Sarah Berkman, Eric Barnett's Assistant Director. Ray inquired, "Hi, Sarah, what's up?"

"Your office is being notified as we speak, there was a laser shot up in Washington State, either up into Space or down to Earth. That is unknown at this time. Several witnesses saw it, but no one could tell if it originated from Matia Island State Park into Space, or from Space to the island. Our grids are set up to see incoming missiles, not things shot straight down. Same deal with the meteorite that hit Russia, none of their missile defense shields went off. It's something we need to work on."

"So no casualties?" Ray asked with curiosity?

"No, but I got word on the personal favor you asked about our mutual friend, Mr. Hurst. I found his family. His parents were on the ferry by all indications. They purchased sundries in the Kingston Ferry Terminal an hour before the bomb. His wife and son are in a hospital in Anacortes. Report is they are both comatose, apparently the victims of some kind of poisoning."

Ray shot back with incredulity, "Poisoning?"

"Yeah, they were brought in from a Seattle Park after the plane and ferry crash. All normal ambulances were dispatched out and this was a transport company. The doctor I spoke to in Anacortes said that they're both comatose, apparent victims of a neurotoxin.

"Hurst was there, but went home to check on his parents and get a travel bag together, as their doctor, Dr. Singh, is set to transfer his family to San Francisco since their vitals are stable. Ray, according to Singh, a shooting happened in the parking lot soon after Hurst left the hospital."

Both Sarah and Ray had a vested interest in Matt's well being. She was the first person to make contact with him inside Manuel's lair after Matt brought them down, and Ray put him back together. Sarah also stood with Matt at the funeral for his pregnant lover, whom he had to gun down to save the world from a great hardship that would have killed millions.

Sarah went on, "Local authorities searched the area after witnesses described a white male driving an SUV that was under heavy fire from a high-powered rifle. The witnesses furthered that the SUV then fled at a high rate of speed while the bullets continued to hit the car and blew out its rear window."

Ray knew that somehow Matt had survived that assault with the high-powered rifle, escaped, and made it home, where he was assaulted again. He then made it out to Matia Island, where the laser shot happened, and now he was gone again. *It had to be. It was the only thing that made sense.*

Sarah continued, "We've stood down local authorities. It's a state park, so the Coast Guard closed it off until our team can ascertain what happened."

"Okay, Sarah, that's a great succinct version, I appreciate it. Please send me the long version in our usual manner so I can compress it."

"Hope I helped."

Ray replied, "You did, immensely. Thanks, Sarah."

They hung up and Ray knew he was asking a lot for her to help him; Eric might not take kindly to it. Ever since Ray had known her, though, he knew if you wanted someone found methodically, Sarah Berkman was the person for the job. She was the former assistant to a sinister man who used to be in her position, but he turned out to be so evil that Matt Hurst had executed him. It was a crime Matt had never answered for, as it was ruled that Beck's victim, Vera, was in deadly peril from him at the time of his death.

Sarah survived Ken Beck and more to the point, Ken Beck survived in his position back then because of Ray and Sarah. Ray knew Beck used him as a psychological analyzer on all of his cases. Beck knew he was also a super sleuth and would not be able to stop himself from coming up with a theory and synopsis that would almost always be right. Then he would use Sarah's incredible tactical skills to coordinate the completion.

Ray knew by definition the hallmark of a great manager was the ability to delegate. Except, when Ken Beck did it, it somehow was sleazy. He wasn't aligning good people he would groom under him, he was aligning people better than him and then he would ride them. It was a brilliant plan, and all it took was for him to be such a major reprobate that no one dared call him on his behavior. Every time Ray thought of Ken Beck, he gained new respect for Ms. Sarah Berkman.

Ray looked out his window. The day had become overcast and it played to his darkening mood. It would appear that Pablo killed Matt's parents and most likely would end up killing his family. And now he was trying to kill Matt for the *coupe de grâce*. Matt never stood a chance, but at least now Ray knew for sure where he would head the first chance he got. And when he got there, he would have a Guardian Angel waiting for him. Maybe he could help extract a pound of flesh and save his friend all at the same time.

His line rang as he was gathering his things to head to the White House. It was Sarah again. The White House was going to have to wait, as Eric was requesting his presence in the homeland threat-assessment room.

He left his office on the double and when he got to the room, Eric had a live TV feed on. The room was silent and he took his seat. It was an interview and within five minutes Ray was pale. Matt was being exposed. Some Internet watchdog/blogger turned reporter had figured out Matt's alias and was now spilling it on national TV. Today of all days! Man, Ray could see it now; every conspiracy-theory nut in the country was going to be going to the hoop hard on this one.

Matt would immediately be linked to today's events, of course, as it was inevitable that the correlation would be made. The Federal Investigation Team was already on the Matia State Island. This was crazy, and Ray knew he was going to be asked some assessment questions real soon. He needed more key pieces of information, but it looked like President Caulfield would have to make a decision on Hurst now. *What a cluster fuck.*

He was so down the rabbit hole that he didn't hear a word Eric said to him until it clicked he was being spoken to, "Ray, are you listening to me?"

Ray snapped out of it. "Sorry, Eric, calculating."

"Okay, like I was saying, we're trying to ascertain right now about what happened on the island. Once we have data to crunch I'm going to need assessments from all Directors. More than anything else, we need to know the source of that pulse. We were lucky enough to have two agents in the immediate area and that is going to save us some critical time. The Feds have the island sealed off and we are waiting. No one is going home tonight people, the sleeping giant just got woke up.

"All of this smells like a foreign threat has already set up shop here and even John Q Public is going to put that together. We need something to report to the White House because this is all coming to a head and the President is going to need to speak to the people."

Sarah looked across the room to Ray and tried to apologize with the eyes as she looked at her tablet and announced, "Matt Hurst's family has been located. His parents were most likely on the ferry and his wife and son have been located in the community hospital in Anacortes, near the Canadian Border. They are both comatose, apparent victims of a biological attack."

Jeff Walton was the up and comer and was in on this meeting because Eric willed it. Of course, Eric also told him to shut his mouth and learn, so he was surprised when he blurted out, "Planes shot down with a Hurst associated pilot, boats blown up, lasers, and now Matt Hurst pops up. It's obvious we are dealing with Pablo Manuel here, but why no transmissions this time? All of this fits his MO except for no transmissions. Pablo liked to talk a lot before, now nothing."

Sarah interrupted, "I have Kim Callahan who is requesting she be fed in live to this meeting."

Eric told Sarah, "Bring her in, but everyone knows to watch their words here," he purposely glared at Jeff.

Kim came live on the monitor at the far end of the conference table. After the usual salutations, Kim got right to it, "What do we know, people?"

Eric answered, as was the normal convention in these types of high-level situations. Dealing with Kim Callahan was like dealing with a mental bully, even worse than Ray, if that was possible. Eric knew his answers needed to be complete as they were being automatically dissected and processed by a supercomputer.

The number one rule was never lie to Kim Callahan. She would sniff out and uncover a lie faster than anyone Eric had ever known. When you spoke to her it must be calculated and it must be truthful—half-truths were just as bad as lies. Eric answered her query, "We're waiting on the assessment from the island before we make a call on this. It appears that the reporter is credible and all indicators are that we are under attack from Manuel. The only variance from his usual MO is no cyber attack or sheep message."

Kim added, "I thought about that Eric, with this Matt Hurst info breaking, it would only seem logical that we hear from Manuel."

"There's more, Kim, minutes ago. Sarah was able to ascertain that Hurst's wife and son are now fighting for their lives in Anacortes, an apparent victim of a biological attack. The community hospital has them; they were brought in comatose from Seattle. We also believe his parents were on the ferry. We have them making a purchase an hour before in the Ferry Building."

Sarah's Comm line lit up and they had a second feed come in. It was Monica Gutierrez, on site on Matia Island. Once she was set up, Sarah instructed her on whom she was addressing and let her go.

Monica narrated, "We found a body here. I'm sending the photo."

Everyone at the table had a tablet and a picture of a small bald man with his throat ripped out and his right arm mauled appeared in living color before them. He had tattoos all over his body, even on his bald head, which was also split open at the bridge of the nose. Sarah had seen this type of man before, as had all the people at this table. This man resembled the video warriors that Pablo Manuel had used to cripple the *USS George H.W. Bush* Carrier Group. They accomplished this with a drone navy and fleet of air flyers.

The presence of this man confirmed that Pablo Manuel was a part of the equation. The agents needed to move the body to get to what lay underneath. Next was a live video feed of a patch of earth that was literally melted, and on the edge of this patch was also a half melted weapon. Upon circumspection, they found it to be a rifle. The fallen soldier with his throat ripped out had a weapon nearby, so this was someone else's. In some parts, the soil had been melted into ashtray like glass, and the collected minds around the CIA's conference table all knew that whatever did this was very powerful.

Eric spoke, "Thank you, Monica, please continue to process the area and let us know what else you find." He terminated the feed. "Okay, we have a lot of work to do people. We need Steve Hatten brought in right away. This laser shot could have come from a plane, and we know the Air Force was up and running around Seattle. Surely they have data we can tap into. Kim, can you talk to the POTUS, please?"

Kim answered, "Of course, I'll see if we can expedite things. I take it we are going to put a lot of resources up in Washington State to support Hurst and debrief him?"

"That would be the plan, Kim, thank you and we'll talk before the hour is up."

The line disconnected and Kim looked at her boss with concern. He was in a real jam. TJAC put them both into power, and Lawrence allowed the implementation of Chase's laser satellite and several others just like it. His fear was that some other foreign power would try to repeat what Manuel almost accomplished and Chase was more prepared than the U.S. Government to get the birds up. *They were never supposed to be used though, unless it was absolutely necessary.* He looked at Kim and was going to speak when the Blackberry on his waistband vibrated.

Kim had an exact duplicate of that phone. It was Chase texting him. Lawrence looked at the phone and reported, "Hurst called in, and according to him, Pablo Manuel is dead, that laser shot took him out. Matt is now heading to the Anacortes community hospital via a seaplane and Doug Sharp is flying."

Kim replied with a calmness that belied the situation, "I would let flow a series of expletives right now to exclaim how impossible that statement must be, but it's becoming redundant as this man is somehow connected to the center of the universe. Well, Lawrence, at least we now know that it went for something good, and we didn't just lose all our jobs for nothing. Now, how do we spin this so we don't?"

The President mused, "I've been thinking about that and I think I've done your job for a change and come up with a solution. Well, first of all, we've been hiding Hurst, so we need a spin. Plus, we used a laser that no one knew about. My dear friends like Eric Barnett are now going to try to have me impeached before this is all said and done."

Lawrence had his hand on his chin, pretending he was working something out, "There is one person, though, who really doesn't like you or me and for that reason he's our key out of this."

Kim's brow was furrowed as she answered, "You said it, Lawrence, I'm the one that's supposed to come up with this stuff and before we do anything with your plan I want to put it under a microscope."

"Well, Kim, you do just that, but your lab session is going to be as long as it takes Steve Hatten to get here, I've already summoned him."

"General Steve Hatten?! What the heck are you thinking, Sir? General Hatten doesn't just dislike us, Lawrence, he hates our guts!"

Lawrence looked like a man who was convinced, "He might really hate us, but you're the one who told me to study him. I know the man and I know what he desires more than anything in the world, so we can use that to our advantage here. If we play this right, we will not expose TJAC. I need you to get a speech together that covers this topic."

Kim looked over the paper the leader of the free world just handed her and commented, "Not bad."

"I'm glad you approve, Kim, I'll sleep better tonight. Now make it happen."

Kim left knowing that although she was the sharpest kid on the block, her boss was no dummy either, and every now and then he had to remind her that he was in charge. She had to admit, his was a solid plan.

* * *

The dealer was waiting for them just as he'd instructed. All the rental cars were gone now, so he called the Mercedes-Benz dealer and instructed them to bring him a new CLS Coupe. The guy on the phone hesitated until Robert made it clear who he was, what he was doing and what his time frame was. It was all black, and the dealer had a big smile on his face as Melvin handed him a check for $75,000.

They headed north and were already across the Washington border when they heard on the news that their secret was not a secret anymore. They had the news radio on when two stories broke out of Seattle. First was a mysterious blue flash west of the city of Bellingham near the Canadian border, and the second was a report that broke the story of Tom Holsinger really being Matt Hurst.

They were stunned, of course. They were hoping for a private conversation with Matt that would convince him to Chair *American Pride*, to use his notoriety to start their baby with a tidal wave. Robert knew deep in his soul that Matt should be embracing this new opportunity, not running away from it. So he and Melvin decided they were going to offer Matt financial security so he could have the means to live a protected life the way many of the rich elite did.

Now though, it was going to be very difficult to get him alone, or worse, someone could now be planning to do him harm.

Robert had a thought now that Matt's identity was out and he texted the blog-group to have everyone meet in thirty minutes inside his online world now that they all had access to the portal. It had suddenly become imperative to know where everyone stood.

He could feel this slipping away—and he just could not let it slip away. Matt had a destiny to fulfill and he was going to see it happen. Robert looked out the window as they were passing a town called Castle Rock. They were in the left lane on I-5 when he observed a big SUV barreling up the on-ramp to the freeway. A striking redhead was driving the monster truck, and as she pulled next to them he could see she had tears streaming down her face and she was in distress.

There was a truck in her lane moving slowly and she started accelerating the big machine with all the engine it could muster, which was plenty. The gap was closing for her to get into their lane, as their car was moving faster than the truck and equal to her.

He saw the woman scream, smash the steering wheel several times with her open hands and scream again. She looked like a Banshee. Then she grabbed the wheel with a purpose and bolted the beast forward with authority, barely creasing the gap between them and the truck. The move caused Melvin to brake and honk. He then let out several expletives that ended with, "fucking asshole!" And that was the nicest of the epithets.

As Melvin was going on about the things he would do to that son of a bitch if he ever got his hands on him, Robert drifted off about her. One of these days he hoped to have a beautiful woman just like that, *but hopefully more stable.*

She was so beautiful, though, he doubted he would ever forget her and even with that kind of crazy, he doubted he would throw her back.

He pulled his laptop up and read through his emails, trying to kill time and wondering how his brethren felt about this new revelation about Tom, as surely they would have heard by now.

Robert knew that a lot of people thought Matt Hurst to be guilty from minute one. When President Caulfield exonerated him, it sent waves of resentment through some sections of the population, especially the law enforcement types. For the most part though, Matt was the one person most people would love to talk to. The sheep followers wanted to know where their Messiah was; the U.S. wanted to know where Manuel was; and everyone else wanted the dirt on him and Nancy Chavez.

What mixture of those answers lie with Matt, Robert had no clue, but would hopefully soon find out. He remembered that they talked about this stuff on their blog, but for the life of him he couldn't remember peoples' individual stands on Hurst. He remembered Tom Holsinger was always pro Hurst, but wasn't really loud about it.

Then it hit Robert. It was Matt Hurst, not Tom Holsinger, who came up with the idea for the game. He was the one that was always adamant that we could make change in this non-violent way.

Now Robert got it.

Matt was exposed to the "wrong way" on enacting change through Manuel and had come to the maturity to know that this type of great change could not come from an iron hand—it had to come from a gentle glove.

It must have killed Matt to see his dream come to fruition and to not be able to grab it because he'd lose his autonomy if he did. Oh, if he only would have known before he tipped Matt's name to the very same reporter that was breaking the story right now. How could he have known, though? He was just trying to kick over the hornet's nest to get Tom to commit.

Then the reality really hit him—as these things often do once you reach the right layers. Maybe Hurst had escaped his captors and his little move to prod Tom had exposed him to Manuel. Robert could unwittingly have been responsible for putting this whole thing into action, including the plane and the bombings. His original idea had been to use Matt's notoriety to catapult the game into the stratosphere, but now he saw that this was now a mission to help a friend in serious trouble.

Robert and the rest of the world were most curious as to how Matt Hurst got away. Was it voluntary or did he escape? Did he have connections to the girl? At any time was he part of this whole thing? Robert was fairly sure the evidence was mounting that he was in witness protection or something. That's why Matt ran when Robert showed him what should have been one of the crowning moments of his life.

It all made sense as he logged in and was brought to the virtual boardroom he created. He was not the first there, which was a relief. He said hi to BostonMike1 and SASPURSRULE29. Soon the other two arrived and they were five.

They sat and Robert addressed them before they could start, "I'm sure you all know by now that Tom Holsinger is Matt Hurst." Everyone acknowledged and he continued, "I just found out as you did and I have to say that this would explain why Matt ran. I believe he got away from Pablo Manuel and was in hiding. I also believe that I inadvertently caused all this by dropping his name to the reporter that broke the story.

"I was only doing it to get him kicked into gear, as I had no idea who he was. I guess my question to each of you is, does it matter? The President cleared him and I believe he was in witness protection. So having him, and knowing him the way we do, it can only be a plus. Not to mention it's his idea. The whole group, I believe, was an attempt by him to try to do this the right way after being around some people who did it the wrong way. Obviously we need to take a vote on this as you might not concur with me. But I say we stand by our man."

Picomann was the first to speak out, "I say Matt is a good man and the things Tom was saying are how he really feels. So we know now that Matt Hurst was no traitor and he must have escaped. I'm standing behind him."

BostonMike1 was next, "If Tom Holsinger is a traitor, then I'm the stupidest man on earth because even though we never met him, Tom is a patriot and if Matt is Tom, then Matt is a patriot. I stand."

SASPURSRULE29 followed, but his was less wordy. "Stand."

TimberJustin12 was next, but his was a news flash, "The local news here just reported that Matt's wife and child have been attacked and are in the Anacortes community hospital. According to an EMT in Seattle, they were called to a park shortly before the plane crashed. Upon arrival, there was a comatose woman and child lying in front of the playground. Their last names were Holsinger, and it has been confirmed that a Jan Holsinger was taken to the Anacortes Hospital. They're also saying that the pilot today was the pilot that took Matt out of the country four years ago and now he's missing."

TimberJustin12 finally added, "I not only support Hurst, but I'm driving up there right now!"

It was more than Robert could have hoped for. Their first test as a group and they were like-minded. He added his final concurrence and said, "I'm heading there too, Justin, we need to support Matt."

They agreed to log back on at 7:00 PDT and share what they'd learned. Robert had renewed hope, and he actually felt good calling them, "His" group.

* * *

It started in San Francisco this time. Last time, the sheep followers started in Central Park and it progressed west. This time it was starting out in the west. Hippy Hill was becoming a place of legend. Just like the Haight-Ashbury district in the Sixties, Hippy Hill was now ground zero for the new millennia fight for marijuana called the 420 Movement. At any given time there was a bongo crowd beating the drums, getting high, and bucking societies' conventions at this grassy knoll at the end of the park closest to the entrance to the Haight. It was also a place to where nearly a quarter of a million people had come when America was under attack.

As it turned out, the sheep followers turned out to be a very mixed crowd. Like the city that was home of the park, difference was the norm. Apparently though, when the chips were down and they thought the good old U.S. had gone too far, they resorted to the ways of their parents, not only uniting, but taking it to the streets. A Hippie is a Hippie for life. You can shave them, cut their hair, and put them in suits or even behind badges, but they will persist in seeing joy in the world first. You can't be any more American than that.

Of course, in such a mixed bag you will have your agitators. They were always present, flagrantly waving their rights guaranteed under the constitution of the United States. Albeit in an antagonistic way, they were the ones currently showing their "True American Spirit." They were ones to make everyone think of the revolution side of things, the "I've had enough sect."

Sandy Burroughs turned his TV sound up. It was all happening again, he could feel it. He knew the way it ended last time was not the end and he had hoped he would live long enough to see it. He had a vested interest in the outcome, as the sheep leader that these people followed and were waiting for was none other than Pablo Manuel, protégé of his dear deceased friend, James Haberman.

James Haberman had found Pablo in an online chess room, of all places. Somehow, in the Super Lotto of life, the two greatest minds of their time ended up being in the same place at the same time. *Jackpot!* Pablo had endured the loss of his family to a cartel vendetta only to then endure the loss of James to cancer. He showed the world that the concept of a World Superpower was not relevant anymore. He obtained an atomic suitcase bomb through a defected Russian agent and used it on the cartel that killed his family. And then, in a different kind of statement, he paralyzed the U.S. Military with a drone army he had created.

The part that no one on the planet truly knew except for Sandy was that Pablo really did have a God moment. He truly believed he was working as a messenger of God—and he convinced James. That scared Sandy to his foundation at the time, as James Haberman was not a man of God, he was a man of science.

Both of them were, so when James convinced him that some biblical wraths were going to go down, Sandy took the inside information and disappeared. He sold his law practice, his house on Russian Hill, and cashed out his stocks. He bought gold and he bought bonds. He married and moved to a secluded box canyon in Marin, becoming a naturalist. There he waited for the final blow to happen to the world, but it never came. Instead, just some lame recorded video that made no sense.

Pablo had mastered many languages, and as a result, could vary his accent. But his main dialect was always audible if you knew him, as it just lay slightly behind in the background. He had a rhythm to his speech and it was not a monotone, but it was soft. Sandy heard the words, but the inflections were all wrong for their young lad. He smelled a rat and figured the CIA was running some kind of a smoke and mirrors routine for the American Public.

The Pablo he knew was not going to be deterred until he'd accomplished his mission, so this probably meant he was dead. Yet they couldn't announce that or there would be serious rioting all over the world. Whatever was happening before surely had not come to fruition, but now it felt like it was back.

Sandy felt it through and through. But time passed, memories got clouded, and lack of confidence in one's rightness started to seep in. Until now, he was pretty much resolved to the fact that the U.S. had killed Pablo and run their cockamamie story to keep everyone at bay.

Better than that, it put out the fire in the hearts of all the followers that were about to start the boat a rocking in every major city in the world. The public was putting it all together quickly now, though. Once the Matt Hurst story hit, everyone was connecting Matt, Pablo, and the attacks. Now there was a story breaking of a laser being used and it suddenly looked like the U.S. was right back where it was two years ago, only the warfare was now being fought on U.S. soil.

After James and Pablo's message of warning, Sandy had created a compound with all the things necessary to survive the fall of civilization, because that was what he was advised to do. Pablo and James really believed that a Utopia was going to rise from their actions, a new era of enlightenment, but not before a cold, hard reality set in and made its new shape on the landscape.

Sandy looked over at his wife, Claire, napping in her chair. He worked hard for many, many years, and she was his secretary through most of them. A couple of years after her husband died they got together. After he found out the truth of what was coming, work didn't seem to matter anymore and together they created this sanctuary.

Although he must admit, when James and Pablo came into his life, he was stagnant and would have plugged along with his old ways until the day he didn't show up for work and they had to do the old "wellness check"' at his house.

He'd had so much to learn these last couple of years. He started off clueless and now he could make wine, can his own goods, and grow a variety of fruits and vegetables. He'd learned to raise chickens and make his own honey from the beehives he kept. No one that ever knew him in the past would have ever thought that Sandy Burroughs, Tax Attorney to the spoiled, would become an earthy type of farmer? Well, he really didn't have much choice, after James and Pablo's revelation. Only a fool would have not taken their dire warning with anything less than total seriousness.

So once again, the stage was set and the fireworks had started, but would he see the finale? Hippy Hill was already completely covered and the crowd started spreading out from there. He could see from the overhead shot that the adjacent baseball field bordering 19th Avenue was now filling up, and Sandy was sure that it wouldn't be long until the movement spread out across the country.

Whether they admitted it or not, everyone wanted to see this play out all the way this time. The truth was, however, Pablo no longer had the full support for his actions, or even close to it. The ferry incident was causing people to start a new non-violent message for the Messiah, "No more bloodshed."

Every single person interviewed was shocked and refused to believe that Pablo would attack a non-military target, seeing that he previously went out of his way to warn people. Conspiracy theories were abounding, and it was all mixing into a big boiling cauldron of anger and despair, mixed with the desire for change.

America was the perfect melting pot to get a serious movement started, and it was happening again. The former middle class, the people who were against this type of anti-government protests in the Sixties were now largely out of work due to America's horrible economy, and they held a lot of repressed anger.

Americans were also over-burdened at work because those who were the lucky enough to survive and were still employed were also now doing the job of three people. America was the most medicated country in the world, in part because their jobs were being erased by outsourcing and modernization at a staggering rate, and the middle class was obliterated in the span of a single generation.

So those same voices against this type of action in the Sixties were in one of two places on this day. They were either pro or they were neutral; but in either case, a major voice against the people hammering the establishment was missing and the resulting lack of resistance was something that the Government should fear if it knew what was good for it.

A little word called revolution loomed right under the surface and those in power must be able to see it. Pablo had actually exposed them in ways they feared way more than they let on. Pablo proved they were not as mighty as they once were. Technology had evened the playing field and Sandy believed that also made the climate ripe for *REVOLUTION*.

Sandy thought of it in inner city speak, the U.S. had lost its *street cred*. They used to be Leroy Brown, but just like in the song, give a man motivation and he will take on a much bigger opponent and do damage. David and Goliath also popped into his head. Everyone loved an underdog and as the people took to the streets and parks all across the country, Sandy was sure that a few of his old clients had their ass's clinched tighter than a frogs. Their establishment was coming apart again.

That was the Government's underlying fear as well, that this congregating in public places would lead in other directions. Some of the people on the fringe liked the anarchy aspect of it all. They spat out their whispered yet sharp words and slowly spread their influence to the ones that were the most ignorant.

Within this large group, Sandy had already identified several sub groups that seemed to have their own agenda. That was what made this unique and obviously terrifying for the powers that be.

He took a sip of his merlot. It was literally his, as he'd made it and did not do a bad job either.

He'd wished there was a way to help the boy, but then again, he doubted he could add anything. Sandy knew Pablo before he was the Messiah for all these people, and also before he was on the most wanted list as the world's most notorious terrorist.

Simultaneously, there was another movement starting, apparently one that began on Facebook and aimed at people connected to the military or police. It looked as though a march was starting in the Presidio and ending at Hippy Hill, according to their spokesperson, a gruff man in his fifties with a wife beater t-shirt and an anchor tattoo, "We plan to march to the park and pick up supporters as we go, then when we reach the park we plan to have a talk with those folks who are supporting this mass-murderer. Anyone who is supporting these sheep dirt bags is a traitor to the United States and a traitor to all those boys who died out on those ships in Ecuador."

His group was currently only fifty strong, but they were announcing their plans to march to the park and confront the sheep followers, and asking for a following of their own.

Sandy had not seen this type of anger and passion since the volatile Sixties, and the result was butterflies in his stomach thinking about those two groups getting together. Claire woke up, looked at his concerned face and said, "What did I miss?"

* * *

Not being able to dry her eyes for the last twenty minutes had already led to three near misses, one of which would have been a rear-end collision that would have ruined her back. Lauren was realizing that her little tantrum was now costing her dearly as she rolled past Tacoma in mounting pain. Her arm that had been broken in three places did not appreciate the open-hand slamming of the steering wheel; as a matter of fact, it downright hated it. But compared to her back, it was a lovely walk in the park.

She had been warned not to exert herself or she would be sorry, and now she was debating if she should pull over and call 911. But instead, she continued to barrel down the highway at nearly a hundred miles per hour. She must have been tensed when she did that wild swinging and it had apparently set her back muscles off in a very bad way. She had taken her pills twenty minutes ago, but this was no joke, she'd made a major mistake with her tantrum. Her repaired left arm was trembling, and the palm of her right hand was still throbbing.

Ever since she'd been about thirteen years old there had been times when she just could not control her anger once she had been pushed too far. Her current tears were mostly from the shame of not being able to control herself over Scott's betrayal. *Why did she always have to fail on the big ones?* This was the one time she'd needed to make sure she did not lose control.

She was passing Tukwila and knew that Anacortes lay ninety minutes ahead, but she would have to go up the 405 as she'd just found out I-5 was out of the question as emergency personnel had shut it down. The traffic on the 405 was very heavy, but the people were still following conventions and the car pool lanes were flowing as normal. She decided she would risk the ticket.

She could see Boeing on her left but the glance cost her a small spasm in her lower back. God what she wouldn't trade for a session with Rodrigo.

Then her mind drifted to that of a subsequent man in her life and thought, *why would Scott have torched any chance he had with me over a story—albeit the story of a lifetime, but just a fucking news story, nonetheless?* She could still see his smug little face on the screen, it seemed to be saying, "You think I'm too stupid to figure you out bitch, well here you go."

Granted, she had not been forthright over the phone, but no matter, that did not give him the right to fuck with her "story of a lifetime." And if he'd ever loved her at all, then he would have known to never fuck with her where her brother was concerned.

She'd decided that she was going to call breach of professional ethics on dear Scott, maybe even embellishing a little to his boss. God she hoped his boss was a weak-minded man. Maybe she would become a tech writer and depose him in his own world. She felt that anger swelling again, but this time was able to put it away as her body could not physically handle another outburst.

Thank God, her pills finally kicked in. She was in so much pain that they did not make her high, they just did their job, which was good since she could not afford to be high right now.

Somehow she was going to make that little weasel pay for what he did. Her need for revenge refueled her, as it had been doing for the last two years. Only now, she could see an end in sight, and it was that motivation that kept her from heading to the nearest hospital right then.

She steeled herself to focus on the road when her phone rang, caller ID said Jerome. She tried to answer normally, but immediately her voice whittled to that of a little girl who'd woken from a bad dream in the middle of the night. She tried to be stoic, but as she started to speak, it all fell apart and the little girl in her uttered, "Daddy . . ."

* * *

Doug set the seaplane down as if he did it for a living, then informed them, "this is nothing compared to landing the big boys." Right at that moment, Storm groaned loudly, his giant tongue lolling back and forth. They all laughed at the timing of the act, and they understood that Doug was not actually bragging. He was stating, in his own way, that if he were anywhere else, the fact he'd landed an airliner in the Sound not a few a short hours before would be a conversation piece. But in this small cabin, that story was even a yawner for the dog. *Talk about a tough crowd.*

There was no doubt that the dog had a smile on his face. He seemed to be convinced that this was all one long training mission and that his master would never have left him. It's a fact of the human condition that when a loved one is in imminent peril, all other things pale, even finding Storm. For the last two years all he could think about was recovering this dog, but now, looking at him so happy, almost brought him to anger. His life was always that way, no joy could be brought to him unless there was a side dish of anguish to go with it—and in this case, it was no side dish, it was the main course.

"What's the plan, Matt?"

Matt figured that question was his own fault. He always acted like he knew what he was doing all the time, so people actually thought he had all the answers, that he was a leader.

"There is no plan, Doug. I killed the one guy who could have saved them or at least given me the name of the toxin that he used. Of course, knowing the man the way I know him, that toxin will most likely be found to be unique and not have any known antidote."

"I have a car you can use to get around to the back of the hospital. My daughter in-law is a nurse there; she'll get you in. Let's just go call my son and have him come down."

"I don't think that will be necessary, Luke; if I'm not mistaken, the young man heading our way at a clipped pace bears quite a family resemblance, might just be him." Matt patted Storm and told him, "*Niza.*"

Luke said, "He's just pissed because he thinks I took a tourist up. One time six months ago or so, I took some people up. He was out and they really wanted to go. I was feeling good, so I took them up. It's not like my plane isn't ready at all times. Apparently, the doctors reported my condition to the insurance companies and if I would have had an incident, it would have cost us everything we own. I was fine and the trip was great, but since then Andy has had neighbors watch to see if I ever try to lift off. Apparently one called him."

The young man in question was the spitting image of his father and Doug immediately saw what this hero looked like in his prime. He could just picture that same rage on his old man's face in a far-east jungle somewhere fifty years ago, and then he began to understand the Silver Star. The young man flung the side door open, demanded to know what he was thinking and stopped talking almost immediately. All he had to say after that was, "You all better come with me," and headed to the office.

When they got to the office, Luke's son, Andy was standing in front of the TV and he was looking more than solemn. Matt had a knot in his stomach because he knew that it was probably going to be some huge story about the laser shot. What he really saw he never would have guessed.

An Internet blog reporter had figured out his real identity. His name was Scott Bailey, and he had been told by Robert Leme that Tom Holsinger was the creative mind behind the newest Leme hit game, and when the reporter followed the story, he got a picture of what he thought was Holsinger. Only after the plane and ferry incidents was Bailey looking at the pictures again and realized that Tom Holsinger was really Matt Hurst.

The next news reported that it was now known that Hurst's parents were on the ferry and his wife and son were attacked in a Seattle park and were now in the Anacortes hospital, as there was no room in the Seattle area hospitals at the time of their injuries. Matt started for the door on a run and Andy called him back.

"You'll never get in. The hospital is completely surrounded by people. Most want to talk to Matt Hurst, but there are a growing number who have painted signs for *American Pride*, which would indicate they want to talk to Holsinger. It's quickly getting out of control."

Matt thought about this and replied with the sound of a completely defeated man. "I have the right to be with my wife and son when they pass. Luke, can I ask you to watch Storm while I go deal with my situation. Last I checked, I was not wanted for anything."

"Of course, Matt, but at least let my son get you close with a car."

"No, I won't be involving anyone else in my life, just ask Doug there what that brings."

Doug's answer was, "You mean more adventure and pussy than ten lifetimes could offer?" He walked over to Matt and stated, "Like it or not, our lives have become interconnected and everything you do from this point on will either lead to a continued existence or instant death. I cannot be negotiated with. So make up your mind right now because if you live, it will be because you let it all hang out."

Matt, remembering his own diatribe to Doug in a hanger in Tahoe, "Your point, Doug?"

"I've seen you in tough spots, you don't give up. For all you know, that Indian doctor you spoke of has cured them. I have a plan to get you in. After all, you're not the only celebrity they want to talk to."

"A diversion, I love it Doug! And I know you're right, self-pity does not suit me well. But life wears on you, all this running for my life and threats. I just want to live a life without threats."

No chord he could hit could ever register with Luke Slate stronger than that one. It was something he related to like a hand in a glove and he let him know, "Matt, I have your back from this point on."

"Thanks Luke, that means a lot to me. Not sure how the general public is going to feel, but I really do appreciate all that you've done and are doing for me."

Before the next words could be spoken, the TV gave an all too familiar announcement that the President was coming on and all of them paused their next move toward the door to listen. This time, it was from the Press Room and not the Oval Office.

* * *

"Citizens of the United States of America and the World. First, let us please hang our heads once again in prayer for our fallen. Once again we have had to endure sadness and horror as we pay a heavy price for our continued freedom. Regardless of the supposed cause behind this cowardly act, or the justifications that will surely arise from the perpetrators, it was still an act of terrorism.

It still robs us of our loved ones and strikes fear into our hearts. We've lost our brothers, sisters, and parents today. The ferry attack was so heinous and vile that even as a person who has had to steel himself over the last few years after hearing so much bad news, I can still barely come to face it. But face it I must, and we must as a nation because that is the nature of things in America. Try as anyone might, they cannot hold us down.

So, even though the next news I bring you is good, it comes with the heaviest price for us all as a nation. In a joint effort, the United States Air Force and U.S. citizen, Mathew Hurst, have brought Pablo Manuel, the terrorist responsible for the attacks in Seattle, to justice. He was wounded and captured off Matia Island State Park in Washington State, where we believed he carried out the attacks on the Southwest passenger plane and Washington State ferry from a command boat.

Unknown to the general public, two years ago, Mr. Hurst was responsible for thwarting a major attack and disabling Manuel's organization in Ecuador. Originally he was kidnapped and held there for two years before striking them and escaping. There is no doubt that his brave actions saved countless American lives back then.

He then volunteered to go into witness protection knowing full well that he would probably be found by a vindictive Pablo Manuel. Matt believed that if he disappeared, then Manuel would have won, for he still had things to do for the country he'd already saved once."

And things were just fine until he met and befriended Robert Leme of the *Top of the Heap* game franchise fame. They bonded and forged an idea, but Matt realized he couldn't be the face of the organization, as Leme and his people all knew him as Tom Holsinger. So he set forth their game plan and backed out, hoping he made the kind of impact that motivated them to move forward without him. He had been hoping to enact those changes himself, but there was just no way to do it and be safe.

Unfortunately, Mr. Robert Leme accidently exposed him by releasing his witness protection name of Tom Holsinger as part of the Leme team working on *American Pride*. Internet reporter Scott Bailey was able to get his picture and release it, which of course led to Manuel finding him. Matt Hurst has paid a terrible price for his patriotism and it needs to be announced now that he was the victim here, never anything more. A stronger patriot the history books will not find.

Apparently Manuel made an elaborate plan to attack the people Matt cared about, as his parents were most likely on that ferry. It has also been learned that his wife and son were chemically attacked in a Seattle park within minutes of the ferry exploding and are now fighting for their lives. There is also a connection to Matt with Douglas Sharp, as he was the pilot that he forced to fly him out of the country four years ago.

Initially, we gave him choices that would have protected him, but he chose to do it this way, never believing there would be enough protection and never wanting to miss out on all the things our great country has to offer. Matt Hurst told me directly, 'What's the point of living in the greatest country in the world if I have to hide in it?' And after what we've seen here, it's hard to dispute his logic. So please, shelve all questions that will put Hurst in collusion with Manuel, it never happened."

President Caulfield looked over the group for some familiar faces that he owed a favor to, "I'm now going to open up for a few questions." He pointed to an eager hand in front.

Linda Breem of the *Dallas Star* got the first question, "Was the Southwest plane and ferry respectively shot by a laser? We have reports of a massive laser used just after the plane went down?"

Air Force General, Steve Hatten, of the Joints Chief of Staff, was flanking the President and the President stepped aside giving the microphone to the General after a small introduction. "The plane was most likely brought down by two small drones. We don't believe they even carried a warhead, as the wings were intact. The drones were apparently designed to just stop the engines. The laser in question was a U.S. weapon and it stopped Manuel's escape."

Spencer Loomis from the *Los Angeles Times* asked the next question, "Did the attack at Tom Holsinger's house on Lummi Island precipitate that laser shot?"

When the President came to General Hatten, he was approaching his biggest detractor among his appointed cabinet. It hadn't always been that way, but more and more he could tell that there was collusion among four of the Generals and one of them was General Steve Hatten.

Now General Hatten had a big secret he could share, one that could have ripped his Presidency apart, one that gave the General the upper hand. Lawrence doubted that the public would have taken kindly to the fact that the data for Manuel's entire military enterprise fell into the hands of his friend, Chase Viana. They would be less fond of the fact he then sanctioned a privately owned company to launch a laser-armed satellite above U.S. airspace.

Chase convinced him of the need to have them up and that he could get them built a hundred times faster than any government entity; no red tape, just get it done. His company was already making the components for many such projects already. At first revelation to the General, Lawrence Caulfield could see a "kid that was going to tell" look all over General Hatten's face, but when the President enlightened him on the advantages of him taking the credit for the whole thing, he noticed a different look.

When Chase agreed to give the Air Force control of the other satellites he had up currently and hand over all test data, the General was getting much warmer to the idea of playing ball. Then when the President of the United States mentioned that it is not unheard of for such a leader as him to make a presidential run, it was like turning on a light switch.

He told Steve knowingly, "Really, all you need is greater positive exposure, I'm sure we can find a way to make that happen." General Hatten and the ego Lawrence always knew he possessed could not pass up that opportunity, even scant as it was. Now he was on the podium and God help Lawrence if he just helped make that man President, because for the first time in his life, he had to compromise himself and it felt alien and contradictory to his nature.

Although General Hatten was not a bad man, he was not someone Lawrence would want to see in his office, let alone endorse him to be there. He watched the General answer with a coolness and likability that made him wince deep inside.

General Hatten spoke, "Well, as you all now know, Tom Holsinger does not exist, he is Matt Hurst. So yes, the attack carried out on the Hurst house was in fact carried out by Manuel. We have confirmed reports that there was also an attack on Hurst prior to that. It occurred in the Anacortes Community Hospital parking lot. Matt had a tracking device that he activated during the attack and was able to lead his assailants out to sea. That's where we disabled Manuel's escape with the laser and captured him. To save time I will answer the next question, Pablo Manuel was captured with one other man."

Phil Martin of the Washington Post got the next question, "Where is Hurst now and why just the Air Force?"

Hatten felt so alive on the podium. And he knew that President Caulfield would have loved to usher him off, but he couldn't, they had a deal, so he was making the most of the opportunity. He used some charm, but not over the top, as this was a solemn time for most. "That's two questions really, Phil, and I know you snuck that second one in because I can't help but talk about the Air Force, but I'm going to allow it.

"Matt's whereabouts are unknown at this time. We've lost his satellite signal, but have not found any evidence that he's been injured or killed. On the issue of a single branch of the Military being used, it's quite simple. We knew that Manuel had previously breached security within our government computer systems and even our military computers that were deemed unbreachable. We also knew he would come after Hurst. So the less that anyone knew the better chances the mission would be a success.

"Of course, few people anywhere realized just how far Manuel would go to make a point. Even though he'd shown just how ruthless he could be in the past, somehow a lot of people seemed to believe he was an overall good person. Well, if he was good, then he obviously went rogue, and when he did, he started killing our troops and sinking our ships.

"No good person would have done these things. The President trusted me and our proud branch of the military to do our job by implementing this. It's just horrible that we were not able to stop this madman before a lot of good people died."

General Hatten let himself get a little misty eyed when speaking about the loss of life. He stepped back with an outer sadness that hid his inner smugness as the President took back the podium to a flurry of hand waving. Unfortunately for the unchosen, he was down to the last question and it went to Susan Bell of *The New York Times*.

"Was Matt Hurst *really* working for the Government the whole time?" The question was asked with a bit of flippancy, and the way she hit "really" and tilted her head made her seem more than skeptical of the whole thing.

The President met her eyes when he spoke, "No, Susan, he wasn't. Strange as the whole thing seems—and believe me I had my moments when I wanted nothing to do with hearing of his innocence—Matt Hurst was drawn into this. I'm going to make it simple and that's not to say you need things simplified, I'm just saying the simplest explanation is sometimes the best one.

"Now I had occasion to talk to this young man two years ago after we brought him back ruined from the horrors of war. I can tell you that once he realized that these people intended to destroy his nation in such a horrifying way, he felt the same as any honest patriot felt during Pearl Harbor or 9/11, he enlisted rather than be drafted. He made it up in his mind right then and there that if any true patriot were in his situation, they would fight for their country to the death.

"So imagine Matt being on a landing craft during D-day. There was no turning back and you could not quit, war was coming. By that explanation, we took him to war, he gave his patriotic all and he survived, which makes him a veteran. So Susan, I guess I was wrong in my initial assumption. He was working for us the minute an enemy of our country took him hostage, and there were people within our Government that were trying to get me on board with that concept.

"Our young hero was sending us messages, but they were very abstruse in nature, as he was limited by time and circumstances when he was sending them. Unfortunately, when you have this job, the rights and safety of an individual pale in comparison to the rights and safety of an entire nation, so it took me a while to get with it. But get with it I did.

"Matt came back to us and didn't ask for anything. He just went on with his life and tried to make a positive change to this great land in new ways. I know practically nothing about gaming, but apparently his game concept, *American Pride*, is based on patriotism. Well, I don't have to be a big fan of gaming to be a fan of that or Matt Hurst, for that matter.

"The fact is, we owe this young man. Sadly, his family and countless others have paid a horrible price for our continued freedom. With that somber note I leave you with the consideration that although we are still a great nation, we now know that with the new millennium comes new technological innovations that can be used for evil as well as good. We also are being forced to see we have weaknesses attributed to these advancements and that our enemies don't care about our values on life, liberty, and the pursuit of happiness.

"So next time you find yourself not valuing your freedom, think about the sacrifices this young man, our military men and women, and countless others have made in your behalf."

Susan Bell looked very touched that her question elicited such an emotional response, especially seeing it was a very antagonistic approach that she had in the first place, "Thank you for your candor, Sir."

"No problem Susan, you know you can always count on me for that. Thank you and God bless us all."

* * *

Doug look bewildered, "Why did they say that, Matt? You killed Pablo and his cohort."

"I don't know. First my mind has to wrap around being on the other end of a broadcast like that. I can tell you, it's a lot less terrifying this way."

He looked over at Luke and Andy and was receiving a very approving and admirable look, the look every soldier who ever stepped off a plane from defending his country should get. His four-legged savior was actually sitting by Luke and looking at him too, with an even toothier grin.

Matt admonished, "I don't know what you three are smiling about, you just stepped in it deeper than you could ever imagine. They had a reason for saying what they did. You must understand that. All of you," he also turned to Doug, "have just stepped smack dab into a major conspiracy. It's clean on their end. Did anyone ever see Manuel Noriega again? But you three pose a loose end and if they ever found out that you know, your lives could be in peril. Don't any of you think otherwise."

Luke looked at him with a twinkle Kris Kringle would be proud of, "Just the same as it's always been, Son."

Doug called Matt over to Luke's office door where he observed the medals, his eyes focusing on the Silver Star.

"I think Luke and Andy understand."

* * *

Dr. Arshad Singh closed his door and sat in his chair. He closed his eyes for one second and started falling down the darkness so quickly he had to jerk himself awake. He gulped the coffee in his hand. It was just above drinking temperature, but he drank anyway, slightly scalding himself in the process. He turned his computer screen on and brought up his reports. He had a few minutes to get some organizing done. Why he shut his eyes he'll never know because now he could not stop thinking about sleep.

Coming from New Delhi, this situation tonight was actually calm given the circumstances. He remembered a bad heat wave one year, hundreds died in his understaffed and overwrought hospital. That and the wailing of the families was one of those things he tried to block out of his memory, but it always surfaced when he thought he had it bad in whatever current situation he might find himself. His Skype light was flashing so he pushed the connect button and his sister Sanji was on the screen live. Apparently she'd heard the news.

"Hello, Brother, how are you?"

Getting his number one concern out of the way, he first asked, "Hello, Sanji, how are Mom and Dad."

"They are fine, they wanted me to call you and make sure *you* are okay."

"They really won't step into the screen?"

"You know them and technology, Brother, so what are you doing? Why aren't you busy helping people?"

"I have been, I needed to get off my feet for a few minutes. You got really lucky reaching me."

"Really, what's the most intriguing case so far?"

"You know I can't talk about that stuff here, this is a very protected place when it comes to medical privacy, but there is one case that bothers me, although it's not related to the plane crash."

"You know I'm in my last year of Medical School, so test me."

"No sister, I'm afraid this is out of your league. It's a neurotoxin case, most likely a planned attack. I have a mother and her four-year-old son battling for their lives. They were brought in stable, but both are comatose. I took the samples I could, but being in a facility that lacks the testing tools I need and lacking credentials in this country I have to defer this. Unfortunately, due to the plane and ferry tragedy, their ride out of here has been delayed. I just know that if I had the right tools, I could be the one to solve this. There has been a steady decrease in vitals over the last six hours and I fear they won't make a long plane ride now."

"Why don't you ask Mansoor to help you."

"Mansoor?"

"For such a smart man, sometimes you can be so dumb. Your cousin is in Brazil, has been for a year and a half. His specialty is neurotoxins. He's working for some big pharmaceutical company on stroke recovery."

"I do remember Mom and Dad writing me and telling me that, but my own life is so crazy, I just let it slip away as information I didn't need to retain."

"Well retain it now."

"I will. E-mail me all his contact info right away. I need to get back to work. Bye, Mom and Dad.

From off the screen he heard a unison, "Bye, Son."

He hung up very happy. He would be able to get Mansoor whatever data he had and maybe he could help the forwarding doctors solve this case. Mansoor could be on it as soon as the Sandler Neurology Center at UCSF sent him the data; which reminded him, his data should be ready by now. He fought off fatigue once more and got moving, half of staying up was moving, although he was pretty sure he was going to fall asleep walking one of these days.

* * *

Malcolm Ward thought he'd heard and seen it all. Although he was just twenty-four years of age, he had covered a lot of the road to manhood in that time; which was the reason he ended up with Frederick Tedesco, because a lot of that road was hard to shake off. The Company can tell you how to handle stress—they have it all compartmentalized for you in manuals and videos and counselors; problem was, everyone was different and each person had his or her own personal breaking point, the point where they'd seen enough children raped and enough fathers left holding their dead families to last a lifetime of nightmares.

His last mission was to infiltrate and eliminate anyone that survived a drone strike on the group that blew up a CIA operated building in Kandahar. One of their informants was apparently a double agent and suicide bombed the building, killing seven agents and analysts. Once they got word of the whereabouts of the compound, he and his spotter set out.

Based on their intelligence report, an air strike was set and he was to pick up the strays. At the designated hour, the drone made its attack. Unfortunately, it only blew up the back of the building leaving many of the enemy in the front. The first man made a move for the warehouse and vehicles to the right. Malcolm shot him in the leg at the knee. It severed his knee and threads of flesh and clothing were the only things holding it together at all.

Arterial spurt abounding, the man was screaming for help, and a second one came out to help the first. Malcolm let him get to his friend and then blew his knee out, too. It was slightly high, so no severance, but the same effect took place. Now two were pleading for their brothers and this is where he got evil. He took several wild shots around the fallen men. Horrible shots that led the men left to believe that those were lucky shots that struck their brethren.

Sure enough, one of hidden combatants came out for his brothers, but he was not the one that he had the scope on. No, it was that gentleman standing in the doorway watching the scene with bated breath. The shot took him through the brick wall right in the heart, the wall puffing in a cloud of brown dust. The third man looked back and upon seeing this understood he had been hoodwinked.

He ran low toward the destination of cover and cars across the compound. Even though the man was crouch running with his head bent slightly forward, Malcolm was able to just blow the top of his head off, the bullet going in just one inch under the scalp and removing the skull plate. When he hit the ground, the contents of his head spilled out in a grotesque show of the horrors of war.

Malcolm then quickly put the decoys out of their misery as surely no one else was coming out. He couldn't be sure he'd gotten them all though, as he had no idea how many where here to begin with. He would have to go in. Seeing it was just the two of them, they flipped. He lost. His spotter, Ashton Paulson, would be his cover. He shouldered his sniper rifle and drew his Colt for the trip. Using the same logic as the enemy, he circled to the warehouse and vehicle cover. He holstered the pistol and re-evaluated with the scope. Nothing.

Switching back to the pistol he advanced on the house on a direct angle with the corner of the house. Once safely against the wall he flattened and drew the flash grenade. He was about to pull the pin and throw it in the window when he heard the sobbing, and then Farsi being spoken, he heard. "Baba, Baba, wake up." More sobbing, "Baba, they will come."

He didn't know why, but he did not throw the grenade and he entered the building with less deadly intent than was healthy for a man in his occupation. He spoke and understood a few words in Farsi and he knew inflection. His wall shot orphaned this person behind this voice, or at least took his father. He turned the corner to meet the terrified eyes of the young man, still pulling on the lapels of his fallen father.

Malcolm spoke, "I won't hurt you," it was one of the phrases he'd learned to say, needing it often. This time the words had no effect; the boy was maybe twelve and obviously had a lifetime of brainwashing against the great evil, not to mention his mind only knew war, and when a child's eyes only see war, then they honestly see martyrdom as a righteous act.

Malcolm said it with more compassion this time, "I won't hurt you." At those words the kid went for his father's rifle that lay on the ground. Malcolm was yelling, "No" when it went too far and he shot the boy in the chest with the Colt. The boy had been wearing sandals and he was literally blown right out of them. He lay against the back wall and as Malcolm approached with the pleading look of why, the boy tried to lift the gun and Malcolm fired again, hitting him in the heart.

According to his spotter, he left the building using no military movements whatsoever. He just sulked as he walked out and broke all the rules on the return trip, including entering the base the same way they had left. He had finally found his breaking point and it put his spotter's life at risk the whole way back.

Malcolm's mind came back to the present as he parked the van, unbuckled, and got into the back through the blackout curtain. The van was a commercial type, which bore no side windows and had heavily tinted windows in the back. There was padding on the back floor, along with a padded resting arch for his rifle; and when he lay prone, there was also a small sliding plate on the door that he could pull back so he could get the rifle barrel out.

The parking structure had railings on the edges of the upper lot, but the van sat high and he was able to scope the front of the building over it. A massive crowd had gathered in front of the hospital, and after hearing the Presidents speech, he knew why.

Malcolm now saw why Frederick had chosen this as his first assignment back. There was no misunderstanding that helping this hero stay alive was a very important and noble thing to do. There was no ambiguity in the mission and he could live with the thought of whom he was helping. Malcolm cared about Matt Hurst without ever having met him.

Frederick helped him accept that if he hadn't killed that boy, he would be the one dead. If he could ever get the kids accusatory and hateful eyes out of his thoughts, then maybe he could really accept that and he could have some recovery. Instead, all he could see in his subconscious were those incriminating eyes of hatred aimed at him.

Malcolm closed the left plate and opened the one on the right side door. There were two office buildings in the hospital plaza. Combined with the parking structure they made a foursquare with the hospital, with grass and benches in the center. Directly across from the van's parking spot was a four-story specialist office where he could see straight across to its roof. On the right was another four-story office building; same deal, he had a good view of the roof. He would have to toggle between the two ports to get the complete picture, but he had a clean shot on anything not directly below him. That thought occurred to him, but he wanted the top of the garage as it afforded the rooftops of the office buildings. If he took a shot from the top, it would be much easier to walk away from the van and rifle, both untraceable. *If he shot?* Malcolm hoped there would be no "if."

Not long ago, he'd promised himself there would never be another shot, yet here he was, bandaged back together, sent back to do that robot thing he did best. *Pull the trigger.*

Malcolm thought about Hurst's story and he'd realized that he was just wallowing in self-pity with his piddly situation. Matt selflessly lost everything in the physical world a person could lose. All he was doing was selfishly battling his own internal demons.

Apparently Frederick considered that he would see this and it would prod him to get back to what had him here in the first place, his loathing of injustice and inequity. It was his driving force—he hated it, hated to see all the injustice in the world.

In college he knew what he wanted the minute the CIA recruiter asked to talk to him. He'd heard stories from the Sixties of this happening, but thought it outdated in today's technological world for the CIA to recruit live like that. He was wrong, of course, and in very short time, he was working for The Company.

All his life he had always been the best at everything. When they'd found him, he was captain of the baseball team, debate team, and a Delta pledge from his father at UCLA. He was definitely going places. Unfortunately for academia, he clearly saw where that would lead and he didn't like it so much. Many of his contemporaries were taking the gold-lined path that privilege provided in this country, and surely he was tempted to be one of them, but then it kind of hit him . . . then what? *Wife, kids, suburbs, GOLF!*

He hated when Frederick, the shrink, was right, and thinking about the unjust nature of Hurst's predicament was exactly what it took for him to snap out of it.

He needed to reconnoiter the parking garage as it posed a threat he could not see. Once that was done, he could rest easier. Malcolm placed the silencer on his HK nine millimeter, and headed out the side door, his six-foot frame hunched, his ball cap pulled low and his hands in the pockets of his jacket.

* * *

Jim Jensen had a nice steady bead on the signal. It stopped in Anacortes for sixteen minutes and was now on the move again. Rather than take the direct path though, he thought he'd play a hunch and follow the signals true path. He could see on the incredible mapping his tablet provided that Matt was heading toward the hospital, which was an obvious destination.

He pulled up to the dock and brought the boat to a crawl. A man and a Rottweiler were on the dock and when Jim slid the boat over sideways, the man obliged and cautiously tied off the boat. The two were looking very wary and Jim could tell it was a look of protection. "I assume you are a friend of my esteemed protégé?"

Luke held the dog while he answered, "Yes we would be. He said that most likely a man named Jim Jensen would come looking for him." Luke added, "This here is Storm. He came back to Matt today, but I will let Matt tell you that story." Luke then directed Jim to the hospital in pursuit of his protégé?

* * *

The traffic was insane. The 405 was an absolute gridlock, the intersections of the two floating bridges that came from downtown were a nightmare of horns and flaring tempers. Melvin kept his cool, but the anticipation of where they were heading left them both bursting at the seams.

Robert had the news on and they heard the reports and then the President's speech. The new car was loaded with options including a screen to sync their phones to. Robert watched the incredible opportunity that he had crumble by the second, while at the same time, he almost could care less because of Matt's situation.

Amazingly, their Chairman of the Board, Matt/Tom was an unbelievable hit. As of ten minutes ago, *American Pride* had sold half its allotted number of the game, which was unfathomable because it was set at five million participants. After the game competition was over, Robert had already announced that they would open the game city up to all for free, as the beginnings of something wonderful.

His staff complained that releasing that information would hurt sales. That people would just wait and get in for free. His exact retort was, "Balderdash." Robert now sat watching Melvin negotiate traffic and thought, *who turned out to be right?*

Their Tom, who turned out to be Matt, had now made the gaming world take notice. Robert pondered the crossover. Matt was now, "King of the Nerds." He was a real life icon, and now he was also the man who was going to lead his new legion into doing all sorts of things that seemed out of fashion, like voting for instance.

It was a pretty big world, and the odds of all this falling into place just like it did were pretty astronomical to say the least. I think an exclamation or two would even be in order. A, "You've got to be kidding me?!" Or a, "That's impossible!" Yet it happened. Somehow, he came together with Matt out of every other person on the planet. *Why?*

Robert really needed nothing from the world; he had his plan and he was self-sufficient. It was something in the way Matt presented himself. It was like the scene in *Scarface*, where Sousa was evaluating Tony and he said something like, "I like you, Tony, there is no bullshit in you." He had that kind of moment in the chat room that day. Somehow this guy was able to manifest his emotions over the web and recruit him into doing something unheard of. Of course, everyone had inherent talents that set them apart from the pack, and one of Robert's main ones was he was the "build a better mousetrap guy." He had been doing some tinkering with Matt's idea, putting a last coat of wax . . . *Just wait until they see the real endgame and what Matt's inspirational actions have spawned.*

The amount of money they would earn was a factor, but it was so much more than that. The game was centered on responsible capitalism. If it weren't for the newly surfaced news about his family, Robert would have been jumping for joy, but as it turned out, no business was going to be discussed any time soon.

Melvin maneuvered deftly around some idle-minded dawdlers who couldn't even manage traffic at a snails pace and pulled up smack next to his angry beauty in the giant planet killer on wheels. The diamond lane had stopped due to a police action and people were merging right, further aggravating the situation.

This time she was not angry, but soulfully crying and talking into what he hoped was her blu-tooth. Robert hated those damn things, as they made one have to really focus at peoples' ears on the streets to tell who was crazy and who wasn't. In the good old days that was the number one way to tell if someone was crazy, if you saw a person talking to themselves, then you could check that box and cross the street. Now one had to find the blu-tooth before you made that check.

Well, if she was talking to herself, it was an impassioned and heartfelt self-talk. Robert could feel how distraught she was and she appeared to be in real pain, maybe she knew someone on the ferry? By now Melvin could see him looking and caught her as well, traffic was moving five miles an hour, so it was easy to see her. Melvin fell in love, too, she was a stunning beauty and she was in such distress. Robert would beg to find a hetero man who didn't feel obligated to helping her.

His phone rang and it was the home office. The game was nearly sold out; by current estimations it would top out in 48 hours. He always put player number caps on his games as they always had prizes to give out and he felt it his duty make sure that if people were shelling out so much money, they should have reasonable chances to win. He was very reluctant to bring it up to five million, so he had added incentives. He hung up with all the possibilities racing in his head. Last year he made sixteen million on merchandise alone.

Robert's mind drifted back to the now and he looked for his damsel in distress, but her lane had moved ahead and he felt cheated as he never got one last look at her. He admonished Melvin, "You let her get away."

"You do realize that you are very rich and can buy love, you don't have to be lonely."

Robert admonished, "Same to you, and I'm not lonely, I have you. The only way it will work for me Melvin is if she has no clue I'm rich when we meet. Otherwise, I will never feel loved the way I really want. I would have made one exception and that was for her. And you let her get away."

Melvin peevishly admitted, "I regularly have Thai Massages and one of the girls there genuinely likes me and she thinks I'm just a limo driver with no money."

"Interesting Melvin. My advice is, if you like her, then sweep her off her feet and out of there and don't worry about what her occupation is or was. Besides, after this year, you will be even richer than the two million I gave you; what a wonderful surprise that would be for her, especially if she has ever had to touch your feet."

Melvin laughed, "You know Robert, every time I test your humanity, you not only show me how amazing of a human you are, but you always add some element, or make some comment that waylays my apprehensions in a way no one has ever done before."

Robert started to smirk and giggle to himself.

The big man acted miffed, "What, do I sound corny or something?"

"No Melvin, as a matter of fact, you sound very, very smart. I don't think you realize just how smart you sound nowadays."

"Cute, now you've made me an egghead."

"Just try to catch *my* woman so I can propose right here on the freeway. Then we can have a double wedding."

* * *

Andy had a truck with a double cab that afforded some cover. After promising his dog he would be back for him, Matt and Doug left Luke and Storm back at the dock, riding in the back seat, as it had tinted windows. They drove across a very bustling Anacortes. Andy informed them that they do get their share of tourist traffic as the ferries ran out to the San Juan Islands from their port, but nothing like what they were seeing now.

Andy looped around some side streets and pulled up at the back of the parking lot where there were a lot of people around, but Matt and Doug were able to slip out and duck into the ground floor garage, hopping a small retaining wall. Matt knew the plan so there was no need to talk as they made their way up toward the front of the garage nearest the front doors. There was a throng outside and now he heard it for the first time. He heard chanting for Matt. *Interesting . . .*

Then he heard something else as they were making their way around the front of a van in a semi-crouch. It was a chant for Tom. *Even more interesting . . .*

Doug looked at him, nodded, and headed toward the ER, but not diagonally from their current position. He crossed the inside lot horizontally and then headed to the door at a straight angle, away from Matt. The affect was immediate and every person in the vicinity swarmed Doug as he made his way to the ER door, acting surprised by all the attention.

As soon as all eyes were on him, Matt made his way across the road in front and entered the hospital lobby where he had talked to Doug a few hours before. He would have been free and clear if the hospital security hadn't lined up inside. After producing identification, he had to sign in, as all visitors did. They gave him a badge and then he left, but it was not lost on him that the autonomy he had enjoyed was over. Those people recognized him and the look was hard to describe, somewhere between, "Awe" and "Disbelief."

That realization brought another and so on, and it wasn't long before he realized, *my life from now on is going to be in a glass house under a microscope.*

The time away from here had let him semi-forget the horrors that awaited him just up the elevator. He was heading to that elevator when he saw the "Chapel" sign. He stopped where he was and stared at the sign. He detested people who were nonreligious and then suddenly found their faith in moments of crisis.

Of course, that wasn't exactly his case now, was it? God had been calling him and he'd been listening. That's the confounding part, he'd answered the call, and he'd done as commanded.

As if his feet were going to defy his stubborn willed mind, the next thing he knew he was facing the alter in the small chapel. No one was there in the physical sense, but there was a cross with Christ on it. Matt had never felt that statue more alive than he did now. Apparently this hospital stood up to the many complaints it must have received from other "short changed" religions that were not represented.

He had never been good at this stuff and he had to keep his anger in check, which was probably how many people felt as they stood there. He did a good job of that until he'd made it half way across the room and his eyes came upon Jesus on the cross. He stared at the statue of Christ for so long that it made him emotional.

At first he was contrite for not being more overt in announcing that he had been chosen as he'd never mentioned it to a single living soul these past two years, afraid of what he would look like to the people in his life. Then anger coursed out of him in a way that even took him by surprise. A person could only take so much and then they just exploded.

His lord and savior took the entire brunt of the out-lashing. He felt indignation at being a pawn in a cosmic game that he never wished to be a part of, but willingly sacrificed himself just to protect his family—only to apparently have them killed anyway, just like Pablo's. That thought wasn't lost on him. Barbecuing his mortal enemy with a laser from the sky did not bring anyone back. The rest of the world might be safer and sleep tonight, but not him, he was going to lose everything. Matt ended up doing the one thing to God that one just doesn't do. He put an ultimatum on his Lord.

He vehemently informed the statue of Christ that if he wanted him as a servant, then okay, he'd accepted, but to take all that was dear to him was too much! He understood that good and evil existed, and that evil had done this to good since the dawn of time, but this time, this one man was taking a stand.

He told the statue that he knew he could be heard and he knew he'd been given direction, but he now wanted to be the one to inform. Looking at the fixed stare, but knowing it was much, much more than an unanimated piece of porcelain, he gave his version of things.

"If you want me to do your bidding then you will give me one more sign and you will save my family. If my wife and son die, then I am going to take all my money, buy a house in the woods with no TV or radio, and I'm going to check out. I'm going to take my free will and turn my back on humanity and you. All I ever hear about is a compassionate and graceful God. And all I ever see is a world of suffering and misery.

"You tap me and tell me to help the world, but do it without wrath. Yet you bring nothing but wrath to me? I know I'm not the only person to be totally confused by your actions and I know I'm not the only person who has threatened to turn his back on the whole thing. Only I'm not turning my back because of my lack of belief, I'm going to turn my back as a conscience objector. I never realized that answering my call to you was going to result in so much horror for the people that I love.

"If I had known, then I would have gone a different path. Of course, one look at history should have told me all I needed to know. So to be clear, there is no reasoning with me, there are no messages that will make me change my mind, other than Jan and Jon waking up normal."

Matt made the sign of the cross, bowed to the Alter, and left. A few minutes before he headed into this scene of absolute horror with the added impediment of massive guilt, but as he pushed the elevator light, he realized his tirade gave him something he needed internally, and that was someone to blame other than himself. He'd been carrying the burden of all this when in fact, he had a co-conspirator who was very culpable in what had happened here. Why does God always get a pass?

He left the chapel and headed left out of the elevator toward ICU, the door was open and he could see nurses bringing in equipment. After washing his hands thoroughly he entered the ward and made his way to the special isolation room Jan and Jon were now in. Dr. Singh was looking Jan over. He looked up at Matt with a renewed respect, but also a new sadness.

"Glad you made it back. There's been a development."

"What's going on?"

"Their vitals are dropping at a slow but steady pace. I had to cancel their flight, Matt. They are not stable enough to fly anymore. I airlifted samples to the CDC Quarantine Station in Seattle. They have a lab there equipped to identify over seven hundred and fifty known neurotoxins. I also have a cousin in Brazil right now and he's working in this field. Currently, I forwarded him their readings for his input. Until then, it's a waiting game."

"If you knew the person who did this like I do, Dr. Singh, then you would know that if there are seven-hundred and fifty known agents, then the one we are looking for here would be number seven-hundred and fifty one. He's not known for making mistakes or having mercy, Doctor, and he told me they were as good as dead."

"Good as dead, Matt, is not the same as dead. Pablo Manuel might have claimed to know God, but he is not God, Matt."

"That's for sure Dr. Singh, he is not God."

"Listen, my cousin, Mansoor, he is the smart one in the family. He's way too smart to be a simple neurosurgeon. His company is trying to cure Alzheimer's itself! We have time, Matt, not much, but we have time."

"What will happen if they don't make it?"

"If you mean will they be in pain, I don't think so. I believe they will just no longer be able to breath, as their respiratory system will shut down. Matt, let me ask you something, have either of them had a cold lately?"

"Yes, actually, they both did over the weekend."

"Were they taking any cold medicine?"

"They were both taking Benadryl. Jan took Nyquil the last two nights. Why?"

"It's the old good news, bad news, Matt. The good news is some anti-histamines can help block toxins. The bad news would be if those weren't present, where would we be? For now, it's a good news thing, so let's take our victories where we can get them. We need you to leave for a few minutes, please, as we have to have several people that need to be in here all working at once."

Walking down the hall in a stunned disbelief, Matt meandered into the ICU waiting room. He was alone, but the TVs were blaring the madness of today's events. Here he was again. In the matter of a few hours, his entire world had been completely undone.

His parents were dead, his wife and child were in imminent peril and he had killed his other woman and their unborn child with a single gunshot two years prior. He was going to be all alone in this world. Uncle Bob died last year and that was it, the only extended family he had. He sat with his head in his hands, as defeated men do. He was contemplating where he would choose his wilderness refuge when his phone vibrated in his pocket. It was Doug; they had exchanged numbers earlier.

He answered it, "Hey."

"How are things up there?"

"Their vitals have fallen and they are not able to fly anymore. They've moved them to ICU. We've turned to the CDC and one of the doctors here has a cousin who might be able to help from Brazil."

"Well, I've got *some* good news for you, Matt. Your parents are alive."

"What?! How can you know this, Doug?"

"Because a good friend of mine works for the FAA." His tone indicated that they were more than friends. "She was on site to help people who were caught in the middle of all this madness. There were two events in Kingston today so the ferry was over capacity and not everyone made it on, some had to wait for the next ferry. Once everything happened, those people waiting for the next ferry were stuck in the middle and then evacuated right out of their cars. As they were getting people back to their evacuated cars later on she came across your dad, Matt. He and your mom are alive. Samantha checked their IDs, Don and Sherry Holsinger."

"Where are they now?"

"Getting an escort here."

"Will you wait for them for me?"

"Of course. Should I brief them?"

"If you could, Doug, it would help, I'm sure."

"Things are swelling outside. Everyone knows you're here as one of the security people must have blabbed that you came in."

"Don't tell me, it's a lynch mob coming for me for causing all this."

"No, Matt, quite the opposite. It appears you have become the new gamer Messiah—on top of everything else you have going on. You went and lived the game, and now a third of that crowd have signs that read Holsinger/Hurst or are just bursting with some kind of support for Tom/Matt. It's like you're two people. I've never seen anything like it, Matt. They sure forgot about me in a hurry, let me tell you."

"Doug, I've been two people for so long now the lines are blurred. Please tell them thanks, but they need to be respectful and leave. My family is fighting for their lives here, Doug. What the hell is wrong with people?"

"That's just it, they're not here to bother you, as they are here to prop you up. A lot have candles now and it's turned into a huge prayer and support group out there. Of course, the media whores are there, but otherwise, it would appear people really care about what happens to you and your family."

"Well, Doug, I hope their prayers can be heard, we're going to need them."

Just then a plump, professionally dressed woman appeared in the room. She had dirty blonde hair that fell shoulder length in soft curls that matched her beige skirt, a square body which Matt thought could block for any running back in the NFL, and sported flat shoes that fit very thick legs with cankles to match stuffed into some support hose. While she smiled, he could tell that that wasn't her norm.

"Hi Matt, I'm Patricia Sinclair, the hospital Administrator. I came up here to ask you a favor at a time when no one should be asking favors."

"And what favor would that be, Patricia?"

"Could you please address the crowd and kindly ask them to assemble in the park just two blocks from here? It's a very unsafe situation out there, and we are really concerned for our patients and visitor's safety. I know it's a lot to ask."

Matt was going to answer her with a civil reply, although he considered the other route, when Dr. Singh went running by out in the hall at a good clip. Never one to waste time slack jawed gawking, he got on his feet, and with a noticeable limp, ran after the doctor, leaving the stunned Administrator to be the slacked-jawed gawker.

* * *

What a cluster fuck this was. Jim Jensen had never seen anything like this without a protest going on. The plaza square was besieged with people—virtually a person on every single spot one could park one's butt. He was standing on the north side of the office that faced the entrance to the hospital and he noticed that the building had been locked up tight.

To his right was another four-story building like the one he was in front of, and to the left was a five-story parking garage. There were people lined up on the railings for the garage, but not on the top as the setting sun was hitting that spot. People were filling the first three levels currently, but no one was lined up on the far end of the parking garage as the medical building had a few trees between itself and the garage, obscuring that view. Jim could get into the parking garage and find a spot, he was fairly sure of it, and by the look of things, that was the best he was going to get.

He made his way around the back of the building with his odd-shaped pack slung over one shoulder. He observed the path that would take him into the parking garage and as he was walking through the landscaping he caught a break. A curious security guard had opened an exit door near the corner and was smoking as he watched the crowd of reporters talking to a passenger from the plane (at least that was Jim's assumption based on the non-professional attire).

The guard was tall, maybe six-foot six, and he had his left arm high on the door with his right shoulder holding him up on the wall. He had quite the wingspan and fortunately his back was to Jim. It was decision time and the decision was to go for it. Just like London Bridges when he was a kid, he slid right under the transfixed guard as the media show went on, much to the man's entertainment. It was fortunate for the guard he'd made it undetected, otherwise it was going to turn into the part of London Bridges, where "they all fall down." He then realized he was mixing up his nursery rhymes, but the point was the same, the guy would have been in a world of hurt.

Jim silently made his way up the fire exit, finding the roof's exit door unlocked and not alarmed. He was able to find the perfect spot up there to stay hidden while doing his reconnoiter. He first meticulously spied every vantage point for counter-snipers and then started checking the crowd. He was a bit frustrated as it was hard doing the work of a whole Secret Service team by himself.

He turned on his tracking pad. Matt was still inside of the hospital, but his dot was moving fast, like he was running. *Man, this guy never stopped*. The beacon finally settled in the southwest corner of the building.

He went back to scanning faces with his binoculars, and every time he saw one of interest he'd push the button and the face was digitally recorded and sent into TJAC's mainframe computer. They spared no expense in their acquisition of data and therefore TJAC had access to some of the best face recognition software money could buy. *So far nothing*.

To the right was the other building identical to his and true to form there was a guard smoking just outside of an exit door on the southeastern part of the backside. Jim could see from his vantage point that he was also crowd watching. It seemed that security was prepared for trouble, as many of the Anacortes police department were on hand and had formed up near the hospital entrance, as well as locking off these two buildings.

At this point in the fall season, the greater Seattle area will stay light until nine o'clock or later, and that was a long four hours from now. Jim Jensen settled in, accepting the concept that he had known since his first minutes in the military, "hurry up and wait."

* * *

Traffic finally cleared enough as they got out of the greater Seattle metropolitan area. Once that happened, sanity returned. Robert was still reminiscing about the phone call he received from the President shortly after leaving Portland. Melvin answered the phone, a number given for Robert, but which was really Melvin's cell phone.

He had answered and slightly stuttered, which caught Robert's attention as Melvin stated, "I have the President on hold."

Robert had to ask, "The President of what?" It was a reasonable question, anyone would have asked it. Of course, not everyone would have gotten the answer, "The President of the United States, Robert."

Melvin simply handed his phone over and in a near whisper, Robert said, "Yes, Mr. President."

At first it was quite formal, as the President had no idea what his and Matt's true relationship was all about, if Robert were a true friend or someone looking to cash in on Matt's notoriety. Robert was looking at the change of scenery as Melvin exited I-5 and headed toward Anacortes. *Once President Caulfield learned how close we were his tone sure changed, that's for sure.*

President Caulfield was a smart man and Robert noticed that he asked very good questions, especially about the true nature of *American Pride*. Apparently his interest was sparked when he heard the premise, yet there was a long silence, and then he said coyly, "Special Interest will not like that very much."

Robert's reply was a cool, "They're not supposed to, Sir, as we're going after them with both barrels." He wouldn't have described the President's emotion as elated because it was hard to read people over the phone, especially a politician; but he would have said that the President *sounded* elated at the prospect of taking it to the greedy. This honestly surprised Robert, as he would have thought by now President Caulfield would have been in cahoots with the lot of them, after all, he'd been there long enough now.

And then a terrifying thought hit him as he looked at his only friend driving them to their destination, *I'm way out of my league here and if I'm not careful, I'll get us both killed.*

Of course, if the leader of the free world was a man of his word, then they had nothing to worry about, because he promised nothing. He offered no aid, just good luck, but the implication was, there would be no resistance either; no low-brow federal tactics to stall their growth or any such hindrances. By the results of the pre-release record sellout, Robert wouldn't need luck, he just needed a few Americans, like their table of five, to stand up and be counted.

Of course, if he was wrong, then he just tipped his hand to the enemy. Could that endearing Southern gentleman be a cold-blooded liar?

Robert was still deriding himself when they made the turn toward the hospital and suddenly had to stop the car. The police had the street blocked off and were sending everyone back. Melvin deftly turned left onto a side street where they found a park not two blocks from the hospital. Every stall was taken, but Melvin made his own stall at the end of one row. As they walked through the lot, Robert spied something that got his attention immediately. In the last Handicap stall was a familiar GMC behemoth, and of course it bared no handicap placard, which he assumed it wouldn't.

As they approached the hospital grounds, Robert was having a walk through an acid trip ala *Lucy in the Sky with Diamonds*. There was a very large number of what one would—for lack of a better term—call nerds here who were pouring in from Seattle, Bellingham, and even north of the border. All of them held some kind of support for Holsinger/Hurst, either in spirit or on some handmade sign in support of their hero warrior and game innovator messiah, Matt Hurst.

It didn't get less weird, it only got more like the song, as Robert was literally walking around inside an actual tipping point right before his eyes. It was happening and the thing they built was already taking on a life of its own right here. Once it did, they would be ready to take on the Special Interest Beasts, and Robert knew from every comic book he'd ever read that beasts don't die easily, *or fairly.*

He was a coward at heart, but actually seeing this kind of support gave him courage that he never knew he had. Then it happened—the signifier. He saw a poster that had a heart on it, and on the heart was written, "Hurst/Leme 2016."

Robert got more than a twang of guilt as he had created this. Regardless, he didn't know that Tom was Matt, he simply wanted Tom so badly that he shucked convention and went to a reporter for help. Now he was in the middle of it, like it or not. Melvin elbowed him as a very hot nerd girl walked by wearing a *Top of the Heap* t-shirt. *This was definitely getting interesting.*

* * *

Dr. Arshad Singh was heading to his office to talk to his cousin as Matt caught up with him. Connected to Mansoor via Skype, they sat and listened to Arshad's cousin from Brazil. The CDC had kept their word and sent him their data. Mansoor was *the* expert on this exact type of neurotoxin, and in fact, he had just published a paper on this type of agent not a few months before.

He edified them that this type of toxin was one that breaks through the blood brain barrier. At that point, Dr. Singh side-barred and explained to Matt that this was why their cold medicine helped them initially, as antihistamines had been shown to help deflect toxins away from that blood barrier. Mansoor concurred and congratulated his cousin on the astute observation.

Matt listened and wanted to shout, "Enough with the niceties already," but wisely restrained himself. Mansoor got back on track, "Anyway, there is a group of former Russian and American weapons scientists who have gotten together to find a cure for Cerebral Palsy. During their research they stumbled upon an antidote for the nasty neurotoxin BoNT.

"It is widely thought that our jihadist friends will most likely end up with this weapon one day and these scientists are trying to get out in front of it with the antidote. I know they were working off a grant, and I know they were starting their own company. Yes, here it is, I was pretty sure they were on the West Coast somewhere. Yes, it's San Francisco. Their company's name is CCP; no idea on what the acronym stands for."

Dr. Singh said, "We need to get a hold of these guys right away." Then he addressed the Skype image of his cousin, "Thank you for giving us some hope here, Mansoor."

Matt extended his sincere thanks as well and then Mansoor was gone after his final condolence to Matt and his family.

Dr. Singh looked at Matt and asked, "Do you have some favors you can call in?"

Matt nodded, "I can definitely do that."

Agreeing to meet in his family's room in a few minutes, Matt stepped out to make the call he'd been avoiding since Chase handed him a dossier a month ago. He was supposed to do a job, but he refused, and ever since, his life had been on a continued downward spiral.

Somehow in the midst of it all, he'd forgotten to be loyal. He should have known that Chase would never have set him up, or tried to harm him in any way. His leap of faith was activating the locator, and his reward was melting the world's smartest man—and biggest killer— even though activating that locator conceded a point and he had to bow his head to his master in the process. It also wasn't the same as a phone call.

The phone rang and Chase picked it up on the second ring. "The prodigal son returns."

"Yes, I guess I had that coming. Sorry for not initially believing in you."

"You don't owe me an apology, Son, I owe you. Our counsel at TJAC wanted a test, they thought you were too likely to have a predisposition for unnecessary violence."

"What kind of test, Chase?"

"In Mexico, the bullets had no primers. There was a sensor in the trigger as well. We even knew you were practicing the night before."

"So if I pulled the trigger on a drug lord, I'm out? What happened when I didn't?"

"Well, first of all, he wasn't a drug lord, Matt, he was an actor. It was the only way, Son. The only way the Board would accept you back and I let them do it. For that, I am sorry. If I might ask, what changed your mind about coming in?"

"Whoever attacked me at the hospital missed the shot. I knew that if it was you that wanted me dead, Jim Jensen would not have missed."

"I can't argue with that logic. Now I assume you have another reason for this call?"

Feeling slightly bashful for being as easy to read as if he were Chases' teenage son, Matt told him the story he'd just heard from Mansoor and like all good father figures, Chase was on it before they hung up. But before they did hang up, Chase gave Matt a solemn promise, "I will never turn my back on you, Son. If you can count on nothing else in this world then you can count on that."

Tears running down his face, Matt said, "Thank you for believing in me, even when I didn't deserve it."

He hung up the phone and turned around to find Doug and his parents standing there. His face was a mess and he really didn't want them to see him like this—he honestly could not remember the last time he'd caught a break. They hugged for a very long time, tears fell, and the phrase, "I love you" was used so many times Matt felt he was breaking it.

Matt let them know that they needed to be prepared because it was not easy to see Jan and Jon as they were. Dr. Singh had been able to set it up so they could be together in ICU. As they turned to leave, Matt's hospital administrator friend, Patricia, was there, apparently persimmons were on sale and she had a hankering, as her mouth was so taut it was puckered.

"Patricia, I'm sorry to have run off like that; but as you could see, Jan's doctor ran by out in the hall and I needed to speak with him."

"I know, Mr. Hurst, and we would normally never broach a subject like this to a family under duress such as yours, but I don't think you really understand how serious this has become."

Patricia gestured for them to head over to a window in the hallway and Matt looked out on a scene that he couldn't believe. It was evening, but not quite near sundown yet. The shadows were falling on the square below and it gave an odd resonance to the overall hue of the atmosphere; it was like he was wearing sunglasses, but he had none on. There were so many people that they flowed all the way down the street he'd come up earlier. *They numbered in the thousands, maybe five thousand or so; it was crazy.*

"You understand our concern now. There's a park two blocks over that way, if you could just address them and ask them to please have some compassion and move over there."

He looked at his Dad for guidance, "What do you think?"

"Go take care of it; we'll stay and watch Jan and Jon."

Matt looked at her and capitulated, "Okay, Patricia, let's go take care of this quickly."

* * *

The information was coming in from so many places that a man with a lesser mind would be going nuts. Ray Callahan was still trying to piece it all together, but for some reason the President needed Director Barnett to play ball about Manuel's death.

Information was on a need to know basis, and not all information was necessary for Ray to know, so he knew he had been kept out of the pieces that would have glued it all together for him. But one thing was for sure; it was a very odd day when General Steve Hatten agreed or conspired with President Lawrence Caulfield. It was well known that the two disliked and distrusted each other very much.

Of course, he could pump his wife for this info, she'd be in the know. The way he'd caught himself saying that, it didn't sound healthy. Ray knew that he needed to keep his compulsion in check. He was a big enough boy to know that one was not invited to every party, and no one liked a "party crasher."

His secretary's phone buzzed; it was Eric Barnett, and he wanted to see Ray in his office right away.

Ray stepped into Eric's very sanitized and impersonal office, "Hey, Boss."

"Ray, how are you? I just got something across my desk that I don't remember us talking about. Can you shed some light?"

"Some light, Sir?"

"Yes, specifically, why are you approving one of Fredericks patients to be released back into active duty and then sending that person out on an immediate assignment without as much as a memo?"

Ray was not used to getting his ass chewed and he responded with a snarky side that he rarely showed, "I followed protocol Eric, which is why you are informing me that you know. Don't forget that we had discussed this earlier and you knew that I was choosing to keep my decision to myself for the time being."

"You know damn well, Ray, that we are all overrun here and this required a phone call."

"Well if I didn't before, I sure do now, Eric."

"Not good enough, Ray, you know better than to try the 'ask for forgiveness' approach. Sorry, but if this little personal decision you made goes FUBAR, then it's your swan song, and even your wife won't be able to protect you."

Tensions had been building between them lately, but he never thought he would see the day when Eric Barnett would threaten his job or throw his wife into the argument when he knew she had nothing to do with any part of his decision process. Having Kim in his life did have one big liability, and it was akin to being the fat kid growing up, as no matter how good your comeback was to a bully, all they had to do was go to the lowest common denominator. "Fatso."

Of course, in his case, it was the, "wife in high places" remarks he must endure as soon as someone was out of ammo and wanted to win the argument.

Eric was openly not happy about his newly appointed Department Head marrying someone in the President's Cabinet, but what could he say. It was frowned upon, but not against the rules. That was when the undermining game started though—the let's undermine and toss a negative on almost every thought out of Ray's head. Well, if that was the way he wanted to play this . . .

"You'd be surprised at the things Kim can do, Eric."

His boss had that hangdog look that he could exaggerate when needed. His head was very round and oftentimes there was a small film of sweat on his smooth cap when things got really stressful. He was able to compartmentalize his face in a way that made his eyes turn like a hound and a furrowed brow that had enough lines to look like a mini pack of hot dogs. He could be very sullen when brought to the precipice of rage, Ray noticed, and apparently his last comment was enough to get him there.

"Be that as it may, Ray, you made this decision alone and you will stand behind it alone. Dismissed."

For once Ray had nothing to say. He had never been dismissed before. Stunned and not sure what to say, he got up and left without a word.

He knew Eric was right; it was a rash decision he'd made without one word of advice from a room full of advisors that worked for him round-the-clock. He'd just sent a newly recovered sniper into a mass of civilians to protect a civilian. Knowing Malcolm's case from Frederick's description, maybe it wasn't the best assignment to send him on. The timing and Malcolm's physical proximity to the situation made his decision the most pragmatic, he was sure of it. But as Ray sat back and looked out over the grounds, he had the gut feeling that what he had set in motion could, in fact, go very wrong.

He was in a business where "what have you done for me lately?" ruled. So trying to stand on his past achievements would get him nowhere—not that he hadn't been there before, but it was never easy being in between a rock and a hard spot, even when you're Ray Callahan.

He mused, *that's why I make the big bucks.*

* * *

The crowd was coming from everywhere, but Malcolm caught a break as the sun was going down, and for the next thirty minutes or so, people would not want to stand at the top because of the glare. They were heading down the stairs in the northwest corner nearest the hospital.

The back windows of the van were mirror like and he'd seen several people walk by and look right in, mostly checking their hair. In retrospect, this might not have been the best place for him to be. There were so many innocent lives everywhere, one false move and another innocent person dies at his hands. He knew Frederick was competent, *but would a competent doc really send him out here?*

He had his field glasses out and it looked like a TV crew was building a small stage up front. *I wonder what's going on?*

* * *

Tears were welling in her eyes as Lauren leaned against the back of the building. There was a crush of people in the square and she had no hope of getting closer; plus some idiot just bumped into her and it sent her confidence spiraling downward. Her back was on fire and she was not even able to get another picture for her own story, *what a drag.*

She needed to resign and get out, as the jerk that bumped her sent her the message that her physical limitation was very real. That was how she ended up on the wall. She was too fragile to be moving in any kind of a crowd. She pushed herself off the wall and started to move, but before she got even a step away, the fire exit door opened with a resounding boom. At the same time, the crowd started cheering and everyone focused on something going on toward the front of the hospital. Then she heard it: Matt Hurst was speaking; it had to be him.

In the doorway was a security guard. He was about five foot four and looked to be Vietnamese, if Lauren wasn't mistaken. He broke out a cigarette and started to smoke while trying to see the action. He could only see the back half of the crowd from his vantage point, so she determined he was just girl watching after seeing his eyes track a girl's ass who was nearby; he obviously could care less what was going on with Hurst. That played right into the move she decided to try. She approached him as coquettishly as possible and asked him if he would let her take some pictures from the roof?

His replay was stern and in perfect English, "I can't do that or I could lose my job."

She realized that if a guy thinks he really has no shot with a girl, he wouldn't be as likely to be falling over himself to help her. She had already thought of this possibility, so she had gathered her cash together for a bribe. Thanks to her dad restocking her bank account, she had a little bit less than four hundred dollars on her. Her new friend in the world smiled and decided that the money was sufficient enough to take the chance; so they waited for the right moment and Lauren slipped in and was then cautiously headed up to the roof via the stairwell.

The trudge was arduous, the camera strap eating into her neck like she was at the end of a day of shooting wildlife in the bush. When one was this messed up, even climbing a stairwell could be too much. It seriously took her two minutes to get to the second floor, with two more to the roof hatch.

Her escort realized that she was not one hundred percent healthy and had a look of consternation on his face as he asked her, "Are you sure you're able to do this?"

She assumed he was more concerned about having to give the money back than about her well being, "I'll be fine, just moving slowly due to a car accident."

The slow moving was making the guard antsy. He was expecting this to be a quick thing, and then he'd move on with his money, the end. He certainly wasn't expecting this to take so long. Escorting a nearly handicap person was trying his patience; she could see it on his face. When they finally got to the last flight of stairs, he told her he was going to the top and open it up. He'd prop open the door too, as he wanted to go see what was going on.

Lauren could see the change in him after they'd heard several large roars from the crowd while in the stairwell. It took another three minutes for her to get to the door.

Outside was still light out, but the sun was minutes from making its final decent of the day. The clouds had that amazing quality to them that happened only at this time of day, like you were in heaven and watching the heavenly light filter through them as you approached the Pearly Gates.

She heard Hurst speak again and the crowd cheered in response. Lauren was trying her hardest not to mess up and trip, but her anticipation was at a level she had never experienced before, so she forced herself to carefully negotiate the best path to take. Directly in front of her were two large square contraptions. If she chose the left path, she would come out on the left corner of the building, farthest from the action. If she chose the right, the angle would be wrong.

The monstrosity in front of her was making a racket that suggested it was an air conditioning unit. Lauren was being very careful not to make sudden movements, while her very concerned escort dumped her for the action. The rooftop was loose gravel and she gingerly made her way over to the opening in the middle.

As soon as she got there, she'd wished she had never come. A man dressed in camouflage the same color as the air conditioning unit was pulling a knife out of the guard's neck. His face was painted in the same metal grey as his clothes and his blackened eyes were now fixed on her.

* * *

The crowd was beyond belief. Robert turned to Melvin, "How will we get up there?"

Melvin smiled at his peevish leader, "I have a small confession."

"And what would that be, Melvin?"

Melvin expounded sheepishly, "I used to be into death metal music; my favorite band was Slipknot."

Robert stared blankly at his protective hulk, obviously not getting it.

"Robert, I used to go to these general admission concerts but my goal was always to touch the stage. I know how to do this. Just follow me and don't back down, I'll be watching my back for you, too."

With that, and much to Robert's amazement, Melvin expertly exerted his will on one person at a time and they began their march toward where Matt was already speaking. One unlucky gentleman tried to take umbrage with them and Melvin's finger found his chest a comfortable place to rest until the man seemed to be suddenly okay with everything.

Robert couldn't believe the number of these people who were tied to his game. He even saw his name on a poster that someone they bumped out of the way was holding.

Matt was talking to the crowd. He said if people remained civil, he was going to come out later and talk if his family somehow recovered. But they needed to move over to the park until that time, and if that time never came, then they needed to understand what that meant and go home and pray for him.

He was tearfully saying that his family was in there fighting for their life and he needed to be singularly focused. Melvin finally muscled them up front and Robert got his first live view of Matt Hurst.

Some people don't meet your expectations when you finally meet them in person, but Matt here seemed to exceed Robert's expectations, and the way he spoke so earnestly and right to the people, Robert was pretty sure a career in politics would not be out of the question. Matt paused and looked around. Just then he did a double take as he noticed Robert and Melvin.

* * *

Jim Jensen was watching the crowd and snapping pictures like mad, sending in image after image for a possible hit. Nothing. The sun was heading toward its last minutes in the sky and then things were going to get dicey after twilight. Fortunately, he brought a scope that would do nicely in sparsely lit areas and he'd already seen enough light poles in the vicinity to know that he should be okay.

At the base of the adjacent building, the back stairwell door swung open and an Asian guard stepped out and started to light up a cigarette. He was enjoying his smoke and looking at all the tail bouncing around as Jim saw him tracking girls more than once. Then, just like that, Matt was on the portable raised podium addressing the crowd. By the time he quickly glanced back at the door, the guard was gone. He scanned the crowd for anyone not intent on this speech, but found none.

He was looking at the crowd in front of the office to the right when he saw a slight movement on the roof above. He quickly looked over and saw his guard on the roof, watching the action; he didn't give off any kind of a vibe or have any habits a good assassin would have, but twice now he had looked back over his shoulder. *Why?*

* * *

Malcolm was scanning the crowd, looking for any body language or face that was malicious. He hadn't seen anything but admiration and tears. There was not one anti-Hurst group or person he could see. As he was looking toward the front, something caught him out of the corner of his eye when he pulled the spotting glasses back for a second. A security guard was standing on the roof of the building across from his position. After a moment of intense scrutinization, Malcolm determined that he was just another enthralled spectator. No real threat would be so overt.

Malcolm knew a trained man such as he would have found a way and it wouldn't have been from the crowd or an obvious rooftop either; he would have taken a distance shot. Of course, with Matt's position being shielded by the buildings, the parking garage offered the only real threat other than the two buildings rooftops. Malcolm was coming to the realization that he was going to have to take the pistol and redo the parking garage again, as his current method of searching was most likely a dead end.

Even if he were to take a shot from here, regretfully, he was sure there was no way to conceal his muzzle flash from detection. The way the sun was hitting the garage, even a single cigarette puff blown from this roof would be illuminated and exaggerated like a cloud from Heaven; anyone in the square would see it. Malcolm knew, of course, that it didn't matter so much to the good guy as it did to the hostile.

He was resolved to a change in his strategy when he decided to scan the building to his right one last time. He noticed an air conditioning unit and a generator, each standing about fifteen feet high, and each offered a blindside that he couldn't see behind. However, for one to take a shot at the target below, one would have to move up in his or her position enough to shoot over the lip of the rooftop. That would put them into play, and he determined that no one was there. He was about to stow his spotting glasses and get to his ground patrol when something on the top of the generator moved.

It might have been a pigeon as what he noticed was a very slight movement. Then his blood ran cold. There was a shooter—perfectly camouflaged—laying prone on top of the generator! He had missed him on several previous passes over of the area. *Damn!* He placed his spotter glasses in the case, carefully opened the right slide port on the van door and acquired his target. His rifle was a Sako TRG-S bolt-action rifle with a specialized .50 caliber round called a "whisper shot" that enabled him to shoot silently at a sub-sonic level, especially with his silencer attached.

As he detected moments ago, he might be able to circumvent the sound of the shot, but the sun was sending the perfect illumination on his location right now and there would be no hiding the tiny puff of smoke that the muzzle flash would emit.

Malcolm adjusted his breathing and was beginning to bring his finger to the trigger when he noted something he should have caught right away. *His target's rifle was not aiming at Hurst.*

* * *

Jim Jensen was not convinced that this apparently inept guard was just hanging out. The two furtive looks this guy made were troubling. Matt was talking and Jim was hearing the anguished voice. *The poor kid.* Unfortunately, Jim had to block the words as his concentration was on its highest level, but Matt's inflection seeped through, regardless of his ability to block Matt's words.

The security guard was quickly convincing him he was no threat when he discarded the cigarette he was smoking on the roof. *No hitter would be leaving cigarette butt DNA all over the place.* He was just about to restart his search when a camouflaged man appeared behind the guard, pulled him down backwards and ended him with a large knife. Jim steadied for the shot when the man moved toward the center of the roof, the air conditioning unit now in the way of a clean shot. His adrenal gland was working overtime and his stress level had peeked. *His hunch was right, someone still wanted his protégé dead . . .*

* * *

Malcolm had the target in sight and it would be an easy extraction, except the target wasn't currently a threat. His shooter was watching the guard on the next building. He looked to be protecting Hurst, too, unless he was just evaluating the possible threat of the guard to his shot.

If he was a hitter after Hurst, then he'd had more than ample time to get the job done. The thought that some other agency had sent this guy here was a cluster fuck beyond all comprehension. *Who the fuck sends two snipers to protect someone and doesn't at least tell one of them about the others existence?*

Malcolm then observed great distress come over his target. It was like watching a spectator at a boxing match. He was going to have to take his eyes off his target to find out what the hell was going on over on the adjacent roof. He deftly pulled out his spotter glasses from the case while never taking his eyes off the target. Once he had them firmly in his hand, then he quickly left his rifle on the bi-pod and looked to see what was distressing the other sniper.

He quickly caught sight of the back of a camouflaged man, in his right hand was a very large knife and he was heading toward the center of the roof, the guard was nowhere in sight. Suddenly, a woman appeared to the guy's left, his body had been blocking her. She was backing away to his left, which meant the air conditioning unit to the left of his new target was now blocking her. His new target was walking toward her location at a clipped pace now and was around the same corner as her four seconds later. *What the fuck is going on?*

* * *

As Matt made his way out of the elevator with the hospital Administrator, he saw something he was going to have to get used to. Notoriety. He was now a very famous guy that people knew where to find. He realized that he did not fully appreciate his previous autonomy until now. Passing through the "lobby of adulation" should have just been a primer for what came next.

In a stunned kind of trance, he walked out and was greeted by some producer who actually wanted to put makeup on him, which he immediately refused and pushed away.

Without further fanfare he was brought up to a podium and thrown to the lions. Immediately, the crowd erupted and Matt couldn't stop them for what seemed like forever. Finally he raised his voice in insistence. The crowd silenced and he addressed them.

"Thank you truly for supporting me here," his voice was loud and strong, so his lack of a microphone or bullhorn was okay. The over-stimulated crowd erupted again and he had to get control back once more by raising his voice, "I really appreciate what the message here is, especially on such a tragic day as this in American history. Many a family is trying to cope right now, including me. Until a few moments ago, I thought my parents were on that ferry, but thank God they are safe. Right now, that situation is playing out all over the place and my heart goes out to anyone going through that."

The emotionally charged situation was too much for Matt and he started to cry and couldn't continue for several moments. He regained some composure and re-addressed the now stoic crowd. A policeman handed him a bullhorn, but he refused. His voice was able to carry to all in the plaza.

"My wife and son were poisoned today by Pablo Manuel. I know this because he told me himself. They are fighting for their lives right now and there is little chance they will survive. So every minute I am here with you, I'm not with them. The hospital asked me to come out here and plead for you all to move to the park two blocks over that way," said Matt, pointing south. "The hospital is basically non-functional as a result of all your support of me.

"Please don't take this wrong, it certainly isn't meant to be offensive, but now is not the time for adulation. Now is the time for mourning— and for me personally, terror. As you all know, my life has been anything but easy to this point, and now it looks like I will have made the biggest sacrifice I've ever made for my country. Right now my wife and little boy are fighting for their lives because I chose to take on a madman. So we all need to keep perspective here.

"Now if you want to stay to support me, then I say thank you, but please don't add one more problem on this day for me. Please just go to the park and let the hospital function. If you really care, it is there you will pray for my family."

During the last part of this speech, Matt had tears running down his face. Never being one to hold emotions in when they needed to be let out, Matt was turning to leave when he heard a small pop that he'd heard before. The square was absolutely silent after his speech and to the untrained ear it could have been anything, but to his ear there was only one thing it could be and he was still alive, so that meant someone else was trying to kill him and Jim stopped the assassin dead.

He looked up to the place where he thought the sound came from and saw a tiny puff of smoke shining off the evening sun coming from the roof of the parking garage; his suspicion confirmed.

No one would have known and he would have made his escape back into the hospital if there weren't suddenly a loud scream from the exact place he had seen the smoke. The voice yelled, "Someone just shot a gun out of that van!"

It was like a light went on in a cockroach-infested room. In an instant, people turned into this frenzied machine of madness. Matt had been so stupefied that he hadn't even noticed the TV cameras. He was speaking to the crowd and in his naiveté had forgotten that this show was being played out live throughout the nation.

Before he could deal with the humility of a few hundred million people being witness to his emotional breakdown, once again, higher duty called him. If he didn't take control of this situation right now, then his country was going to be wounded in a way that would make them feel vulnerable for a generation or more.

To kill him would have been such a coup for evil—especially coming on this day, at a time like this time in his life, where to kick him on the ground would be the cruelest of insults. Not to mention it would make everyone feel the type of post 9/11 anxieties that all terrorists go for— like there was no safety for anyone.

So no matter how badly he wanted to be with his wife and child, he needed to take control of this situation right now. He stood back up to the podium and shouted in his most commanding voice, "STOP!"

* * *

Malcolm used the field glasses to quickly look back over to the distressed shooter on the roof to his right who was now off the generator and forsaking cover was making his way to the southwest corner of the roof. He was obviously looking for an angle to get the target that was on the other roof. He made a decision—and that was that the distressed shooter was somehow a friendly.

He replaced the spotter glasses and opened the left side doors port. He fixed his rifle on the other roof just in time to see the female walking backwards obviously pleading with an unknown figure. As she was backing up, she tripped backwards to the rooftop. The unknown assailant suddenly became visible, appearing in full-camouflage. The assassin hesitated a split second before he made a move to leave his feet and plunge his knife into her.

Malcolm's world froze. It was only a millisecond before he took the shot, but in that fraction he was able to replay his whole career right up to point where he killed the kid in Afghanistan. He joined the ranks of the CIA to help be the executor of justice in an unfair world. He hated that the tough guys always pick on the weak. Although it all went bad in Afghanistan, that didn't change what he was here for in the first place, and why he fought so hard to prove to Frederick that he was over it. In that small fraction of time, he was able to right his perspective as he squeezed the trigger for what was surely a clean headshot. The crimson spray confirmed it so.

* * *

After seeing the guard attacked, and throwing all standard procedures aside, Jim scrambled off the generator that he was laying on and expeditiously made his way to the southern corner of the roof which would allow him an angle if the hostile showed himself again. In position, he could see the part of the adjacent roof past the left side of a probable generator unit. Although he still had a slightly obscured perspective, he could now at least see that side of the roof and if the shooter were going to try to get to Matt, then he would have to come into his line of sight.

Suddenly a woman appeared, walking backward and she was hysterical and pleading with the hitter that took out the guard. Jim was sure it was his target. The woman was Caucasian, rust colored hair, and was not moving right, like she was injured, Jim noted.

As she was backpedaling, she must have backed into an object that tripped her up and she went straight backward onto the roof. Jim tensed immediately as his camouflaged target came back into view, knife at the ready and heading to where the woman fell back. Jim pieced it all together in that small time frame. Guard one interrupted the shooter, but was dispatched in hopes of saving the opportunity, but the girl must have made her way to the roof for pictures—as Jim recalled a moment before she fell that she had a camera around her neck—so she stumbled onto his target that had just felled the guard.

Right as the camouflaged man was going to make his move to finish the woman, Jim steadied for the shot; his finger was flexing the trigger, but he had not depressed it yet. As he was in the final process of the shot, the man's face quite literally disappeared in a red spray. Jim heard the suppressed shot as it came from right over him to his left. He looked up and saw the small puff of smoke hitting the setting sun and magnifying it significantly. *There was a second shooter protecting Matt?*

Jim was still processing that information when a civilian on the top deck of the parking garage put two and two together and sounded the alarm.

The D.C. sniper case had warned people about the possibilities of someone shooting out the back of a vehicle like that. The resulting scream had the effect Jim thought it would, complete pandemonium. Then he saw something that made his heart swell and he forgot what the hell he was doing for the first time in his profession career.

It was not so much that he forgot; it was more like he had the realization that he was living a moment in history, one that would be replayed over and over again, but not to be missed live. Matt turned back around and did what every true leader was able to do. He commanded immediate attention.

* * *

"Stop what you people are doing right now! I don't want to see another person run. This is a perfect example of what the hell is wrong with us right here! First of all, I heard no gun report and if it were the kind of gun that was silenced, then I wouldn't be here anymore, would I? Because if someone is shooting anyone here today, it's either someone shooting me or someone protecting me, and I'm still here." Matt saw that stopped them. Now all eyes were on him again and it was time their ears got it too! *Enough of this sheep mentality!!*

This was it…the moment. He somehow knew that God would lead him to this moment, as he had faith. Faith. For all of Pablo's wisdom, he had very little faith. He was always trying to steer his destiny, where Matt had chosen to take the path of least resistance and not try to put his own spin on God's plan. He felt it now, as this was his moment to put forth a plan that had God's spirit at its core.

But the angst over his family had not subsided, for God was known to make sacrifices—or have others make them would be more specific. His Divine belief was going to override all other things here though, it just had to. In his memory, Matt was suddenly driving back from church with his parents when he was just sixteen-years old.

That day's sermon was about loving Jesus over all other things, about loving Jesus over even one's wife or children. Matt's parents had said that they understood this and they agreed, but he would not relent that point. He argued it from every angle he could until his dad had to finally kill the conversation completely. Matt argued that *if* God gave us the capacity to love and he made us in his image, then how could it be a sin to love one's wife as much or more than the being that created her? Weren't we all God?

It just never made sense to Matt, yet here he was living it out in a real life or death situation. He knew that to say what he had to say was going to take a speech, and time—time he did not have. Before he knew it, a microphone was placed in front of him and he now had an impromptu speaker system to address the crowd through, the speakers were on top of a news van.

As if there was any doubt he was going to go ahead with this, that doubt was laid to rest. Like Abraham, Matt was asked to forgo his instincts as a father and husband and do the Lord's bidding—or he was out of his mind; one of the two.

Contrite, yet resolved to get his diatribe out, Matt spoke to the crowd passionately. "Our reality as a country changed in nineteen sixty-three." He expected some feedback from the speakers, but this was a different blue-tooth world than the one he grew up in. "In November of that year, a sniper sent a message to all of us, and the message was, 'They kill the good guys.' And the first question everyone wants answered from that statement is, 'Who are *they*?'

"Most people think anyone who dares to say things like there is a 'They' have to be a conspiracy theory nut, or some other dismissive or derogatory remark designed to cause everyone else to disregard them and their thinking outside the box. Unfortunately the people deriding the brave and different would also be the people hiding it all. That's really the beauty of it—if you're the perpetrators.

"Unfortunately for people like me, there are some conspiracy theory nuts that are obviously mentally distressed individuals, like the Una-bomber. Such people have little or no connection to reality, and these are the people who the oppressors love the most, because they cloud the water, they make us all seem unbalanced. Once that happens, the masses will be less likely to believe the truth when it is presented."

As Matt paused and cleared his throat, a policeman handed him a bot-tle of water, which he took and drank half of. "That's where America is now, people. We're in trouble because we are now run by the 'They,' instead of our actual Government. We got so greedy and powerful that we have nearly destroyed the natural earth in less than two hundred years and have given away the power of our Government for money. And I am not talking about our great and honest President by the way, as he is just one man against an army. I am talking about our lawmakers.

"There is an obvious plan to erode our middle class and it is almost complete. Who is doing it, you ask? Who are *They*? If you don't know the answer to that question by this point in your lives, then shame on you, because you are the problem that's causing our great country to implode.

"The answer is the *One Percenters*; they created this and you created them. You bought their products as loyal customers, then, when their companies hit what would be a natural ceiling of growth, they hacked jobs to keep investors happy, and you let them; you kept buying. When it again reached its ceiling, they started taking their manufacturing overseas to make better profits. And that's where it went all wrong, people. That single issue is the one that we need to inspect.

"There is a difference between allowing countries to sell their products in our country and moving manufacturing out—a big difference. These companies are putting higher profits over being patriotic Americans, and you all let them get away with it by still buying their products."

Matt looked at the people in the front row for a second, then he realized another face in the crowd was familiar as Justin from his group was listening intently. He went on to say, "We all have, we're all guilty. We built the very thing that is now killing us, and those are multi-national conglomerates. They're a beast that doesn't count you as individuals, and they have no face of responsibility. You're just a marketing number to them. And now their Special Interest Army has taken over our Government. This is no conspiracy theory, it's a fact.

"Think about it people. We know that corporations have sent in their shills to bribe their way into legislature. In short, the rich guys are now controlling the people that write our laws. So, if that's true, every single law passed must have some advantage for them. Given that, what would you suppose would be the reason for our insane immigration laws? Assuming what I said is true, what do you think that reason would be?

"It's obvious that our immigration laws are a joke by world standards, so let me tell you my theory, if I may. I think it's because they know that if you separate us enough and don't enforce English as the only spoken and written language, then you have weakened us as a people because our freedom of speech and communication are a HUGE POWER. It's a power we all take for granted, but they understand that all too well.

"Why do you think the Iranian authorities always take away the cell phone relays during unrest? If keeping people from communicating is an act of repression, then having the ability to communicate is the opposite. My family emigrated here from Germany in the late 1700s; I did my family history. My family still honors many German traditions and my father speaks a little as well, but we are Americans first. The only reason that the recent immigrants to this country have all these laws passed to help them remain factionalized is because it's obviously in the best interest of the powers that control us.

"I grew up in a very multi-national, multi-cultural mecca in the San Francisco Bay Area, and anyone that has ever known me knows that I have not a racist bone in my body. I think we should all embrace different cultures. But let's face it, cultures don't run free countries, people do, and the people running this country are taking advantage of us. They don't care about the color of our skin, or our religion, or what cause we care about. These people have figured out that our parent's generation had about thirty percent disposable incomes, and now they're targeting ours to make sure they have it and we don't."

Matt was on such a role that he didn't dare to look at another face or a monitor; he had turned everyone into a blur as he went on.

"Although my family is waiting for a team of specialists right now and I have to be there, I am going to take another five minutes to tell you how we can fix it, but will anyone listen? Even when my sacrifice could be that I might never see my wife and child again . . . the first thing we have to realize is there can be no disagreement in the solution. The solution is simple, and if it's followed, it will work and it will work on the principle of the tipping point.

"One of the main powers of the One Percenters is that they get us to argue about everything. They get us to omit their treasonous acts and fight like idiots over the most mundane things. They've created pundit television to counter every good thought that might come out, and they push partisanship over patriotism. We must stop arguing! That's what the game *American Pride* is all about; and it starts with the second problem for me.

"If you want to know what that is, then look no further than the answer to observation number one, and today proves it, 'They always kill the good guys.' What am I saying, you ask? You want it in plain English? Then here it is. I'm not going to lie to you as you're used to nowadays. I'm also not going sugarcoat it so we don't offend any sect or people. To know me and know my words is to know a man who does not see people in colors, I just see us as all in the same boat, and the boat is sinking.

"Today, just a few moments ago, a person tried to kill me right in front of all of you. I can almost guarantee you that the person who perished moments ago was the very beast we speak of. I offered my life and the life of my family for my country. Only through the grace of God did I survive both encounters with Pablo Manuel, and these people were going to callously blow my head off right in front of you because they might not be able to make their shareholders expectations the next quarter if I'm able to pull this game off. If you're asking how I know all this, let me tell you."

Matt observed Robert's hulk in a stupefied trance, it was almost off putting as he continued, "Before the person screamed about a shooter I heard the silenced shot. I've had some training in this field now and I recognized it, faint as it was, the sound carried in this hushed plaza, which meant that my protector killed or deterred someone from killing me. For that reason, although the idea for *American Pride* was mine, I asked Robert Leme to not include me in the design team, as I inherently knew what was coming. Like that day in sixty-three when we lost Kennedy, I knew I would end up leaving a wife and child behind if I did this alone."

Matt fought back the misting that came from that thought, "So not only was Pablo Manuel trying to kill me, but the 'They' I've been speaking of must have tried, too. Either that, or maybe one last sheep follower, time will tell." He finally broke his unfocused outlook and gazed down to Robert and his hulking bodyguard and winked.

Matt re-addressed the crowd, "This is the beauty of what Robert is bringing to life in the game. *American Pride* is a real game with real prizes, but it's also a free market place governed by a counsel of eight. Working off our principle of 'They always kill the good guys,' we set up a counsel of eight, knowing it is much harder to kill eight people than it is one, much like the Hydra.

"Currently, there are only six at the counsel table, but that's by design. We decided to add real incentive and as part of the Grand Prize, we're going to give away at least one of those two remaining seats to a winner in the game. This game will be a virtual world, except that in this world, it is American made products only. If your character walks into a store to buy something, it can only be sold there if it was made in the USA.

"I hold no grudge against Robert; he was just trying to motivate a man he thought was afraid in Tom Holsinger. He had no clue it was me and that's why when presented with the opportunity to make my dream a reality, I had to turn Robert down. By that time, he had already given Scott Bailey the release with my name, and as he didn't know that my alias was Tom Holsinger, he assumed he was just prodding a reluctant man.

"I turned down the job then because I couldn't afford the notoriety; but before I leave all you people to go be with my wife and son, I need to ask Robert Leme if that job offer still stands."

Matt looked down at Robert and he said, "Yes," which Matt repeated loudly. The crowd cheered and he asked Robert to come up and say a word.

* * *

Robert Leme had been avoiding this moment his whole life. He never thought he would get a turn in this world because in his mind he was such a dislikable loser. Even after his success with *Top of the Heap*, he still felt like a loser. A lifetime of ridicule will do that to even the strongest of spirits. Robert felt embarrassed, though. Matt had just handled the fact that someone probably tried to kill him with great grace and bravery, yet he himself was too scared to even walk up to the podium.

Robert watched as several police cars sped through the parking garage up to where the person was alleged to have seen the shot. That person was still up there, but on the other side of the structure now, away from the van. Robert didn't have Matt's kind of bravery, but he did have something to say, as his idea had a time and that time was now. All he had to do was garner more nerve than he'd ever had in his entire life.

Frozen, eyes all on him, he suddenly felt two giant hands on his back, gently pushing him toward Matt and the microphone. Robert mused that Melvin was like a mother bird finally telling her fledgling to go out and fly. He reluctantly made his way up to Matt, who briefly embraced him as a greeting, not the customary handshake.

Trying not to focus on the thousand faces staring at him, Robert started with, "Matt is right, but what he doesn't know is I have a much grander idea now. Sometimes inspirational things spin off other ideas and I'm not ashamed to admit that Matt's idea spawned one that won't go away in my head." He looked at Matt, "I believe we can let Matt go to his family now and we can go to the park and re-set up this talk; then I will tell you all about it."

The crowd applauded as crowds do, but right when Robert got control back and was going to speak on, a shriek erupted over the crowd, sounding crazed and frenzied, "MURDERER!"

A woman was on the roof of the building to his left. When he put his glasses on, Robert had good eyesight and what he saw was very disturbing. She was splattered in a red substance that he supposed was blood and Robert thought she looked like Sissy Spacek in *Carrie* right after the bucket of blood was poured on her.

She yelled again, "You murdered my brother, you're no fucking good guy, you're a killer! You're nothing more than a no good killer!" Then she was gone. She disappeared back onto the roof. Robert looked at Matt, who looked more than concerned; he looked downright mortified at the accusation.

Robert tried to turn it around and addressed the crowd as if he was blowing that off to madness, "Looks like someone did a few too many mushrooms today, and unless the President of the United States is wrong, then Matt would have to argue that horrible accusation with her."

As it turned out, the distraction gave Robert a reprieve from the anxiety he was feeling and he was better able to articulate his thoughts now that he remembered Matt was his friend and he was here to not only support him, but to protect him. The latter reason ignited in him indignation and that was one thing in this world that brought the ire out in Robert Leme.

With a purpose he spoke now, "Matt's idea for *American Pride* was great, there's no doubt about it, but it was also the beginning of me realizing my own true calling. By creating the game counsel the way we have, no one person will have control, so stopping us by removing one of us will not work. Stopping all eight of us would, of course, but that would be taking the mask off of the people who would wish to stop us, so you won't see it happen that way—but make no mistake, the battlelines just got drawn.

"Matt's idea has brought me to my calling and I have realized how to make *American Pride* the most pivotal program ever written, at least for the survival of this country anyway. After paying off all the designers and production people, I am going to take all my profits for this game and..."

Right then the glass entrance doors to the building on Robert's left opened and the shrieking started once again. It was the girl from the roof and she was wailing, "You're no hero, Matt Hurst, you're no hero." She was labored, though, Robert could see, as there was something wrong with her gait. That wasn't the only thing. There was something else about her that seemed familiar. *And what was the purpose of her covering herself in blood like that?*

* * *

Malcolm watched as the woman he'd saved made her way toward Matt. He'd been watching the cops check out the van that he'd left locked when the shrieking starting. He had easily slipped out the driver's door after the shot and escaped unnoticed. It was an unfortunate development that he had to abandon his vehicle, but he still had his sidearm and his comrade on the other roof had surely put two and two together by now. So he probably had help in watching Matt while he dealt with the matter at hand.

After her tirade from the roof, he made his way over toward the building she was in. When she breached the entrance doors, he was quickly able to ascertain she wasn't armed. It was a crazed scene as his shot had obviously hit some bone that resisted. He believed his shot hit the temple and the residual fallout was not pretty to look at.

Suddenly his previous target was moving toward the girl. He had been tracking a hulk that had been bullying his way through the crowd to get to the front, with a small nerdy guy in tow. He definitely had caught Malcolm's interest until he got right near the front, only to let the nerd step inside. He was a bodyguard. Now that same hulking bodyguard was heading straight for her. She wasn't looking good, obviously hindered by some physical ailment that prevented normal movement and the exertion of her roof experience and her tirade apparently left her drained.

Malcolm was watching the hulk advance and the girl wobble at the same time, both at the edges of his left and right peripheral vision. He relaxed his grip on his pistol and started advancing toward the two, trying to anticipate what the hulk would do to her once he closed the gap.

* * *

Robert was stunned, as was everyone else in the plaza. He remembered something from his childhood that he wished he could have made go away a million times in his life, but it never would leave his subconscious. He only had one pet as a child, Hugo the rabbit. Hugo was a gray Netherland Dwarf and he was Robert's pride and joy, so full of life. In the summer, once the sun was down and things cooled off a little, Hugo would start his routine. He would zip around the apartment, from one room to the next at full speed. Robert would be watching TV and finally Hugo would spring himself onto his lap, climb his chest and lick the salt off his nose with his rough little tongue.

One night, after Robert returned him to his large steel cage, Hugo decided to bite the wire and he got his teeth stuck in the wire cage. The next five minutes of his life were the most terrifying he could ever remember. The rabbit screamed. It was a scream that he would never forget. He had no clue rabbits were capable of making any sound other than a grunting noise Robert observed while Hugo was rutting in springtime. Hugo was screaming this banshee wail that until now, Robert had never heard before. Now he'd heard it again. It was a scared and vulnerable wail.

Once she came out the front entrance, he got a good look at her and his blood ran cold. It was his dream girl from the freeway. He quickly whispered into Melvin's ear and he didn't have to say it twice. He gave Melvin an objective and he was taking on the task without hesitation, much to the anger of the displaced crowd as he covered the distance to completing his goal.

* * *

Matt was watching this insanity play out and albeit at any other time in his life, you couldn't have pried him away from there with a crowbar, right now, at this moment in time, all he wanted to do was leave. Robert's hulking friend was blazing a path toward his accuser. *What new madness is this going to turn out to be? What new piece of information is now going to spiral my life further into the abyss?*

His accuser was staggering like a prizefighter who had taken a solid punch and was one jab away from going down. Robert's assumed bodyguard was plowing a path toward her and it was a good thing because she appeared to have passed out. Just as she was falling forward, the giant deftly caught her and cradled her like a small child in his mother's clutch. Matt saw her lift her head and speak into the man's ear.

Matt assumed the entire nation was watching as the massive man walked the bloodied and crazed girl toward the makeshift podium. For some reason, Moses and the parting of the Red Sea popped into his head. You could literally hear only background noise—the people silent as the girl spoke into the giant's ear. He in turn looked at Matt and was apparently going to speak for her.

"She says you murdered her brother, Homeland Security Agent, Joe Raley."

Matt was stunned now that he understood what this was about. He was trying to find some words when she spoke into the hulk's ear once more. God, she was a bloody mess and then he saw something on her shirt he never wanted to see again, something that brought him back to the most terrifying day of his life, the day all this was set into motion when he had picked the same substance out of his Vera's hair. The substance was brain matter.

Robert's bodyguard listened to her and spoke for her once again directly to Matt, "You're no hero, you are a murderer and I've been chasing you since the day you killed my brother. Your friends in Ecuador nearly killed me just for mentioning your name. No decent person has friends like that."

Matt remembered Mauricio telling him that his daughter Cecilia chased off a female reporter that was hunting him down. Of course, he didn't ask Mauricio for that kind of help, his daughter and he had acted on their own free will. He knew Mauricio to be ruthless, but decent. Then he remembered the day the man unloaded his Colt .45 into two men that tried to kidnap his daughter and understood that she probably spoke the truth.

Matt replied, "I'm so sorry about your brother. I've replayed his death in my head over and over again. I was undercover and they were undercover. I was wrestling with his partner for control of his gun, as I had tackled him trying to intervene in what I thought was the attempted kidnapping of my shoplift suspect. When I looked up at your brother during the scuffle, he had the girl in a chokehold and was trying to shoot me in the head. I was never more terrified in my life and in a surge of strength I raised his partner's gun and squeezed his hand. I did this thinking I was saving my life. That's the only reason I would *ever* take a life—to save my life or someone else's.

"As for my friends in Ecuador, none of you would be standing here today if it weren't for a man I met who made the impossible happen for me, a man whose daughter I saved from vicious kidnappers, and under his code, is forever in my debt. So if you came across that man, in their country and you were looking for me, you are very lucky to be alive, for sure.

"None of these situations were in my control and the only way your brother could be here today would be if I just let him, an unknown person to me, kill me without a fight. From my point of view, I was battling two perpetrators that were going to kidnap a woman and there was no talking going on, only a struggle for my life. Miss, I don't like talking to people I don't know, so can I please have your name?"

She whispered to her mouthpiece once more and he spoke her name, "Lauren Betton."

"Thank you, Lauren, and I am not trying to be insensitive, but you have to understand, your brother's life is not the only one that ended that day, and I've investigated every one of them. That is what I formerly did for a living before that day—I investigated things. I have read all the information about the case a hundred times. It is a fact that if your brother and his partner would have called in for back-up or simply identified themselves, this whole thing would never have happened—including my life and reputation being stripped from me."

The silence was palpable. No one dared speak because they might miss a second of what her next words were, but they didn't come. She was crying into Robert's bodyguard's chest and wouldn't pause. After a minute, some talking started, but everyone was still intent on waiting this out. To Matt's amazement, the hulk barely looked like he was holding anything. He once had to endure such a situation in which he held Vera for ten hours. Matt wondered how the giant would look after that long, probably the same as he did. Then she whispered into his ear for a long time. Before he spoke, she reiterated what she had said so he got it.

He spoke, "She says that if what you say is true, then you won't mind being a completely open book and letting her do your story—she is a Journalist. But be warned, she intends to do the piece with every intent of exposing you."

"No problem," was Matt's reply.

Before Matt could speak anymore though, Robert stepped back into the spotlight, literally pushing his friend back, and Matt intuitively understood that this was a purposeful move to allow him to extricate himself from the podium and the scene.

Robert tenderly informed her, "Lauren, I'm going to take it a step further. I'm going to make you part of the counsel for *American Pride*. Absolute power corrupts absolutely and we need a watchdog. Some diligent person, such as yourself, to make sure we keep an honest path with open books. If you take the job, it's yours for life and no one will tell you what you can and cannot write. I know Matt, I can't tell you how, but I know him like we lived in another life together. He does not lie. If that's what he said happened, then that is what happened and it's time we all moved on. Even you must admit that the record does not lie, and it's full of mistakes made by the Department of Homeland Security.

She buried her head in Melvin's chest as Robert continued, "We are going to do some wonderful things and you are going to bear witness, if you'll take the job. My plan is simple; that's the most important part about all this, simplicity. Will you join us?"

For the first time, she lifted her head and looked at both of them. Matt could see she was beautiful under all the madness. Ignoring Robert was between them, their eyes locked. Her eyes seem to be saying, "Do you swear, because if you are lying, the punishment is death." His eyes met that expectation with a pleaded, "Yes, I swear." She looked back at Robert and said, "Yes."

"Great, now Melvin, please get her into the hospital and let us all do as the hospital requested and leave for the park. One last thing though, I was interrupted mid-sentence and I would like to finish the thought. Matt opened up my path and for that I will be forever grateful. I had a vision recently of how this is going to take off, and take off it will. I'm going to donate all the money I make from this to start manufacturing in the U.S. Not just once, but over and over again. We're going to have towns that have been devastated by a manufacturing plant leaving register with us. We will put a matrix of skilled labor together, then as a group we will target a company that has moved its manufacturing outside of he United States, build a better product than they currently have, and knock them out of the lead, one company at a time.

"Once a target has been set, we will open a plant and their wares will be for sale in *American Pride*. Anyone selling there will have all the free advertising they want inside the game and any subsidiaries of

Robert Leme, Inc. Once the plant is making a profit and the employee/ owners have taken care of themselves, the future profit can go into their expansion, but controlled by them so they can reinvest in new product lines and equipment.

"We are going to focus on doing things the old-fashioned way and not replacing people with innovation. People need to work and that is one of the big focuses of the group. Just because we can make a machine that can replace ten men doesn't mean we should."

Matt decided that this was his chance to get away. Robert had the crowd and he was very proud of his friend. He suspected that his body-guard was a big part of his strength. The giant was walking the girl to the ER amidst a throng of reporters following. With this many leads, one had to choose, and about eight reporters decided Lauren and Melvin were the story.

Matt went to step off to the left and follow them even though he wasn't going into the ER. Some of the nearest spectators started it and before Matt could stop it, the crowd was asking for an ovation of sort. Although they'd just met him, they were expecting a goodbye apparently.

A helicopter took off from a nearby landing pad. Matt remembered seeing such a landing pad at a different hospital in California, so it wasn't a difficult concept to grasp. He figured it had something to do with Jan and Jon Jon.

As usual, whenever he tried to use distractions as a way to avoid reality, the clock was always the winner. Matt was a most torn man, as seemed to be his norm. He had opportunity here to further their cause in a most impressive way, but his life was like kettle corn: salty-sweet. His life was always salty-sweet. He looked back up at the hospital and saw his dad in the third floor window, the same window he had been looking out of not long ago. His dad gave his son the thumbs-up sign and then he pointed toward the inside of the hospital. It was his way of telling Matt that there was no immediate crisis inside the hospital. That helped.

Not to deny the crowd and justifying it out of obligation to civil tranquility, Matt approached the microphone again. "That helicopter took off to retrieve my family's last remaining hope, the doctors it will bring back offer our last chance. I need to leave and be with them as this could be their last moments if those doctors fail. But as has been the case since the day I was kidnapped at gunpoint in Palo Alto, I have had to adapt to having two lives. I've had to learn to survive in one world and hold onto my other at a distance—for you people, for my country, for everything I love.

"The day I was kidnapped I realized my abductors were going to kill me. I knew my life was going to be lost and I also knew the people that had me were going to hurt my country. So I enlisted myself into the military, the CIA specifically. I was very well read and knew what my role would be. I was going to take a page from the book our enemies use against us, the one entitled, *How to be a Fanatic.*

"I had made up my mind to sacrifice myself for my country. It was an opportunity that offered me a way to gain access into their organization. As they had kidnapped me, they knew I was not a planted spy, so all I had to do was act like I wanted in.

"Two years later, opportunity allowed me to get America out of the crisis Pablo Manuel put us through. I was in a very tough position then, and it took a great physical and psychological toll on me. When I returned home, I was put back together in the same hospital as any other soldier. Why did I tell you this? Because we are about to lose our way of life, people, and if there are other veteran's out there, I want them to hear me and take action. One soldier to another, that's why. We need everyone on our side."

Matt garnered a look of admonishment with the his next statement, "I risked my life for this place and my family is up there dying because some nut-job took the word of God way out of context by committing all these heinous acts. Now the least you all could do is listen to Robert tell you how to reclaim our country sans the idiots who are running it now. And we're going to do it based on the two greatest powers we have left: communication and our power and right to purchase freely.

"If we try to have this 'Revolution Without Wrath' and they stop us by blocking these freedoms, then the answer will be plain to see who really is in control. And if that happens, only a new American Revolution will cure our woes. And from where I sit right now, our woes are mighty."

As Matt made his way to the hospital, a throng of reporters mobbed him and out of nowhere, Doug showed up lending a stalwart hand. He began pushing and shoving reporters out of the way and got Matt out of there. Completely lost on all of the frenzied journalist was that the second biggest news story was ushering the biggest one by, and no one even knew Doug was there.

Doug looked back at Robert addressing the crowd and realized he was only the second biggest story for his fifteen minutes of fame. This time around, Doug's fifteen minutes was a literal one and he couldn't be happier as he and Matt got into the elevator and its blissful silence. Matt was facing the wall, not wanting to make eye contact. Doug placed his hand on his friends shoulder, "That was amazing Matt, I'm sorry it had to come at a time like this."

The elevator door opened and Matt stepped off, his small break from the reality looming inside these walls was over.

He had forgotten in all this that he really twisted his ankle and subsequently Doug had to catch him from hitting the deck when he tried to turn up the hall. He looked at Doug with a pained expression. "Thanks, I had forgotten I nearly broke my ankle earlier, I guess the adrenaline will do that."

Doug reached into his pocket and extracted a travel tube of ibuprofen, "I remember when you gave me four of these during our adventure flight. Now I can return the favor."

Matt stopped at the water fountain and took them, then proceeded up the hall with a slight limp.

* * *

Scott sat back and watched the television screen in disbelief. He also witnessed his own fifteen minutes of fame go by in that same amount of time, and he was not happy about it at all. At the very end, when she raised her head and looked at Leme and Hurst, she quickly glanced at the cameras and sure as shit, through her smattered red face, she gave a one second glimpse of smarmy.

Scott knew her facial expressions like his own and he purposely gave a look at the end of his interview intended for her. Apparently she had caught it and although she was in the middle of the second greatest story ever told, she took the effort and pulled it off. Apparently she had the anger of his betrayal so much on her mind that she had to let him know, even in the midst of all that? *Hell hath no fury . . .*

* * *

Jim couldn't be more proud. In his life he had seen greatness in many forms, and as a West Point instructor, he'd had the privilege of mentoring some great minds, some of who were currently running this country.

He watched Matt leave and he had goose bumps; he felt like he'd just watched the birth of a new national figure. Only the man that Matt had referenced in President Kennedy could have matched the kind of charisma Jim just witnessed right now.

It wasn't just about his charisma, but Jim felt if Matt desired, that alone could launch him into the political arena. There was something else though, what was his draw? Swagger? That was is it. Matt was able to pull off swagger without being condescending. He was able to convey confidence without hubris, and it was contagious. Jim felt very attached to the boy, so he was biased, but he looked into the crowd when Matt was crying. There was seriously not a dry eye in the house and his mentor burden grew at that moment to the point of absurdity.

Chase had hired him to mentor the boy and prepare him for the real world—to place some philosophy in his head and make sure it was screwed on right. Jim never had children of his own; his life had been too chaotic to even entertain the thought of a long-term relationship, let alone kids. But to Jim, watching Matt today was as close to watching his own son's valedictorian speech as he was ever going to get.

Now of course, this situation with Matt and TJAC was much more than a "getting the kid ready" mentoring project. Jim made the conscious decision to become Matt's guard until the day he died. Matt was going to need someone with his back that could not be compromised.

Then it struck him. That slick son of a gun; Chase had set him up. He knew that once he got to know Matt that he would take on this role. He knew all along, but somehow, it never clicked for Jim until Matt talked to a nation in a way that very few people could. By touching on the fact he was now a veteran, Matt opened up a whole new demographic. *This boy could actually get us back on the right track.*

Jim had already packed and left the roof minutes earlier. He made it back to Slate's tour guide business about the same time the troops showed up. And show up they did: State, Federal, regular Army even. The Anacortes Hospital was on lock down and the crowd and Mr. Leme moved to the park.

* * *

Antonina Krutova was washing dishes and looking into the reflection on the kitchen window in the Oakland hills. She was watching *Dancing with the Stars*; well, technically she was listening with periodic glances at the reflection in the window. She preferred to wash dishes the old fashion way, even though Igor had purchased one of the nicest contraptions that ever washed a dish. So nice in fact that she had no idea how to use it. Her scientist husband always assumed she was so inclined.

Oftentimes men of such intellect chose women that were more like their mothers than their contemporaries. Antonina knew, of course, that Igor's interest in her came from the dance floor. Igor's father was a world-class dancer and had performed all over Ukraine. It was dancing that brought them together. That's why she never missed her favorite show, even if it's listening and watching in the reflection.

Antonina always recorded the show and watched each episode many times. Tonight was her third re-watch of this week's show. After hours of all the horrific news stories, she had had enough and needed a break. After Matt Hurst went into the hospital, the media began the repetition thing and that's where she got off the train. How can any man be so unlucky as this Matt Hurst?

Only knowing her Igor, a man who she had known only to cry a bit at funerals and nowhere else, it was unusual for her to see a man be able to cry and still have her feel that he was a "real man." She liked stoic men and loathed men who lacked character or strength. As she watched this Matt Hurst, she never felt for a single moment that he lacked strength. In fact, he seemed to turn weakness into strength as his impassioned speech went on. She would pray for him tonight.

Their house sat in a cul-de-sac and her kitchen window looked down to the end of her driveway and to the end of the street. That's why she was able to see the odd procession from the beginning. Four cars turned the corner without stopping at the stop sign and were headed straight for her house. They all screeched up and personnel in black windbreakers that read FBI filed out of their respective cars.

If that wasn't enough of a spectacle, the mother of all spectacles landed in the street in front of their house and before she could call Igor, he was in the kitchen, dressed, with his laptop carry case in his hand.

"Igor, what is going on?"

"Not to worry, my dear, we are in no danger. These men have come to take me to Seattle. Matt Hurst's family was poisoned by a neurotoxin; apparently that is what's wrong with them, my dear. I received a text not five minutes ago from Steven and he told me to get ready immediately. Our hypothesis is now going to be tested and made a fact. Or not...

Igor looked at his wife, as she was still very beautiful even in her late fifties. She never let her figure fall and looking into her eyes was what an astronaut must feel like looking back on earth and seeing this amazing blue marble. Those things would be enough for any man to fall in love, but that was not why he fell in love with his wife. She thought it was because he fell in love with her on the dance floor and he'd allowed it; why not, it made her happy. Only he knew that he fell in love with Antonina because of her absolute compassion for all things.

When they were dating as teenagers they would walk everywhere—it was their way to slow the world down. Igor remembered the first time he saw it. They were walking down to his parent's house and in the street they spotted the biggest green caterpillar either had ever seen. Igor remembered having to have it, so he made his way into the street. At the same time, so did a robin. It had the insect on its lunch menu and was now in a race for the large meandering treat. Unbeknownst to the robin, a car was coming and Igor relented, of course.

The bird was not so inclined, and with the single mind of the meal, it threw caution to the wind and grabbed the insect, but it was not able to get out of the way of the car and it was struck. It wasn't a deathblow and the bird was thrown to the side of the street stunned. Although that scene was sad to watch play out, Antonina's response was quite shocking.

Igor had always likened it to a person watching their child get hit by a car. It was the same terror, the same absolute loss of composure. She literally broke down over the bird. Of course, he felt guilty because had he not interfered, the bird would have lived, but in his mind, it was just an unfortunate incident. She pleaded with him to try to capture it, but when he did it mustered the strength to fly a short distance and get away.

Igor had never seen anything like this display in his life, and at first he thought the whole thing to be high drama over something as simple as a bird. Time passed though, and the incident was put into the vault, but it was just the first of what would prove to be a lifetime of over empathy for the smallest of things.

Most people would find that an annoying trait, what with all the hysteria that surely went along with it. He guessed he wasn't most people because that would be number one on the list of things he would miss about her if she were no longer here.

He replied, "I will do my best, you know I will."

Her eyes were already misting as she wanted to be emotional, but over the years she had learned to not burden him when he was leaving for business. She understood the stress he was under.

"I know you will, Igor, I will pray for them."

* * *

Matt watched as the team of scientists applied their antidote. Antidote? He would have never guessed in a million years that a word like antidote would be involved in his life. His parents and Doug were in the waiting room. He wanted to be alone with Jan and Jon Jon during this procedure. Apparently the dose had to be delivered in such small quantities that they brought in a special micro-infusion device. Matt couldn't even tell it was delivering the contents of the syringe, but he was assured it was. Currently Dr. Singh was bringing the former weapons scientists up to speed on every nuance of the case.

It never was lost on Matt just how much could transpire in a single day. In a single day, he had done more then most people would do in a lifetime—as far as heart-stopping action went anyway. Not a few short hours ago he felt the bullet Pablo shot pass through him and take him to the next life. Although the bullet never actually hit him, he thought it did. The blinding light of the laser that came down made him believe he was on the other side. He remembered that he only had one regret as he was leaving this earth: his wife and son.

Dr. Singh said their vitals were slipping fast and if this procedure did not work, they would not survive the night. Matt remembered what it looked like to see someone die this type of death. He had poisoned all of Pablo's followers and watched them die horrific deaths on the closed circuit monitors that Pablo had installed.

With a heavy sigh of a burden too much to handle, his mind went to a very selfish place. If he watched that here tonight, he was going to take his own life. His parents not being on that ferry now complicated the fact that he would not stay here with the daily remembrance of his wife and son dying that same type of death.

Then it hit him, the thing he kept trying to ignore. God. God had played a role throughout this whole thing. Why did he keep denying it? If his family died tonight, he could do no such thing as kill himself. If he did that, then he would never see them again. It was like he was being held hostage in this game of life and death.

If he took his other idea into play and just checked out into the wilderness, he would have to endure the memories of this for the next forty years. He seriously decided that he would become a daredevil, maybe a rock climber. Eventually that would lead to an early death—whatever it took to not have to be the person who thought about nothing else but tragedy for the rest of his days.

Matt looked out on the team of doctors talking around a computer screen. The Russian one, whose name escaped him, was very optimistic. He said all the right things were in place for his wife and son to come out of this. The toxin fit the right profile and the fact they both had a cold and took an antihistamine prior to them being exposed no doubt saved their lives.

Now it was another game of watching and waiting. He wanted to pity himself so badly. He sat silently and as always, the reminders of his newly appointed piety did not take long. When one felt sorrow for oneself, one took away from God's plan for all. Matt knew this. He knew it all too well. In light of all this awareness, he felt like a rebel without a cause, because he was so infuriated, even in face of all the evidence, he was angry with God, and his inner child was defiant and smiting.

That's when a teenage girl was rolled in, her mom unraveled at her side. Matt was eavesdropping, as they were just outside of Jan and Jon's room. The girl was seventeen. She was at home with her mother and started complaining of a headache. Within minutes it was a 911 call, then the mom doing CPR until the emergency units arrived. She was getting the doctors report currently. It was an AVN, a type of aneurism that is caused by a genetic birth defect in one of the brains arteries and connectors. They can burst at any time, but usually in teenagers around this girl's age.

Matt actually forgot his problems for a moment, he was glued to this poor kid's story. Here she was, happily going about life and suddenly God's plan for her was that she was going to go through this, for whatever reason. In a profound moment of understanding, Mathew Hurst understood that all these doctors with all their innovation meant nothing in the face of our preordained path.

The woman was alone now and their eyes met. They both had the same dilemma. Both of them were in the hands of God. Matt rose from his chair and went to her. Without a word he placed his hands on her shoulder. She burst into tears and he pulled her up to him.

He comforted her for a quite a while. His mother and father came in and were rather confused seeing him with her in his embrace. He motioned for them to be with Jan and Jon. Befuddled, they obeyed, moving into the room with his wife and child. He could tell the Russian doctor wanted to talk to him. He gently let the woman know that the doctors needed him, but he would return if she needed someone to be with. She said she was embarrassed because after everything he'd been through, he shouldn't have had to deal with her problems, too.

Much to Matt's chagrin, his autonomous days were over. To this woman, he wasn't just some guy in the same hospital ward with a similar plight, he was a national celebrity who took time out for her—the complete opposite of what he wanted to be. He extricated himself and headed over to the waiting doctor, Igor something, Matt finally recalled, but the last name was lost on him. This Doctor Igor had a hard, yet gentle face. He was one of those people you expected to have a totally different personality than he ended up having.

"How are things, Doctor?"

He looked stoically at Matt, "There is little change yet as the drug is not even halfway administered. We have seen a slight decrease in their vitals, but nothing dramatic. We're hoping there is a war going on in them by now. A war the good guys are winning."

"How long before we know if you are successful."

"It's going to be several hours, Matt. We are going to need to have personnel in there now, so please wait for us in the ICU waiting room. I will come for you soon."

As Matt turned to leave his mom called his name in a way he knew all too well. Anytime there was a grave issue, whether it be a dead pet hamster or a cat found lying in the front yard, Sherry had that tremulous voice. Before he could react though, Jon's machines went into alarm mode and rushing personnel came sweeping in and immediately got his parents out of the room and then all of them out of the ICU unit, pulling a curtain to seal off the woman he shared a moment with.

As he was ushered out, he went into that slow motion mode, a mode that had happened to him several times in his lifetime. It was that mode where lives were on the line and one could hear one's own heartbeat during the event.

Everyone around him was flying in fast motion and he was in slow. Although his gunshot wound was superficial, he suddenly became very aware of it when a medical cart slammed into him as it rushed by. The doctors had triaged it prior, but he was sure the impact of the cart re-started some bleeding; not to mention his twisted ankle, he had almost forgotten about that. When he was chasing the doctor earlier he was so pumped that he did not even feel it.

But that wasn't the only thing he'd noticed in slow motion. The woman he comforted had a pall on her face as they closed that curtain around her. He could see Jon being attended to and the woman's face, she was just blankly staring at him, in that stare of a million words. He would never forget the anguish and despair on her face; it would haunt him forever. He knew why, too. She had that horror movie quality about her, like she had the inside story that Jon was going to die.

They were outside the waiting room in the hallway. Doug saw them and came running. Matt's mom was a total mess, using crying, hysterics, and madness in abundance. His dad was trying to be the rock, and Doug was helping them both inside the ICU waiting room.

Just like before, Matt's feet were taking him where his mind and spirit did not want to go. Before he could stop himself he was in the elevator and walking into the empty chapel. He walked right up to the statue of Christ and curled up on the floor, completely contrite and completely defeated. There was no way possible for him to face what was going on there, he was just not that strong. This was a place that no man should ever be, and the place where one found out what ones breaking point was. Matt had found his and he began to weep uncontrollably.

* * *

Ray Callahan sat in the most comfortable chair in his mausoleum of a living room. He and Kim agreed on most things but not home decorations—well, at least not what one can do in them. Ray had bathrooms with towels he was not allowed to use, bedspreads that could not be lain on, and a living room one could not sit in. Of course, tonight he was going rebel, as he also had a cup of coffee in his hand when his wife walked through the door.

Her face told the story, she knew something was up immediately and dropped her briefcase where she stood and came to her husband asking, "What's happened?"

Ray gave her a serious look of disapproval, "You mean other than the fact that I am sitting here waiting to find out if part of my extended family gets to live or not?" Ray looked regretful as he said, "Matt called me, but I screened the call with the intention of returning it after our lunch. But with all the things going on, I, Ray Callahan, forgot to call back." Ray adjusted his posterior while balancing his coffee with expertise. "I just got news that a specialist team was flown in to try to save them."

Ray then took a sip of coffee and his wife's eyes bulged at the prospect he might spill a single drop, "Of course, now I will have the sound of Matt's frantic voice haunting me forever. The one time ever that I ignored a call from Matt Hurst it has to be 'the call.'"

Ray then mustered a condescending tone, "And how did your day go, Kim?"

"Ray, you know damn well how my day went. I am here to get three hours of sleep, shower, change, and leave. I would assume you are in the same boat."

In as sarcastic a tone as he could muster to the woman he loved, Ray said, "I'm sorry, I cannot talk about Agency business. It is a breach of protocol to talk about active cases with non-agency personnel."

"Well up yours, too, Ray, I don't have time for this shit."

As she was picking up her briefcase, her husband dropped the bombshell. "I told Eric that once we clean this all up, I'm out."

"What are you talking about Ray, the Agency is your life."

"No Kim, you are my life."

Blushing, Kim replied to her husband, "What will you do, go into private practice?"

"I was thinking I could go to work for your friends, Kim. I believe I have something to bring to the table."

"What are you talking about, Ray?"

Ray looked admonishingly, yet coyly, "Why Kim Sullivan-Callahan, did you really think you could keep secrets from me?"

His astonished wife gave him his favorite look, the one where he appeared to her as the smartest man in the world, "How long have you known?"

"For a long time. I knew something was up the minute Matt turned down a job that he told me he had always wanted just the week before. You'll have to be better than that if you ever want to pull the wool over my eyes, Dear."

"Bringing Matt Hurst into our fold was one thing Ray, he wasn't an Agency legend. You'd be missed. What did you tell Eric? You're a Director."

"Eric accepted my resignation because he has grown weary of me. I'm like a stone stuck in his shoe. Lately the friction has gotten to the point where Eric is chaffed by the sight of me. Plus, I made a big mistake."

"Those are words I've rarely heard from you, and when I have it's usually involving the edibleness of our steak. What did you do?"

"When I pieced together that we had essentially used Hurst to lure Pablo out without as much as telling him, I placed an asset to protect Matt. Unfortunately, I rushed my decision, semi-coercing Frederick into releasing said asset back to active duty even though I knew he was being treated for PTSD. My concern for Matt compromised my judgment."

"Sounds like it worked out to me. You saved his life from what I hear."

"Yes, but when word gets out of how this all went down, it's going to look like I power-played Eric again for the spotlight. That's why he accepted my resignation."

"Are you sure you want to do this, Ray?"

"Chase Viana seems to be a very fair guy, Kim. Don't think for a second that once I pieced this together, that I didn't vet him. It's a well-funded group of patriots and that appeals to me."

"Truthfully, once the shock wears off, you will be embraced by them and then you will be empowered in ways you've never thought possible."

"Can't say that sounds bad."

"I would be okay with all of this if you would show signs you are upset, like with me earlier. You obviously just had a very rough day, yet one could never tell. I know that you are an intellectual force, Ray, but even men like you are allowed to cry, be frustrated, and show emotion. Look at Matt. If there was ever an example of masculine crying, he's mastered it.

"What can I say, Kim, I was mentored by Bob Thompson, a man who showed no emotion. He believed that emotion was a weakness. Showing any emotion at all, even in the midst of September Eleven, was unacceptable. The guy was like my father and I emulate him to this day, I'm not embarrassed to say."

"Well, Ray, I'm sure to get a lot of heat, but I'm just going to deflect it with humor. I've already decided, and I've got lines all ready. I'll have you in a maid's outfit with a feather duster, or a Chef with a big white hat; I will have you painted as a real kept man. Soon, as things constantly roll forward, even Ray Callahan will be forgotten."

"That's good perspective, my dear. Don't forget, in a few short years, you will be in the private sector, too. Walk up to the average person on the street and ask who Bill Clinton's Chief of Staff was. Our country has "Short-Timers." It's what allows us to move on so quickly in the face of adversity, but it's also a negative when we fail to permanently embody the ideals of great men."

Kim looked at her husband sitting in her antique Versailles Palace chair, drinking a cup of coffee and realized that this was not a marriage that was going to be in the fifty percent failure category. If this was how her husband managed his worst day, then she had the inner belief that she chose wisely, "Well, I'm glad we had this discussion. Chase and Company had a running bet on when I would cave and tell you about TJAC. That is our name, you know. It stands for, Thomas Jefferson Action Committee. They just called me in to talk about you and me."

Kim eyed Ray in the chair for at least the tenth time.

"Why do you keep looking at me in a way that would indicate we should leave this room and specifically that I should vacate this chair, Dear? When one pays a hundred thousand dollars for a single chair, then one should be elated that someone sits in it. It has a lot of butts to rest before it can make up for that kind of money."

Kim smiled at her husband. He knew that if there was a fire, she was saving her living room first, "This was a onetime pass, but if I ever find you here again, the tyranny I will perpetrate will eclipse that of our dearly departed shepherd, Pablo."

Ray rose out of the chair, careful not to spill a drop of the half-filled cup in his hand. He walked into the kitchen and Kim followed asking, "Do you think they will live?"

Ray turned and tears where flowing down his face. No words were needed; Kim just hugged him, as even the great Ray Callahan had a breaking point, it appeared.

* * *

Brian Franklin cleared his throat audibly. Ever since his windpipe had been crushed by a vicious throat chop by the woman he loved, he had had to clear his throat every thirty seconds or so now as a tick. When one had a crushed windpipe, one tended to get conscious about an action others take for granted, and that would be swallowing. Swallowing became so excruciating that they had to switch him to blended foods. Even then, swallowing was something Brian loathed for many months after his encounter with the woman that started all this madness to begin with.

He would never forget the day when she altered his life. If it weren't for one of the fast-thinking PhDs at Conceptual, he would have died a choking, gasping death. Instead he bore the scar where his own knife was used to cut a slit right at the base of his throat. Unfortunately, no one had the right type of pen and it took three more minutes for a straw to be retrieved from the cafeteria. In that three minutes, his only breathing happened when Dr. Varosh squeezed his skin and muscle together to make a small gap. Brian tried to calm himself, as thinking about those three minutes usually brought on a panic attack. That was one more thing he could thank her for, the need for Xanax.

Before the woman he knew as Nancy Chavez destroyed his life with a single throat chop, he was a confident man; he did not fear life, nor had he ever had a single bout of anxiety. After the incident at Conceptual Labs, he tried to return to work, but the minute he stepped foot into that building, the anxiety started. He went on medication but still could not return to work. Conceptual offered him a severance package and he took it. But living alone and not working, he soon got homesick.

Growing up in Anacortes, Washington, Brian loved to go home to visit whenever he could after moving to the Bay Area, but would always joke during long bouts of rain that he was glad he could go back home to Sunnyvale, as Sunnyvale was just as one would think it would be, very sunny.

It didn't take too long after moving back, however, that he found he had to get out of the house, no matter what he did for work. That's when he found the hospital security job he currently held. Of course, no one knew who the hell he was or the fact that he was there at the beginning of this unbelievable rollercoaster of death and mayhem.

He was trying to stem the rising anxiety, but seeing Matt Hurst run by brought it all back. Matt was, after all, an even bigger victim of hers than himself. Right after killing and maiming her way out of Conceptual Labs, Nancy Chavez went right to Matt's store and ruined his life as well. *That one woman ruined so many lives, why would I still give up everything for her?*

Brian was able to hear Hurst's speech from just outside the main entrance door. Of course, he had to agree with what the guy said—it was all the truth—but be that as it may, Brian really doubted that Hurst or the tech nerd guy, Leme, would be able to make any sweeping change to the country.

It looked good for a show here, but how many of these people would get home and never take action? Brian bet even money he was one of them. Everyone had delusions of grandeur on how to fix this place, but none of them ever seemed to pan out due to all the infighting this country was known for these days.

Just then, to Brian's amazement, Robert Leme appeared through the automatic doors. He looked different than he had earlier. He had obvious concern, as did most that walked through those doors, but he also had a swagger that he'd missed before. Brian felt himself being drawn to it as Robert approached and asked to see Lauren Betton in the ER.

Brian checked the list, he knew he could deny the man since he was not family and it was family visitors only right now. The hospital was under lock down at the moment—there had been more cops, federal agents, and Department of Homeland Security personnel coming through than he had seen since that fateful day in Sunnyvale that started all this. Instead, he let the man through with a visitor badge. He knew he was a friend of Hurst's as well, so it was the right thing to do. As Robert left, he thanked Brian and then put his hand on his shoulder in a gesture that showed he knew that he could have been turned away, but instead was given a favor. Brian felt his magnetism as he walked off. *Maybe this really is the guy to make change for our country.*

Robert made his way into the hectic emergency room. Fire, military, and flown-in medical staffs were triaging patients in the ER waiting room itself. A makeshift treatment tent was set up in the parking lot and any patients needing minor treatment were being routed outside. Robert did not see Melvin or Lauren. His guess was that hers was not a minor injury. He made it to the front counter where there was an insane amount of people who hadn't even checked in. Feeling his frustration mounting every time the double doors opened as a patient was being released, new Robert took action and walked straight into the ER unchallenged.

It took checking several rooms, but he finally found them. She was lying on the patient table with Melvin holding her hand and staring at the door. Lauren was sleeping. As soon as Melvin saw Robert, his hang-dog expression lifted. It was obvious he had been torn between duties, and of course chivalry won out and Melvin remained at Lauren's side.

"How is she?"

"She was screaming so bad from the pain that they shot her with morphine. She is going to have to be immobilized for a minimum of two weeks. According to these docs, she never should have been out of a hospital."

Robert looked at Lauren and his heart ached. Even in her battered and unkempt state he would love her forever, given the chance. "Her need to confront Hurst was too much."

"There's more Robert, so much more. She was worried that she didn't document her last two days well enough, so she filled me in during her pain. That guy that broke the story, that Scott Bailey, well he was her college boyfriend. He betrayed her by exposing Matt. She was coming here to blow the lid off this whole thing, but her friend beat her to the punch as she was en route."

"Oh my God, Melvin, that explains her suicidal driving when we first saw her—and the crying." Robert thought for a second and continued, "So she pushed herself to get here and confront both of these guys, I'd imagine."

"You have no idea. She was flying from South America since the day before, even after the doctors had begged her not to leave. Then while traveling here, the plane and ferry tragedy happened and grounded her plane in Texas, but she still pushed on to Portland and rented a car. This is a very tenacious girl, Robert. You chose well to bring her on."

Robert wondered if it were creepy to fall in love with someone at first sight. He knew that he never stood a chance in hell with a world-class beauty like this one, but that didn't mean he couldn't protect and admire her. *No, there was no rule against that.* "I'm going to make sure she's safe, Melvin. No, strike that. We're going to make sure she's safe and we're going to watch her grow."

"How'd the park go?"

"It went very well, Melvin, I think people are ready for change and this offers a new kind of hope."

Melvin looked admiringly at Robert, "That's true, boss, all it took was one great American to stop filling his pockets long enough to care."

"Any word on Matt?"

"No, and strangely, that pilot was running around looking for him not twenty minutes ago. I meant to tell you that. Maybe you should go see what is going on, I have things to do here."

The two men stared at each other. They knew that their paths were now set. Like it or not, they were the face of a movement. Robert left and when he did, Melvin felt a new power coming from him, a power that wasn't there five hours ago. Was it possible for a man to realize his dream and make peace with it in such a short span of time? Melvin realized he was watching it—no need to run the variables, sometimes all one had to do was open one's eyes.

* * *

Doug was watching Doctor Igor Krutova and his American medical team talk to Matt's parents. He was eavesdropping. Krutova was telling them that although both of them had stopped breathing, they had been able to provide ventilation to get them through long enough for the antidote to work. After nearly an hour, both vents weaned them back to breathing on their own as their own respiratory systems came back into function. All their vitals looked good and it really looked like a miracle was at play here.

Doug stepped over and hugged Don and Sherry, and then told them he would find Matt. His parents were now really worried about him and what he might do if he thought Jan and Jon were dead. Doug took off and they sat and prayed.

* * *

Eric Barnett didn't dislike the President, but he did note that the man went out of his way to always remind him he was the subordinate. Usually it was with something subtle, like bringing him in, yet extending a phone call he was on that wasted his time—like he was an idiot and time did not matter to him, only to the President. Eric got the game. Meanwhile, back at the ranch, his office was a caldron of stress swirling around like some witches brew. The man finally extracted himself from the call.

"Eric, how are you?"

"Okay, given the circumstances. Our country is in shock and thank God this time we had some answers to give."

"What do we know about the shooter in Washington?"

"He's an unknown. No prints and Malcolm's shot removed his face. So it will be a long and arduous process finding his origins."

"You mean his country of origin, don't you, Eric? Not having finger-prints is a pretty good indicator that he was an outside contractor. My people think he was sent by Pablo Manuel as a insurance plan."

"I will not assume any of that Chief, and you know it."

"Very well, keep me posted on any new developments. Anything else?"

Eric looked at Kim. She did not allude to anything so he blurted, "Ray Callahan put in his resignation, effective after the dust settles here."

The President was flabbergasted, "Why would he do that Eric? Kim, can you shed some light here?"

"Well, first of all, I just found out last night. I believe he's doing it to clear the obvious conflict of interest our nepotism creates. He claims he just wants a simpler life. Either way, Sir, he's earned it. I'm sure he will always make himself available in case anyone ever needs him to help solve a case."

Kim made sure she used her "dagger eyes" on Eric while she said those words.

Getting into a pissing match with the boss's favorite pet was never a good idea and Eric ate the words he really wanted to tell Kim after that last statement, "That will probably happen more than you like, Kim."

"Okay, Eric, well please keep me abreast of any new developments about that shooter. I want to know who wants our boy Hurst dead or was that the last act of Pablo Manuel?"

As Eric was rising to leave he thought he would let these two know exactly who they were fucking with, "Oh yeah, we were able to track the laser shot, as you know."

"Oh, we were unaware of that, how come that data was not available to us."

"Because our country is fractured enough right now, and they don't need to know that there was no Air Force satellite within five hundred miles of that laser shot. So the next time either of you pull this, "we're better than you" shit on me, then I promise you there will be a thorough investigation into that laser shot. You two just do your time, vacate the job, and let the next man try to pull any of this stuff and watch what happens."

Kim looked at Eric with her usual disdain, "Who says the next person in here is going to be a man?"

Eric laughed the laugh of a man who had won. He left the Oval Office with his tail feathers in a plume, not cropped as most who left here were. Overall, he was the big winner here. Pablo Manuel was dead and he removed Ray from his job, thus removing a spy within his House of Spies. He had also just one-upped two people who needed a little reality check. Eric was walking on sunshine as he stepped out of the White House and headed back to his job.

Albeit he now had to replace Ray, as far as he was concerned his building was full of Ray Callahans who just hadn't had the chance. He doubted he would ever stoop so low as to ask Ray Callahan for help in the future. That was just a political statement he'd made to appease those two idiots—and those two fools would be gone soon enough.

* * *

Doug was frantically walking back to the elevator after talking to the front security guard, who said he had not seen Matt recently. Doug had checked every conceivable place. He'd checked all the floors, including the ER. He'd checked the roof, the stairwells, and the chapel. Matt was nowhere. He walked by the chapel and thought he would look in one more time, but it was still empty. Confounded, he was closing the chapel door when he noticed the tip of a shoe sticking out of the pew nearest to the Alter. Doug went running over to find Matt unconscious. He was lying at the base of the Jesus statue.

Then Doug saw movement and could tell he was sleeping by the heaving of his chest. He knew he needed to let him know in the fewest words possible that his family was okay so as to not give him one second of anxiety, "Matt, wake up. Matt." Matt opened his eyes and Doug immediately stated, "It worked, their okay."

"What? Are you sure?"

"Yes, I heard Doctor Krutova tell your parents. They ventilated them till the antidote worked."

Like an action figure from some eighties movie, Matt was running off again, badly hobbled from his ankle injury. Doug wondered when the poor guy was ever going to get to stop running?

* * *

Sandy Burroughs watched the TV and as usual, nothing made sense. He was now to believe that Pablo was culpable for the attacks on the innocent people of Seattle, then captured in a "clean the slate" move that reeked of Manual Noriega. No one was ever going to get the real story, and no one was ever going to see Pablo again. Sandy's face was so troubled that Claire immediately noticed and went to sit next to him, staring into his worried face.

He looked at her and only spoke one sentence, but it carried all the weight it needed to, "We have to do something."

* * *

As the man of industry looked out over his complex from his seat on top, he contemplated the last twenty-four hours. The person they needed removed still breathed and it complicated his corporation's plans. His secretary buzzed his line and let him know his appointment was here. Ten seconds later a large blonde man entered his office and sat. The subordinate could not see his face, as he sat in the shadows.

He looked at his subordinate and questioned without salutations, "Can they identify him?"

The blonde man answered, "No, the CIA shooter removed his face."

"That was a very fortunate thing, as this CANNOT get traced back to me in any way." His face was very flushed and the man who worked for him was beginning to understand that he was in the wrong place at the wrong time.

"It will not, rest assured."

"Your life depends on it. Dismissed."

The man of industry knew that he would not be able to remove Hurst right away, but he would sit and wait. He had time—and when the time was right, Matt Hurst was going to become a distant memory.

* * *

Matt sat between Jan and Jon. His parents, Doug, and Robert were on the fringe of the room. Matt had each of their hands and Jon's hand started to squeeze Matt's in a way that indicated he was coming out of it. Soon they were playing finger games and Jon started to giggle even though he still had his eyes closed. He opened his eyes and his first words were, "I have a headache."

Matt started crying and said, "Okay, son, we'll get the nurse in here to check you out."

"Where are we, Daddy?"

"We're in the hospital, Jon, but we're okay now."

Matt was stroking his boy's head as Doug made the move to get the doctors. Just then he heard the voice he was sure he would never hear again. Jan asked with her eyes still shut, "What did you do this time?"

Matt took her hand and said softy, tears streaming down his face, "It's a long story, Babe, a very long story . . .

* * *

Rodrigo Arrologas grabbed his keys and hat, and then headed out of the care facility he worked for. He had a second job taking care of an elderly woman across town and he barely had time to stop home and eat before he headed out again. He was working so hard because he had to save money to go surprise his American love interest, Lauren Betton.

She was a patient at the hospital and he was her therapist. Rodrigo supposed that people always wanted what they couldn't have. He had many girls who were interested in him here, some that rivaled Lauren's looks even, but none that could match her aura.

Plus her looks were amazing—from her startling green eyes and the way her freckles sat gently on her face, or the way they ran to her breasts. Rodrigo flushed. Lauren did things for him that no other woman had even come close to, and he missed her daily. That was why he was saving his money to go sweep the woman he loved off her feet. He did not care what person she might be with, or what the circumstances he might find her, he would not be denied!

He put his key into the door lock of his Toyota Corolla, and as he was turning it, he'd heard the woman's voice ask, "Can you give me a ride to the airport?"

He turned and asked her with incredulity, "Why are you here?"

"Why do you think? I came to take you home with me, so I can finally get some sleep."

"Why your home?" His machismo showing a little at the "take the lead" stance his woman just took.

"Because I have a job I cannot leave."

"I saw, you are quite the Internet sensation."

"Will you go back with me?"

He drew in closer to her and got excited, especially at the thought that one day she would be fully recuperated. He always had to be so careful before when they made love, as she was very incapacitated. The thought of the two of them acting like animals was titillating him beyond all reason, "I was already saving my money to come and get you."

The two embraced for a long time and Lauren finally felt the kind of love that she always thought she'd deserved . . .

To continue the saga of Matt Hurst and Pablo Manuel, watch for the fourth book in the Harbinger of Change Series, *Chesed*.

Other Books from Timothy Jon Reynolds:

The Harbinger of Change

When store detective Matt Hurst went to work that morning, he didn't expect to see himself on the evening news as the target of a manhunt for the most wanted terrorist in the country. He didn't dream he'd be seducing a beautiful spy and betraying his wife and country in order to save them. He didn't imagine he'd be battling for his life against a psychotic CIA hitman. He didn't guess he'd be playing a deadly game of mental chess with the most dangerous terrorist mastermind in the world. And he didn't expect that by the end of the day he'd be the only person who could save America from World War III. If you like political thrillers in the spirit of Robert Ludlum and Tom Clancy, you'll want to read Timothy Jon Reynolds' latest page-turner, *The Harbinger of Change,* the first of the "Harbinger of Change" series. *Available now.*

And the Meek Shall Inherit

Now, two years after American citizen Matt Hurst was kidnapped and coerced into betraying his family and country in order to save them, his time of waiting for revenge is over. He has bided his time effectively and has now placed himself in a position to achieve his end game of redemption. In order to survive, the American abductee has had to immerse himself in his captor's world, so much so that now that the time has come for him to act, will he be able to pull out all the stops to avenge his country's and family's honor? Or has the ideology of his captors taken ahold of him so deeply that he is now willing to act against his own country, something he'd already been falsely accused of doing? *And the Meek Shall Inherit,* the continuing saga of Matt Hurst and Pablo Manuel, is a rollercoaster ride of international intrigue and military action, coupled with the inner-turmoil of the man who can stop it all—if he has the will to do so. *Available now.*

Chesed

Shortly after the one-year anniversary of the attacks on America and his family in Seattle, Matt Hurst can no longer duck the public's need to know all the facts about the exploits of his life. Hoping that clearing the air will be the salve he needs to live down his notoriety, Matt and his family host a television special that clears up all the speculation once and for all. Unfortunately for Matt, destiny has other plans for him, and once again, he is thrown into a world of international intrigue and suspense. And yet again, if he wants to get out alive, he will have to pull out all the stops as his enemies are far more reaching and powerful than ever. *Chesed* balances action, intrigue, and the ruthlessness of the corporate world with brotherhood and hope, lifting the reader to believe there really could be so much more for us all. *Coming December 2016*

Timothy Jon Reynolds formerly worked as a criminal investigator for the Dayton Hudson Corporation. In his tenure there, he literally oversaw hundreds of criminal cases of almost every nature. It was there that started writing in his mind—even if he didn't know it at the time. After leaving that career for a safer one, he began working as a manager in the biomedical industry, eventually moving on to owning his own company. Nowadays he travels the northwest as a Sales Manager for the company that bought his, taking in and absorbing the places and people he visits and meets. All as fuel for his stories. His feeling is that writers, "need fresh faces and stories around them constantly, otherwise they will stagnate and the writing will suffer." When he is not traveling, Tim enjoys being a Northern Nevada resident with his wife and children, complete with all the civil liberties that great state provides.